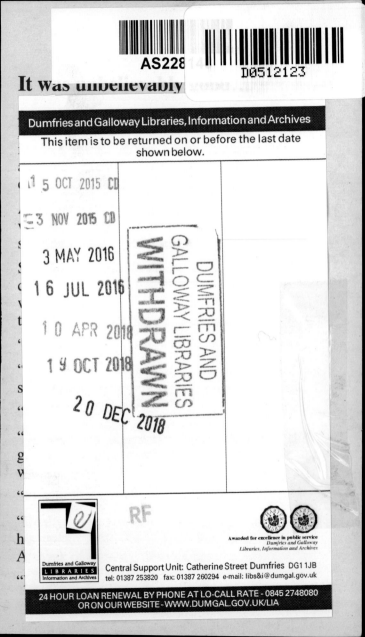

AS228

D0512123

It was unbelievably

Now what? Addie was lying half-underneath Derek—instead of Kevin—and Derek was kissing her, sweet, perfect kisses that made her feel as if she was melting into the mattress. She wasn't exactly objecting.

Addie gasped. Derek had started tasting the curve where her shoulder left off and her neck began, sending shivers...everywhere.

She should either continue the seduction, or she could—and should—be honest: tell Derek she was sorry, but she'd made a terrible mistake. And then he'd stop sending her into orbit.

"Derek."

"Yes, Addie." He sounded amused. "What was so funny?"

"Um. The thing is."

"Ye-e-s?" He kissed her bare shoulder, a slow gentle kiss that made her pause, because she wanted to enjoy it.

"I made a mistake."

"Really." He lowered his head to her breast; his mouth took her nipple. Wet heat. Pressure. A shock of pleasure through her.

"I thought you were Kevin."

HALF-HITCHED

BY
ISABEL SHARPE

MILLS & BOON

All the ... ... ion of
the auth ... ... name
or name ... ... own or
unknow ... ... are pure ...

All Rig ... ... or in
part in ... ... lequin
Enterpr ... ... of may
not be r ... ... onic or
mechan ... ... mation
retrieva ... ... blisher.

This bo ... ... rade or
otherwi ... ... e prior
consent ... ... that in
which i ... ... ndition
being in ... ...

® and ™ are trademarks owned and used by the trademark owner and/or its
licensee. Trademarks marked with ® are registered with the United Kingdom
Patent Office and/or the Office for Harmonisation in the Internal Market and
in other countries.

First published in Great Britain 2013
by Mills & Boon, an imprint of Harlequin (UK) Limited,
Eton House, 18-24 Paradise Road, Richmond, Surrey TW9 1SR

© Muna Shehadi Sill 2013

ISBN: 978 0 263 90319 5
ebook ISBN: 978 1 408 99692 8

14-0813

Harlequin (UK) policy is to use papers that are natural, renewable and
recyclable products and made from wood grown in sustainable forests. The
logging and manufacturing processes conform to the legal environmental
regulations of the country of origin.

Printed and bound in Spain
by Blackprint CPI, Barcelona

Isabel Sharpe was not born pen in hand like so many of her fellow writers. After she quit work to stay home with her firstborn son and nearly went out of her mind, she started writing. After more than thirty novels for Harlequin—along with another son—Isabel is more than happy with her choice these days. She loves hearing from readers. Write to her at www.isabelsharpe.com.

To all the world's creatures of habit.

1

THE SOUND OF the ocean swelled through Addie Sewell's bedroom. She stirred in the soft cotton sheets and listened, picturing waves tumbling, sea foam forming lacy patterns that rushed in, then retreated across soft white sand. Somewhere far off a seagull called.

Addie groaned and threw off the covers on her twin bed. "Alarm off."

The ocean stopped. Or rather, the ocean sound stopped, made by her talking alarm clock, which she'd affectionately nicknamed Tick. The real ocean would have to wait until the following week, when she flew north to attend her friend Paul Bosson's wedding on his family's island in Maine.

She should be looking forward to this vacation a lot more. Been a while since she'd been anywhere except her parents' new house in Florida, and it would be great to see high school friends again. But honestly, she could use the time better staying home and going through boxes of old family photos and papers her great-aunt Grace had left behind, and to get serious about looking for a condo.

By living with her elderly aunt for two years before Grace's death, Addie had inherited this rent-controlled apartment a block from Central Park on Manhattan's E.

97th Street. With her actuary's salary, she'd saved enough for a down payment on the right condo. She just couldn't seem to find time or enthusiasm for the search.

To be honest, she was not a big fan of life changes, and the apartment was not only in a great location, but held lovely memories of Great-Aunt Grace.

Yawning, she stretched and blinked blearily at the freshly painted ceiling, a nice change from the crackling that had progressed for years. Desperate pleas to the landlord had finally been answered.

"Time."

"Seven o'clock," Tick replied.

Seven o'clock. Her eyes fluttered closed, shot open... closed again. Usually she had no trouble jumping out of bed in the morning, especially in the summer when it was so bright out. Lately it had become harder. Maybe she should get her iron checked. Or her vitamin D level. Or work out more.

The chime of an incoming text forced her eyes open again. Pretty early for anyone to be in touch. Mom and Dad were cruising the Mediterranean and her brother, Gabe, was off hiking somewhere in Nepal...

Anxious curiosity got her out of bed; she retrieved her phone from its charger and checked the message.

Oh, my. She was awake now. Wide-awake.

The message, seven words long, was not from her world-traveling family members, but from her childhood best friend Sarah Bosson, twin sister of Paul, next week's groom.

Kevin Ames will be at the wedding.

Kevin Ames.

Addie gave a short laugh, shaking her head. Look at her, all excited over something so silly. Kevin was two years older than Addie, Paul and Sarah, but he'd been on the cross-country team with Paul since middle school at John Witherspoon in Princeton, New Jersey. Addie and Sarah had seen him constantly at the Bossons' house. Last she heard, Kevin had some work conflict in Philly, where he lived, and couldn't make next week's Maine trip.

Ignoring her responsible side nagging that she should be in the shower by now, Addie texted back.

Since when?

Wow. She headed for the bathroom, still clutching the phone. Kevin Ames was The One That Got Away. Everybody had one. That person you never went out with that you really wanted to, or maybe you almost did, but something went wrong—the timing wasn't right, or, in Addie's case, when finally presented with the opportunity to start something with Kevin the summer before her senior year at Princeton High School, she'd totally messed it up.

Another text from Sarah:

He got someone else to go to his conference. Paul just found out.

Addie pressed her lips together to keep from grinning like a fool. She hadn't seen the guy in eleven years. He was undoubtedly married. In fact, she'd looked him up online several years back and yes, he was.

And guess what…he's single now!

Addie lost the battle with the smile. Okay, not married anymore. But that didn't mean anything. He could have put on four-hundred pounds, lost his hair and…

He's into marathons.

Oh. Four-hundred pounds was unlikely, then.
Well.
Addie shook herself. "Time."
"Seven-twenty."
Argh. She was behind on her morning schedule, which she'd developed specifically to avoid having to rush. From an early age her parents had modeled the importance of routines. Addie had scorned them in her rebellious— mildly rebellious—adolescence and her brother had no use for them at all, but she'd come to realize that routines could save you a lot of time and effort and trouble. You knew what to expect. You didn't have to think or make decisions, everything was already in the works and you simply stepped in and did your part.

Sarah again.

I told you about that jerk playboy Derek Bates being there? I so wish he wasn't coming.

Addie rolled her eyes. Sarah was pretty judgmental, but her anti-Derek rants were over the top, even for her. There was definitely something she wasn't telling.

Yes, you told me. But only about a million times. Gotta go to work. TTYL.

In her tiny apartment's tiny bathroom, Addie turned on the shower spray, counted to seventeen to make sure the water was hot enough and stepped into the iron claw-foot tub where she washed her hair and scrubbed up, thinking about…
Kevin Ames.
Who could help it? Not that he'd been all that remark-

able looking. Handsome, sure, but not striking. Bland all-American good looks, brown hair and eyes, straight teeth and an athlete's lean body. But he was so magnetic that women went nuts over him as if he were a knockout. Both Sarah and Addie had been smitten.

When Kevin Ames smiled at you, it was like no one else in the world existed.

Of course since Kevin was a really fun, friendly and popular guy, he smiled at a lot of people, including a lot of girls who were more beautiful and more stacked and more whatever-else guys found essential at that age. He'd always been big-brother sweet to Sarah and Addie, so they contented themselves with worshiping from afar.

Then that one August night, almost exactly eleven years ago, when Kevin was about to start his sophomore year at Brown, someone had told Addie that Kevin was interested in her. Addie couldn't remember who. But she sure remembered the feeling when he asked her out. Stunned, then euphoric, then terrified. She and Sarah had immediately started planning: clothes, makeup, attitude, everything he'd be sure to say and every way she should respond when he said it...

Get going, Addie.

She yanked the water off and dragged her towel briskly over her body. Back in her bedroom, she pulled on the clothes she'd ironed and laid out the previous evening, giving an exasperated groan when her first attempt at pulling on nylons ended in a run—and now she had no precious cushion of time left for disasters.

This was why she got up at the appointed hour every day and had everything prepared. Because she hated this flustered perspiring mess she got herself into when she deviated from the plan.

Great-Aunt Grace, her mother's aunt, had been even

worse—or better, depending on your perspective. Since she'd died, sometimes Addie went crazy, like she had cereal on Thursdays when Grace's cereal day was Friday.

She giggled, pulling on her black pumps. Wild woman!

The smile faded. She hadn't felt like a wild woman in a long, long time. Maybe never.

Kevin Ames.

The night of their date he'd picked her up in his gold Nissan sports car. He'd chatted easily with her beaming parents then they'd gone out for pizza on Nassau Street, and driven to Marquand Park, where she'd played as a child. Kevin had switched off the engine and produced a surprise fifth of vodka Addie had felt too intimidated to refuse, ignoring the voice that told her drinking was not a great idea for either of them.

At the fizzy height of her buzz, he'd taken her face in his hands, looked deeply into her eyes and kissed her.

Oh, that kiss…

She relived it until she realized she was standing on one foot, clutching her other shoe, and it was not getting any earlier.

"Time."

"Seven forty-five."

Eek!

Addie raced to the living room and snatched up her briefcase, stomach growling for breakfast she'd have to grab at work, headache demanding coffee. She let herself out of her apartment, snatched up the *New York Times,* which she usually read over breakfast, and ran down the hall, punched the button for the elevator, punched it twice more, as if that would do anything. Slowest elevator in Manhattan. While she waited, she checked her work schedule for the day.

Hey. She grinned at her phone. It was her half birthday. Addie Sewell was now officially twenty-nine and a half.

In another six months she'd be thirty. Still at the same job. Still living alone…

No, no, she *liked* living alone, loved the independence and the freedom. Though sometimes she wondered about venturing out to the humane society and adopting a cat. Cats were supposed to be good company, and more suitable for a small apartment or condo than a dog. Dogs were a lot of work.

The elevator doors opened to a good day getting better. *He* was in there, Mr. Gorgeous, the guy from the tenth floor, one of the most good-looking guys Addie had ever seen. In the three years she'd lived here, she'd never once had the guts to say anything more than hi.

So…she would again. "Hi."

Mr. Gorgeous nodded. "Hey."

The door closed, leaving that peculiarly charged silence in elevators that Addie tolerated with this guy because saying something and then relapsing to silence would be even more charged and peculiar. But if she started a conversation that lasted all the way to the first floor, then what, would they walk together into the street? What if he were talking to her only to be polite? Better not to say anything. So she stayed silent, watching the lighted numbers at the top of the door descend.

Kevin Ames.

He'd kissed her again, and again. His hand had traveled inside her top to stroke her breast, which felt wonderfully intimate and very hot. Except then Addie had started thinking about his last girlfriend, Jessica Menendez, and the size of her you-know-whats, and the girlfriend before that, Isabella Tramontina, and how she had a body that made men fall like dominoes when she walked down the hall.

Addie had compared them to her own pudgy small-chested big-butt body and virgin status, and panic had erupted. Was this all he wanted from her? To make out in a car drunk on vodka in a public park?

Then came the part that still had the power to bring the sick burn of humiliation to her stomach. Words slurring, she'd told Kevin she *loved* him. She'd told him she wanted their first time to be on a bed. But not just a bed. A bed of *white linen* strewn with *roses*.

Oh, God. She was blushing even now.

Addie would never forget the look of utter bewilderment on Kevin's face. He'd mumbled some kind of apology, said something about a misunderstanding, and had driven her home in a silence even more painful than the one on this slow, slow elevator. Kevin had gone back to Brown. Addie had gone back to high school. She'd heard about him now and then through Sarah or Paul, but hadn't run into him again.

Okay, for a few years, she ran *away* from him so as not to relive that mortification.

But she had enough self-confidence now to laugh about the incident with him when she saw him again next week. She was no longer a virgin and she no longer confused sex with love. Or at least she understood that for most guys they were separate entities.

The elevator door opened and she surged out ahead of Mr. Gorgeous so as not to burden either of them with forced contact.

On E. 53rd street at the offices of Hawthorn Brantley Insurance Company, she grabbed a bran muffin and cup of coffee from the cafeteria then met with teams to design a new life insurance plan and to work on storm damage models, then she formulated spreadsheets dealing with expected drunk driving deaths in Wisconsin the following year.

At lunchtime, back in the cafeteria, *New York Times*

crossword puzzle section tucked securely under her arm, she selected her usual sandwich, carrot sticks and apple, then threw caution to the wind and picked out a cookie. Special occasion! Her half birthday!

Eating the same thing every day meant she knew how many calories she was getting, and that they'd last through her workout and that she'd be healthily hungry for dinner.

Unfortunately she was a little late and her usual single table was taken. Heading for her second choice, Addie noticed Linda Persson, assistant director of Human Resources, seated by herself at a table for four. Linda was a lovely woman, but a little…well, she wasn't very attractive or very funny or very talented or very interesting, and at age sixty wasn't likely to become so.

Addie couldn't bear to see her sitting alone in her beige suit and ivory blouse, forking chef salad into her mouth, trying to look as if she'd chosen to be without a friend in the world because she so enjoyed the experience.

Sigh.

Addie put her tray down on the table. "Hi, Linda."

"Hey, Addie!" She smiled with such obvious relief that Addie banished the doomed feeling and put herself in the Glorious Martyr column.

"May I join you?"

"Of course." Linda pulled her tray toward herself as if there wasn't plenty of room already on the large table. "I was just thinking about my plans for the weekend."

"Fun ones?" Addie hoped they were special and interesting, because then she could think about something other than Kevin.

"I'm getting a new mattress Saturday afternoon. And then I'm going to see a movie." She pushed her too-large brown glasses up her nose. "I like going to movies by myself, do you?"

Addie nodded reluctantly. She did, but was ashamed not to want a lot in common with Linda. "I don't mind, either."

"I like getting there early because I like to sit in the middle of a row, not too close, and because I like to watch the previews, and have popcorn all to myself. And since no one talks to me, I can really disappear into the film."

"Same here." Actually…exactly the same.

"And then after the movie I'll probably go home and organize my kitchen. It's driving me crazy that the flour and sugar canisters are on the opposite side of the counter from the measuring cups and spoons. I've stood it this long, but no more." She tossed her mousy-brown curls, beaming triumphantly.

Addie took a long sip of skim milk to wash down her suddenly dry sandwich. She'd made similar changes after Great-Aunt Grace died.

"Sunday's my weekly brunch with my friend Marcy." Linda finished peeling a banana and took a bite. "We have sesame bagels with whitefish salad and read the *New York Times* travel section to plan fantasy vacations."

"Have you been on any?"

"No, no, they're just for fun."

"Why don't you go on one?" Addie was as surprised as Linda by the edge to her voice. She read plenty of travel articles, had the money and could take the time, but hadn't been anywhere, either. "Or two, or three or all of them?"

Linda shrugged. "I'm an armchair traveler. Saves me trouble and sunburn and storms and delayed flights."

Oh, dear. She forgot lost luggage.

"I'm a creature of habit I guess." Linda polished off her banana and picked up a brownie. "Like I have the same thing for lunch every day."

Addie stopped with a big bite of apple in her mouth.

"I feel comforted by routines. I like knowing what to expect."

Addie told herself to keep chewing, that she was never going to finish the apple while frozen in horror.

"I was thinking after work today I might stop by the humane society and look at cats."

Steady, Addie. She could panic, or she could take this lunch as a sign that maybe she was a tiny little bit stuck in a very small rut.

"They're supposed to be great company. Perfect for an apartment. And not as much work as a dog."

Large rut. Moon-crater-size rut.

Help.

Be rational. Rationality was one of Addie's best superpowers. She'd use it now, like this: it was good that Addie was faced with the person she could turn into. Especially today, her half birthday, because she had time to change before she turned thirty.

So she'd change. Starting today. Right after work, instead of going to the gym, then showering and having dinner in her apartment reading whatever parts of the *New York Times* she'd missed at breakfast and lunch like she did every evening—except when she had book group or dinner with a friend, she was going to…do something else. Like…

Well, she'd think of something.

She said a grateful goodbye to Linda and charged off to finish her day. By five-thirty, her plan had been cemented into action. After work she was going to Blackstone's on E. 55th. She'd have two drinks and look available. If nothing happened, one point for going and good for her, it was a start. If she talked to at least one guy, two points and a pat on the back. If she was asked for her phone number, three points and a high five.

Given that it was a hot sunny Thursday in late August,

when people were already looking ahead to the weekend, she'd give herself excellent odds on making two points and call it even on three.

Done.

Blackstone's was crowded and noisy, not usually her thing, but today exactly what she was looking for. She pushed her way into a spot at the long bar and managed to get a glass of Chardonnay from the bartender, thinking it might seem more feminine than the beer she was really in the mood for, and wondering if a navy skirt and cream blouse was any kind of come-on outfit. She was pretty sure it wasn't. But hey, Addie was alive and she was female. That was enough for plenty of guys.

She stood resolutely, sipping. Looking around. Smiling.

And sipping.

And looking around.

And smiling.

"Excuse me."

Addie turned hopefully to look into dynamite blue eyes. *Oh, my.*

"I was wondering." He quirked a dark brow. Even his eyebrows were sexy. "Is this seat next to you taken?"

"No." She tipped her head seductively. *Two points!* "Help yourself."

"Thanks." He didn't sit. But…his *girlfriend* did. Then the guy practically climbed into her lap and the two of them started sucking face.

Okay, then. Time to go.

She exited the bar, staggering into a guy as the alcohol kicked in. Did he catch her and did their eyes meet and did choirs of angels sing?

No. He said, "Hey, watch it, lightweight."

Right. Fine. Whatever. She'd go back home to her rut and stay there.

On the way she stopped into the supermarket on Lex-

ington Avenue for a deli sandwich and a cupcake—
chocolate with chocolate frosting.

Girl gone wild.

She made it home, hungry and cranky, managed a halfway nice smile for the doorman and stomped onto the elevator where she turned and saw Mr. Gorgeous coming into
the lobby. Oh, just great. She rushed to push the button
that would close the doors so she didn't have to face more
man-failure, but she hit the wrong one and kept them open.

He got on. "Thanks."

"Sure."

The doors closed. They stood there in their custom-
ary silence. Addie took a deep breath. She had nothing to
lose. Face it, she couldn't even see over the top of her rut.

"I'm Addie." She stuck out her hand. "I live on eight."

"Oh, yeah, right, hi, Addie." He couldn't have been
friendlier, took her hand in his strong warm one. "I'm
Mike. On ten."

She grinned. Maybe her rut wasn't quite so deep after
all. "Nice to meet you, Mike."

"Same here." He looked her over, but not in a leering
way, more polite and appreciative. "My great grandmother
was named Addie. Not a name you hear a lot anymore."

"No." She wrinkled her nose. Men never associated her
name with hot babes they'd lusted after their whole lives.
Always great-aunts and grandmas. Addie's mom had named
her after a Faulkner character in the novel *As I Lay Dying*.

So cheery.

"Any fun plans tonight, Mike?" Ha! Listen to her. No
one could accuse her of being boring now. Maybe Mike
would even like to split a cupcake.

"Yes." He nodded enthusiastically. "My boyfriend and
I are going to make enchiladas and listen to *Madama But-
terfly* live from the Met on Sirius radio."

Addie tried as hard as possible to keep her features

from freezing in dismay. Boyfriend. Of course. "That'll be great. It's a great opera."

Or so she assumed, not having heard a single note of it. "How about you?"

"Oh, well. I'm going to…" Sit around and cry until her hangover started. "Meet some friends. Later."

Like next week in Maine. Where Kevin would be. Though at this rate, he'd turn out to be gay, too.

Growl.

She escaped the elevator and let herself into her apartment, stalked to the living room and whapped the bag with the sandwich and cupcake down on the dining room table, not caring if one interfered with the other.

Let the celebration of her half birthday begin—alone with her take-out meal. And hey, after dinner, she'd meet up with Linda at the humane society and they could each buy eight cats and a truckload of kibble and litter and lock themselves into their apartments for the rest of time.

She got a big glass of water and opened the sandwich, wolfed it down and opened the cupcake to wolf that, too.

Her incoming text signal chimed. Addie put down the cupcake and dug out her phone. She could use good news. Maybe Sarah had some more.

Really glad you'll be there next week. Seems to me we have a lot of catching up to do. Maybe some unfinished business to attend to, as well?

Addie drew in a huge breath. Forget guys in bars. Forget Mr. Gorgeous. And definitely forget the cats.

Next week Addie Sewell was going to blast out of her rut and sail over the moon with The One That Got Away.

After eleven long years she'd finally get a do-over with her first love, Kevin Ames.

2

LAND HO. Derek stood at the front of the Bossons' forty-two-foot cabin cruiser, *Lucky,* as she made her way from Machias to Storness Island, which Paul's family had owned since the 1940s. First boat Derek had been on besides his own in a long time…seven years? Eight? Being a passenger felt strange. Or maybe it was the jet lag from the fifteen hours of travel, Honolulu to Portland, and the five-hour drive that morning, Portland to Machias, to meet Paul.

Lucky left the chop of open sea and purred into the protected cove on the island's north side, a mile from the mainland. Derek had visited the Bossons here only once, several years earlier, but the place was as picturesque and familiar as if he'd just left. The cove boasted a sand beach—unusual along Down east Maine's rocky coast—with the same driftwood branch he remembered lying across it. The white boathouse still stood among the birch, spruce and firs, its doors padlocked. Birds darted over the rocks on the cove's other side. Peaceful. Remote. Hard to imagine any of the world's constant turmoil still existed. Same way he felt leaving civilization and taking to the sea on *Joie de Vivre,* the eighty-foot yacht in which he'd invested—his parents would say wasted—a good chunk of his inheritance from Grandma and Grandpa Bates.

Paul directed *Lucky's* bow toward the mooring, which Derek snagged with the boathook, inhaling the cool air's clean pine-salt scent as he tied her on.

"Nice place you got here." He and Paul were the only ones on the boat. Most of the wedding guests had already arrived, but Derek hadn't been able to get a flight out of Hawaii until after his last charter ended yesterday. Or was it the day before? God he was tired. But he wouldn't miss Paul's wedding for anything.

"Yeah, it works for us." Paul grinned and slapped him on the back. He had one of those eternally youthful faces, round cheeks, sandy hair and bright blue eyes. At twenty-nine he didn't look a day older than when Derek found him ten years earlier vomiting up too much summertime fun, lost and disoriented in a not-great part of Miami. Derek lived there at the time, working jobs on whatever boats he could, in the years before he got serious about his maritime career and enrolled at the Massachusetts Maritime Academy. Since Paul had had no idea where his friend Kevin lived, Derek let him crash on his floor in the tiny apartment he'd sublet when he wasn't at sea. Didn't take him long to figure out Paul was a good kid caught in a bad situation—a delayed adolescent rebellion against real and imagined pressures of adulthood.

Derek got Paul a job on a boat for the summer, helped him get off booze and back on track to finish college at Notre Dame. In the ensuing years their friendship surpassed big-brother mentor and younger screw-up, and became close and satisfying. About as close and satisfying as any relationship Derek could have these days.

He helped Paul load last-minute supplies into the on-board dinghy and lower the boat into the smooth water.

"You won't know a whole lot of people." Paul climbed into the dinghy and manned the oars. "Sarah, of course."

Of course. Derek settled himself in the bow seat. He'd emailed Paul's sister before coming, hoping she'd put aside her grudge against him, but Sarah was a passionate woman prone to the dramatic, and apparently hadn't forgiven him for thinking it was an extremely bad idea for them to sleep together. Her reply had been coldly formal, but at least she'd replied. "How is Sarah?"

"She's Sarah." Paul spoke of his twin with exasperated affection. "Two parts fabulous, two parts crazy-making. She has her best friend Joe here, and her friend from grade school Addie Sewell."

"Addie." Derek frowned, trying to get his tired brain to function. "That's a familiar name, have I met her?"

"Nope." Paul corrected his course with a few strokes of his right oar. "Grade school friend of ours. I was crazy about her for years."

"Oh, right, the woman who walked on water." Derek had been curious about her. Paul was easygoing about pretty much everything—once he stopped drinking—but this Addie had him in knots. As far as Derek knew, Paul had never let on to Addie how he felt.

"Yeah, I had it bad." Paul shook his head, laughing. "Ellen finally exorcized her completely. Addie's a great friend now."

"Okay. Sarah, Addie. Who else?" The boat nudged onto the generous expanse of sand exposed at half tide. Derek jumped out and grabbed the bowline, pulled the dinghy up onto the beach. At high tide, there was barely enough beach to walk on. At low, twelve vertical feet out, there was ample sand, then ample mud, sprinkled with rocks and starfish, clusters of mussels, and a hidden bounty of steamer clams.

"Some friends from college and a few from work in Boston. Nice people. Oh, and Kevin Ames, who can't make it until tomorrow. I think you met him once." He gave Derek a sheepish look and started unloading the skiff onto a waiting wheelbarrow. "Maybe not under the best circumstances."

"Right." Kevin had been the friend buying Paul booze in Florida in spite of his obvious issues with alcohol, and encouraging him to drop out of college and "find himself." He'd reminded Derek of his own brothers: wealthy, self-centered and entitled, sure rules were for other people and that they'd automatically rise to the top—like most scum. If it wasn't for the sea, which had started calling to Derek in middle school and soon after took him away from the life his parents planned for him, he'd probably be that way himself.

Years of hard work clawing up the ranks from deckhand to captain was enough to beat the entitled out of anybody.

They finished loading the wheelbarrow, secured the dinghy against the rising tide and made their way through the Christmas-tree smelling woods, then up a wide bumpy path through blueberry bushes to the back door of the house, a rambling two-story Victorian with weathered gray shingles and dark green trim and shutters. Pitched in nearby clearings were several colorful tents, obviously for overflow guests, though the house had six or seven bedrooms from what he remembered.

"Hey! Hurry up. Ellen needs the cheese you bought for nachos." Sarah jumped down from the house's back deck and strode to meet them, followed by a tall, dark-haired guy in jeans and a Green Day T-shirt. "Hi, Derek."

"Hey, Sarah." He smiled, relieved when she managed a chilly grin back. Apparently she'd be on good behavior for her brother's wedding. "It's good to see you. You look great."

He wasn't lying. She'd dropped the few extra pounds she'd carried, had shortened and shaped her curly blond hair, and moved with more mature grace, though she still evoked a tall firecracker about to go off.

"Thanks. You look…" She scowled at him. "Like you haven't slept in years."

"Not sure I have. Hi, I'm Derek." He offered his hand to the guy hovering behind her, noting the wary look in his eyes. Was this Joe? Looked like Sarah had shared her I'm-the-victim version of their story with him.

"This is Joe." Sarah pointed.

"Good to meet you." Joe shook Derek's hand then picked up a grocery bag under each arm. "I'll take these up to Ellen."

"Come on in. We're having drinks, getting organized to take a picnic supper down to the beach." Sarah turned and charged back up the stairs to the house, throwing Derek an inscrutable look over her shoulder that made him a little nervous. He'd had to put her off gently on that same beach five years ago, and he really didn't want to go through that drama again.

The pine and faint wood smoke smell inside the house was instantly familiar. Paul's parents were on the mainland, so instead of Mrs. Bosson at the stove, there was a blonde, attractive woman Derek identified as Ellen by the adoring look she sent Paul, and whom he instantly liked by the bright smile she sent him. The aroma in the kitchen was fantastic.

"Welcome, Derek." She gave him a sincere hug, Southern accent warming her words. Paul had met her through a mutual friend in Boston two years earlier and his fate was sealed pretty quickly. "It's good to meet the man who saved Paul's life."

"I don't think it was quite that dramatic."

"I know it was. He's still grateful and so am I." A timer went off; she grabbed lobster oven mitts and peered into the oven.

Derek looked around the large, airy eat-in kitchen, amused and pleased so much of it was exactly the same as the last time he was here. The loon sculpture, the blobby painting of a seal Sarah had done as a girl, sand dollars and sea glass, a tide clock hanging next to an iron candle holder forged by a local blacksmith. He'd only been here a week, but would never forget the strong sense of love surrounding the Bosson family, and their joy at being together. He hadn't had much of that in his life, still didn't, and he'd unapologetically eaten it up. Paul had invited him back a few times, but their schedules never seemed to mesh.

"Can I help, Ellen?"

"No, no." She set a pan of fragrant rolls onto a cooling rack. "I just got rid of my army of helpers and am finishing in here. Grab a beer and go on outside, I'll join you in a minute."

"Here you go." Paul pulled bottles of beer and lemonade from the old gas refrigerator and tossed the beer to Derek, who was afraid drinking would send him into a coma of exhaustion, but hell, it was a celebration. He'd risk it.

He followed Paul outside, where Paul was immediately pounced on and dragged into conversation. Derek paused on the front stoop, newly entranced by the Bossons' view. The house sat high on a hill. The land in front—you couldn't really call it a yard—was covered by juniper bushes and sloped to a steep cliff with a breathtaking panorama of ocean and islands. More tents were pitched to the west of the house, and a tiny cabin, built for the twins to overnight in, perched to the east. At this hour the sun's full strength had started to wane and colors were deepening—the blue of water, the dark green of firs, gray-brown shades of the rocky coastline, and the puffy white of clouds. One of his favorite places on earth. And given that he'd been all over the world and was working out of Hawaii these days, he had plenty of Edens to choose from.

Taking a deep breath of the cool, salty air, he shifted his focus to the other guests, in groups on the front porch and down on the grounds. Fifteen to twenty people. At thirty-five, he probably had five to ten years on most of them. It had been a long time since he'd been in this type of social situation. On his boat, he was the authority, keeping just enough distance from guests and employees, making the ship's safety and smooth operation his first priority, the comfort of his passengers a close second. Onshore, he was a temporary or occasional friend to whomever he knew or met wherever he was.

He took a bigger slug of beer than he needed. Paul caught his eye and raised a finger, indicating he'd be right back. Derek waved him off and took another drink. He was a grown man; he could introduce himself to—

"Hi." The woman was right under his nose, smiling at him, about to come up the steps as he'd been about to go down.

"I'm Addie." She pointed to her chest, as if he might not know for sure she was talking about herself.

So this was Addie. To put it mildly, she was not what he expected.

The way Paul had described her beauty, wealth, breeding and untouchability in his besotted way had Derek imagining a chilly, elegant brunette dripping sophistication and disdain. The kind who'd show up at a casual island wedding like this one in stiletto heels, linen and pearls. The kind Derek had taken around the world in his boat, the kind with rich older husbands they were always looking to cheat on.

This woman was wearing soft-looking midthigh black shorts, a casual rose-colored scoop-necked top half covered by a gray hoodie, and flat natural color sandals on slim feet. She had deep coffee eyes and striking dark brows, curling short dark hair—a sexy-schoolgirl fantasy come to life. She reminded him of a down-to-earth version of the French actress Audrey Tautou.

He had major hots for Audrey Tautou.

"You're Addie Sewell."

"Yes." The expressive brows lowered in amused confusion. "How did you know?"

"You're world famous."

"Ha!" Her wide mouth broke into a smile that took away a good deal of his weariness. "You must be a friend of Paul's."

"Derek Bates."

"Oh." Her smile faltered, her eyes clouded over, the temperature around them dropped forty degrees. Brrrrr. "Sarah's told me a lot about you."

"That's funny." He forced himself to chuckle, visualizing a roll of duct tape over Sarah's mouth. "Sarah doesn't know a lot about me."

He expected an insult, an argument, a stinging defense of her friend, and was surprised to find her considering him thoughtfully. "I just know what she told me."

Derek sighed. He'd leave bad enough alone. It was his word versus Sarah's and this was her territory and these were her people. "I'm pretty sure I'm sorry to hear that. When did you arrive, Addie?"

"Three days ago. Sunday evening."

"From…?"

"LaGuardia." She glanced around, apparently not sure she should be talking to him.

"Into Portland?"

"Bangor."

"Okay." He nodded too many times, at a loss what to say next, how to act around a lovely woman who'd undoubtedly been told by her best friend that he was something you should avoid stepping in.

"Weather been good here this week?" *Really, Derek? The weather?*

"It's been okay." She fidgeted with the zipper on her hoodie. "Not great. But at least no rain."

"What have I missed so far?"

"Oh. Well. We've gone hiking on the mainland. Done a lot of hanging out…" She laughed nervously. "I can't really remember."

"It's okay."

"Oh, Quoddy Head. We went there. The easternmost point in the U.S."

"Nice." He nodded again. This was torture. He wanted to skip the small talk. Go straight to what mattered, how she felt about life, whether she was doing what she loved, whether the world was a gorgeous place or a disaster, whether she was seeing anyone, and whether she liked kissing all night under the stars…

He nearly hugged Ellen when she clapped her hands from the front stoop.

"Hey, y'all, we're ready. Come through the kitchen, grab something to carry and we'll head down to the beach."

Derek finished his beer and tossed it into the recycling container set up outside. If he wanted to have fun this week he'd need to do better than this socially. Part of his job was chatting with passengers, so making small talk should be second nature. Instead he felt as if he were trying to exercise a muscle atrophied from years of disuse.

After grabbing a cooler, he joined the procession to the beach, aware of Addie's presence in the crowd as if she was lit up in neon. He still couldn't get over how different she was than he expected, or how much she aroused his…curiosity.

The beach was cool and comfortable; a light breeze kept the mosquitoes manageable, though repellent was passed around before everyone settled in. To his relief, Derek eventually got a second—third? fourth?—wind, and was able to relax and enjoy himself. The guests were friendly and easy to talk to, all interesting people with solid views on life and their places in it. The food was simple and abundant: excellent crab rolls, nachos, potato salad and coleslaw, and the beer flowed like…beer.

A few times—more than a few—he glanced over at Addie and caught her just looking away, though she made no move to approach him. He wasn't sure what to make of her surreptitious inspection. Was she repulsed? Fascinated? Attracted? He was certainly attracted. The more he looked at her, the longer the evening went on, the more he remembered stories Paul told about Addie, the more he was intrigued, and the more beautiful she became. Maybe it was the softening light. Maybe it was the beer. He wanted to talk to her again. Alone.

As the sun lowered, there was a move to light a bonfire and gather around it. Not enough sleep and too much beer, food and conversation propelled Derek to his feet. He could use a break and had a deep need to watch the sunset from a remote corner of the island he remembered as a prime viewing spot. A quick look showed him Addie was missing from the crowd. He'd have liked to invite her along, but that was probably a terrible idea given what she still thought of him, so it was just as well.

Excusing himself from Sarah's friend Joe, who'd turned out to be an interesting and friendly guy, and Carrie, a piece of work who'd settled on Joe after flirting with pretty much every male at the party, Derek left the beach and headed back into the woods up the hill toward the southwest where he could best watch the evening light show.

As he crested the hill, he glanced back at the house; its shingles glowed majestic gray-pink in the evening light, tents providing a festive carnival atmosphere.

Addie Sewell was coming down the front steps.

Derek stopped short. When she caught sight of him, she did the same. For a few bizarre seconds they stared at each other across the grassy space, then what-the-hell, Derek beckoned to her. She frowned and looked down toward the path to the beach.

This might take some persuading.

"Hey." He spanned the distance between them across the top of the hill, brushing past goldenrod waving in the breeze. Addie held her ground, chin lifted, watching him approach. "I'm going to take a walk, to check out the sunset."

She pressed her lips together. An adorable dimple appeared in her right cheek. "Sounds like a good idea."

"Want to come with me?"

"Oh." She blushed crimson, eyes darting again to the apparent safety of the woods. Poor woman, trapped by the big bad sexual predator Derek wasn't. "I don't know...."

He'd wait. He swatted a mosquito. Stuffed his hands in his pockets and rocked back and forth on his heels. Began whistling.

She giggled. A good sign.

"The sunsets here are breathtaking...."

"Well." She gave him a cautious sidelong look. "It has been either cloudy or foggy since I've been here."

He grinned. "I'll keep my clothes on and my hands to myself, I promise."

"Oh, no, you don't need to—" Her eyes shot wide. "Wait! No, yes, you do!"

He laughed and she laughed with him, and then bang, the tension was gone, and he felt lighter than he had all day.

"What I meant was, I'm not worried." She arched a brow at him. "I have a spectacular right hook, three gold medals in track and a black belt."

"Weaponry?"

She pointed emphatically into his face. "That, too."

"I'll remember." He smiled, trying to look as blandly safe as possible, so she wouldn't guess the depth of his attraction. After what she'd probably heard from Sarah, he should act like touching her had never occurred to him.

Though it was starting to be all he could think about.

"So you must have been on Storness Island before, Addie?" He gestured her onto the narrow path in front of him, being the perfect gentleman. The perfect gentleman who wasn't wrong in thinking her rear view would not exactly be a hardship.

"Actually, no. Sarah invited me a few times, but my parents always had me in summer camp or some program, or we were traveling. So this is new to me."

"Sounds like you were a heavily scheduled kid."

"Oh, yeah. They played Mozart while I was in utero. I got infant flash cards, only educational toys, organic food before it was mainstream, you name it." She spoke matter-of-factly. Was she grateful? Resentful? Resigned? He wanted to get at more of her, only barely understanding his fascination.

"How was that?"

She shrugged, keeping her eyes on the path, an obstacle course of rocks and protruding tree roots. "It was all I knew, so it was fine at the time. Now, it seems a little over the top. They'd lightened up some by the time my brother came along. He's five years younger. What about you?"

"I'm the oldest of four brothers. My parents did the overachiever conditioning on us, too. It worked pretty well on my brothers. I wasn't interested." He reached to touch her shoulder and pointed into the bay where the sunset was gathering force. "Look at that."

"Beautiful." She stopped walking, then smiled rapturously and stretched out her arms, as if wanting to embrace the bay. "Don't you wish all of life was that simple and perfect? After living in the city so long it's like...well, I miss things like this at home."

He knew how she felt. "What city? Wait, near LaGuardia obviously, so I'll guess New York?"

"Manhattan. Where's home for you?"

He quirked an eyebrow. "That's a tough question to answer. I don't have one in the traditional sense."

"Oh, right." She turned and kept walking. "You're the yacht captain."

He expected the slight sneer. Most people had no idea what the job entailed, how serious his responsibilities and how wide his range of duties. "I'm based in Hawaii right now."

"Ooh, *that* must be tough."

He caught up to her as the path widened down a cranberry-covered hillside, red berries a stunning contrast to the carpet of dark, shiny leaves. "It has its moments. What do you do in Manhattan?"

"I'm an actuary for an insurance company."

"Ah, a numbers woman." And a very smart woman.

He was impressed. Maybe she'd like to take over for his bookkeeper, Mary, who was due to go on maternity leave in another month. "How do you cope with Manhattan being Manhattan?"

Her mouth puckered a little while she thought. The sun landed on her cheekbones and lit her eyes. He was hit with a strong urge to kiss her. But since he'd only just met her and was trying to show how wrong Sarah was about him...not a good idea.

"In Manhattan you have to retreat into your head. You can't go out there every day and let the chaos get in your face. At least I can't. It's strange what you get used to. A friend on the phone the other day said she could barely understand me over sirens in the background and I hadn't even heard them."

"Noisy, crowded, sounds perfect."

"Oh, but there's so much culture. So much energy. Anything you want to eat, buy, hear or see, you can find in New York." She smiled mischievously, mouth generous, lips full. "How do you deal with all that total isolation in the middle of the ocean?"

"Ha. Good question. My answer would probably be something along the lines of, 'I retreat into my head. You can't go out there and let the emptiness get in your face.'" He loved the way she laughed, soft and low. "And of course there's so much beauty. So much peace."

"Speaking of which..." They'd arrived on the rocky ledge he remembered as the best spot for sunset watching. He wasn't wrong. The sight was spectacular. Addie crossed her arms; her breasts rose and nestled against each other. She sighed in pleasure.

Derek swallowed. Lack of sleep, beer, this woman...

He was beginning to understand what had happened to Paul.

"I'm curious." She turned to face him, eyes doe-wide and questioning. The gods were putting his resolve not to touch her to an excruciating test. He wasn't sure he'd pass. "Did you always want to be at sea instead of settled in one place?"

"Yes. Did you always want to be in the same office and house every day?

"Not specifically, no. But it didn't surprise me I ended up there." She tipped her head, mouth spreading again, this time in a troubled smile that was both vulnerable and bewitching.

Derek should step back from her. Derek should stop thinking about her and start thinking about tragedies or trash heaps or tarantulas. Derek needed a good night's sleep. Or twelve. "Why not?"

"I didn't have a childhood dream like yours. I always did what was expected of me. My parents prepared me well for my future, and I felt I owed it to them to be successful."

Ah, a good girl. She was really turning him on now. He wanted to teach her how to be naughty sometimes. "There are all kinds of success."

"True." She brushed a stray lock off her forehead. "I guess I'm pretty traditional. Not that exciting."

Ha. He wasn't touching that one. Instead he turned her and pointed out into the bay. "Look now."

"Oh." Her face brightened; it was all he could do to make himself watch the sunset he was here for. "Incredible."

"Yes. Beautiful." She could think he was talking about the glorious colors if she wanted. The sun was slipping through a vivid combination of orange and maroon at the horizon. Higher up the clouds had turned baby-girl pink. Seagulls flew overhead; cormorants skimmed the water, heading toward the navy-colored east. The moment was powerful, primal. Addie had him under a spell he barely understood.

He moved up close behind her until he could practically feel the warmth from her body. She tensed and went very still.

"Addie." His voice came out low and husky. She made a small sound, but didn't answer. He barely knew what he was going to say. "Did you…ever meet a guy and know you'd be kissing him very soon?"

She flinched, but didn't move away. "Derek…I don't even know you."

"I'm just asking." Like hell he was.

"Oh. Well. Yes. I mean…I guess so." She cleared her throat. "Have you?"

"I'm not really into kissing guys."

A nervous giggle exploded out of her. "I meant—"

"I know what you meant. Yes, I have."

"Oh." She sounded carefully neutral. "Why did you ask me that?"

"I wanted to know."

Addie turned her head to the side, her features darkened by the light behind her. "What happened between you and Sarah?"

"She obviously told you."

"I want to hear it from you."

He was absurdly pleased. She was giving him a chance. But since she was already on Sarah's side, he'd have to choose his words carefully. "Sarah and I…mixed signals one night. When things didn't work out the way she expected she was angry and hurt. She's a great person, I respect her and would go back and change that night if I could."

Addie turned around to look up at him, stopping mere

inches away. God help him. "She told me you came on to her."

"No." He held still while she examined his face, wanting to touch her so badly he was having trouble breathing, aware that he'd just called her close friend a liar.

"Did you ask me about kissing because you wanted to kiss me?"

"What do you think?"

He expected a giggle. A blush. A coy glance. Instead she looked distraught. "Derek, I'm...I'm here to be with someone."

A solid kick to his stomach. "Yeah? Who's that?"

She dropped her gaze. "Someone I've known a long time."

He would have noticed if she'd been hanging around any guy in particular tonight. As far as he knew all the guests had arrived.

Except...*him*.

Aw, crap. "Kevin Ames."

"How did you know?" She was blushing.

"He's world famous." He kept his voice light, not wanting to sound as disappointed and pissed off as he was. "I've met him."

"Really?" Her voice got all eager, which made Derek even grouchier. "Where?"

"In Florida." He was not going to comment further. If Kevin was the type she fell for, she wasn't going to want a man like him.

He shouldn't care. For God's sake, he'd only met Addie tonight.

Maybe it was the booze, the loss of sleep, too much loneliness for too long, but there were plenty of attractive women here, many of whom he'd spoken to at dinner—

hell there had been plenty of attractive women crawling all over his boat for the last eight years.

It was crazy, it made no sense, he was exhausted, out of his mind, he'd known Addie all of a few hours.

But he'd never wanted any of them the way he wanted her.

3

SARAH LAY ON a grassy patch at the edge of the island's northern beach, where they'd had dinner that evening, listening to the waves lapping, gazing up at the night sky in search of shooting stars. She'd gone inside with everyone else hours ago when the party broke up, but after people headed off to bed she'd come back out here, knowing she wouldn't sleep. Too many emotions, her head spun with them. She hated feeling half-crazy like this.

For whatever reason she'd been born feeling things more intensely than most people, which earned her all kinds of lovely labels: diva, drama queen, yeah, yeah, she knew. She did overreact, she did get more upset, more happy, more…just more. But short of drugging herself, there was nothing she could do about it. She was who she was, for better or worse.

Right now worse.

She swallowed awkwardly over the mild burn of thirst in the back of her throat. One beer too many and not enough water to balance out the alcohol. But it was so lovely lying here watching the sky, indulging her tortured thoughts, that she didn't want to go back up to the house for a drink.

Derek Bates was the most gorgeous, sexiest, most intelligent, incredible man she'd ever met. And Sarah was nothing to him. She always fell for men who didn't want her. Before Derek there'd been Ethan at Vassar, captain of the baseball team, a great friend. She'd lusted, but he never thought of her "that way" and had dated cheerleaders and dancers and other varieties of perfect—from her perspective perfectly vapid—women, while maintaining a closer relationship with Sarah than with any of them. Before Ethan there'd been Kevin Ames. She'd had it bad for Kevin for a long, long time. But when he finally stopped chasing big-boobed wonders, he'd wanted Addie, not Sarah. Maybe he still did…that would be great, actually. If Sarah couldn't have him, at least one of her best friends could; for Addie's sake Sarah would do whatever it took to bring them together this week. Addie needed someone. She had no idea how fabulous she was.

But back to Sarah's favorite topic: Sarah. What if she never got Derek out of her head or her heart, even knowing he'd never belong to her?

That night five years ago on this beach, she'd been a total brat, which she was still so horribly embarrassed about she could barely look at him.

Although seriously, who could not look at Derek? She still did, just not when he could tell.

Anyway, it had been a cool and moonless night, like this one. They'd sat on this very spot talking for an hour after Paul and their parents had gone to bed. Sarah had been drunk on too much wine and had started bawling over something, she couldn't even remember what. Derek had comforted her, put his arms around her, stroked her hair. She'd thought that was the signal she'd been dreaming of and had tried her best to make something happen.

Yeah, well, nice fantasy, Sarah.

Then, in an appalling show of immaturity, she'd bolstered her crushed ego by accusing him to Addie and then to Joe, who when she came back to Vassar had been able to tell right away that something was upsetting her. It didn't help that she'd also overheard comments from Paul about Derek's sexploits in harbors around the world. A woman in every port, sometimes two, and in St. Thomas, three, two of whom were apparently twins. So even not caring much who he had in bed at any given time, he still hadn't wanted Sarah.

She coughed. Man, she needed water. Her throat was practically sticking to itself.

Footsteps rustled and snapped in the woods. Sarah lifted onto her elbows. A man's form, stepping onto the beach, well-built, tall. Her heart starting to race. Derek? Coming to finish what they started?

"Sarah?"

Joe. Her heart slowed. She sat up. "Yes, it's me."

"What are you doing out here?"

"Couldn't sleep. How did you know where I was?"

"I heard you leave, didn't hear you come back so I came looking." He plunked down on the grass beside her and handed her something cool.

A can of sparkling water. "Joe, you are a god."

"Wait, you're only realizing that now?"

"No, no, I knew." She cracked the top to the can and took a long, grateful drink. "Heaven. Thank you."

"You're welcome. So what are you doing out here besides not sleeping?"

"Watching for shooting stars. Thinking."

"About what?" He scootched down to lie next to her. His warm side adjacent to her hip made her realize she'd gotten chilly.

"About…how I always fall for guys who don't want me."

"No kidding. You're batting about a thousand on that one."

"Ha." Sarah giggled. "Thanks for the vote of support."

"I mean how can anyone be so clueless?"

"Hey." She shoved him with her hip. "Your deep empathy is much appreciated."

"You can't see what's right under your nose, Sarah Bosson." His voice descended to a melodramatic growl.

"Okay, okay. So what do I do?"

"Come to Dr. Joe. He will rewire your brain using everyday household items."

Sarah's laughter was interrupted by a horrific burp from the soda bubbles. She laughed harder. "Oh, no! Joe, I'm so sorry."

"It's fine, don't worry, really. I still have hearing in my other ear."

"Stop, stop." She waited for her giggles to die out, loving that she could belch in front of Joe and not feel more than slightly embarrassed. He had no illusions she was perfect. He had no illusions about her at all. And for some reason he still wanted to be her friend.

They'd met at Vassar and became close right away. After graduating they'd both moved to Boston where she got a job fund-raising for Harvard and he did something with computers she couldn't begin to understand. They saw each other a few times a month and talked and texted often. He was her absolute rock. She'd die without him. "Anyway, so I was thinking about this one unattainable guy who—"

"Derek."

Sarah's jaw dropped. That was psychic, even for him.

Or maybe she was pathetically obvious. "How did you know?"

"You mooned over him all night."

"I did not!" Yup. Pathetic.

"Because he's so hunky and sexy and sooo super hot!" Sarah made a sound of exasperation. "Well, he is."

"I know, I know." Joe's sigh was heavy in the darkness. "Go ahead, Sarah, talk. You know I can take it."

"Well, I have to tell you something." She hunched her shoulders, hugging her knees, hoping he wouldn't be angry. "That night with Derek on the beach."

His body tensed next to her. "Yes?"

"He didn't attack me. I was drunk and I sort of…tried to make something happen."

"I figured it was something like that."

"Wait, what?" She released her knee to whap his shoulder. "How dare you undermine the power of my dramatic bombshell?"

"Aw, Sarah." He reached up to push her bangs off her face, let his fingers drift tenderly down her cheek. "I've known you for nine years. If you were really attacked by some guy, he wouldn't live long enough to see the next day, let alone the next five years. The way Paul talks about this guy, the way you talk about him, it didn't add up. I didn't know exactly what happened, but I'm not surprised."

She lay down next to him, throat tight. "You don't blame me?"

"For what?"

"Lying?"

"I didn't think of it that way. You just weren't ready to tell the whole truth."

Her heart was full to bursting. She had to blink through

tears to bring the stars back into focus. "Seriously, Joe, are you perfect or do you just pretend to be?"

"I'm the real deal, Sarah. Maybe someday you'll realize—"

A white streak blazed across a good portion of the night sky. Sarah shrieked and pointed. "Did you see *that?*"

"Whoa. Yes. I did." He sounded as awed as she felt. "It means you get to make a wish."

"Why not you?"

"You saw it first."

"How do you know?"

"Because." He reached over and rubbed her head until her already messy hair was a total disaster, making her shriek again, with laughter this time. "I said so."

"Stop! My coif! My stunning updo. Ruined!"

"Now." He let her go. "Make a wish."

"Okay, okay." Sarah thought—took her about half a second to decide—then reached up to the sky and wished with all her might that she might love a man who loved her back. It was all she'd ever wanted. So many people managed it. Her parents. Paul and Ellen. Why not her?

"Finished?"

"Yes."

"Should I check?"

Sarah frowned. "Check what?"

"To see if the six hottest members of the U.S. Navy are waiting naked in your room?"

She giggled. "That's *not* what I wished for."

"Then I hope you get whatever it was." He got to his feet, reached down and pulled her up opposite him as if she weighed nothing. "And I think you need to go to bed."

"Yes, Dad." She didn't resist when his arms came around her. He was such a good friend. So patient with her, so nonthreatening. Why couldn't she fall in love with him?

"Listen to me."

"Mmm?" She laid her head on his solid shoulder.

"You are going to sleep really well tonight." He started stroking her hair, working the tense muscles at the base of her scalp. "And tomorrow you are going to wake up and realize you've put this Derek demon totally to bed."

"Okay." She closed her eyes. As if. She'd be happy if she could think about him without getting wet. And talk to him without getting so flustered and guilty she could barely form words.

"And." Joe rocked her back and forth. "You are going to remind yourself that I love you no matter how insane you get, no matter how completely and insufferably annoying, no matter how—"

"Uh, Joe?" She patted his chest. "Yeah, um, thanks. That's enough."

"No problem." He squeezed her then took her hand. "Let's go."

"I'm ready." She followed him across the beach, fumbling for her flashlight. "Hey, who was that girl you were talking to all night? The cute little one."

"Carrie?"

"Yeah. Where's your flashlight?" She tried to remember seeing him use one, still not having any luck extracting hers from her sweatshirt pocket since it was on the side of the hand Joe was holding.

"Don't need one. Just follow me."

"Wait, seriously? Through the woods? The path is treacherous and it's pitch-black. I've come here all my life and even I wouldn't do it."

"I have cat eyes."

"Joe…" She hung back, still trying for the flashlight, until he tugged her impatiently forward.

"Just lift your feet so you don't trip. You'll be fine."

"Okay. But if you kill me I'm suing." She followed him a few more steps, getting braver as it became apparent he was navigating nicely. "So…what about Carrie?"

"Nice girl. What do you want to know?"

"I don't know." Her voice came out too high and she had to relax her throat to get it back to normal. "Do you like her?"

He snorted impatiently. "No, I talked to her all night because she repulsed me."

"Okay, okay. Never mind." Sarah's giggle felt forced. What was wrong with her, she was so self-absorbed she couldn't even be happy for her best friend? "I'm glad for you. I hope something comes of it. You deserve someone wonderful."

"I think so, too." He pulled her up unerringly through the trees, finding the path past the blueberry patch and up to the house, supporting her when she stumbled. It was actually kind of mysterious and cool.

"I don't know what I'd do without you, Joe."

He chuckled and opened the back door for her to go inside. "I hope you never have to find out."

She kissed his cheek and crossed through the living room toward the bedroom she shared with Addie, noticing how much calmer and lighter she felt, how much more clear and slow-moving her brain was. Joe was good for her. He always had been. Knew her inside out, tolerated her worst faults and adored her strengths. What more could a woman want?

Macho alpha sizzle. Daring, adventure, challenge.

Sarah sighed and used the hall bathroom, then climbed into bed, careful not to disturb Addie.

Sometimes she thought she must be the most shallow person alive. But if she was deep-down wired to be attracted to guys like Derek, Ethan and Kevin instead of guys like Joe, there wasn't a single damn thing she could do about it.

4

ADDIE WAS CONFUSED. Standing on the cliff in front of the Bossons' house, drinking champagne punch, keeping an eye out for Kevin's arrival, she was in a thorough state of turmoil. And since confusion didn't visit her very often, thank goodness, she could safely say that she didn't like it. At all. Most of the time her emotional life was, if not under control, then at least comprehensible. She was single or she was in a relationship. She was friends with someone or she wasn't. She had a crush on a guy or she didn't.

She'd come to this island with a head full of Kevin. Her past with him, the promise of intimate time with him this weekend, and the vaguest whisper of possibility that they could continue some relationship into the future— Philadelphia wasn't that far from New York City after all. Over a decade of mooning and fantasy about to come true.

And then she met Derek.

Her love of the simple and the clear—statistics and probabilities and interpretable data—did not prepare her for a man who, during their first-ever meeting unsettled her to the point of blathering, who wanted to watch the sunset alone with her, and who, in a low, dreamy voice, as much as said he wanted to kiss her. Frankly, for a few seconds—okay, many seconds—she'd wanted him to kiss her more than she'd wanted to go on breathing.

Even if Sarah's story about Derek wasn't one-hundred percent accurate, as Derek claimed, he was still a girl-in-every-port guy in his mid-thirties, while Kevin, at thirty-one, had already been totally committed to one woman in a marriage, faithful until divorce did them part.

Shouldn't that clear everything up? A rational conclusion drawn from the available information, leading to a sensible low-risk recommendation for future action. Derek was a womanizer. Kevin was a sweetheart. Only an idiot would still dream about Derek. Or do something completely foolish like keep peeking over at him on a kayak trip earlier that afternoon. She'd interrupted perfectly wonderful chances to stare into the water, spot orange and purple starfish, waving seaweed that looked nearly floral, blue mussels and splotchy pink growths on underwater reefs by looking up every three seconds to keep track of where he was and with whom. Worse, she'd caught him several times in the act of looking over at her, too.

For a while he'd paddled alongside her kayak, and they'd chatted easily about his extensive travels and her not-so-extensive ones. About movies and books and favorite foods. Through it all, he'd shown no signs of anything more than friendly interest, and then he'd quite naturally steered his kayak over to chat with someone else.

Well, of course, right? He was here to get to know Paul's friends, too. Plus the guy had put himself out there with her last night and she'd stomped him flat, why *would* he continue to show interest?

And why couldn't she stop wanting him to?

Greedy Addie, wanting her hunk and to eat him, too.

She giggled at her own thought and nearly spit out the sip of punch she'd just taken. The group was assembled after quick-as-possible showers to save the water supply, enjoying a predinner drink or two.

The group minus Paul. Paul was not on the island because Paul had gone to the mainland to pick up *Kevin*.

Eek!

Addie was as light as the champagne, as bubbly as the…champagne, as fizzy as the…um, well…champagne. And clearly not big on similes.

Paul had been gone over an hour, which meant any minute he'd be back. Addie had come down by the cliff here, hoping to catch the first glance of *Lucky's* approach, so she would know exactly when to start freaking out.

Or she could get a head start and do it *now*.

Closing her eyes, she inhaled deeply, fighting a sudden deep desire to be home organizing Great-Aunt Grace's papers. So easy. So uncomplicated. This paper goes in this pile. That goes in that one.

"Hello, Addie."

She started at the sound of Derek's voice, luckily not standing close enough to the edge to pitch over. She immediately had to put the brakes on a fantasy of Derek saving her from certain death by hauling her back into his arms.

Honestly. Addie pulled herself together. "Hey, there, Derek."

Then she made a fatal error. She turned to look at him.

He was breathtaking. A touch more sun on his cheeks made the contrast even sexier between golden skin and his white shirt, and made his vivid eyes practically jump out of his face.

No, no, *Kevin* was coming soon. Once glance at him and everything she'd ever felt for him over so many years would come rushing back again, and this Derek guy would be forgotten.

"Enjoying the view?"

"I am." She put on a casual smile—ho-hum, nice to see you—and concentrated on the view, which she'd just been pretending to look at before. Yes, it was lovely. A sailboat was cruising in toward the bay, sails crisp white in the sunshine. A lobsterman was hauling traps just beyond the next island, his white and green boat bobbing gently in the waves. Breezes ruffled her hair; the air was sweet enough to drink. Why hadn't she been enjoying this all along? "I don't think I'd ever get tired of this view. The sea is always changing, the light, the birds, the boats…"

Derek chuckled. "Well, Ms. Manhattan. You're describing the view I see pretty much every day. Maybe you need to give that life a try."

She snorted, having to suppress yet another picture, this one of herself sunbathing on the deck of his yacht. "Do they pay full-time salary and benefits for someone to project the odds of running aground or sinking?"

"Um…" He tapped a finger on his very sexy lips as if trying to remember. "Not really, no. But I have an on-board bookkeeping position opening up in a few weeks. Are you interested?"

"Don't think so, but thanks." Addie made another serious mistake. She smiled at him. Then he smiled at her, and it was as if the scene around them wrapped itself up neatly and disappeared, the way backgrounds did sometimes in cartoons, leaving the two of them alone in nothingness.

Worse than how she'd felt the night before when she'd had to force herself to watch one of the most magnificent sunsets she'd ever seen. All she'd wanted to do was gaze into those cinnamon-brown eyes and drool.

Okay, Addie. Engage rational superpowers immediately. Like this: fine to look, fine to appreciate, but no touching.

An upswell of voices by the house made her turn to see what was happening.

Kevin was happening. Somehow she'd missed being first to see the boat, hadn't heard it, either, and now he was right here, standing on the front porch, being hugged by Ellen, two or three others crowding around for their turns, grinning that old familiar straight-toothed grin that could still knock her for a loop.

And just like that, as if she'd been released from a sorcerer's spell, Addie was able to move again, to walk away from the awesome but evil power that was Derek, and into the pure heavenly light of Kevin.

"Ad-*die*." The last syllable of her name came out on a shout. She'd forgotten the special way he said it, and the memory made her legs move even faster. And there he was, disentangling himself from the other woman and sailing down the steps on his strong runner's legs to grab and whirl her around in a joyous embrace that made her laugh and gasp for breath and nearly spill her punch.

Kevin Ames.

"God, look at you." He held her at arm's length, his face glowing. Eleven years later, he looked exactly the same. Maybe his face was thinner, maybe his skin was a bit weathered, and now that she looked, had he lightened his hair? But really, exactly the same. "You've turned into one seriously hot babe, Addie!"

His face might be glowing, hers was on fire. "Thanks, Kevin. You really—"

"Addie all grown up." He shook his head, looking her closely up and down. Somewhat disturbingly, she noticed his eyes were the exact shade of brown as Derek's. Medium caramel. Only for some reason they weren't doing quite the same things to her. "Addie Sewell. I can't believe it. You're a real woman now."

"Oh, well." She was taken aback by his seductive tone then chided herself for being such a prude. Kevin wanting her was the whole point. "I just did the normal grow—"

"What were you, seventeen, eighteen last time I saw you?"

She nodded, unable to blush any harder than she was, or she'd try. "Eighteen."

"I remember that time very well, Addie." His voice lowered, his gaze turned tender. He touched her under the chin, making her shiver. "We never quite got synced up, you and me."

"Uh, no. Not quite." She peeked up at him under her lashes, trying not to be mortified by the memory of her outburst at their last meeting. He certainly didn't seem to hold it against her. "I was a little naive."

"You *were?*" One eyebrow rose suggestively. "So that means you're not anymore?"

Man, her blush mechanism was going to wear out at this rate. But this was what she had come for. No matter how loudly Aunt Grace's boxes were calling to her, no matter how uneasy and rattled she felt around Kevin, she wasn't going to be the shy hide-away girl anymore. "No, Kevin. Not anymore."

"I'm really glad to hear that, Addie." He leaned in close, caught and intertwined her fingers with his, gave them a squeeze. "I've always had a soft spot for you. Actually… sometimes a *hard* spot."

She caught herself just before she cringed, and smiled up at him without shame this time, waiting for the world to disappear around them the way it had around her and Derek.

Waiting…

And…

Hmm.

Well, she felt all warm and melty and sweet, that was something, right?

Plenty.

"Kevin!" A guy Addie barely knew—John, she thought—one of Paul and Kevin's old track buddies charged out of the house and Kevin bolted away for the chest-bumping man-hug.

Addie grinned at the macho ritual then on impulse turned around, feeling eyes burning into her back.

He was still there, feet planted apart, hands on his hips, looking grimmer than she'd ever seen him, or pretty much anyone, look.

Not because of her and Kevin?

No. He didn't look sulky or immature or sour-grapes. He looked…angry. And strong. And nobly determined.

And sexy as hell.

Turning head away, lalala, can't seeeee you!

"Addie." Sarah bounded toward her, drink in hand. "We have *got* to talk."

"Now?" She peered around Sarah at Kevin, relieved to have an excuse not to look back at Derek again. "Can't I have a few more minutes?"

"No." Sarah grabbed her hand and pulled her away from the crowd, across the top of the hill where Addie and Derek had walked the night before.

"What is it, Sarah?"

"I have to tell you something."

"I figured that much." She was used to Sarah's drama, but this time Sarah seemed uncharacteristically uneasy. Usually Addie had the feeling that underneath the wailing and gnashing of teeth, Sarah was enjoying herself immensely. Not this time. "What's going on, are you okay?"

"Fine. Better than ever. But I should have told you this

before. Years ago. Coming here made it really clear." She took a deep breath. "It's about Derek."

"Yes?" Addie had a feeling she knew what was coming. If Sarah's story matched the one Derek told, that meant he'd been telling the truth.

"That night with Derek and me. He wasn't— I was the one—" She gripped Addie's arm, blue eyes wide and earnest, then seemed unable to go on.

"You made the move on him."

"Yes." Breath exploded out of her, Sarah-size relief. "Yes."

"It's okay, Sarah."

"I'm so sorry I—" She frowned. "Hey, how did you know?"

Addie took a leisurely sip of punch, deciding how to answer. She could tell Sarah that Derek let it slip, but wasn't sure it was her place to frame him. And she'd definitely had her own doubts about Sarah's story. "Your anger at him was a little over the top. I wasn't sure, but I thought something didn't feel right."

"Jeez, you, too?"

"Who else?"

"Joe. He said he figured it out pretty much right away." She looked suddenly troubled. "That girl Carrie is really after him, have you noticed."

Addie studied her friend closely. Was she jealous? Addie could only hope. Joe had been deeply in love with her for so long. It was heartbreaking to watch. Sarah had to realize on some level how perfect they were together. He calmed her down and adored her; she spruced him up and gave him purpose. But who knew if she'd ever let herself admit it. "Can you blame her?"

"No, of course not." She laughed too carelessly. "Joe is the perfect man. I tell him so all the time."

"Exactly." Addie smirked, enjoying the situation. Sarah was jealous! Addie would be so pleased if Joe got his happy ever after with her. "Maybe they'll end up together."

"Maybe." She bit her lower lip. "I'm not sure she's his type, though. She's too…obvious."

"Uh-huh. Yeah, men hate when women make them feel totally sexy and desired."

Sarah glared at her. "Not helping."

"Trust me, he won't even notice her extreme beauty and large breasts and—"

"So you're not angry about Derek?" The abrupt subject change nearly made Addie laugh, but out of pity she switched gears, wondering if Carrie might be the answer to Joe's prayers in a way Sarah didn't even suspect.

"No, I'm not angry. He hurt you, and you lashed out, and then felt trapped by the lie. Welcome to the human race."

"Aww, thank you, sweetie. I'm not sure I deserve forgiveness." Sarah gave Addie a fierce hug. "But now wait, we need to talk about the most important thing. How are you going to seduce Kevin?"

"Seduce him?" She blinked stupidly. "Me?"

Sarah rolled her eyes. "Isn't that the point of this weekend? I mean besides Paul getting married of course. The secondary point, then?"

"I thought he'd handle that." The minute the words left her mouth she wished them back. Guys had always been the aggressors in her relationships. This week was about getting out of her rut, not settling back into it in a different place. "No. Forget it. Forget I said that."

"Gladly." Sarah fanned herself. "I thought I was going to have to smack you."

"No, no." Addie took a gulp of champagne punch for strength. Seduce him. *Dear God.*

"I'm thinking tonight you can play a little hard to get, just tease him." Sarah wiggled her fingers gracefully. "And then tonight when everyone is in bed, sneak into his room and *bang.*"

The dancing fingers made a vicious grab.

Good Lord. Was she crazy? Just walk into Kevin's room and attack him? Addie pictured him asleep in one of the second-floor bedrooms where Paul and Ellen had put their closest friends. Imagined fitting her naked body to his, waking him with a gentle kiss.

Well.

That would take her pretty damn far out of her rut.

"If I do this…" She shook her head as Sarah started a massive victory dance. "Sarah, I said *if.*"

"No chickening out." Sarah waggled a warning finger, eyes flashing excitement. "You can do this. He wants you to, you saw his text and you saw how he greeted you."

"True." Deep inside her, little flutters of excitement, even though the concept was still surreal.

"Come on." Sarah took her arm and dragged her back toward the house. "You need more punch."

A second glass of punch later, Addie and Sarah were in line at the buffet near tables set up in the middle of a circle of tents, loading up on hamburgers, hot dogs, potato chips and bean salad.

"Now we strategize." Sarah surveyed the tables. "We want to sit somewhere empty, not too large, so you can get cozy with Kevin when he comes to join us."

"And you with Joe."

Sarah made a face. "I do not do cozy with Joe. That's Carrie's job."

"Ha. I think if you ever wanted to get cozy with Joe he would be more than happy to."

"What?" Sarah was still analyzing the table situation,

effectively using her habit of blocking out what she didn't want to hear. "Small ones are taken. That one will do."

Addie followed her to a table for six set up at the perimeter of the clearing.

Sarah put down her plate, patting the place diagonally across from her. "You there. Then Kevin can choose if he wants to be intimately close to you on the bench, or to gaze longingly into your eyes across the table."

Addie pretended disgust, giddy inside. "You are a piece of work."

"Aren't I? Hey, Joe." She beamed as Joe sat next to her, and managed to keep the smile going when Carrie sat opposite him.

"May I join you?" Kevin's rich voice—not as deep as Derek's—came from behind Addie's left ear.

"Absolutely." She made a show of giving him room on the bench, then after he was settled, scooted back until their thighs touched. "Isn't it great to—"

"Boy this looks good." He grinned around the table. "Joe, how are you?"

"Not bad." Joe's features turned stiff.

"And you are Carrie?"

"That's me!" Carrie gave a Miss America smile and giggled. She was a tiny redhead from Atlanta, who was so perky and cheerful and enthusiastic about everyone and everything it made Addie want to step on her. "I'm a friend of Ellen's from grade school!"

"Welcome. This is a great gathering. And perfect weather. Supposed to keep going until the ceremony, too. *Hey, Paul.*" Kevin turned, leaning back into Addie, so his shoulder pressed against her breast. He raised his beer to his friend a couple of tables away. *"This one's for you, buddy!"*

Addie turned to see Paul's reaction, but her eyes never

made it that far. Derek, holding a plate and a beer, was making his way…oh, no…straight to their group. Worse, he sat opposite her, where she'd have to look at him.

"Addie, my hot woman." Kevin had turned back to the table and was gazing down at her. "Have I told you how fabulous you look?"

She nodded, laughing. "You have! And then I told *you*—"

"Yeah, I remember now." His eyes skimmed intimately over her. A sudden movement across the table made her glance at Derek, who was giving Kevin another I-would-kill-you-if-it-were-legal glare. Addie turned determinedly back to Kevin, who was still ogling. "You lost a bunch of weight or something, right?"

"Fifteen pounds."

"Good for you. And *you*." Kevin put his elbow on the table, pointing at Derek. "I know you."

"Derek Bates." He said it like a challenge.

"Derek, right. Right." Kevin did a quick drumbeat on the table. "The *s-s-sailor* man."

"And you're the *s-s-sales* man."

Kevin's smile froze slightly. "Vice president of IT sales. Small company but we're making big, big money."

"Impressive." Derek glanced at Addie. "You've known each other a long time?"

"Oh, yeah, Addie and I go way back." Kevin draped his arm casually around her shoulders, and then let it slip across her back and down, landing on what the bench wasn't using of her rear end.

Oh, my.

His hand was warm. His fingers started moving back and forth. She pressed her thighs together experimentally. No, she wasn't dying of lust. But then they weren't in a private room, able to concentrate only on each other and on their feelings.

"We met after Paul and Kevin became friends in middle school," Addie said. "Kevin was—"

"John Witherspoon Middle School in Princeton, New Jersey. Cross-country team. I'd hang out all the time at Paul's house." Kevin leaned in to stage-whisper to Addie. "I always had a crush on you."

She smiled into his gorgeous blue eyes, and then she felt it, a little tingle of chemical connection. Good. It was coming back. For a while she'd worried.

"Nice story." Derek looked as if he'd eaten something that made him sick. The tingle died, and she felt slightly sullied and shamed.

What the heck for? What weird power was this guy starting to have over her? She didn't know, but this had to be the beginning and the end of it.

"Hey, Addie, you ready for a refill on that punch?"

She nodded emphatically. "Definitely. Thanks, Kevin."

"No problem. *Hey, Sarah.*" He shoved Addie's glass toward her. "Addie wants more punch. Could you go get her some?"

Small beat of silence at the table.

"I'm *kidding.*" Kevin laughed; that loud warm laugh that could still make her fizzy, though this time mostly in relief. The rest of the table joined in. Probably not Derek, but Addie couldn't bring herself to check. "I'm getting Addie some punch, do you want some? Carrie? Joe?"

Kevin collected cups and walked off. Addie stared after him, noting the breadth of his shoulders, the elegant tapered line down to slender hips and wiry runner's thighs. She'd have that body next to hers tonight.

Fear and adrenaline hit her hard. She needed more punch. Now. *Hurry, Kevin.*

"Addie."

Derek. She turned reluctantly, dreading what those brown eyes were going to do to her.

Yup. They did.

"What?" She sounded irritable. Because she was.

"You don't have to do this."

She froze, eyes open wide. How did he know about the seduction? Sarah didn't...no, she couldn't have. He couldn't have any idea what he'd just said. She needed to calm down.

"Don't have to do what?"

"Be with this guy if it doesn't feel right."

"I know. I know that." She sounded like a petulant child. "I do."

He pressed his lips together. That grim look again. She wanted to slap it off him. Or kiss—

No.

"Okay." He picked up his plate and his beer. "But I think you're making a big mistake."

"Who's making a mistake?" Sarah turned rather sloppily to stare at Derek. "Addie? What's she doing wrong?"

Addie jerked her head toward where Kevin had gone.

Sarah gasped. "You *told* him?"

"Told her what, what's this?" Carrie was perkily fascinated, "What's goin' on?"

"Addie told me she wants to start a round of female naked cliff diving after dinner." Derek shook his head somberly. "I told her she was making a mistake. We should wait until midnight. And it should be co-ed."

The table erupted into shouts of laughter, then into a cacophony of increasingly bad suggestions.

Addie sent Derek a grateful look. He gave a curt nod and strode over to join Paul's table, where he was immediately pounced on by a blonde big-boobed woman

Paul worked with who was probably incredibly nice—
any friend of Paul's had to be—but at that moment Addie
hated her. And then herself for caring at all when she had
The One That Got Away waiting on her, hand and foot.

"Here we go." Kevin handed drinks around, then sat
close to Addie, clinked his beer bottle with her glass and
leaned forward to speak privately. "Here's to finding you
again, Addie. I think you're a remarkable woman and I
look forward to getting to know you again this weekend.
I feel like I made a big mistake letting you out of my life."

Ooh. Serious melt. "Thank you, Kevin. That was really sweet. I've thought of you a lot over the years, too."

His grin would be able to charm a cobra. "Cheers."

She clinked with him and raised the glass to her lips,
holding his eyes. Definite tingles that time. Big ones. She
was transported right back to his car, eleven years earlier, and the way he kissed her, with such sweet reverence,
again and again, until passion took them over and turned
the kisses hot and breathless.

Sorry, Derek. She'd made up her mind.

Tonight she was climbing those stairs and finishing off
eleven years of foreplay.

5

"BEDTIME, JOE." Sarah pointed toward the stairs leading to the Bossons' second floor. She, Joe and Addie were sitting in the living room in front of a fire crackling in the brick hearth, warding off the evening's chill. Other guests were already in bed or on the beach stargazing. Kevin had just gone upstairs, kissing Addie's cheek and smiling meaningfully—maybe?—as he left. Which meant he was probably now in bed. Which meant seduction was imminent.

Addie was terrified.

Joe didn't even glance up from his book. "No way. This is getting good. I can't light the kerosene lamp to read in my room or I'll bother my roommate."

Sarah huffed. "Addie and I have to talk."

"Yeah?" That got his attention. "About what?"

"Girl stuff. Kevin left for bed, your turn now."

Joe snorted. "Kevin was in bed right here. Even my dad doesn't snore that loudly."

Addie cringed. He had been loud. Mouth wide-open, drool glistening in the firelight—not particularly sexually alluring.

"So?" Sarah glanced at Addie then bounced up to stand

an inch from Joe's knees, hands on her hips. "You never snore? The guy traveled today, he had to get up practically in the middle of the night to catch a plane. Now go."

"Okay, okay. I'll go." Joe picked up a bookmark, closed the book and stood, nearly bumping noses with Sarah, who faltered but stood her ground. Addie smiled. *Go, Joe.* He should throw her over his shoulder and take her somewhere private. "But you owe me, Sarah Bosson."

"I do not." She took a step back, wrapping her long black sweater tightly around herself. "Git."

Joe took hold of her arms and planted a lingering kiss on her forehead, waved goodbye to Addie and left, grinning and shaking his head. Addie sighed after him. What she wouldn't give for her own personal Joe. "He's the greatest, Sarah."

Sarah snapped over to look at Addie from where she'd been staring after Joe. "What?"

"Joe." Addie smirked at her. "The best."

"Oh, yeah, he's great." She rubbed her hands briskly together. "So now, Sweet Addie-lide, or should I say, 'Addie-*laid*,' we have plans to make!"

The bottom dropped out of Addie's stomach. "I don't know, Sarah."

Sarah's eyes narrowed. "What do you mean you don't know?"

"I'm not sure this is a good idea."

Sarah threw up her hands. "I *knew* you'd chicken out."

"I am not." She'd been so sure during dinner. Kevin had been so sweet, so attentive, so obviously interested. But it was one thing being on the receiving end of a flirtation and quite another to barge into his room his first night here and demand sex. "I just think…maybe it's bad timing."

"Uh-huh." Sarah tapped her foot, fists planted at her waist. "Try again."

"I'm…having my period."

"Are not."

"I've got a raging case of…whatever."

"Sor-ry," Sarah sang. "You're go-ing."

Addie flopped back on the couch and stared up at the planks of the ceiling. "I don't know, it just doesn't feel right."

"You're chicken."

"I'm *not*—" She lifted her head defiantly then scrunched her face at Sarah's skeptical expression. "Okay, yes, I am, a little. But it's not just that."

"Of course it's just that. How can wild beast seduction feel right if you've never done it before? You have nothing to compare it to. Now." She started pacing the room, braided rug to pine boards to braided rug, *thud thud thud, tap tap.* "You'll want to get in the mood. Obviously sitting here talking to me isn't going to do it. We need to picture the whole thing."

Addie groaned, thinking Sarah was probably right. Jitters were perfectly natural, and this weekend was about throwing off her fears and reaching past her comfort zones.

"I've got it." Sarah went around turning off gas lamps until the room was in semidarkness, lit only by the flickering fire. "That's better. Now close your eyes and think of—"

"England?"

"Kevin."

Addie did close her eyes, but only after rolling them in exasperation. "Okay."

"Now imagine him completely naked." Her voice lowered to a seductive drone. "In bed, waiting for you."

She did. Kevin. Naked. Top to bottom, bottom to toes. Hmm, that wasn't bad. Not at all. "That actually helps."

"Of course it does. Now imagine he has gold skin and just enough body hair to be manly, stopping well short of gorilla."

"I should hope so." She formed a vivid picture. Definitely helping.

"Minimal body fat. Well-defined muscles. Bologna-size schlong."

Addie burst out laughing. "That does *not* help."

"Eyes closed." Sarah waved at her impatiently. "Now imagine yourself naked sliding into bed next to him. Imagine him waking up and touching you everywhere with really good warm hands, kissing you, murmuring incredibly sweet things."

"Yes." Addie smiled dreamily, imagining her little heart out. "That's working."

"Repeat after me, 'I am a sexual goddess.'"

Addie snorted laughter. "I'm who now?"

"Ahem. This will only work if you cooperate."

"Okay, okay." She suppressed a giggle, still enjoying her private naked picture of Kevin. "I'm that, a sexual goddess, whatever."

"With feeling."

"I *am* a *sex*-ual god-*dess!*" She ended the phrase with a ridiculous squeal.

Sarah collapsed onto the couch next to her and folded her arms over her chest. "That's it. You're hopeless."

"Am not."

"Are, too." Sarah punched her shoulder. "You *can* do this, you know."

"Yeah?" Addie turned and looked at her friend, thoughts spinning around a confusing maze of yes-I-will and no-I-won't. Kevin was attracted to her, he obviously wanted her and he might even be harboring feelings for her. So what was the problem?

Maybe she was just chicken. Or maybe she was experiencing a wise instinct warning her away. How could you tell the difference?

One concept kept her from ditching the idea entirely. One very important concept. If she went back to New York without trying to do this, she'd spend forever wondering what would have happened if she had. She'd never get out of her rut if she never took that first big step. Better do it tonight. Get it out of the way so she'd be able to enjoy him and not spend tomorrow nervous all over again.

"Okay." She squeezed her eyes tight shut, then opened one to peek at Sarah. "Okay. I'll do it."

Sarah's head lifted off the couch. "Really?"

Addie nodded, spirits starting to bubble with excitement. "Yes. Really. I'll do it. Now, before I lose my nerve."

"Yay!" Sarah applauded silently. "So what will you do exactly?"

Addie's brave expression slipped. "Exactly?"

"Well, no, not *exactly,* but I mean, like, for example, are you going to go into his room naked?"

"Sarah!" The outrage was automatic, but she did have a point.

"Come on, you have to work out these details."

"You're right." Addie jumped up to start pacing herself. *Thud thud thud, tap tap.* Repeat. "I can't be naked because someone might see me out in the hall."

Sarah got up and started pacing opposite her, doubling the thuds and taps. "So strip in his bedroom, then?"

"He might wake up prematurely."

"Get in bed with clothes on?"

"That's no fun."

They both stopped and stared at each other in dismay.

"Oh!" Sarah started taking off her sweater. "This is perfect. Go up there naked with this wrapped around you.

If someone sees you, you're covered, but once you're in Kevin's room, all you have to do is drop it and voilà, birthday suit."

"That might work."

"Plus you get to feel like Venus on the half shell." She posed, Venus-like, voice high and dreamy, and let the sweater fall. "Letting your garment drop and po-o-ol around your feet."

"Sheer poetry." Addie giggled on her way to their bedroom, already taking off her clothes, nervous and excited—not really in a sexual mood, but that would come later, when the nerves had subsided and she could relax in Kevin's arms.

"Here." Sarah handed the sweater through the door.

Addie finished undressing and draped it around herself then emerged back in the living room and struck what she hoped was a practiced seductress pose. "How do I look?"

"Perfect." Sarah clasped her hands together, beaming. "International woman of mystery. I'm practically hot for you myself."

"Yeah, I wouldn't bother with that."

"Go look." She pointed toward the bathroom they shared.

Addie floated in and peered at herself in the old mirror hanging over the white sink. She did look really good. Her cheeks were flushed, which kept the black material from washing out her complexion. But the dark color made a wonderful sexy contrast to the pale skin of her neck and chest, and plunged dangerously between her breasts.

Her courage rose. She looked like a seductress. No, she *was* a seductress. Not a woman staring at thirty from the bottom of her rut.

She emerged triumphant from the bathroom. "I'm ready."

"Not quite." Sarah brandished a kid's glow stick and bent it to mix the chemicals. The plastic began to glow eerie green.

"Where did you get that?"

"My parents keep a supply in case someone needs a night-light. It's going to be pitch-black in his room since there's no moon tonight. You don't want to trip over anything."

Addie cringed at the thought. Nothing would ruin a seduction faster than falling on your face. "You are brilliant, have I ever told you that?"

"Not nearly often enough." Sarah handed over the glow stick. "And it doubles as a great light saber if you want to do battle with random Jedi. You remember where his bedroom is? First on the right?"

"Absolutely."

"Good luck, Addie Baddie." Sarah hugged her tightly. "This is the start of something really wonderful for you. I can just feel it."

A lump rose in Addie's throat. Sarah suspected, but couldn't know how important this was. A chance to change her life. A chance to redeem her mistake with Kevin that night so long ago. A chance to find romance that might really count.

"Thanks, Sarah. I hope so." She kissed her friend's cheek and turned to walk up the stairs, leaving Sarah to sleep alone in the downstairs bedroom they shared.

Kevin Ames.

The wooden stairs creaked sharply a few times; her feet padded across the bare pine boards on the upstairs landing. First bedroom on the right.

She stopped outside the door, closed with an iron latch like all the bedrooms.

Eleven years later, she'd feel that wonderful mouth on

hers again, would feel those strong arms around her, would feel his hand on her breast. And so much more.

Another surge of that odd panic. She closed her eyes, fiercely ordering fear to stop ruining her life. Addie Sewell was going to do this. She deserved this. No matter what happened. Just walking through his door represented a victory—for her and for her future.

Addie reached for the iron handle, pulled the door toward her so the latch would lift silently and walked into the room.

Done!

She closed the door carefully behind her, listening for any sign that Kevin had heard her.

He was still, his breathing slow and even.

She was in.

For a few seconds Addie stood quietly, amazed that she'd actually done this, that she, Princess Rut, had snuck mostly naked into a man's room in order to seduce him, when for years she'd been too scared to say hi to a guy in her elevator.

A sudden calm came over her. This was right.

She took the time to breathe deeply, inhaling Kevin's masculine scent, surprisingly free of beer fumes. He'd had quite a few more than his share. But then this was a celebration weekend. She'd had one glass too many of punch herself.

As silently as possible, she walked toward the bed, glow stick held behind her so it wouldn't be bright enough to wake him. In the dim light she could see a swathe of naked back, his head bent, partly hidden by the pillow.

A rush of tenderness. *Kevin Ames.*

She gently laid the glow stick on the floor, let the sweater, yes, Sarah, pool at her feet, where it covered the stick and reduced the light to the barest glimmer. Addie left it like that. She knew what Kevin looked like. She wanted to feel her way around him, get to know him by touch.

Totally naked now, heart pounding, she climbed onto the edge of the bed then slid down to spoon behind him. His body was warm against hers, his skin soft, his torso much broader than she'd expected. They fit together perfectly.

She knew the instant he woke up, when his body tensed beside hers.

"It's Addie."

"Addie," he whispered.

Addie smiled. She would have thought after all he had to drink and how soundly he'd been passed out downstairs, that she might have trouble waking him.

She drew her fingers down his powerful arm—bigger than she expected. "Do you mind that I'm here?"

He chuckled, deep and low. Addie stilled. She'd never heard Kevin laugh like that.

Before she could think further, his body heaved over and she was underneath him, his broad masculine body trapping her against the sheets. And before she could say anything, gasp or even breathe, he kissed her, a long, slow sweet kiss that made her feel like she was melting into the mattress.

When he came up for air, she knew she'd have to do something. Say something.

But then he was kissing her again. And this time her body caught fire without her permission. She made a funny helpless noise she'd never heard herself make before, and her mouth opened to his kisses and it was all she could do not to open her legs as well and let him inside her right then and there.

Because it was so, so good.

Beyond good.
Unbelievably good.
It just wasn't Kevin.

6

Now what? ADDIE WAS lying half underneath Derek instead of Kevin, and Derek was kissing her, sweet perfect kisses that reached all the way around her body and pulled her closer to him in every respect. She wasn't exactly objecting.

Which left her with a terribly painful choice to make. Either she could pretend she'd meant to come into Derek's bedroom all along and go through with the seduction, or—

Addie gasped. Derek had started tasting the curve where her shoulder left off and her neck began, sending shivers…everywhere.

This was a time for rational superpowers.

Like this: either continue the seduction, or she could—and should—be honest, tell Derek she was sorry, truly sorry, but she'd made a terrible mistake. And then he'd stop sending her into orbit.

As he'd sent dozens and dozens of other women, all around the world.

That did it.

"Derek." She put up a hand to ward off his next kiss, which he was aiming for her mouth.

"Yes, Addie." He sounded amused. What was so funny?

"Um. The thing is."

"Ye-e-s?" He kissed her bare shoulder, a slow gentle kiss that made her pause, because her shoulder had never been made to feel quite that way and she wanted to enjoy it.

"I made a mistake."

"Really." He lowered his head to her breast; his mouth took her nipple. Wet heat. Pressure. A shock of pleasure through her.

She closed her eyes and forced out her new mantra: other women. Many other women. Probably *all* other women.

"I thought you were Kevin."

He lifted off her very, very disappointed breast. "Yeah?"

Completely unconcerned. Addie blinked up at what she could see of his face. "But—"

Another gasp. His mouth had decided it couldn't neglect her other nipple.

"But…" She struggled to remain coherent. Her hips really wanted to strain toward his, and she needed to get them under control. "I didn't come in here to have sex with you."

"So it seems."

He moved the rest of the way over her. Addie nearly shrieked in protest, until she realized he was wearing underwear. Soft, distended underwear, which was currently transferring amazing amounts of heat to a certain spot between her legs she was very, very fond of.

"But, so that means you need to let me go." No, no, he needed to let her come.

"Does it?" Derek moved his chest back and forth over her breasts, the hair—stopping well short of gorilla—a stimulating male texture across her skin.

Then he started kissing her again in earnest. Powerful

teasing kisses that turned her on as if he was…doing other things. Which she desperately wanted him to be doing.

All of them.

But she'd come in to rekindle something with Kevin, an old friend she could trust with her body and her heart, and it was sort of awful of her to be playing with Derek like he was the shinier, newer toy.

With resolve borne of strength she wished she didn't have, Addie wrenched her lips away from his. "I can't think when you're doing that to me."

"Doesn't that tell you something?"

"Yes. It tells me I can't think when you're doing that to me."

He chuckled and moved back. Immediately her body felt chilly. And lonely. "Better?"

No. "Yes, thank you."

"You're welcome."

Now what? She should get out of this bed immediately, throw Sarah's sweater back on, have whatever conversation they should have while standing safely across the room and then go to bed, after she smacked Sarah silly for giving her the wrong directions to Kevin's room.

"So you were hoping to jump in bed with Kevin. It's not too late, you know. He's right across the hall."

She gaped at him, prickling with outrage. "You think I could make out with you and then go across the hall and seduce Kevin?"

"Why not?" Derek shrugged in the near darkness, lit an eerie Shrek-green shade by the glow stick. He was still sexy. And very unogre-like. "It's not like we exchanged rings."

"No, no, I know, but…" She wasn't sure how to explain it. "I can't. I mean, after this kind of a…connection."

"Connection?"

Argh! What had she used that word for? Thank God for the dim light to hide her blush—but didn't green and red mix to make muddy brown? "No, not that. You wouldn't understand."

"Why not?"

"Because men like you don't." She spoke more harshly than she meant to and swung her legs over the side of the bed, confused, hurt and more confused because she didn't understand why she was hurting. Embarrassed, she'd understand right away. Appalled ditto. But *she* should not be feeling rejected. *She* was the one who'd put a stop to this.

"Hey." His hand settled on her thigh. His voice was gentle. "I'm sorry. Really. This was a shock to both of us."

"No kidding."

"But the connection wasn't."

She turned to him. Another shock. "You felt that?"

"From the beginning." He drew his hand down her cheek. "I knew we'd be good together."

"Physically." Well, duh, Addie, what did she think he meant, spiritually?

"That much for sure. Don't know what else, yet. You felt it, too."

"I…yes, some. A little. Yeah." Little like the universe was little. "Okay, a lot."

He gave that deep chuckle that had become familiar and very attractive. Like pretty much everything else about him.

In defense, she tried to conjure up a picture of Kevin, and got him snoring and drooling on the sofa.

Oops. But really, that made her feel tenderly toward him for being a normal flawed human being. She might lust after Derek, but tenderness counted for more.

"So tell me, Addie. What did you mean a 'man like you'?"

"Oh." She struggled with how to explain, more aware than she wanted to be that she hadn't left his bed yet, and that it wasn't really difficult to figure out why not.

"One with...considerable experience...in the area of... physical relationships."

Silence for half a beat, then they both started giggling.

"Translation?" he asked lightly.

"Um...you get laid a lot?" That threw them both into another round of suppressed giggles. Very dangerous. Sharing a private joke in bed together made the darkened room seem even more intimate.

"Where did you get that idea, Addie?" He held up his hand. "Wait, don't tell me. Sarah."

"Oh. Well...yes." Addie wrinkled her nose. Sarah, who had lied about him being sexually aggressive on the beach, and whose hobby was inflating gossip. "She said she heard it from Paul."

"Ah." He rubbed his head. "I get it now."

"So...it's true?" Addie bit her lip. Jeez, could she have sounded any more disappointed?

"Paul and I joke a lot about the girl in every port thing. With my career it's hard to have any kind of long-term relationship. I'm never around. But I don't use women, and I don't hunt them just for sex."

Addie drew her knees up, hugged them to her chest, feeling suddenly exposed even though she'd been naked all along. His playboy reputation was the only reason she had stopped her seduction of the wrong man. "You don't ever want to settle down in a real home somewhere?"

"I've thought about it." He pushed hair back that had fallen over her forehead. "But I love what I do. It would take an extraordinary woman to make me want to give up this life."

She nodded, more confused than ever, knowing she

needed to get up and leave and wanting more than ever to lie down in those amazing strong arms and escape into bliss.

What about Kevin?

"So what now, Addie Sewell?" He touched her chin, let his hand fall to the mattress. "Would you like to spend the night with me?"

Yes. She wasn't going to answer that way, but her soul did, loud and clear. "I don't think it's a good idea, Derek."

"No?"

"You're leaving for the other side of the world on Sunday. I don't have to commit to every guy I sleep with, but I generally hope for more than three days."

"And with Kevin you have that option."

"Yes." The answer came out automatically. After what had just happened in this bed, she couldn't picture spending the next three days with Kevin. But she wasn't going to tell Derek that. She needed about a week to sort out her feelings. Why hadn't she stayed home with Great-Aunt Grace's boxes?

"Okay, Addie."

Three beats later, she realized that was her cue. *Bye, Addie, don't let the door hit you...* She slid off the bed and crossed to where Sarah's sweater was covering the glow stick, which burned unpleasantly bright when she slipped the black garment over her shoulders like a cape, wistfully reliving her hope and excitement when she'd let it drop.

Behind her she heard Derek's body swishing over the sheets, then silence. He must have lain down again, and was trying to sleep. Or was he watching her leave? Would he lie awake thinking about her and what might have been? Would she?

At the door, she reached for the handle then heard his footsteps behind her. His arms came up on either side of her head to keep the door from opening, trapping her inside. The sweater fell. She could feel the heat of his body behind her. "Addie."

"Yes." Her voice was a breathless whisper.

"If you change your mind…" His lips landed on her shoulder, stubble a delicious rasp on her skin, making her shiver with desire.

"I will." She froze in horror at what she'd implied. "I mean I *will* let you know."

That gorgeous chuckle again. Then silence so tense she screwed her eyes shut, desperate to leave, but unable to until he chose to let her, desperate to lean back into him and absorb the feel of his skin against hers, to give in, let him take her back to bed and to places she had a feeling she'd never been before.

His arms came down. She was free to go. "Good night, Addie."

"Night." Not bothering to finish covering herself, she grabbed the sweater, pulled the door open and launched herself out into the hall.

Where she collided, butt naked, with the wiry-haired bare chest of Kevin Ames.

7

"KEVIN." Addie clutched Sarah's black sweater around herself, covering her breasts, which had obviously been waving around in full view seconds before because Kevin's eyes were still popping out of his head.

"Addie, what…" He gestured past her with his flashlight. "Wait, that's your room? I thought you were sleeping downstairs with Sarah."

"Oh. Uh." God, could this be any worse? "Actually—"

"I thought that was Derek's room."

"It…is." Her stomach gave a sickening lurch. What would have happened if she'd taken the right turn…or rather the left turn? She certainly wouldn't have to be explaining her way out of this mess.

Kevin looked hurt, then angry. "What the hell, Addie? I thought you and I were on to something. Now you're with him?"

"Kevin, we need to talk." Addie pulled him away from the door on the other side of which Derek was undoubtedly laughing his very fine ass off. "Somewhere private."

"Here." He escorted her across the hall and waited expectantly, arms folded, flashlight pointing downward so his face glowed with eerie shadows as well as monster-green from the glow stick.

Addie looked at him questioningly. What was so much more private about this side of the landing? "What about your room?"

"We're fine here. No one will hear us. Why are you coming naked out of this guy's room in the middle of the night?"

"I…" Addie closed her eyes. This was horrible. Since she hadn't made it into Kevin's room, she still had no idea how he might react to the idea of her seducing him. "I thought it was yours."

Kevin was silent for so long, she opened her eyes. Well, one eye. Just for a peek.

His arms were no longer across his chest. He was no longer looking as if he could growl. He looked rather stunned, in fact. "So you slept with Derek instead?"

"No! Of course not." She felt herself blushing in the dim light. It would help nothing to mention how much she'd wanted to sleep with him. "I went in there thinking it was your room and when I realized it wasn't, I came back out."

Just…not quite immediately.

"Addie." His voice was gentle now. "You were going to seduce me?"

"Yes." In sudden horror she realized he could easily say okay, then, let's do it. The only thing she wanted to do less than seduce him now was to explain why she no longer wanted to. She wasn't even sure why herself, except that it had something to do with Derek.

Okay, everything to do with him.

"Wow, Addie. What a surprise." He didn't sound as if he meant a fabulous Christmas-day-biggest-package sur-

prise. More like a so-you've-gone-back-to-drinking surprise. "I didn't think you were the type."

Of course she wasn't. But he didn't need to point that
out. "Obviously I'm not. Look how I screwed this up."

"See…to be honest here, Addie, I'm a take-charge kind
of guy."

"You are?" She had no idea what he was talking about,
and it irritated her. This was Kevin. *Kevin Ames.* Addie
was supposed to be melting into a big puddle at his feet,
and that was absolutely not happening. Not even close.

Addie, Addie. Be rational. Like this: she was tired,
confused, humiliated and so far out of her comfort zone
she should probably be wearing an oxygen mask. All she
needed was some recharge time, a good night's sleep and
a little space to sort through her emotions. Everything
would be okay in the morning.

"See, I'm not that into women making the first move."

"Oh." So going into the wrong room and being humiliated had saved her from going into the right room and
being humiliated. How nice.

"Yeah, I kind of thought we'd go off alone somewhere,
like to a beach or something." He patted her shoulder awkwardly. "Maybe have a few drinks…get to know each
other again. Ease into it."

Addie's irritation vanished. Get to know each other
again. Yes. *Yes.* She'd been going about this as a theatri-
cal fantasy. Kevin was talking down-to-earth reality. It
had been eleven years; they'd both changed and matured.
They had a lot of catching up to do, many things to find
out about each other as adults. He recognized that, while
she'd been planning to jump him his first night here like
a horny frat boy.

"Kevin, thank you." Her relief was immense. Re-entry
into the comfort zone complete. She covered his hand

on her shoulder with hers. "I had put all this pressure on myself and was listening to other people instead of to my instinct and…basically trying to be someone I'm not cut out to be."

"You should never do that, Addie. You want someone who loves you for who you are. You're sweet and adorable. Part of what makes you so sexy is your innocence. You should never try to be anything else."

Addie blinked. She took her hand off his and pulled Sarah's sweater more tightly around herself. He was right about her. Of course he was. But she couldn't help feeling the loss of that moment imagining herself as a wildly sexual seductress.

"Listen." Kevin crossed the distance between them, took her in his arms for a long, comforting hug that—

Oh. Well, now she got the beer fumes. But under them, a nice sweet aftershave that she…pretty much liked. "You go to sleep now. Forget all this. Tomorrow we'll take a walk or something and catch up, okay?"

"Yes." She pressed her cheek against his shoulder. He understood her better than she'd understood herself. "Thank you, Kevin. You're wonderful."

"Aw, I'm just a normal guy, Addie."

Exactly. And that's what she needed and wanted. Her two previous long-term relationships had been solid and comfortable—not dull, but not a passionate thrill a minute, either. She wasn't cut out for that much excitement. It would exhaust her.

"Good night, Addie." Kevin brushed a kiss across her mouth. No wild sparks, just lovely comfort. Which was exactly what she needed just then. He was remarkable.

"Good night, Kevin. Thanks for saving me from myself."

"No problem." He grinned and stayed in front of his

door, watching her descend the steps. At the bottom of the staircase, out of his sight, she heard him open the door to his room—on the *left*—then an odd high whimper, a squeak and a thud. Addie gasped and whirled to stare up into the blackness of the second floor. Had Kevin hurt himself?

A few seconds later, normal footsteps. Addie relaxed and continued into the living room. If he'd been injured, he'd have called her for help. She was not walking into any other guy's room again on this vacation unless she was sure she was invited.

In fact, all she wanted to do was sneak into her room, and drop into a dead sleep.

She passed the glowing embers of the fire, used the bathroom and came back into the living room to stare out the window at the water. It was peaceful and contented tonight, reflecting the brightest stars in two glittering lines across its gentle waves.

So beautiful. So uncomplicated. She could learn a lot from an ocean.

At her room's door, she stopped, put firm, careful pressure on the latch and eased the door open.

Dark. Quiet. Soft steady breathing from Sarah. Addie wilted in relief. The last thing she wanted was to have to explain any of the bizarre comedy of tonight's errors to her friend.

She crept into the room, laid the glow stick on the small table next to her twin bed and fumbled under her pillow for her pajamas. Sleeping naked was sexy with a man, but alone it felt all wrong and cold.

Sarah's sweater dropped off her easily; her pajamas bottoms went on easily. But when she swung her arms after pulling on the tops, she bumped the table and knocked the glow stick to the floor. Not only did it hit the boards with a bang, but it rolled noisily before she could grab it.

"…Addie?"

Argh!

"Hi, Sara-a-ah," she whispered soothingly. "Don't wake up…I'm just going to bed."

"Don't wake up?" Sarah was already up on her elbows, eyes wide, turning on the electric lamp next to her bed. "How can I possibly sleep? What happened? Why are you back so early? Tell me everything."

Good Lord, zero to sixty in two seconds. "In the morning, Sarah, I'm exhaus—"

"What do you mean morning? Are you kidding me? I'll go out of my mind." She tossed aside half the covers and patted the mattress next to her. "C'mon. Spill."

Addie sighed. If she wanted any sleep tonight, she'd have to tell everything. Otherwise Sarah would be at her until the end of time. She crossed reluctantly and sat next to her friend; let Sarah fuss putting the covers back over their legs.

"Now, tell."

"Okay." Addie blew out a breath. "First off all, Sarah, Kevin's room is on the *left* at the top of the stairs."

"No, it's not. It's on the—" Her eyes shot wide. She slapped a hand over her mouth. "Omigod. Omigod."

"Yeah."

"But if you turned right…wait, *did* you turn right?"

"Oh, yes."

"So you went into—" She gasped. "Derek's room!"

"Yup."

"You walked in and took off your clothes in *Derek's room?*"

"Uh-*huh.*"

"No!" She gave a strangled yell that could have been

laughter but probably wasn't. "Tell me you didn't climb into bed with him."

"I did."

"Oh, God! At least tell me he threw you out right away or you bolted. At least tell me he didn't touch you."

Addie turned to look at her incredulously. "Uh, Sarah?"

"He *did*." The wail was anguished and unexpected. "I knew it."

"For heaven's sake." Apparently any contact between her and Derek was highly offensive to everyone tonight. "I apologized, we talked for a couple of minutes and I left the room."

Sarah was nearly in tears. "I'm sorry. I am being ridiculous. It's just that you always…"

"Always what?"

"Get the guy!"

"Sarah!" Addie was more stunned at that moment than she'd been all evening. And it had been one hell of an evening. A vision of her neat and ordered rooms in Aunt Grace's apartment floated temptingly. Maybe she wouldn't get a condo. Maybe she'd stay there forever with her lovely routines and cats, flossing regularly, and never change anything in her life ever again. "I didn't 'get' Derek. I don't even want him. And I have no idea who else you could mean."

"Kevin."

"Wait, you want Kevin?"

"No!" Sarah wailed.

Addie pressed a hand to her temple. This was going to make her insane. "Do you want me to finish the story?"

"Yes." She sniffled. "I'm sorry."

"Okay. So I charged out of Derek's room, still pretty much naked, and I bumped into Kevin. Literally."

Sarah gaped at her. Let the record show that for once Addie had managed to render her speechless.

"You. Did. *Not.*"

Speechless at least for one second. "I did. And you know what? When he found out I'd been going to seduce him, he said he'd rather get to know me again slowly first."

Another gasp. "Oh, Addie! That is adorable. I knew you and Kevin were right for each other. Derek is seriously bad news."

For a weird second Addie wanted to defend Derek. Quite hotly. But that would get her exactly nowhere. Besides, she had no proof that Derek wasn't a player, just Sarah's word, which, depending on Sarah's mood, might or might not mean anything.

"So now you and Kevin are good?"

"We're good." Actually Addie had no idea what they were, but she smiled and squeezed Sarah's leg anyway by way of saying good-night, and got up, completely drained, not wanting to think about Derek or Kevin or any combination thereof for the rest of the night if not weekend. Sarah turned off her lamp and Addie got into bed by the nauseating green light of the glow stick, which she never, ever wanted to see again.

"Addie? Are you going to go after Derek now?"

Addie paused, about to bury the offending light under her pillow. What the hell was she talking about? "Of course not. Why, do *you* want to go after him?"

"Me? *Me?*" Sarah laughed loudly. "As if. I would never go after a player like that. His criteria for choosing a sex partner is female and breathing. No, no, I was just worried you'd get hurt."

"Okay, then." Addie sighed, feeling like she'd been hollowed out and filled with sadness. Maybe she'd give up this whole man thing. At least for now. It had all become way too complicated.

"Hey, Addie. I had a great idea."

Addie groaned. "If this has anything to do with men, I don't want to hear it."

"Aw, Addie. C'mon. You…" Silence, while Addie could practically hear the wheels turning in her head. "No, nothing about men, it's to cheer you up."

"Go ahead." Addie yawned and nestled into the pillow, immediately having to banish memories of lying nestled against Derek.

Oh, dear.

"There's a secret cove on Storness Island. No one knows about it but our family. The entrance to the path is camouflaged and you can't see the beach from the water, either, because there's a spit of land in the way. Let's go there and sunbathe nude tomorrow. Take a break from guys and everything.…"

"Sure," Addie murmured drowsily. Sarah was up to something, but right then she didn't have the energy to care. "Fine. Whatever."

"It's great, you'll love it."

"Mmm…"

She was asleep in about ten seconds. When she woke up, she was sorting boxes in Great-Aunt Grace's old bedroom, patiently and meticulously organizing the contents, letters here, photographs there, all spread out on Aunt Grace's four poster bed.

Where suddenly Derek was lying naked, smiling devilishly.

Impossible. He didn't know where Aunt Grace lived. He was in Maine.

A blink later, she was naked in bed with him, but not at Aunt Grace's anymore, he was back in Maine, and she was kissing him ravenously until her body caught fire. Literally. And then Kevin was in bed with them, too, not seeming to mind the heat, making odd sucking sounds through his lips. Derek, not at all fazed by the bed being in flames, kicked with incredible power and sent Kevin flying across the room, where he curled up fetal and was instantly covered with seaweed, dribbling sand and water onto the braided rug.

Awestruck, Addie looked up at Derek, looming over her, the two of them within a circle of fire now, like Siegfried and Brünnhilde from Wagner's Ring cycle, which her parents had dragged her to as a teenager over her violent objections.

You are mine, Addie. You know it as well as I do. We belong together. I felt it the second I met you, and you did, too. Kevin isn't fit to wash your underwear.

The dream changed and slowed. The fire was gone, the bed, clean and white again, floated on the sea, rocking gently, blue water all around, white clouds overhead, sweet breezes blowing it toward the sunset. What didn't change was the passionate heat in Derek's eyes, and the figurative fire in her body.

He moved over her, and kissed her. She spread her legs and he slid inside her, his motion echoing the rocking of the bed and the waves, making love to her in time to nature's rhythm, back and forth, in and out…

As her arousal grew fierce, Addie began waking up.

No, no. Not yet, not yet!

She kept her eyes shut, keeping out reality, holding on to the feel of Derek's body on top of hers. Her hand crept between her legs. In her mind she was still with him, out on that bright sea, tasting the salty breeze on his skin, moving her hips in time with his, feeling him moving deep inside her.

Her fingers rubbed faster, then faster. The orgasm hit her hot and hard, alone in the dark.

Derek Bates.

Kevin Ames.

What the hell was she going to do?

8

DEREK LIFTED THE ax high into the air and brought it down with a satisfying *thunk*. The small birch log split neatly down the middle; he added the pieces to the good-size stack he'd already cut. That morning he'd run twice around the island, done a punishing calisthenics workout, taken a ball-shrinking dip—couldn't really call it swimming, more like flailing, splashing and gasping—in the icy sea, and was now involved in chopping enough wood for the Bossons to burn for the next twenty summers.

Hey, he was happy to help them out. Less charitable was the fact that every time the ax bit deeply into the wood, he was imagining Kevin Ames's head.

Thunk.

Last night he'd barely slept after Addie left.

For one thing, he couldn't erase the feel of her. The softness of her skin, her lips, the gentle swell of her breasts, the warm length of her body under his.

From the first shock of discovering her in his bed, he'd suspected she'd made a mistake. Last night at dinner she'd made it quite clear that she was still determined to go after Kevin. God only knew what kind of Freudian slip brought her to his bed instead, but he didn't believe for a second it was only an accident. Somewhere deep in her subconscious, Addie had known exactly what she was doing. For that reason Derek had no qualms about trying to prove she was in the right place with the right man.

He'd almost succeeded, too. Together they'd generated serious hunger and heat. But while he wasn't above a little underhanded persuasion, he wasn't going to tie her down and force her to stay.

Thunk.

Ha. Derek had thought letting her go was agony. No, he'd tasted true agony when he realized she'd walked out of his door straight into the arms of the man she'd intended to have all along. He'd stood there, incredulous, still smelling her scent on his skin, listening to them talk for a few seconds before he moved away, not interested in hearing anything they were saying, not wanting to think about what might happen next.

Thunk.

Could Addie respond to him the way she had and then jump into bed with Kevin? He'd sure as hell like to think not. Whatever was between Addie and himself, whether it was simple chemistry or something deeper, he'd never experienced anything close to it. And he'd be willing to bet by Addie's clear struggle between wanting out of his bed and wanting to stay in it, that she'd been surprised and overwhelmed by their passion, as well.

So now what? Spend the next three days watching her throw herself at a drunken jerk who wouldn't let her finish a sentence or express a thought? A guy Derek had caught the day before flirting outrageously with Carrie, who'd been puppy-dogging after Joe, who was tagging after Sarah, who was still semi subtly presenting herself to Derek, who was going crazy for Addie, who wanted Kevin?

Thunk.

If Addie was trying to land a really great guy, it would still be hard to step aside, but Derek wouldn't hesitate. He had nothing to offer a woman long-term but a nomad's life on the sea or a lonely life in port, waiting for him to come home. There were undoubtedly some women out there who'd embrace that life, but Addie had spelled out quite clearly that she wasn't one of them. Nor was she the type to enjoy the here and now and to hell with later.

He laid the ax across the stump he'd been using as a chopping pedestal, enjoying the faint breath of breeze across his bare torso. Hot day. At this rate he might make it back into the ocean for more ball-shrinking fun.

"Hey, Derek." Incredibly the object of his ax-wielding fury strolled into the clearing and lifted his fist for a bump. Derek hated fist bumps. "Puttin' in some good sweat there, huh?"

"Yeah."

Kevin put his hands on his hips and slouched into a casual pose, apparently settling in to watch. He was wearing plaid shorts. Derek hated plaid shorts. With a yellow polo shirt. Derek hated yellow.

"Nice day." Kevin yawned wide and long, without covering his mouth.

"Rough night?" Derek couldn't help himself, even knowing he should shut the hell up.

"Man, yeah. Crazy night." Kevin laughed, scratching his head enthusiastically. "Amazing night."

Derek picked up the ax, sweat turning cold, stomach sinking. Addie had gone from his bed to Kevin's.

No, he couldn't believe she'd do that. Did that make him perceptive or in denial?

"That girl is a gymnast." He put his hands to his lower back and bent side to side. "Wore me out."

That girl? Derek's grip tightened on the handle. Did he forget her name already? With the amount Kevin had to drink last night, Derek wouldn't be surprised. Though until he heard that Kevin had for sure been with Addie, he wasn't going to believe it. Not totally. She was an intelligent, passionate, exciting woman, and Kevin…wore plaid shorts. "Congratulations."

"Yeah, thanks." He yawned again. "Have you seen Addie around this morning?"

Derek blinked. Something about the way Kevin emphasized her name—as if he'd been talking about someone else before—gave him some hope. "Not lately."

"Thought I'd see if she wanted to go on a walk with me this morning."

"Yeah?" He hauled up the blade for his next swing, trying to look as casual as possible. "When did you last see her?"

Thunk.

"In the middle of the night." Kevin smirked. "Guess she paid you a visit by mistake first."

Derek held Kevin's gaze. Very bad idea to taunt a man holding an ax. "She spent some time in my room, yeah." *Not sure she thought it was entirely a mistake.*

Kevin's turn to look uncomfortable. "Well, I haven't seen her this morning."

Damn it. Still no definite answer. She might not have spent the whole night with him.

Sarah sprang into the clearing holding a towel around herself, cheeks rosy, body glistening. She stopped short when she saw the two men, then her eyes lit up and she pursed her lips as if about to whistle. "Well, gentlemen, hello."

"Are you naked under there?" Kevin's eyes were practically shooting out of their sockets.

Derek snorted. Didn't the guy ever listen to himself? "I think what he meant was, 'Hi, Sarah, great to see you.'"

"That's what I thought." Sarah spared Derek a glance then turned to Kevin. "Addie and I were sunbathing in the altogether."

"Where?" Both men spoke at once then glared at each other.

"Ha!" Sarah snapped her fingers at each of them. "Like I'd tell you?"

"Okay." Kevin turned to Derek, all pretend business. "We'll split up. You take that way, I'll take this way, we'll search the island."

Hilarious, Kevin.

"Yoo-hoo!" Carrie bounced into the clearing, beaming. The woman made Sarah look low-energy and depressive. She sent Kevin a slow, sexy wink that made Derek straighten up and take notice. *"There* you are."

"I'm here." Kevin laughed nervously, looking from Sarah to Derek and back.

Well, well. Wasn't *that* interesting.

"Hi, Sarah!" Carrie gave a cute little finger-wiggle at Sarah who gave an even cuter finger-wiggle back, wearing a gruesomely overbright smile, which went right over Carrie's head.

"And hel-*lo, Derek.*" She looked him up and down in a way that made him want to put his shirt back on. "You are lookin' fine this morning."

"Derek's helping the Bossons out with their firewood supply," Kevin said. "I was about to take over."

Like hell.

"So, Kev-i-i-n." Carrie sashayed over to him, and tiptoed her fingers up his arm, sticking her face up close to his. "How's my wild man this morning? You tired from last night or ready for more?"

The last sentence came out in a stage whisper that everyone heard. Kevin's face turned cranberry-red. He stuttered out a few syllables. Somehow Derek managed not to pump his fist and shout, *yes!*

Sarah froze and blinked at Carrie, then at Kevin. Then back. Her eyes narrowed into furious slits. "What the hell is going on here?"

"What?" Carrie gaped at her in wide-eyed surprise. "Oh, no. Y'all aren't dating him are you?"

"*No,* I'm not dating him."

"So what's the problem?" She looked so bewildered Derek nearly felt sorry for her. But yesterday she'd been all over Joe, now Kevin, so he doubted she cared much for anyone but herself.

"Uh, so, Carrie." Kevin pried her fingers off his biceps. "What are your plans this morning?"

Carrie beamed and tucked her arm all the way through his. "Whatever *you're* doing."

"You know, Kevin, in case you feel like a long walk…" Sarah smiled with dangerous sweetness. "There's this short pier on the other side of the island."

Kevin had the sense to look mortified.

"Ooh, maybe we'll do that." Carrie pulled him around, clearly missing the insult, which Derek remembered as one of Sarah's father's favorites. "Come on, Kev. See y'all later!"

The second the two of them disappeared between the trees, Sarah abandoned all pretense at civility. "What the hell was that?"

Derek did everything he could to look appalled and furious, but he was ready to sing hallelujah. Not only had Addie *not* been with Kevin last night, Kevin had shown his true colors to Sarah, who would waste no time passing the information along to her best friend. And that would very nicely take care of Kevin. "Looks like they're an item."

"He was supposed to be with *Addie* last night."

"Addie was exactly where she was supposed to be."

Sarah glared at him, then stalked over and poked him in the chest. "Listen to me."

He caught her finger. "Hey. Hands off the merchandise."

"You listening to me?"

He suppressed a smile. He liked Sarah. "I'm listening."

"Why didn't you sleep with me that night? No bullshit."

"Because you were drunk, because you're my best friend's sister and because I had nothing to give you beyond that one night. No bullshit."

She was quiet awhile, digesting that. Actually he'd never seen her hold so still. "So are you really not a player?"

"I'm not." He held her gaze. "Never had the time or inclination."

"Why did I overhear my brother talking as if you were?"

Derek kept himself from rolling his eyes. That again. "Because he likes the cliché of sailors. Woman in every port, ha-ha-ha. It's our little joke. Not very funny, but we're guys. We like that stuff."

Sarah nodded, still frowning, but clearly calmer. Derek picked up his shirt and put it back on. He was done chopping wood.

"You like Addie don't you?"

"I do." He was surprised by the question, surprised by his immediate answer and by the emotion in his voice. Yes, he liked her. Against all logic, a woman he barely knew, he liked her a whole hell of a lot.

Sarah twisted her lip. Started to speak, changed her

mind. Folded her arms across her chest and glared at him some more.

He gave her a brotherly punch on the shoulder. "Spit it out, Sarah."

"Hey. The merchandise!"

"Sorry." He raised his hands in surrender. "Truce?"

Her expression softened. "Okay, truce."

"Good." He risked a smile and actually got a warm one back. "Now what were you going to tell me?"

"There's a hidden cove on this island."

"Yeah?"

"One you can't get to unless you know where to find the entrance. It's a total family secret."

"I see." He didn't yet, but was willing to be patient.

"Addie's still there."

Derek eyed her warily, not sure what she was getting at. "Okay."

"Naked."

He swallowed and said the only thing he was capable of: *"Glrmph."*

"Listen to me. Pay close attention." Sarah leaned closer, blue eyes direct and no-nonsense. "Because I'm only going to say this once."

SARAH SAT ON the ledge near her favorite rock, a white crystalline boulder dropped in the middle of jagged gray granite, as if the gods had been playing sky golf and lost track of one ball. At high tide the rock was near-covered, but now it sat exposed in all its glory.

Newly slathered with SPF 50 after sunbathing with Addie, loving this stretch of sunny days after the fog and clouds earlier in the week, Sarah was shucking corn. Forty ears, in preparation for the rehearsal dinner that night. The bag of unshucked sat to her right, the paper shopping bag for husks on her left. The naked ears, she was laying in the family's huge midnight-blue enameled pot with white specks she'd always thought looked like snow. They'd use the pot again to cook lobsters for the wedding feast the following night, when weather forecasters predicted more perfection. Paul and Ellen deserved nothing less.

From the clearing where she'd confronted Derek and learned the truth about Kevin's snakelike character, Sarah had gone straight to the house and volunteered for a job, needing a steadying task. She still couldn't believe Kevin, the guy she was so sure would find love with Addie, the guy she and Addie had been so crazy about for so many years, was a complete jerk.

She ripped off a handful of husks, threw them in the bag. And she still couldn't believe she'd told Derek where to find naked Addie. *Derek!* The guy she wanted. The guy she'd lusted after for years, pined after for many point-less hours, hoping this week that she could finally change his mind.

Pointless. She could see that now so clearly. Maybe she'd finally gotten sick of all the years chasing men when that one crucial concept was missing: them wanting her, too. Maybe she was growing up. Definitely she was ready to string Kevin up by his balls and she was ready to change her opinion of Derek. Definitely she was trying to be happy for Derek and Addie, even if they only had through Sunday together. She and Addie had talked that morning and it was pretty clear to Sarah that Addie was smitten with Derek, even as she'd tried to pretend Kevin still had a chance. Funny how you could figure out other people's crap much more easily than your own.

Kevin. And *Carrie!* Jeez. How typically male. Sarah rubbed an ear free of the last few strands of silk. Though, really, in her new mood of analytical maturity, she should examine that statement, too. What was a typical male? Not fair to say Clueless Neanderthal. Paul wasn't like that. Joe wasn't like that. And now it seemed Paul had been right all along and Derek wasn't like that, either. So there were exceptions. She just couldn't seem to fall in love with exceptions. Look what she did with Derek the second she realized he was a good guy—gave up on him immediately and handed him over to her best friend. And she should have known immediately that if she'd wanted Kevin at some point, he must be bad news.

A strand of silk escaped the garbage and flew on a welcome puff of breeze toward the water. Following it with her eyes, she saw Joe coming toward her, striding easily across the rocky beach, hair wet and tousled. Joe would understand. He'd listen. He'd tease her if she was being ridiculous and support her if she wasn't.

She should really work on falling in love with Joe.

"Hey, Sarah. I've been sent to help you."

Sarah beamed at him and gestured to the ledge. "Pull up a rock."

"As soon as I find one that fits." He tried a few places, attempting the difficult task of getting the shape of the human butt to match comfortably with the craggy formations. "There."

"Just showered?"

"I went swimming."

Sarah gaped at him. "What are you, a polar bear?"

"Warm day." He picked up an ear and started working with her. "Sure cooled me off in a hurry."

"The breeze should pick up in a minute. The tide is changing."

"Yeah?" He glanced at her admiringly. He looked handsome today. The bit of sun on his face helped brighten his complexion, heightened his cheekbones. "How can you tell?"

"Lobster buoys." She pointed at the nearest, yellow and white striped. "They point out when the tide's going out, in when it's coming in. Right now they're starting to swing around."

"Cool."

She added a corn ear to the pot and wiped her hands on her shorts. Time to confess, since she confessed pretty much everything to this man. "Joe?"

"Sarah?"

"I'm afraid I've done a terribly unselfish thing." She sighed dramatically. "It's awful."

"Sarah, I'm so sorry." He picked up on the game right away, features contorting with worry. "How can I help?"

"I don't know. I've never done anything like this before." She pressed diva-fingers to her temple and closed her eyes. "I think I'm in shock."

"No!" He gasped comically. "What did you do?"

"Believe it or not, I'm about to tell you." She opened her eyes and resumed her normal voice. "I realized Kevin is a complete A-hole. But Derek is a good guy."

"Agreed on both counts."

"Yeah, well." Sarah shrugged. "Took me a while to figure it out."

"You should have asked me. I know everything."

"Uh-huh." She took his corn and added it to the pot, tore more husks from her own. "I also decided it was stupid to hold out hope for Derek."

"Really?" He stopped with his hand in the bag of corn, dark eyes clear and watchful. "You gave up on him? Really?"

"Yes." She let out another heaving sigh, enjoying her role tremendously. "Completely."

"Why?"

"Because, Joe." Sarah smiled sadly, feeling wise and old, and the way Joe was looking at her, maybe lovely, too. "He didn't want me."

"The fool."

"And there's more."

"Sarah…" He cringed, putting a hand to his chest. "I'm not sure my heart can take this."

"I gave him a green-light push toward Addie just now. He really likes her and she really likes him."

"Wow, Sarah. That was a really generous thing to do." He tsk-tsked, eyes twinkling. "You must feel terrible."

"I should." She wrinkled her nose, surprised by what she was about to say. "But I don't. I feel sort of glad for them. And sort of relieved."

A slow smile spread over Joe's face, making him even more attractive. Maybe it was the light? The beautiful Mainescape around them? "I'm speechless."

She nodded, proud inside, but not wanting to be gross about it. Joe's approval meant a lot to her. For nearly ten years since she met him when he stepped in to help her out with a cranky customer at the campus bookstore, their friendship had consisted of Joe being a steady, stable source of comfort and support, while she flailed and wailed and stumbled through life.

"Joe?"

"Sarah?"

She frowned down at her next ear of corn. "What do you get from this friendship with me?"

"Uh. I— Huh?"

She giggled. Maybe he could be a clueless male, too. "I mean, you give me total acceptance, unconditional support, lifts and reality checks when I need them. What do I give you?"

"Aw, Sarah…" He tossed husks toward the garbage. They missed and fell onto a sandy patch below the ledge.

"I'll get them." They spoke together, both scrambling down to pick them up, each gathering half. He didn't answer her smile with his usual bright one. Looked down at his feet. Out to sea. She shouldn't have asked him the question.

"You don't have to answer, Joe." Especially if his answer was, *You bring me nothing.*

"I don't have the words right yet."

Sarah bit her lip, feeling queasy. "Tactful phrasing required?"

"No." He took the husks from her hand, tossed them into the garbage bag and came back to stand in front of her, looking down at her earnestly. "Risky phrasing."

"What do you mean?" Sudden fear. She knew what was coming. A truth she'd denied for years because it suited her to. God, why was she seeing everything so clearly today? Couldn't she space it all out a little? She wanted to turn and run back to the cove, interrupt Addie and Derek and tell them sorry, but she changed her mind and they had to have a threesome immediately.

Then Joe did something she'd never seen him do. He changed. He got taller and broader and more muscular and more masculine. Before her eyes. She couldn't breathe.

He took her hand, put it to his lips then pressed it to his heart. "You are loyal and generous and you make me laugh and cry and suffer and celebrate and always, always hope."

Sarah's breath went in as if it would never stop. No one had ever said anything that lovely and romantic to her. Ever.

"Joe, that was so beautiful," she whispered.

The breeze she'd predicted sprang up, playing with his now-dry hair, sending strands of hers across her face. For

one terrifying moment, she thought this new version of
Joe was going to kiss her. He had that look in his eye, one
she'd seen plenty of times, but never on Joe. The preda-
tory my-woman look.

No, no, no, not Joe, that wasn't right, he wasn't—

Oh, dear. He was.

Would she let him? No! She wasn't ready!

God took care of her. The breeze strengthened and
knocked over the garbage bag, spilling husks everywhere.
By the time they got those cleaned up and went back to
their work, Joe was himself again, the moment was over,
and they were back to being comfortable friends.

Almost. Sarah couldn't quite forget. For that one second the thought of kissing Joe had been terrifying, yes.
But also just the tiniest bit…thrilling.

And maybe, if she allowed herself to think about it—
absolutely right.

ADDIE WOKE UP, bleary-eyed and cranky and very, very
sandy. What time was it? Where was she? What was she—

Right. Storness Island. The secret cove. She'd been
there all morning with Sarah. They'd had a long conversation analyzing the world and all men in it, noting particularly how unworthy way too many of them were.

That part was mostly Sarah.

Addie struggled to sit up, brushing back a tangle of
hair. Then they'd moved on to discuss, specifically, Kevin,
Derek and Joe, and how maybe Sarah had been wrong
about Derek. And how Addie should give him a chance as
well as Kevin and see what happened because you couldn't
have enough eggs in different baskets.

That part was mostly Sarah, too.

After she left, insisting Addie stay on for a good
while to relax, Addie had been exhausted. Give Derek a

chance this weekend? *And* Kevin? The woman who'd been tempted to spend this week filing? Please.

Since the day was hot, she'd retreated to a banana shaped spot at the edge of the beach, where bushes and vegetation had formed a sheltering canopy, and covered herself with her towel. Apparently she'd kicked it off at some point while she was asleep and, just as apparently, a warm breeze had come up and blown more sand on her, plus the sun had moved and taken away a lot of the shade. So now she was naked, sweaty, thirsty and probably a little sunburned.

She stood up groggily and shook out her towel in the stiffening breeze, eyes squeezed shut and head turned, then tried to brush the sticky sand off her sticky body.

Ouch. Sand grains brushing over sunburned skin equaled sandpaper. Addie looked longingly toward the water. A skinny promontory and a kind of zigzag in the island's coast formed a natural pool that looked perfect for swimming, and hid whoever was in the cove from passing boats. The tide was low now, but should be on its way in. Sarah told her the best time for swimming was sunny days when high tide had been creeping up over pre-heated sand and rocks all afternoon. This water wouldn't be warm, but it would get this sand off more effectively and a lot less painfully.

She marched down the beach, which was relatively steep so the tide hadn't gone out that far, and gingerly stepped in.

Brrrr. Cold. Especially on heated skin.

She stuck her other foot in.

Really cold.

This would take considerable courage, but if Addie did a superfast wash-off of sand and sweat, her body would feel great when she was back in the warm sun again.

She hoped.

Another step, and another, until she was up to her knees, then thighs, then…*oh* that was cold. Men would *not* want to do this. Not if they wanted to have children someday.

A few more steps and the coarsening sand under her feet turned to pebbles, then rocks. She had to pick her way carefully, testing with her feet to be sure stones were stable before trusting them with her weight.

It would be much easier to swim.

In past her waist, she paused, swirling her hands in the greenish depths, following shafts of sunlight picking up tiny particles, not unlike sunbeams shining through dust or mist.

So. This swimming thing. She needed to dive in and get it over with.

Ready?

One. Two. Three. *No!*

Chicken.

One more step, then she'd dive for sure. Addie stepped bravely forward onto a stone that toppled and threw her. She shrieked and fell, tried to regain her footing, floundered, then lost the bottom entirely and went under. She flailed to the surface, treading water, gasping, already turning so she could get back to shore as fast as possible. One long stroke in, she got the bottom back under her feet. Whew. Another step and she stumbled and fell again into what she had now decided was fresh iceberg melt. Feet scrambling, she fell twice more, sputtering and shrieking, before she finally reached sand and stability in waist-high water, so she could stagger safely back to—

Derek.

Oh, my God.

Derek was standing on the beach, feet spread, hands on his hips, grinning.

Her eyes shot open about as wide as they could go; her hands sprang to cover her breasts. Thank God water was still covering…the rest.

What the hell was he doing here? Sarah said no one knew about the cove. How did he find her? What was she going to do? Why was he standing there staring at her?

Her teeth started to chatter.

She was *naked* and the water was *freezing*.

"Uh. Hi, Derek."

"Hi, there."

She wanted to growl at his cheerfulness. "Um, could you turn around so I can go get my towel?"

"Nope." He was enjoying himself, the rat.

"Nope? What do you mean nope?"

"What do you think?" He walked forward a few steps and guess what, did some more grinning and staring.

Damn it, Derek, this was not fair.

Time for her rational superpowers. Like this: she could run for her towel, giving him only a speeding peek, which might not be all that terrible considering he'd had his hands all over her last night.

Or she could just say to hell with it and walk to her towel at a normal pace, letting him know she was not ashamed or embarrassed about her body. Yes, okay, her hands were currently cemented over her breasts, both of which were joining the rest of her body in being covered with oh-so-not-sexy goose pimples, but she'd chalk that up to panic and forgive herself.

Once covered, she'd be in a good position to discuss whatever he was here to discuss. Or whatever she wanted to discuss. Like maybe that she and Sarah had talked about—

Addie gasped.

Derek was walking deliberately toward her. *Prowling*

was a better word, because his intentions were quite clear in his expression and in the animal way his body was moving. Everything about him was broadcasting what she'd felt from him last night in bed.

I want you.

Oh, help. Addie had to run for the towel *now,* while she could still feel her legs.

The water covered Derek's feet. He didn't even flinch.

His ankles were gone now.

His shins.

Go! Now!

She wasn't moving.

Why wasn't she moving?

Move!

There! Good! Now she was moving!

But *wait,* what was wrong with her, she was not walking toward her towel, she was walking toward *him!*

Stop, before it's too late!

Four feet away from him her hands dropped from her breasts to her sides.

It was already way too late.

9

ADDIE KEPT WALKING. She walked straight into Derek's arms, naked, dripping wet and salty, and she kissed him. Hard.

What was she doing?

Something utterly, deliciously and completely spontaneous.

What about Kevin? What about how he wanted to get to know her slowly, see if they could have something real together?

Addie's lips faltered, then it hit her. She didn't want Kevin. The moment she'd seen him she'd known. The only reason she'd been hanging on to the idea of reconnecting was that it was her *plan* and God forbid Addie Sewell not stay the course and go through with one of her plans.

Derek's arms came around her, and he kissed her back. And how.

But this man has nothing to offer. He'll be back at sea in a few days.

Nothing to offer? She pressed herself against him, felt a rather impressive swelling in his shorts. Seemed to her he had *plenty* to offer.

And guess what? She was taking it. And that made her, right now, about the wildest she'd ever been.

Addie turned off the voice in her head and gave herself over to what she was feeling. Warm, soft lips taking hers, warm hands stroking the line from her waist to her hip. Warm sun and breezes drying her skin. And hot, hot longing throughout her whole body.

She'd never felt like this, never experienced this overwhelming and desperate need. Not for anyone ever.

"Addie." He led them out of the water, working as hard as she was to control his breathing. "Shouldn't we talk about—"

"No." She took hold of his shirt and pulled him back to her. The feel of the fabric under her fingers became annoying. She wanted skin.

Up came his shirt; she helped him drag it over his head and oh, my goodness, what a chest. It should be on permanent display at a treasure chest museum.

Her hands fumbled at the button on his shorts, got them open, unzipped, down. No underwear. Oh, my goodness. That part of him should be on display at the rock-hard hall of fame.

Hard because of her, and this incredible want they generated together.

He pulled her close, pressing her body against his, and oh, the sensations were incendiary, exciting…and not enough. *Not enough.* She wanted more of him, all of him. *Now.*

Good Lord, what kind of wanton creature had she turned into?

The best kind. She'd never felt so primal, so real, so… herself. No expectations, no role to fill, nothing but what her body wanted and needed.

Even if she and Derek lasted only a few days, this new

sense of herself and her power would forever be hers, Derek's gift to her, lasting until death.

She lifted her leg to wrap around his hip; he reached down to stroke the softness between her legs. Addie moaned and clutched his shoulders, distantly aware of the gurgling swish of the waves and the occasional call of gulls. Beautiful spot. Beautiful man.

And speaking of beautiful spot. His fingers…

Too soon he stopped and spanned her waist with his strong hands, preparing to lift her. She grabbed him around the neck and gave a little hop into his arms to help him, though he could probably have lifted her without it.

Mmm…

Kissing her—open, wet kisses that were making her lose her mind—he walked her up the beach then set her on her feet by a towel he must have brought with him. How long had he been there watching her before she noticed him?

"Wait here." He strode back toward the shorts he'd dropped on the beach.

She giggled, pushing hair back from her face. "Like I'd leave now?"

Derek tossed a grin over his shoulder and picked something out of the shorts' pocket.

Condom. Good man.

She watched him walk back toward her, muscles bunching and releasing, utterly natural and unselfconsciously naked in this lovely place.

Come to think of it, she felt the same. Not worried he might find her flawed, not comparing her body to anyone else's. Her brain knew he wanted her. Her heart knew he wanted her just the way she was.

Come on, Addie, you're romanticizing him the same way you were romanticizing Kevin.

Maybe. But with Derek it wasn't so much a thinking process as an instinct.

He came up close, arms around her waist, and leaned back to examine her face. "I take it you changed your mind."

"Apparently." She tried to make eye contact, but the depth of his gaze was too intense, made her insides shuddery and sweet, so she contented herself with gazing at his chin, his shoulders, his chest, only chancing a glance up at him now and then, as much as she could take.

"You're sure?"

"Very." She traced the line of his collarbone with her finger. "How did you find me here?"

"Sarah."

Addie's finger stopped at his sternum. Her mouth dropped open. "*Sarah* told *you* I was here?"

Why hadn't she sent Kevin?

"Yeah." Derek nodded, looking unexpectedly wary. "Right after she found out Kevin spent last night with Carrie."

"Kevin—" Addie's mouth dropped wider. "He—"

"I'm sorry, Addie."

She stared at him, trying to process all this, waiting for the pain, the rage, the feeling of betrayal. That rat Kevin. Not wanting to let her in his room. All that crap about wanting to get to know her before they slept together. The funny high-voiced whimper she heard....

Addie burst out laughing. What an idiot she'd been.

Derek blinked in surprise. "You think that's funny?"

Addie shrugged. "Parts of it are. The whole night was practically farcical. Me with you by mistake, then bumping into Kevin who had another woman with him the whole time. And it's funny in a sort of sad way how hard I worked not to see Kevin as he is. And it's funny in a sweet way that Sarah relinquished her need to attack you long enough to let me try."

"Mmm." His eyes warmed. "I like the way you attack me."

"After Kevin…well, you're not exactly a booby prize."

"No." His eyes dropped appreciatively below her neck. "I get that one."

"Aw, jeez." Addie pretended disgust at his pun, disgust which crumbled when he darted forward and fixed his mouth onto her breast.

Mmm. She let her head fall back, concentrating on the wet heat of his tongue and lips tugging her nipple, sending pleasure signals traveling through her body down between her legs.

"Make love to me, Derek." She dropped slowly to her knees, pulling him with her—not that he resisted.

"I definitely plan to," he whispered. "I wanted to from the moment you said hello on the front steps of the house."

"Me, too." She held out her arms for him. Their words were strictly carnal, but somehow Addie felt as if they were speaking from the heart. Even though they were in this for only a few days, it didn't feel like a hit-and-run relationship. It felt much richer, more important to each of them.

Oh, please, Addie, you're getting laid, stop trying to make it into something more.

Telling the critical pain-in-the-butt voice in her head to shut up, Addie clasped Derek's warm, wide body to hers, reveling in its power, how small he made her feel, but how safe.

He paid her breasts more attention while he ran his hand up and down her belly, slightly lower with each stroke until he touched the top of her pubic curls, then lower and lower, making her gasp.

"You like that?"

"Oh, yes." She arched her hips up, inviting his hand to explore further, her arousal building again to a fever pitch. *"Yes."*

"I like it, too, Addie." He lifted his head to gaze at her while one finger traveled slowly over her pubic bone, nudging her clitoris, stroking over it, making the slide down between her labia.

Addie whimpered, eyes cemented to his, helpless under his touch. His finger dipped inside her. She gasped at the intrusion, hungry between her legs as she'd never been before. Derek withdrew his finger and painted it, slippery wet, over her clitoris, warming where the sun's weight already lay.

Addie nearly came right there, had to breathe and back down. She wanted him inside her. She wanted him coming with her.

Again, his finger slid and thrusted and painted. Again she fought the orgasm, trembling in his arms, her breath a series of stuttering gasps. Again, and again he brought her to the edge, until she was ready to scream.

"I can't do this much longer," she whispered. "I want you."

He pulled on the condom, spread her legs wide and knelt between them, making her feel open and vulnerable to him, breeze blowing intimately on her sex. His eyes traveled her body, rested on her face.

"You're beautiful, Addie."

He made her feel beautiful. Inside and out. Nothing else mattered right now. "Come to me, Derek. Please."

He walked forward on his hands, his body held over hers. Addie lifted her head and they both looked down. At her—wide-open. At him—hard and ready.

Then he lowered himself, only halfway. Addie reached

for his erection, impatient to guide it where she wanted it so badly.

"Addie."

"Yes." She was breathless with anticipation. Why was he holding back?

"Look at me."

She met his eyes and he pushed inside her, slowly, an inch, back out, then farther, stretching her, filling her. She closed her eyes—the connection and emotions were too intense—and let herself concentrate only on the animal, on the thrust of him way inside her, friction slow and steady in spite of how wet she was. The weight of him on top of her, the clean just-showered smell of his skin. The way he moved leisurely in and out, showing no impatience. She didn't want him to hurry. They had the beach to themselves and the rest of the afternoon.

For a while, his rhythm went on unchanged, as they got to know each other's sounds and movements, exploring textures and shapes.

Then Derek pulled almost all the way out, made love to her with only the first inch or two of his penis, causing a light tug on her clitoris, just enough to make her crazy but not quite enough stimulation to come.

Torture. She moaned involuntarily, began breathing harshly, nearly panting. She had to come *now*.

When she was about to put her hand down and take care of it herself, Derek thrust all the way in and began an earnest, powerful drive.

Addie gave a yell, more noise than she'd ever made during lovemaking, but she was no longer in control of her body or herself. The orgasm was coming so slow and hot and hard, she wasn't even sure she'd survive it.

Just before its peak, she opened her eyes in surrender and locked on to Derek's.

"Yes," he whispered. Somehow he knew. How did he know? "Let go, come for me."

Gripping his shoulders, bracing herself, Addie yelled again, lost in the explosion of pleasure, and the doubling of its intensity as she realized he was coming with her, inside her, pulsing as she contracted over and over until the waves of pleasure subsided, leaving them locked together, breaths heaving.

When she could speak again, Addie stroked the dark head resting on her breast. "That was wonderful, Derek."

"Mrhgm."

She giggled. "You're welcome."

He lifted his head unsteadily and blinked down at her. "Are we still alive?"

"I…think so."

"My God, Addie." He was smiling, but she heard the awe in his voice and saw it in his eyes. "That was… I'm kind of glad you changed your mind."

"I'm kind of glad Sarah told you where I was."

"And that Kevin got laid last night."

"And that I found your room by mistake."

He kissed her then, long slow kisses that instead of heating up her body, heated up her heart.

Uh-oh.

See? You can't handle casual sex. You are not a wild woman. What made you think you could?

She kissed him back, only letting herself enjoy the smooth masculine feel of his mouth against hers, her hands stroking the long muscles in his back, sweeping up to his powerful shoulders.

He pulled out reluctantly, removed the condom and lay facing her on the towel. For a while they were quiet, gazing into each other's eyes. She didn't find it hard to do anymore. He seemed almost familiar; there was some part of his gaze that now jumped out and included her. It was not the way she'd ever imagined looking at someone she barely knew. There was no fear, not even of judgment. This was so new. So different.

And she'd have to say goodbye to him in only two days.

"You know what?" She stroked the side of his face, unable to stop wanting to feel his skin under her fingers. "That's the most spontaneous thing I've ever done."

He turned to kiss her palm. "It certainly got my attention."

"I'm not usually like that."

"You don't generally flaunt your very beautiful naked body in front of men you don't know very well? I'd say that's a good thing."

She laughed. "I mean...I didn't think that was something I would do. Or even could do."

He turned her gently onto her back and lay half over her. "Maybe it's the Maine air."

"Maybe it's some mind-altering drug Paul and Ellen put in breakfast."

"Maybe you were possessed by aliens."

"Maybe I feel safe with you." She wrinkled her nose. "Nah, that's ridiculous."

That deep chuckle again. Addie wanted to bottle it and bring it home with her. They had two more days and she already missed it.

"I hope you do, because you are safe with me. As for not being spontaneous, we all have busy lives, duties, things we need to accomplish every day. Spontaneity is a luxury. You're on vacation now, you can afford it."

"True." She frowned thoughtfully, outlining his lips with her pinky. They were beautiful lips. Of course right then she was so infatuated, she'd probably think he had beautiful toenails. "But I do tend to be uncomfortable with anything not planned ahead."

"Maybe you'll embrace the dark side a little more now." He kissed one cheek, her other cheek, her nose, her forehead. "It's not as if you have to strip for every guy you meet for the rest of your life. Try new things, see how they feel. Baby steps."

Addie stroked the hard curve of his shoulder. It meant a lot that he took her neuroses so calmly and seriously. "You feel really good, Derek."

"So do you, Addie."

They smiled at each other. Incredible happiness and incredible peace, an amazing combination. "Tell me something."

"Mmm?"

"No, I mean tell me something. Anything. Everything." She grinned at the alarm on his face. "Tell me about your childhood."

"Ah." He rolled onto his back, lips curved in a wistful smile. "My childhood was a study in conflict. Between me, the boy who'd wanted a life on the sea since he was old enough to read *Kidnapped,* and my parents, who'd planned for me to go to business school like my dad and brothers ever since I was born."

"Ah, the family black sheep!"

"Baaa."

She propped herself up so she could see his face. "Tell me more."

"Let's see. I worked crap jobs on boats in Boston Harbor till I was old enough to leave home. Then I got crap jobs on boats in Miami until I went to school, graduated and worked my way up, saving every penny. At what I felt was the right time, I let everyone know I was looking for the right boat. And then one day I heard about her."

"Love at first sight?"

"You have no idea."

Oh, great, she was jealous of a boat. "Picture in your wallet?"

"Nope." He half lifted his head to peer at her. "I should have one, huh?"

"Absolutely." She stroked the firm, rounded planes of his chest. "I'd love to see her."

"Who knows what life will bring. Maybe you will someday."

"Maybe." She paid close attention to his body, not wanting to look at him. The topic was too charged to be under discussion this soon. "So you met the love of your life...."

"I had some money set aside by my grandparents, and landed a loan with help from a guy I worked for as first mate for years."

"He didn't mind you were leaving?"

"He knew he had no choice." Derek adjusted his head on the towel, expression fiercely proud. "He was a good guy. I enjoyed working for him. But I wanted to be boss. It's in my blood I guess. All Bates boys are bossy."

She loved the idea of him working hard, making his dream come true all by himself, becoming captain and owner of his own little kingdom. It was kind of a turn-on. But then calling something about Derek a turn-on was sort of like saying the sun was warm.

"It's amazing what you've done. I admire you."

"Oh." He looked embarrassed, but in a way that told her he was pleased by her compliment. "Thanks."

"It took courage and determination."

"Hmm." He sat up and squeezed her hand. "I think it was just what I wanted to do, so I did it."

"But a lot of people don't get to do what they want. Or can't. Or are afraid to."

"Yeah?" He studied her chin then planted a kiss in the perfect spot. "What would you do if you could?"

"Oh." She cast her mind around, mortified not to come up with anything thrilling. Maybe she should invent something—skydiving or hiking Mount Everest. But when she looked into Derek's serious brown eyes she couldn't tell him a lie. Even a little one. She wanted this to be real for the short time they had. "I'm pretty contented, actually."

"Hey, a lot of people can't do that, either. So you're just as remarkable."

Addie rolled her eyes. "Nice try."

He laughed and kissed her everywhere he could reach, teasing playful kisses that made her squeal and giggle like a silly schoolgirl.

Except she didn't feel silly. She felt…fabulous.

"What do you say we go rinse off, Addie?"

Addie pretended to shudder. "In that water?"

"In our private pool." He stood and held out his hand. "Which happens to be filled with that water, yeah."

"Tell you what." Addie was already getting to her feet. "You go, I'm outta here."

She took off toward the path. He caught up to her in about three strides and snagged her around the waist. "Oops. Ocean's the other way."

"Help, help! *Torture!*" The word ended in a squeal as he picked her up and ran with her to the water. "So help me, Derek, if you dump me into that freezing—"

Of course he did. She found her feet, and lunged up, flung her arms around his neck and knocked him off balance so he fell in, too.

There. They were even. With a shout, he rocketed up out of the water as fast as she had, grabbed her hand and pulled her back out onto the shore and back to his towel where they sat absorbing the sun's warmth, bodies glowing from the cold, lungs working to overcome the shock.

Addie had never had this much fun with a lover. Her first serious boyfriend, Todd, had been intense and bookish, a lovely sweet guy. Her second, Leo, had been a little sunnier maybe, but neither were the type who liked to play like this.

Addie apparently liked men who played. As long as they respected her in the morning.

"I suppose we should think about going back?" The minute she spoke, she regretted it. Practical, sensible Addie. Had she always been such a spoilsport?

"Yes, we should." He frowned hard then his face cleared. "There, we thought about it."

Addie burst into giggles. She was enjoying herself a ridiculous amount. And if he wanted to stay, then he must be feeling the same. "That's settled, then?"

"At least until we get hungry."

"Gosh. Now that you mention it…" She blinked at him sweetly, reclined onto her elbows and let her knees open slowly all the way to flat. "I'm getting *hungry* right now."

"Addie Sewell. Beautiful, funny *and* a nymphomaniac." He waggled his eyebrows and adopted a lounge lizard accent. "*Now* how much would you pay?"

"Oh, that is just *nasty*." She pretended to struggle away from him, letting herself be overpowered of course. He grinned wickedly, then turned one-eighty and positioned himself with his hands on either side of her hips, his knees to one side of her head, his face…lowering.

Addie lay back blissfully, desire responding to his skill, noticing deeper intimacy with him this time, not only from their already having explored each other's bodies, but from the joy of letting loose and being silly and child-like together. Two different kinds of vulnerability, both bringing them closer together.

She could fall for this guy.

Yes, yes, she knew it was too soon, way too soon. But everything about being with him felt so different from any relationship she'd—

Ooh. His fingers had joined his tongue. He was spoiling her. She reached over and pulled at his leg, wanting him to feel this good, too.

Derek understood, moving to kneel astride her head. Addie guided his penis into her mouth; he tasted clean and salty from the sea. She tried to vary the speed and pressure of her lips, listening to his breath hissing when she hit a rhythm or spot he really liked, but what he was doing to her at the same time made it very hard to focus on anything but her gathering frenzy for him.

Just when she was about to cry uncle, Derek pulled back, flicking gently with his tongue, then lowered his mouth and sucked firmly, pushing two fingers deep inside her.

She was lost. Her orgasm hit fast and intense from the beginning. Barely keeping herself under control, she fingered the shaft of Derek's cock, keeping the rhythm going with her mouth at his tip, then reached under and past his balls to the hidden root of his penis.

He inhaled sharply, moaned and seconds later erupted, his muscles contracting, making the sexiest sounds of ecstasy she'd ever heard.

Oh, my.

She lay, blissful, panting, heart swollen and aching with all she felt. What they'd done was nothing she'd ever consider a loving or sweet act, and yet…that's exactly how it had felt with him, each giving to the other. Derek turned around shakily and collapsed next to her, pulling her to him, cradling her head on his chest, nearly bringing tears to her eyes with his tenderness. The breeze had picked up, blowing cooler sweet air over them. The tide was coming in, waves rolling lazily toward them over the warm sand.

This was paradise.

"Addie." He took her face in his hands. "You are incredible."

Then he kissed her, differently from the way he'd kissed her before. Gently, reverently, over and over. Her heart swelled larger, dangerously so, that intense sweet ache in her chest told her she was in serious trouble over this man.

Could she fall for him?

Yes. That worry had been there since the night they watched the sunset together, Addie just hadn't been able to admit it to herself.

After today, however, she had a brand-new worry. Not whether she'd fall for Derek Bates, but how far she already had.

10

"ARE YOU HUNGRY? For food this time?" Derek drew his hand down Addie's firm stomach, over her pelvis, fingers brushing lightly through her curls. He could touch this woman all day long. In fact, he intended to.

"Actually, yes." She turned to him, face rosy and bright. "I've been in denial, though, because I'm enjoying this so much I don't want to go back up to the house."

"What would you say if you found out I have a cooler up in the woods packed with lunch?"

"Hmm." She bunched her mouth, thinking it over. "I guess I'd have to say you're the world's most perfect man."

Derek laughed and got to his feet. "That'll do."

He climbed the small rise into the woods, heading toward the spot where he'd left the cooler. Around Addie he felt more natural and relaxed than any woman he could remember being with. Something about her made him feel he didn't have to hide any part of himself. He'd been playing a role so often on board *Joie de Vivre* that he'd apparently made it a habit to turn his real self off, turn on the charm and say only safe and appropriate things, acting with professional decorum at all times—even onshore to a certain extent—so that his clean and sober reputation stayed intact.

Something else was surfacing now, too, from deep in his subconscious, rising slowly, about to break through. He'd noticed it first around Paul and Ellen, who were constantly connecting with a look, a touch, a murmured word or two. They had a future of that special linkage ahead of them, years and years, for the rest of their lives. Watching them had made Derek aware of how much time he spent alone, even among people.

He couldn't say he'd bonded deeply with anyone in his family, though of course he loved them all. At his first jobs at sea, he'd contented himself with "buddy" relationships with crew members, and there was always distance from his superiors—the same distance he kept now as captain. Paul had probably been his first substantive friendship. He'd had relationships now and then with women, but they'd always been secondary to his career, and never very consuming. With Addie, he felt truly connected.

He grabbed the cooler and jumped back down onto the warm sand, brought it over to her, feeling like a commoner proffering gifts to a queen.

No, that wasn't right. She never made him feel common. She made him feel like a man worth loving.

It would be easy to qualify his feelings for Addie, saying they must only be superficial, that he and she had only known each other such a short time, yadda yadda, all the common sense stuff. But deep in his soul, where there existed only truth, he was getting the beginnings of a message so huge he was afraid of hearing it, afraid of dwelling on it, not sure if he was afraid it was true or afraid that it wasn't.

Addie was The One.

Crazy talk. He was way, way ahead of himself.

"Here we go." He plunked the cooler onto the sand and arranged the towel so they could sit together facing the water, then opened the lid. *"Les sandwiches du jambon."*

"Good Lord, what have you made for me?"

"Ham sandwiches."

Addie giggled. "So chic, Pierre."

"Ain't it?" He unwrapped a sandwich he'd made when he stopped into the main house for a lightning fast shower after chopping all that wood, and for condoms. It had occurred to him if his plan for Addie's morning worked out he'd want to spend a lot of private time with her that afternoon as well, so lunch was a good idea. Paul and Ellen had nothing planned for the group until the rehearsal dinner that night. Many of the guests had decided to spend the afternoon on the mainland. They were free and clear until early evening.

"Thank you. It looks delicious." She took the thick sandwich—of ham, cheese and cucumber slices on whole wheat bread, and a can of lemon-flavored sparkling water.

They ate for a while in comfortable silence, then Derek started smiling—he couldn't help it. Addie had that adorable frown across her forehead, which he was starting to learn meant she was working something out in her mind.

"It's funny," she said eventually. "I almost didn't want to come to this wedding."

"Yeah?" A tiny shock jolted his chest, as if he was suffering the idea of never having met her. For crying out loud. She *did* come.

"Anything that promised to take me out of my comfortable everyday routine felt like a threat. It's kind of scary to look back now and see how stuck I was. I hope I never go back to that."

"You won't if you don't want to. And for the record, I'm very glad you came." Understatement of the millennium. She'd already changed his life. From now on he wouldn't settle for less than this remarkable level of affinity and of intimacy.

"Me, too." She smiled at him, her dark eyes warm and a little shy, dimple sweet in her right cheek. His heart seemed to double in size, straining to get out of his chest. "Tell me more about your life as the big romantic yacht captain."

"Ha." He took a sip of water. "Nonstop fun and glamour."

"I knew it!"

"Let's see. Which would be more thrilling, talking about managing a hardworking, squabbling crew stuck in close quarters for weeks at a time, or discussing the hours spent charting courses and worrying about weather, or dealing with annoying entitled passengers, or managing the budget, or hey, I know, understanding the paperwork and health regulations required by different ports, rarely getting a day off...are you still awake?"

"Wow." She chewed solemnly on a bite of sandwich. "I guess every job has its downside, huh. You still love it, though."

"Most of the time, yeah."

"There must be some glamorous parts to it."

"There are." He chased a bite of sandwich with water, realizing he'd been starving and glad he'd packed lots of food. Not only had he worked his body plenty today, he'd also been through an emotional Tilt-A-Whirl. "I've anchored at some of the most gorgeous spots in the world. Seen places I never would have dreamed of if I'd stayed in Massachusetts with my family."

"Hmm." Addie took another bite. Derek was intrigued. Usually this was where women sighed and batted their eyes and said they'd give anything to be able to come along on a trip, that it sounded so romantic. But Addie sat still, that slight frown creasing her forehead.

"It must be a lonely life."

For about three seconds he sat, stunned and oddly moved. She was right. It was a lonely life. But not that many people—no one he'd met—had ever figured that out.

"It can be." His voice had gone husky. He cleared his throat.

"It's also not a life conducive to having a family or a home. Not in a traditional way anyway. So it must seem like there's no real solution to loneliness."

Derek took a last big bite of sandwich to delay answering. What was he going to say, *You're right. And quite honestly, I didn't even consider marriage and kids until I met you the day before yesterday?* It would be a great way to see her gorgeous rear—running away from him as fast as possible. He wouldn't blame her.

What was happening to him? His career, his boat, they'd been everything to him his whole life, first as a dream, then a reality.

"I think I'd have to meet the right woman." He wanted to roll his eyes at the cliché. "Well, obviously. I wouldn't want to be with the *wrong* one."

"No kidding." She gestured with her sandwich. "You need to find someone who'd be fine on her own all the time. Raising kids with no help whatsoever."

He did roll his eyes then. "Yeah, piece of cake, there are probably five or six on the planet."

They laughed together, though a part deep inside him felt vulnerable and pained, like they were poking fun at something too personal. "What about you, you want the traditional marriage?"

"I…" She stopped, looking pensive. "Funny, I was going to say yes, immediately, but you know, I'm starting to question a lot of stuff about myself this weekend. Maybe I need to think about it. I definitely don't want to be home alone raising kids, so…you know, just to spare you asking me."

More laughter, strained this time, no, not too funny. Painful and vulnerable times two. "Tell me more."

She tipped her head to one side, considering. "It's funny, having been here, seeing Kevin, meeting you—this week is about Paul and Ellen's wedding, but it's also feeling like a crossroads for me, as if I'm coming to a place in life where I can choose to be different going forward."

"Different how?"

"More adventurous. Taking more risks. Trying new things."

He nodded and took a bite of sandwich to hide his reaction, which was a fierce possessive need to drag her back to Hawaii and onto *Joie de Vivre* so she couldn't try this new wildness out on anyone else.

The power of the feeling shocked him. Maybe this was a crossroads for him, too. The idea of leaving here, the camaraderie, the community and Addie, and sailing off with his crew and a bunch of strangers—the life he'd chosen, the life he'd worked so hard to be able to live—it was not appealing the same way it always had.

"What would you do? Take up skydiving? Start a career as a stripper?"

"Ha!" She made a face. "Not likely. I'm still me."

"I like that about you."

"Mmm, thanks." She closed the space between them for a kiss. Maybe she intended it to be brief, but Derek had other ideas. Her mouth was warm and soft and tasted like lemon sparkling water. She was delicious. He cupped his hand around her head and held her close, kissing her until his desire started rising again. And by the whimper she gave, he knew the excitement was mutual.

What torture next week to be on his boat thinking about this woman and knowing he couldn't hold her again. The *Joie de Vivre* had always been his ultimate refuge, his sanctuary, his kingdom. This woman could change all that. He wasn't sure he liked her having that much power over him and his life. But he wasn't sure he had a choice.

"Tell me the wild things you'd like to do," he murmured.

"Hmm. Maybe I'll take ballet." She didn't resist when he took her plate and put it on the sand then returned to kissing her, dragging her across his lap, wanting to keep her safely close to him. "I loved ballet when I was a girl. Maybe take that up again."

"Mmm, Addie in a tutu. I like the idea."

"Or maybe…" Her voice lowered and became slightly husky. She tipped her head to give him better access to the soft skin of her neck, tasting of salt, cocoa butter and Addie. "Maybe I'll take an online lit class."

Derek sucked in air, as if she was wildly arousing him. "A *lit* class. Addie I'm not sure how much more I can stand."

"And…" Addie sat up and put her hand to his chest, her gaze smoldering. She pushed until he was forced to lie back on the towel, then she straddled him on her hands and knees. "Maybe I'll learn French."

"Oh, la la." He growled and pulled her down to kiss him, molding her body on top of his. "Addie, I just want you to know that if you feel the need to try out anything different, you know, to bring out this wilder, primal, sex monster side of yourself, seriously, feel free. Right now. On top of me. I can take it. Really. I promise."

She was giggling madly, which made her wiggle just a

little, which was doing some truly great things for his man parts. Then her laughter subsided. She rested her head on his shoulder and went still. They lay there together, breathing in the clean sea air. A boat passed somewhere not too far off, engines throbbing, radio occasionally crackling to life.

Addie lifted her head, hair spilling over her forehead, cheeks flushed, eyes sultry, lips parted. "You're on."

He lay there, hardly able to believe the change in her. His cock reacted, hardening nearly fully in record time. All she'd done was look at him.

"You need to put on another condom."

He said nothing, scrambled to obey, had it on and was lying back down within seconds.

She straddled him again, lifted herself to her knees, the strength in her thighs controlling the height of her hips.

Not low enough.

As if she heard him, she lowered herself until she was sitting at the base of his erection, pressing it against his abdomen. His cock felt nestled in the warmth of her sex. He knew more was coming. He couldn't wait.

Addie lifted her arms over her head, pulling her breasts up, lengthening her torso. Then she began to sway, sliding her sex over him, stimulating his cock, undulating her body, eyes closed, like a belly dancer in a trance.

It was the sexiest thing Derek had ever seen, all the more so because he knew what she had to fight to be this free with him, because he knew this was a vote of confidence and trust in their intimacy and in him, that she felt comfortable and safe enough to let loose.

He groaned and grabbed her hips, pushing his up to increase the pressure, going from aroused to nearly desperate in a matter of a minute.

She caught his mood, began to ride him gently, rocking her hips up and back instead of side to side.

When he wasn't sure how much longer he could stand that, she pressed her hands into the sand on either side of his head and lifted, allowing his penis to come to full attention. Allowing him to feel the loss of warmth and the coolness of the breeze.

Only for a moment. Thank goodness.

Her hips lowered again, just to the tip of his cock, trapping it, then circling gently, making him use all his strength not to shove inside her, pump into her softness until he found release.

"I'm psychic, did you know that?"

"Nope." He spoke through clenched teeth.

"I am. And I'm getting something from you…" She gazed sightlessly off into the distance. "Wait… Yes, got it. You want to be inside me."

"Amazing." He sounded as if he was strangling.

"All the way."

"Yes. *Yes.*"

"Hmm." She came down farther. An inch of him disappeared. Her sex was warm and tight around the tip of his penis. He fisted his hands, swallowed convulsively.

"Do you like that, Derek?"

He nodded, sweat breaking out on his forehead, completely under her control, and not minding at all.

"How about this?" She moved lower; another inch of him slid inside her, another inch sensually enveloped. He wanted to pound his fists in the sand.

"Yes. I like that, too. More, please."

"Like this?" She hesitated, poised, making him wait. Then bore down powerfully and took him all the way in.

He gave a yell he was ashamed of then forgot his shame as she moved fiercely up and down. He tried to slow her movements, tried to stop her, somehow. But she was relentless, gripping his cock with her body, releasing and gripping again, panting in his ear, whispering what he felt like inside her, hot and hard and making her crazy with pleasure.

He was lost, too far over the edge to stop. With another shout he came so hard he felt as if his body was trying to turn inside out.

Oh, man.

"Addie." He could barely say her name.

"Mmm?" Her eyes were bright with triumphant pleasure. He'd never seen anything so beautiful.

He had to catch his breath, pulling her down to clasp her in his arms. "I want you to understand something."

"Yes?"

"It is physically impossible for me to come three times in this short a time."

"Really." He could hear the smile in her voice.

"I think you must be a witch. Or a shape-shifter."

"Supernatural sex." She kissed his neck contentedly. "Cool."

"Except for one thing."

"What's that?"

"You didn't get your third."

"Oh, no." She lifted her head. "I can't come that many times, either. Seriously, that was wonderful just like that."

"Uh-huh." He was already traveling down between her legs, aching to taste her.

"No, Derek, I really don't think I...*oh.*"

He'd gone to work, loving her taste, the supple give of her sex, the way she writhed under his tongue and his fingers.

"Maybe..." She stopped for a gasp as he changed his rhythm. "Maybe *one* more."

When she came apart, minutes later, moaning and gripping his arms, he felt her pleasure and satisfaction as if he'd come again himself.

He was falling for her. How could this happen so fast and so intensely? It made no sense…went against everything he thought he believed about love and about caution and about common sense.

Worse, and far more foolish, the idle fantasy of taking her out on his boat to live with him instead of returning her to the city had begun to change into the beginnings of a serious idea.

_11_

PAUL AND ELLEN'S rehearsal dinner was ending. The last lobster had been ravenously consumed, rolls and salad demolished, blueberry, raspberry and chocolate cream pies decimated. The group was lolling around the bonfire on the beach where they'd eaten, chatting while they finished off the keg. This was to be their last night on Storness Island. The next day, Saturday, they'd spend the morning cleaning and packing, then the trip back to the mainland for Paul and Ellen's late afternoon wedding and reception at the beautiful house in Machias owned by the Bossons' close friends, the Brisbanes. Sunday they'd all go home.

Sarah sat watching the flames, full of lobster, pie and confusion, nursing a last beer. She hadn't had many—this was her third in three or four hours. She wasn't in the mood for drinking. Most of the evening she'd smiled and chatted and acted the part of the happy groom's sister—which she was, no question, very happy for Paul and for Ellen, whom she adored. But the reason for her uncharacteristically somber mood eluded her, and therefore its solution was similarly out of reach.

Every time she felt some understanding approaching she'd do everything in her power to go inside herself and grab it—but always at that instant whatever she was after, whatever part she'd managed to comprehend, disintegrated again into confusion.

In other words, something was massively bugging her and she was effing clueless as to what to do about it.

This was not like her. She'd always thought of herself as sunny and optimistic, knowing what she wanted and how to go about getting it—as long as it wasn't a man. This weekend had dislodged her from that certainty, and tossed her into a who-am-I? abyss.

She hated that.

One of the guys Paul worked with, Evan she thought his name was, stood up on the other side of the bonfire and hoisted his cup of beer. "Thought I'd say a few things about the bride and groom taking the big plunge tomorrow."

Murmurs of encouragement came from around the fire. Evan went on to talk about his friendship with Paul, and told a funny story from Paul and Ellen's early years dating, when Paul bought her the world's most hideous sweater which Ellen pretended to like and still wore.

Sarah smiled at the couple, her heart contracting with a wistful pain. Envious? Yes. Their faces were glowing; they were constantly touching each other. It was sickening.

Sarah had wondered for a lot of years whether Paul was in love with Addie. She'd never asked, because she was so afraid the answer would be yes, and then she'd have to cope with an impossible situation since she knew Addie had never noticed Paul as anything but a buddy. Around Addie, Paul had either been quiet and worshipful, eager to please, or trying too hard to be cooler than he was.

After he started dating Ellen, he'd become steady and mature, yet also able to be entirely and proudly his goofy charming self. No posturing, no going quiet, no puppy-dogging. This was the real deal.

Imagine, being accepted so entirely in love that you didn't have to hide any of yourself, didn't constantly have to fear judgment and rejection. To relax so completely into someone that you might even discover parts of yourself you didn't know were there. Paul had found his inner alpha and had stepped up to the plate for his family, for Ellen's family and for their friends on many occasions, where before he might have wanted to, but ultimately have talked himself out of the risk.

How ironic, to have to feel safe enough in yourself before you could take any risks, when finding the person who could help you feel that safe took the biggest risk of all—making yourself completely open and vulnerable to someone else.

Would Sarah ever find that safety? Not if she kept falling in love with the men who'd risk nothing.

Evan finished and sat down. Another friend rose, a girlfriend of Ellen's. She talked about how cynical Ellen had gotten about men and about dating, so that for the first six weeks of her relationship with Paul, she kept saying he had to be some kind of total pervert or criminal because no one could be that wonderful. Of course her friends saw through this, and knew she was mentally shopping for a wedding dress after their second date.

Sarah sighed. More of the irony of love. Finally finding someone perfect for you and not being able to accept that lightning had struck, because so much of dating was wading through utter crap. She could vouch for that. She'd be suspicious, too, after all she'd been through, if something so great was simply handed to her.

"Hi." Joe's whisper made her automatically shift to make room next to her, still mulling over the mysteries of love and life, still not sure what to conclude when it came to her own situation. He sat and casually extended his arm behind her back, leaning on his hands, listening attentively with her to Ellen's friend, then to a few others who stood and told stories—funny stories, sweet stories, poignant stories, all demonstrating what a good match Ellen and Paul made. After a few minutes, Sarah leaned into Joe, enjoying the moment and his arm behind her, feeling a little more relaxed now, and steadier. Joe did that to her.

The last toast finished, Paul and Ellen stood up to say good-night. They'd be spending the night separately as tradition dictated. Ellen would stay in their bedroom in the house, and Paul would bunk in Kevin's room.

Poor Carrie. Sarah snickered. Yes, she was glad the little you-know-what wasn't after Joe anymore. Joe deserved a lot better. But it was pretty disgusting that she'd gone so obviously after him and then jumped into bed with Kevin the second the opportunity presented itself. What was up with that? Pathetic if you asked Sarah. Which no one had.

Around them, people were standing, stretching, forming new groups or heading off into the woods toward the house or to their tents. Sarah wasn't ready to go to bed. She knew she wouldn't sleep with this dryer load of un-identifiable emotions tumbling inside her.

"Hey." She turned to Joe, who seemed nearly as moody and distracted as she felt. "Want to take a walk?"

"Sure." He stood and held out a hand to haul her to her feet. "Which way?"

Sarah shrugged. "Doesn't matter. How about sunset point?"

"Okay."

They stopped at the house to get flashlights and a couple of old quilts to wrap up in since the night promised to be chilly. Fall came early to Maine, and late August nights could offer a pretty convincing taste of September.

They made their way down the cranberry covered hill to the prominent outcropping where they spread one quilt on the soft ground above the ledge and huddled under the other, flashlights off, staring out over the dark water.

"Nice rehearsal dinner."

"It was great." He yawned.

"Tired?"

"Yeah. We introvert types get worn out by all this fun."

She laughed. "Poor Joe, all those annoying good times."

"Uh-huh." He nudged her affectionately with his shoulder. "I'm not sure how I survived enjoying myself."

"Well, it's almost over."

He was silent so long she turned to look at him. "Joe?"

"Sorry, what?"

"Hello?" She'd obviously startled him out of some deep thought. He wasn't generally the brooding type. "I said the week is almost over."

"Yeah, I know."

Sarah frowned. Something was bothering him, too. "Guess we go back to the old routine, huh. You at your job, me at mine, seeing each other once in a while."

"Could be."

"We could make a pledge absolutely to have dinner once a week. At that Thai place you like down near Symphony Hall."

"Maybe."

Maybe? Really? Okay, this was serious. "What's the matter, Joe?"

"Me? Nothing."

"Come on." She nudged him with her shoulder, too, but hard, punishing him. "This is me you're talking to.

What's going on? Is it Carrie? Are you devastated having lost her to Kevin?"

He snorted and sent her a look she didn't need to see clearly to know was toxic. "Please."

"Sorry."

"No, you're not."

"You're right. I'm not." Her voice came out harder than she expected. "If you'd gone for her I would have had to sock her. Or you. Or both."

"Sarah…"

Her stomach turned over. She knew that tone, one he almost never used. Last time was when his mom had been diagnosed with late stage cancer. "Yes, Joe."

"I've been offered a job in Phoenix."

"What?"

"You heard me," he said calmly.

Yes. She had. And she felt as if she'd been given that sock in the gut she was saving for Carrie.

Joe had been looking for a job without telling her. He'd gotten a job without telling her. He was going to move… and was telling her.

"Wow." Sarah swallowed convulsively. She'd need to try harder to sound pleased for him. "That's great, Joe."

"Thanks."

"You're welcome!" Ugh. Now she sounded perky. Her face was heating; there was a weird rushing sound in her ears, but she sounded like Miss America on speed. Or Carrie. "What will you be doing?"

"More of the same. Computer geeks are pretty indispensable. But I like the culture of the new place a lot. And it's more money, a good move up."

"Great!" Now she sounded manic. Very close to insane. She could not process this, could only keep asking the expected questions, trolling for basic information, when all she wanted to do was ask how in hell he could do this to her. "When did you hear?"

"They called me a few hours ago."

"Well…wow." She tried desperately to sound happy. She would not make this about her. If this was what he wanted, this was what he should have. Phoenix. Jeez. Wasn't that on the other side of the planet? "This is thrilling."

"Yeah."

Sarah forced a laugh. "You don't sound very thrilled, Joe."

"You don't, either."

No. She'd tried. But she couldn't bullshit Joe. Never had been able to. Maybe she needed to stop bullshitting everyone, and then the Joes of the world would find her.

Not damn likely.

She summoned all her strength, while her heart felt as if it were going to explode. Not have Joe around? Not see Joe? Be far away from Joe? She couldn't get her brain to comprehend a change that huge. Boston wouldn't be the same. "Trust me, I am incredibly happy for you. You deserve this. When do you start?"

"I haven't accepted the offer yet."

Hope. Giant shimmering globs of it, surrounding her like a bubble bath gone wrong.

"But you will?" The end of her sentence quavered, betraying her hope. She hadn't meant it to be a question. She hadn't meant to show her vulnerability.

"I'd be a fool to turn it down."

"You would." She nodded vigorously, voice too high and too loud. "You absolutely would. And you're not a fool."

He laughed bitterly. She'd never heard him sound like

that, and it frightened her. "I've been a fool for a long time."

"What's that supposed to mean?"

"Sarah…one of the reasons I applied for this job, was because I was starting to realize that I need to get on with my life. Career-wise, but also…I'd like to get married someday. And hanging around you so much, I realized was a way to avoid finding a woman I could really be with."

Sarah forced her eyes open as wide as possible, blinking rapidly. Joe in love. Joe married. Joe at home with babies and a wife.

Joe with a woman who wasn't Sarah.

Of course. Of course he deserved that. Of *course* he did. And she was going to be freaking crazy happy for him. Her new mantra: the world was not about her. She was done being Selfish Sarah. No one on earth had suffered more from that selfishness than Joe.

"Thank you for telling me." Her voice cracked. "I completely understand."

"Sarah." He turned to her, put his arms around her and drew her down so they were lying together under the quilt, fresh Maine air cooling their faces, waves gurgling and tumbling down under the cliff.

She burrowed against him, trying to relax, forcing her breathing as steady as she could manage, and feeling as if someone had just hollowed her out with a giant drill.

"I'll miss you, Sarah."

"Stop." She spoke sharply then made herself giggle as if it was all a big joke.

Her panic rose. This was no joke. She had to get out of there. She couldn't lie next to him anymore and pretend. She was going to cry, she was going to scream, she was going to throw up. This pain, this dread, it was all her fault.

"You'll be busy, Joe, you'll have a new city to get to know, a new…everything." A smiling blonde with Joe's babies, Joe's arm around her, Joe's mouth on hers. Joe, the man she would depend on for love, support, friendship—everything Sarah had been greedily lapping up for the last near-decade, giving nothing in return.

She threw off the quilt and stood. Nausea threatened. She ran from him, behind a clump of alders and fell to her knees, breathing deeply.

"Sarah! What happened? What's the matter?" He spoke sharply from worry. He'd cared about her so deeply for so long and she'd taken it all for granted.

The cool air slowly settled her stomach. She collapsed back onto her bottom on the mossy ground.

"Just…too much beer. I thought I was going to lose it. I'm fine. Really."

"Sure?"

"I should get to bed." Where she could fall apart in earnest. "Thanks for telling me your news. And congratulations, Joe. I'm proud of you."

"I'll walk you to the house."

Of course he would. If she'd thrown up he would have stood behind her and stroked her back, held her hair out of the way. He'd do that for his wife, for his kids, always steady, always reliable.

A real man.

She let him help her up, waited while he gathered the quilts, let him take her arm and guide her back, lighting the way with her flashlight.

Inside the house, a few who'd deserted the beach fire had built another one in the fireplace, sipping something from steaming mugs and chatting or reading.

At her bedroom door, Sarah smiled gratefully at Joe and gave him a quick hug, sickened by the irony of having realized how much he meant to her now that she was losing him. What a cliché. She felt utterly stupid and defeated.

In her room alone, she changed into her pajamas, used the bathroom and crawled into bed, not even trying to sleep, just letting the misery and pain wash over her, quietly bearing it, knowing this was what she deserved.

She could try to stop him. She could plead with him, beg him to stay, promise things would be different. But she wouldn't. She had no right to sabotage his happiness. And she was too confused right now to be sure of what she could offer him, and what she could realistically promise.

Sarah groaned and pulled the covers over her head. This maturity stuff was the absolute freaking *pits*. She wanted to cry, but if she cried she'd look like hell for her brother's wedding, and worry everyone, so she couldn't even do that.

Hours later, or not, she had no idea how long, Addie came in. Sarah pretended to be asleep, turned toward the wall, clutching the covers under her chin, breathing slowly and a little too loudly. She couldn't talk to anyone, even though Addie might need an ear or a shoulder. She and Derek must have had a hell of a morning and afternoon. They'd shown up just as the rehearsal dinner started, looking blissfully stunned. Sarah would ask tomorrow, listen tomorrow. Do what she could to advise. Not right now. She hadn't become that selfless.

Hours later—or not, she *still* had no idea how long—Addie's breathing slipped into its own slow, regular pattern, only Addie probably had no reason to fake being asleep. Sarah lay still awhile longer then threw off the covers. This was torture. She couldn't lie here anymore or she'd go stark raving nuts.

Tiptoeing across the pine floor, she unlatched the door

as quietly as she could and shut it behind her, hoping she hadn't disturbed Addie.

In the living room, watching the dying embers of the fire, sat Carrie.

Ew.

Sarah hesitated, not exactly jumping at the opportunity to share her insomnia with Carrie, then gave a quick wave and made a beeline for the bathroom, buying time to decide what to do. She could go outside, but it would feel cold and lonely out there. Back to bed wasn't an option, at least not yet. Maybe she could light a lamp and pretend to read something? Find another room in the house where she could sit? The kitchen?

In the end she decided to stay in the living room where it was warmest. Maybe Carrie wouldn't turn out to be such bad company. Or maybe she'd shut up.

"Mind if I join you?"

"Nope." Carrie lifted the blanket she'd been sitting under and offered half to Sarah.

The gesture reminded her of Joe, and brought on a fresh wave of pain. "Thanks, I'm fine."

"Insomnia a regular demon for you?" Carrie asked.

"Not usually." Sarah sat near the other end of the couch, hoping she could answer in monosyllables and then lapse into miserable silence and that Carrie would get the hint.

"It's my regular companion." Carrie got up and put another log on the fire. "My mom was the same way."

"Yeah?" Sarah wondered why Carrie wouldn't rather enjoy the warmth of Kevin, then she remembered Kevin and Paul were in the same room tonight. Ha.

"So if it's not a regular problem for you, what's up tonight?"

Sarah shrugged.

"Did y'all fight with Joe?"

Huh? Sarah stared at her. Joe couldn't have told her. He wouldn't.

"I saw you two together when I was coming back up from the beach. You both looked miserable. I thought maybe you were on the outs."

"We're just friends."

"Oh, I know *that*." She chuckled, making Sarah feel like an idiot for protesting against something Carrie hadn't implied. "Believe me, I know. Joe is totally the friend type."

Sarah bristled. She did not like this woman and she did not like the way she was talking about Joe. "What type is Kevin?"

"Kevin? He's a jerk."

Sarah blinked in surprise then snorted. "Good choice, then."

"I always go for jerks." She spoke as if she was talking about shopping for a type of shoe. "They're perfect when you don't want to get serious."

Sarah started feeling queasy again. "You go after jerks deliberately?"

"Well sure, honey."

"What about Joe?"

More of that annoying laugh. "I wasn't going after him. Just flirting. He seemed the type who needed to be flirted with."

Sarah made herself breathe. And unclench her fist. And not think any more about putting it into Carrie's face. "I'm sure he was grateful for whatever crumb you tossed him."

"I know, right?" Carrie completely missed Sarah's sarcasm.

"So why don't you want to get serious about anyone?"

"Are you kidding?" She gave an ugly guffaw. "Me?

Marriage? No, thank you, ma'am. I saw what it did to my mom. I'm steering clear of that slavery."

Sarah swallowed audibly. Her mother had described marriage the same way to a friend. Sarah had overheard her, and even though she'd been too young to understand, the tone of her mom's usually sweet voice had made the words stick in her head. "Well, then don't marry a jerk."

Carrie snorted. "They're all jerks. And if you make the mistake of thinking you found a good one, as soon as you fall for him, trust me, he turns jerk."

This was sounding familiar. Wheels started turning so hard in Sarah's brain, she would not be surprised if her scalp started steaming.

And then, there it was, what she'd been on the edge of figuring out all day. She was always falling for unavailable men and jerks, all along thinking what she wanted from them was a serious relationship. But, like Carrie, she was essentially making sure she'd never have one. The only difference was that Carrie knew that about herself and acted that way on purpose. Sarah had been ignoring her subconscious, acting on pure denial, moaning and bitching and playing the poor-me victim to whomever would listen.

But she'd just figured it out. And she knew she really had because now instead of waves of pain, she was getting a huge sense of relief, like her subconscious had been trying to tell her this for years and she resolutely ignored it, but now thank God she had finally paid attention.

Sarah was choosing the men deliberately out of fear. She was setting herself up to fail because she was afraid of taking that risk she'd been thinking about earlier, the risk of being that vulnerable.

That night on the beach with Joe, she'd wished on a falling star that she'd find someone to love who'd love her back. Joe had told her she couldn't see what was right under her nose. Tonight when she found out he was leaving Boston, her whole world threatened to collapse.

Oh, Joe.

She could totally see it now. See everything she'd been lucky enough to have for the last decade, and all she'd done was try to find it somewhere else.

Maybe…maybe if she hadn't screwed this up too badly, after the wedding she'd be able to show Joe exactly what she'd learned about men, and about relationships and most of all, about what this new Sarah wanted to try. With him.

12

DEREK THREW OFF the covers. What time was it, 1:00 a.m.? Two? He'd given up trying to sleep. What a messed up day. One of the most blissful afternoons he'd ever had, with a woman who affected him deeply, then during Paul and Ellen's really fun rehearsal dinner—lobsters that put every other one he'd eaten to shame boiled in a huge pot right on the beach—the whole afterglow aura had drifted away. He wasn't even sure when the downshift had started, or at what point he noticed. The evening started with warm glances between him and Addie and occasional surreptitious touches. By unspoken agreement, they both seemed to want to keep their new bond private.

As the evening drew on, as the partying intensified, as Paul and Ellen became more demonstrative, and the toasts longer and drunker and funnier and more poignant, the obvious hopelessness of his and Addie's situation had hit him. And it must have hit her, too, because her eyes had dulled, her smiles and cheers became as forced as his own. Not that he wasn't happy for Paul and Ellen, he couldn't be happier. Theirs was a strong and good relationship that would only grow stronger and better through marriage.

The problem? He and Addie had that potential, he could

feel it in his gut no matter how much his sensible side tried to explain it away with theories about animal attraction and infatuation, the fool's gold of love.

But there was no way they could make their happy-ever-after happen.

Part of what he loved about Addie was her strong and sensible side; she'd be a woman he could depend on to tackle life's decisions calmly. She'd never be a woman like Sarah, a maelstrom of impetuous and random choices. But that very characteristic meant she was unlikely to give up her life after a short affair and go trotting around the globe with him. Derek couldn't blame her. Neither was he willing to give up life aboard *Joie de Vivre* and stick himself into a suit and between four walls.

After dinner as the crowd dispersed, he'd taken Addie into a private place in the woods for a quick good-night. He'd kissed her, and they'd embraced fiercely. His body had responded to hers, he'd lowered his lips to her hair, inhaling her scent. She'd clung to him, pressing her face into his neck. Then they'd gone to bed, neither suggesting they do so together in his room. He wasn't sure of her reasons, but Derek knew his: if he got the chance to hold Addie in his arms all night, leaving her on Sunday would be that much more painful.

Now, body tortured by physical memories, and brain tortured by emotional ones, he was giving up the farce of trying to sleep and going downstairs. Maybe get a glass of milk or herbal tea or whatever he could find that might help him relax.

Though he had a feeling nothing would help get Addie out of his system.

He clumped downstairs with his flashlight and headed toward the glow emanating from the kitchen. Someone else up? Or had someone left a light on?

Joe was slumped over, face pressed against the wooden tabletop, a bottle of Irish whiskey by his head. Derek took two steps into the room and he sat up, squinting blearily to see who'd disturbed his beauty sleep, hair sticking up on one side, cheek and forehead red where they'd been resting on the table.

"Joe, man, what happened to you?"

Joe shook his head wearily. "Love."

"Love, huh." Derek opened the refrigerator, searching. Milk, water, lemonade, beer… He glanced back at the table. If they were going to be talking about love, maybe he needed whiskey, too. Though he'd get a bottle of water out for Joe. Looked like he could use a little dilution of the alcohol in his blood. "It's that bad?"

"It's worse."

"Uh-oh." Derek got a glass down from the cabinet and poured himself a couple of fingers of Jameson's, his favorite. Poor Joe. Something must have happened with Sarah. "Tell me about it."

Joe frowned. "Tell me about it like, 'yeah, I know what you mean,' or tell me about it, like really tell you about it?"

"Both." Derek lifted his glass in a toast. "You talk first."

"Mmph." Joe stretched and yawned, then hunched back over his whiskey. "I got my dream job offer today."

"Yeah? Congratulations." That clearly wasn't the bad news. Derek toasted Joe again and took a sip of whiskey. Its smooth burn coated his throat. Delicious. He should start stocking the stuff in his cabin for when he was there alone every night and needed anaesthetizing. "That's a very big deal."

"Thanks. The job is in Phoenix, which means I'd have to move."

"Ah." There was the problem. "Yeah, that'd be a helluva commute from Boston."

Joe acknowledged the joke with a bleak nod. "If I take it, then I have to say goodbye to Sarah. Which also means I'm saying goodbye to—"

"Don't tell me. Let me guess. All your hopes and all your dreams about a future with her." He laughed bitterly. Yeah, he sorta knew what that could feel like.

Joe looked bewildered. "How did you know?"

"I have my ways."

"Addie?"

Derek's turn to look surprised. "Uh…"

"Shit." Joe glowered at the table. "Just shit."

"Well put." Derek took another sip of whiskey. Looked like he and Joe had a lot in common right now. "So that's that with Sarah?"

"That's that."

No. Not after all they'd been through together. Derek couldn't accept that. He'd seen Sarah around Joe; she lit up like the moon. "She won't go with you?"

Joe laughed bitterly. "Oh, like *that* would happen."

"Did you ask her?"

"What, are you kidding me?" He laughed again, so painfully Derek had to hide a wince. "I think I've suffered enough humiliation tagging after her like a puppy for the past however many years."

"Hey, Joe. You love her."

Joe snorted, noticed his glass, picked it up and tossed back the tiny amount left. "The saddest part? I know exactly how long I've been her puppy. Nine years, eight months and four days since I met her at the Vassar bookstore in the checkout line. She'd cut in front of someone by mistake, and he was all bent out of shape. I stepped in and smoothed it over for her. We got talking. I fell for her in about five minutes."

"Does she know?"

"Of course she knows. *Everybody* knows." He flung out his arm and nearly knocked over the bottle, grabbed it at the last second, looked at it in surprise, then sloshed another finger into his glass. "Good old Joe, panting after Sarah while she goes after every guy she meets who's my most polar opposite. Including you."

Oof. Yeah. Derek would go back and erase that for Joe's sake if he could. "But look, none of those guys worked out. Including me. I never touched her by the way."

"Yeah, I know." He blew out a frustrated breath and let his head hang. "I'm not angry. It's not your fault you're incredibly good-looking and charming and exciting, or whatever else she needs that I'm not."

Derek contemplated the top of Joe's head, half feeling sorry for him, half wanting to tell him to grow a pair. "What do you think she needs?"

"The whole bad-boy shtick. That's not me." His head was nearly touching the table again. "It's never going to be me."

Derek leaned toward him, prodded him in the shoulder. "If Sarah really wanted that she would have stayed with at least one of these guys, right?"

"They all dumped her."

"Oh." This was not easy. Derek frowned, struggling to organize his thoughts. "Okay, here is my advice. If I was you, I'd start by telling her straight-out how you feel."

Joe's head lifted, eyes dull. He looked like hell. No way would Sarah go for him that way. "What if she tells me to get lost?"

"Dude, you're moving to Phoenix, how much more lost can you get?"

Joe nodded thoughtfully. "Good point."

"Then…" Derek gestured with his glass, gaining hope

as his proposal gained momentum. "Then, you ask her to move to Phoenix with you."

Joe reacted as if he'd been stung by a bee. "Huh?"

"Well, isn't that what you want?" Derek thumped his glass down on the table.

"Yeah, but…"

"It's what you want. Do it. You don't feel like you have the kind of confidence she wants? Fake it. Eventually it becomes real."

He waited for Joe to process the concepts, enjoying his whiskey. For several seconds Joe appeared stunned, then his face seemed to thaw some. His eyes hardened in determination.

"I'll do it." He slammed his hand on the table. Even though his hair was still sticking up on one side, he seemed to grow from a lost kid into a man right before Derek's eyes. If that didn't impress Sarah, nothing would.

"Good. Good for you. I bet you won't regret it." God he hoped not.

"I'll do it. I'll do it right now." He struggled to his feet and then had to sit heavily back down.

"Uh." Derek held up his hand. "I'd wait until tomorrow. Maybe after the wedding, in case things get…emotional."

"You're right." Joe grimaced. "Besides, I probably smell like a distillery."

"Could be." Derek pushed Joe's water toward him. "I'd switch to the soft stuff now. Make your plan tonight. Tomorrow you'll be in much better shape."

"God, if this works, Derek…" Joe laughed nervously. "You'll have made me the happiest guy on the planet."

"Wait, you two are getting married?" Paul walked into the room and grabbed a bottle of water from the refrigerator. "That'll make tomorrow a *really* big day."

"No. No. Not him." Joe put both hands up. "I want to marry your sister."

"Yeah?" Paul grinned and took a sip of water, clearly not surprised by the news. "I was just in her room talking to her. She's pretty bummed."

"Because I'm leaving?" Joe asked hopefully.

"That would be a big fat yes."

"See?" Derek gestured to Joe, then to Paul. "Hey, Paul, tell us how you feel getting married."

"Oh, good, is this my groom interview?" Paul pulled out a chair and sank into it, pretended his water bottle was a microphone. "Well, I'll tell you how I feel, Derek. Ellen is the best woman I've ever met and really right for me, so I guess that means I feel pretty freaking great. In spite of the fact that I can't sleep."

"Nervous about marrying her?" Joe asked.

"No, no, not nervous about the marriage." Paul put the bottle on the table. "Maybe nervous about all the details. Mostly excited about how important the day is to both of us. And also because up in my room lies the mighty Kevin, who snores like an angry yak."

Joe burst out laughing. Derek drained his whiskey glass, thinking of how the story of Paul and Ellen's rocky start might help Joe.

"So you met Ellen and that was that?" Derek knew the answer of course, but when Paul looked at him incredulously, he tipped his head imperceptibly toward Joe.

Paul's face cleared. "Oh, no. I nearly let her get away from me. I didn't, but I still panic sometimes thinking how close I came to messing up my whole life. Just because I was afraid."

"Hear that?" Derek pinned Joe with a meaningful stare. "You know what you want, you gotta stop hanging around feeling defeated and go after it. You want Sarah to go with you next year to Phoenix? Ask her. You have strong feel-ings for her? You need to…tell…her."

He froze in his chair, feeling as if he'd just kicked him-self in the chest.

Holy shit.

"Derek?"

Derek found himself on his feet, gaping at Paul and Joe. He forced himself to focus on his friend's concerned face. "Paul. Was Addie in the room when you were talk-ing to Sarah?"

"No, why?"

"Any idea where she is?"

"No."

Derek was already half out the door. How stupid could he be? Had he told Addie how he felt? Had he told her what he really wanted?

He'd just given Joe the exact advice he needed to hear himself.

ADDIE SAT ON the promontory where she and Derek had walked to watch the sunset his first night on the island. Wednesday night. Today was Friday—or rather the wee hours of Saturday. Three days. It was ridiculous to be feeling that strongly about him so soon, and it was stu-pid to be sitting out here this late. She should be in bed so she could enjoy Paul and Ellen's wedding the next day without being exhausted. Where was her common sense?

She didn't know. All she knew was that at the moment, she couldn't move. The hypnotic rhythm of the sea, the glittering reflection of even the tiniest crescent moon, the sense of wild wide-openness around her—who wanted to be confined to a cabin, to a bed? If she could, she'd blast off into space and just keep traveling to infinity for all eternity.

No, she wouldn't.

She'd summon Derek here with magic powers she didn't have, and cast a spell to force him to fall in love with her so they could live happily ever after.

If only it was that easy. Her superpower was not the ability to summon hot men; it was being rational and practical. Like this: she knew that the intense feelings she was experiencing right now were simple infatuation, and that they'd pass easily once she was back to her old life, away from this seductive and wonderful-smelling place. And away from Derek.

The rehearsal dinner had been so lovely, the intimacy between Paul and Ellen so beautiful. Watching the way they knew each other inside out and were so looking forward to making the ultimate commitment—the more Addie saw, the more she realized how silly to think she could have fallen for Derek in such a short time. He must have realized it, too. They'd started the evening with longing glances, not ready to show the gang their new status as…what? Not a couple, yet. Lovers, anyway. A concept well demonstrated by Kevin and Carrie, who were practically humping each other into the bonfire.

But over the course of the evening, the tenuous tie that had been formed between Derek and Addie on the private beach started fraying, strand by strand. Their hot looks turned lukewarm, their conversations with people around them intensified. They didn't seek out or spend time alone. Not that there was that much opportunity, except to say good-night.

Such a comedown. But good. The hurt showed her that she was really no good at this wild woman thing. Jumping into a sexual relationship wasn't something she could handle. The sharing of their bodies so soon after meeting had only confused the issue, making her think their feelings were deeper than they were.

But, oh, they had felt so deep. Everything about Derek Bates had been intense from the moment she first said hello to him on the house's front steps. She should have known their lovemaking would seem to engender intimacy so soul-wrenching it put all her other relationships to shame.

So. She'd made a mistake. If they had truly connected that deeply, if their souls really had been…uh, wrenched… that connection would not have eroded a mere hour or two later. They'd be upstairs in his room right now making wrinkles in the sheets.

She stiffened. A rustling through the woods behind her. A light bobbing closer. Someone was coming.

Immediately Addie told herself not to get excited, that it wasn't necessarily *him*. And even if it was, she shouldn't get excited. There were twenty plus people on the island, which made the odds of it being Derek a mere—

"Addie." His deep voice shot thrills through her. *Oh, Addie. Be sensible.* "What are you doing out here so late?"

"Hi, Derek." She turned her head to acknowledge his presence, awareness of him making her skin feel as if it were coming to life, nerve endings reaching for his touch. Shameless little buggers. "I'm sitting here soaking in the atmosphere. I wasn't sleepy."

"It is beautiful." He sat down next to her, turned off his light. Addie held still, every cell in her body screaming at her *not* to be sensible. Hadn't she just told herself her deep reaction and emotional tumult around this man had faded?

Yeah, uh, never mind.

And hadn't she just told herself that those feelings weren't to be trusted anyway?

Uh-huh.

"You okay?"

"Sure." She stared out at the water, annoyed at herself for avoiding a meaningful answer, but what was the point? She wasn't okay, and wouldn't be until she was back home in New York among all her familiar people, places and things and thoughts of Derek had finally left her alone.

He took her hand, lazily stroking up and down her fingers. "We need to talk, Addie."

Nerves burned through her in spite of her being sure there was nothing to say except hey, that was fun, seeya later. She should tell herself instead that it was nice of him at least to want to do that. Many men wouldn't bother. "Okay."

"I don't want to talk here."

"Why not? What's wrong with here? It's beautiful, it's private and it's got a great long drop onto jagged rocks in case I need to push you off."

He laughed and her heart soared with pleasure. *Stop it, Addie.*

"I want to talk to you out on the water in a rowboat under the moonlight." He glanced up at the toenail clipping of a moon. "What there is of it."

"What?" She turned to gape at his dim shadow. "Are you serious?"

"Yes, why?"

She couldn't believe he had to ask. "It's the middle of the night."

"Yeah…?"

"As in dark."

"Dark, yes."

She gestured toward the water. "*Very* dark."

"It sure is." He squeezed her hand. "Want to go?"

"But…" A giggle was trying to come up her throat. He had the perfect amount of patient amusement in his voice, which had made her listen to herself to find out why he was amused, and to discover that she sounded like a dork. He didn't have to say a word and he got his message across.

Addie didn't want to be a dork.

"It's dead calm. We'll stay close to shore." He got to his feet and held out his hand, his palm a pale invitation in the black night. "Yes?"

She put her hand in his, and let him help pull her to her feet where he held her inches from him for a few charged seconds that had her heart beating up a storm. "Okay."

"Good." Keeping her hand, he turned the flashlight back on and pointed it toward their feet, guiding her safely into the woods and back down to the beach, where *Lucky's* skiff was waiting.

Ten minutes later, Addie couldn't imagine what she thought might have been remotely bad about this idea. The air was cool and fresh, the stillness mesmerizing, the creak and splash of oars a wonderful atmospheric addition. Hard to imagine the vastness of the water they were part of when the darkness made the space feel so intimate. And being with Derek made her so agitated and worked up, but also, very strangely, content. If you could be content while filled with a violent longing for wild sex.

"So." Bumping sounds of wood on wood as Derek stowed the oars. "Let's talk."

"Okay." She sighed. How much better just to keep drifting, away from land, away from troubles and issues and everything that had seemed so important?

"We probably should have had this talk at the beach this afternoon. But we were too busy…being active."

Addie smiled. "Is that what we were doing?"

"And, in my case anyway, being waylaid by emotions

I didn't expect or, frankly, want to have. Which made it hard to sort them out."

Addie held her breath until it occurred to her it would be pretty hard to have a conversation if she wasn't breathing. "What emotions?"

She didn't expect him to answer right away. Or at all, really. It was unfair to ask him to be so vulnerable by exposing his feelings when she hadn't been planning to let out any of what she'd been—

"I feel very strongly about you." He spoke easily, in a steady voice, as if he was telling her he liked her outfit. But the effect on her…thank goodness she was sitting down or she'd have pitched off the boat. *I feel very strongly about you.*

She had no idea what to say. She had to say something. She couldn't leave him hanging out there.

"Oh."

He laughed. "Well, not quite what I'd hoped for, but okay. I'm a patient guy, we have time."

"That's one thing we don't have."

They drifted farther, the white sand beach a barely visible crescent, stars crowding the sky above them, the sliver of moon showing just above the island's treetops.

"It's funny, when we were kids thinking about our futures, even when we were just out of school, didn't it seem as if whatever we did would be under our control? Maybe we wouldn't get the exact job we wanted right away, or the apartment we wanted, but somehow we'd work it so we had it all eventually. No matter which doors we picked, the others would still be open to us if we wanted them to be."

Addie thought about her life and which doors she'd chosen. Always the safe ones, the ones that would take her where she'd already planned to go. She hadn't really considered any other paths. They'd been closed in her mind all along. "I never really wanted too many doors open at once. But I do know what you mean."

"These days every now and then I come up against a door that's locked in my face. I bought *Joie de Vivre* understanding that life with her would be all-consuming. It was and still is what I wanted. But, Addie…" He took a deep breath. "I didn't count on meeting someone like you."

Addie stifled a gasp, feeling torn in half. Part of her was thrilled. He'd said exactly the right thing at exactly the right time, and how often did that happen? And yet… it wasn't the right thing, because there was no point admitting feelings for each other. She didn't want a pen pal for a boyfriend.

"I agree, it would have been nice to have more time together to understand what we started." Addie stopped her speech abruptly, rolling her eyes. Derek had been passionate, sincere and direct, and she sounded like she was talking about developing a new insurance policy. She'd try again, keeping firmly in mind that she had plans to start a new, more interesting and involved life back in New York. This man was not her final and only chance for happiness or personal growth. "Knowing we have to leave this here…is really hard."

"You have no idea how hard."

"Ha." She snorted. "I'm sure you'll be back to women in every port very soon."

"Doubt it." He eased himself off the seat onto a waterproof cushion on the boat's floor and opened his arms. "Because you're the only one I want. Come here?"

"Derek…"

"Yes?"

She sighed heavily. The sensible, rational Addie thing to do was to explain that there was no point in them indulging in any more romance because it would only make it worse when they had to leave each other.

But…Derek must again be bringing out the wild woman in her, because she was finding it very hard to convince herself that sitting here on a cold seat alone was a better idea than sitting in his lap with his warm arms around her.

She pulled herself together and addressed his silhouette. "I don't think it's a good idea for us to touch each other."

"Not a good— Are you *nuts?* It's the best idea I've had all day."

His response was so unexpected she burst out with a nervous giggle. "Derek…"

"I get what you're saying, Addie. I really do. But I need to ask you something, and it would be a big help to hold you while I'm doing it."

Ask her what? Addie stared at his dark form. How could she refuse him? She couldn't. She didn't want to. Relief swept over her as she moved toward him, giving in to what she'd wanted all along, and sat down between his legs on the other half of the cushion.

His strong arms came around her, his chest was broad and warm at her back. He laid his cheek on her hair. She felt sheltered, protected, cared for.

Irresistible.

"So." She'd meant to speak in a no-nonsense tone, but her throat was thick with emotion, and all she managed was a gentle syllable. "What's so frightening that you can't face it alone?"

"My life on *Joie de Vivre.*"

She laughed. "I'd say you've done pretty well alone so far."

"I have." His arms tightened around her. "But I don't want to do it anymore."

Her brain started a tornado of thoughts. Her heart was pounding. *Be sensible, Addie.* He'd met her three days ago. He was not about to do anything crazy, like sell his boat and move to New York.

Was he?

Of course not. She hated when her brain went sailing ahead into unlikely waters.

"I was talking to Joe." His jaw moved against her hair when he spoke. His chest rumbled.

Addie turned her face closer to his, unable to resist the temptation. "About what?"

"I was yelling at him for not taking the risk of coming right out and telling Sarah how he felt about her, and what he wanted and needed from her." He kissed her temple, bent his head to lay his cheek against hers. "And then I realized I was doing the same thing with you."

Addie closed her eyes, struggling to stay calm. "Derek, he and Sarah have known each other for almost ten years."

"Doesn't matter. It's the same deal. If I don't ask you this now then I lose you for sure."

Her argument died. Her heart was hammering, blood hot in her cheeks. Was he going to change his life for her? For *her?* "Ask me what?"

"Addie." He paused, long enough that she nearly started to panic. "I want you to spend the next year on *Joie de Vivre*. Working and living with me."

13

"WHAT?" In Derek's arms, Addie stiffened into an iron statue, exactly as he'd expected her to. *"What?"*

He smiled in the darkness. Anyone would react that way. And, strangely, instead of being in an agony of suspense waiting for her answer, he felt relaxed, freer and happier than he'd felt in a long time. Too long. He hadn't hidden, hadn't closed down and entered the hell of "what if?" He hadn't held himself aloof, gone about his own business and let others do the same. Because he wanted Addie to be his business, and vice versa. What she decided was beyond his control, but he'd gone after what he'd wanted, the same way he'd gone after *Joie de Vivre,* even knowing it would be a long, tough fight.

Until he met Addie, he hadn't recognized how far he'd stepped back from life after getting the boat. Addie had brought him screaming—and shouting and skipping and laughing—back into it. For that he'd always be grateful, even if she fried his heart by turning him down.

"I asked if you'd come live with me on my boat next year."

"You… But I can't just… I mean…" She struggled

to sit up straighter, away from him. "We've known each other three days."

"True." He let the silence hang, listening to her sputter, practically able to hear the wheels turning in her head, knowing he probably came across like a crazy person. "Don't answer now. Just think about it. This might be the change you're looking for in your life, or it might be too much change. We might find we're meant for each other, or we might want to hurl each other overboard after two weeks. I don't know. I just know that I haven't met anyone like you in a long time, maybe ever. I want to find out what's here, and I think maybe you'd like that, too."

"If course I would, but…" She slumped down then straightened again. "Derek. Look, this is really sweet of you, but I can't—"

"Shhh." He pulled her back against him, nuzzling her hair, leaning her to one side to gain access to her beautiful neck. "Don't use reason. Not now."

"Not *now?* Now is the perfect time. There probably won't ever *be* a more perfect time than now."

"Why?" He pressed his lips against the smooth skin under her ear.

"Because…something like this, something this big… We have to be sensible."

"Why?" He slid his hands up her rib cage, stopping just under her breasts, then let his thumbs explore their rounded underside while his mouth explored her throat.

"Because this is a huge, vitally important decision that affects every aspect of our lives, and you can't—" She gasped and arched against his hands, which had moved up to cover her gorgeous breasts. He shifted under her, getting hard. This woman drove him wild. "Um, you can't just… I mean— Will you *stop* that?"

"Why?" He slid his hand under the elastic waistband

of her shorts, and moved between her legs, over the cotton of her panties. She gasped again, but held still, letting him finger her.

"I, um… Oh, hell, there was some reason." She moaned as he lightly stroked back and forth, barely touching her through the thin, soft material. "Derek, you're not playing fair."

"Do you want me to?"

A long sigh. The tiny gurgle of waves against the planks of the boat. The far-off cry of a loon.

"No." She turned her face to his and he took her lips in an explosive kiss that made his erection swell so painfully against her beautiful bottom he was nearly ready to come himself. Somehow he kept his cool, kept up the gentle brushing touches across her cloth-covered clitoris. She was breathing fast, moving in jerky bursts as if it was getting harder to control her body.

She was turning him on like crazy.

"Derek." His name came out a breathless plea. Addie tried to wriggle around to face him, rocking the boat dangerously.

"Shhh. Wait. Hold still."

She obeyed, breath coming in pants, her skin getting damp. Derek returned to torturing her, increasing the pressure and speed of his fingers—but only slightly.

"Derek. *Oh.*" Her cry was desperate; her fingers clutched his arms so hard it hurt. He kept her on the edge, stroking slowly, holding her tight against him so she couldn't move from his grasp. *"Please…"*

"I'll make you come. I'll make you come so hard you'll scream. And next year on my boat I'll make you come every day. Every morning, with my tongue between your legs, and every afternoon bent over the seat by the helm, and every night in my bed." He murmured the words into her ear, voice low and passionate, his cock harder than it had ever been in his life. But in spite of the pure eroticism of his words, he felt caveman protective, possessive and oddly tender. He wanted to give her those moments, every day, show her how she was desired, wanted, respected.

And maybe someday more.

Instead of terrifying him, the idea of falling in love added new power and excitement to this time with her. Why else would he want her to move onto his boat? He'd never invited any woman he was dating to do more than experience *Joie de Vivre* for a day or two.

Addie. He gave in, gave her what she wanted, what she needed, slid his fingers underneath the by-now damp cotton and found her clitoris.

She exploded nearly instantly, her body tensing, a long, low cry ripped from her.

He plunged two fingers inside her, feeling her heat, her moisture, the contractions grabbing at him. It took everything he had to keep his own needs under control while she came. He wanted to turn her around, have her straddle him and bury himself in her as deeply as he could go.

As if she read his mind, instead of coming down slowly and savoring her afterglow, she gathered her legs under her. He could feel them trembling. "Addie."

"Shh." She pulled down her shorts then offered him her gorgeous rounded behind.

Derek groaned and yanked open his jeans, jammed on a condom while she waited, keeping his eyes on her beautiful shape, nearly out of his mind with desire.

Protected, he grabbed her hips and positioned her over his vertical cock, which was so eager for her it was jumping and pulsing like a creature with a mind of its own.

Around Addie, he'd started to wonder.

She took hold of his erection with warm fingers, making his breath hiss out between his teeth, then, using her strong thigh muscles to keep herself up and balanced, she lowered herself onto him.

Almost.

He could feel the hot entrance to her vagina nudging the tip of his erection.

Oh, no. Payback for the way he'd made her wait for her climax. He tried to thrust higher, but she straightened, lifting herself so his cock stayed only that tantalizing inch inside her no matter how far he strained.

"Addie, you don't understand."

"No?"

"See, it's okay for me to tease you. But you need to give me what I need when I need it."

"Ahhh, really." She started manipulating her body, squeezing, releasing, squeezing, releasing.

"Addie." His teeth clenched. Sweat gathered at his hairline.

He might not survive this.

"Ye-e-s?" She swiveled her ass in a gloriously sexy circle, taking his cock on the ride of its life. Then, she sank an inch lower, pulled back up immediately. Did it again.

Too slow, too shallow. He wanted to come *now.*

And yet. This was elegant, sensual torture like he'd never had before, even more intense than on the beach, and the part of him that wasn't ready to scream was enjoying it—and Addie—very, very much.

He wanted her with him next year, all year, every day of it.

Another inch, another, then she froze, held still with him halfway home. She could probably feel the impatient jumps of his penis inside her. Derek waited as long as he could, ragged breathing betraying his true state.

"Addie. Have mercy."

"Like you did on me?"

"Well, eventually…"

She laughed and half twisted her upper torso, started playing with her breasts for his benefit—or detriment as the case might be—pushing them up in a sublime offering, drawing her palms across the nipples, letting her head drop back with the pleasure she was giving herself.

That was it.

He took hold of her waist and pushed her firmly down on top of him, letting out a hoarse sigh at the tight, slick feel of her around him. All of him. Finally.

"Derek!"

He ignored her outrage, lifted and dropped her, pushed and pulled, thrusting his hips up and down, making her have to steady herself by grabbing the gunwales of the boat, her head bouncing, moans showing her own pleasure.

His orgasm didn't wait long. He lost control in a few more seconds, pumped her savagely, and came in a huge burst that made his mouth open in a long, silent yell.

Holy moly.

It was a few moments before he could move again.

"Addie."

"Yes?" Her tone was soft, tender, sweet. He lifted her off him, cringing with regret when he slid out, a regret that was swiftly over when he pulled her back against him, wrapped his arms tightly around her, even knowing their time was nearly over, wanting to keep her close.

She wouldn't move to be with him on *Joie de Vivre*. Why would she? She had a job, an apartment, a whole life. It was completely absurd for him even to entertain hope that she'd give it up for him.

And yet…if he'd let huge odds keep him from trying, he wouldn't be a yacht owner at all.

"What would you say if I asked you again, Addie?"

She laughed, relaxed and warm against him. "This answer wouldn't count."

"No?"

"No. Sexually induced slavery is not a fair bargaining tool."

He grinned. "I'm pretty sure the slavery goes both ways here."

"Derek." She was serious this time. "I have a job."

"I know."

"An apartment."

"Yes."

"It's not like I can just leave."

"No."

"I mean…" She gestured in exasperation. "Jobs aren't exactly a dime a dozen."

"Right. I understand."

"And rent-controlled apartments are even rarer."

"Got it."

"Besides, I'm thinking—"

"Come on, Addie. Are you trying to convince me or yourself?"

She giggled in his arms, and he felt a powerful piercing sweetness in his heart that could only be one thing. He loved her. It had happened, much sooner than he thought after meeting her, much later in life than he expected. So he was capable of the emotion, he just hadn't been in the right place at the right time with the right person. And now, he'd fallen within a few days of knowing Addie, as if his capacity for love had been hiding in the wings his whole life waiting impatiently for him to get it right, and now couldn't wait to let him know he had.

"Right now I'd do anything you asked me to."

"Yeah?" He pretended to think it over. "How about swimming over to that island and picking me some—"

"Except that."

He laughed and kissed her, then kissed her again, and since it didn't seem as if there could possibly be anything more wonderful in the world to do, he settled in to kissing her, tasting her mouth over and over, holding her warmth to him, immersing himself in their cocoon of intimacy in this tiny boat on this vast, dark ocean.

"Jobs can be put on hold," he whispered. "Apartments can be sublet."

"I know. But…" She sighed, running her fingers down and across his arms in a gentle caress. "I'm just not the kind of person who can make such a huge decision on the spur of the moment. Honestly, I wish I was. It's tempting, it sounds as if it would be incredibly exciting. I certainly feel closer to you than I should after such a short time, but it's just… Well, it's completely crazy."

"You're right. No question."

"When I was a girl, my parents taught my brother and me that there was a right way to do everything. A right way to speak and behave and eat and dress and wash… right programs to watch on TV, the right people to know. Everything was so black and white for them, everything was so carefully worked out. My brother rebelled in a big way. He spent his whole life doing as much wrong as possible. Drugs, women, dropping out of college to wander around the world, making just enough money at whatever job he could find in order to take him to the next country and the next job, making friends with the lowest of the low, in short rejecting everything they taught us."

Derek chuckled. "He sounds like someone I'd like to meet."

"He's great. He really is. I admired his rebellion as much as I was appalled by it. I bought into my parents' version of life because I was so shy that any form of rebellion would have plunged me into anxiety and panic." She twisted around to peer up into his face, though neither of them could see much. "Do you see what I'm saying? If I said to hell with it, I'll come with you, it would probably destroy us, Derek. I'd be a complete wreck away from everything I know and feel safe around."

He wanted to point out that she'd changed her life several times already. Going to college, moving to New York, that life on a boat wasn't nearly as foreign as she probably imagined. That after a few weeks that life would start seeming normal and everyday as well, full of the same dull moments and repetition and routine as any.

But instead he gave her a final squeeze, understanding that he'd get no further tonight. It was beyond late and they were both exhausted. He'd back off and enjoy Addie tomorrow at the wedding, then ask her once more Saturday night and then again Sunday morning before they left if he had to.

"I understand, Addie." He kissed her lightly. "Want to go in? Big day tomorrow."

"We probably should." She moved out of his arms regretfully and sat in silence on the row back to Storness.

At the top of the hill the house was dark and quiet. Derek led the way in and to the bottom of the stairs, and then gave Addie one last kiss, guessing neither of them would sleep much during what was left of the night.

But as he said good-night and watched her walk through the living room to the bedroom she shared with Sarah, his arms and body itching for the feel of her, he knew that even if his hopes of returning to the *Joie de Vivre* with her beside him were obliterated this weekend, he'd still find some way, any way, that they could be together again.

Because having found a woman like Addie Sewell, he was not going to settle for anyone else.

14

PAUL AND ELLEN'S wedding day dawned sunny and clear.
Well…it had *probably* dawned that way. Dawn happened
during the one or two hours of sleep Addie managed to get
before the household was up and working, taking down
tents and cleaning and closing up the house. Right now
Addie was carrying a load of borrowed sleeping bags
down to the beach so *Lucky* could transport them back
to the mainland.

The previous night, she'd dragged herself away from
Derek's warm arms and kisses to lie awake in tense bewilderment over the enormous decision he'd handed her.
Of course her practical side thought the idea of ditching
everything she knew to follow a near stranger out to sea
was completely ridiculous, and that she'd never allow herself to do such a thing. That side of her was cranky and
exhausted by the turmoil and change and utterly unpre-
dictable nature of the past several days. That side of her
wanted to climb onto a plane and go home, get a solid
night's sleep and wake to peace and blissful routine, and
not give crazy ideas another moment's consideration, because what was the point of torturing herself pretending

there was a decision to be made? There was no decision. The answer was clear.

But…

The side of her that had recently been awakened, that had just started to tune into all the things she'd been missing since she was a girl, carefully scheduled out of any control of her own life and decisions by well-meaning parents who saw themselves merely as guides, not tyrants— that side, which was only just starting to be tired of always playing it safe, was tempted enough to want to keep the options alive, to keep more than one door open, as Derek had put it last night. That side, so long deprived, was now hungry. The beast had awakened. It wanted to make up for years of hibernation, to explore and indulge these new and powerful feelings, to shake up her life and for once do something completely irresponsible and totally unlike herself.

But…

This was not the way she would have preferred to awaken that beast. She would rather it awoke bit by bit, comfortably, leisurely, getting used to each stage of awakening before it progressed to the next. Small risks? Like finding new and exciting places and ways to seduce Derek? Yes, yes, bring them on. Risk finding herself out of a job and an apartment, floating around in a new life she could turn out to hate with a man she might not ultimately be compatible with? That was like being woken from a deep sleep because your house exploded around you.

So…

Maybe there was a compromise? Some way to indulge her new hunger for change—and for Derek—without completely abandoning the woman she'd always been? She could visit him in Hawaii, or wherever he happened to be, and go along on a short cruise to wherever he was scheduled to go. He could visit her in New York. They could meet somewhere in between.

But...

If they really wanted to test the viability of their relationship, long-distance with only occasional passionate too-short reunions was hardly the way to go about it. Addie was nearly thirty, she wanted to settle down, and who knew when or if Derek would ever be able to do that.

And yet...

Addie groaned. She'd been going around and around on this for the past twelve hours. That morning, she'd seen Derek, but apart from a warm smile and a surreptitious hand-squeeze, there had been no chance to mention the importance of their possibly life-changing discussion the previous night. All of which left her feeling it had not been quite real, and that maybe she was angsting for no reason.

"You okay?" Ellen fell into step beside her on the path to the beach.

"Oh." Addie gave an embarrassed laugh. Apparently she'd made her frustration audible. "No, it's fine. Just... a lot on my mind."

"Hmm." They crossed the sand and handed over their bundles to the crew working to load the skiff. "Tell you what. Let's take a break."

"Really?" Addie gestured back toward the house. "There's still a lot to do."

"We have plenty of people working and plenty of time. The ceremony's not till four."

Addie looked doubtfully at the line of burdened wedding guests approaching *Lucky,* reminding her of a colony of ants. "I'd feel bad if we didn't—"

"Ahem." Ellen crossed her arms across her chest. "I'm the bride, and I get to decide."

Addie giggled and curtseyed meekly. "Yes, ma'am."

"C'mon, let's go." She took Addie's arm companionably and led the way back up the hill toward the house, turning left onto a narrow trail Addie had noticed before but never followed. "Have you been down here? It's one of my favorite spots."

A few dozen yards later they emerged from the trees onto a part of the island dominated by great granite ledges that sloped into high tide, which, along with a good breeze, was sending waves crashing into shore, causing spectacular eruptions of white, foamy spray.

"Ellen, this is wonderful."

"Come on." Ellen strode out onto a section of ledge near a large crevice in which small stones had collected; a gift from the power of the sea.

"I love to sit up here and chuck rocks in the water. It's crazy but fun. Good stress relief, too. Want to?"

"Sure." Addie couldn't say stone-throwing tempted her that much, but this was Ellen's parade and she wasn't going to rain on any of it.

"Wait up here, I'll climb down and get us a bunch." Ellen scooted down, leaping the last few feet and landing with a clacking crunch at the bottom of the crevice. A minute later she reemerged, grinning triumphantly, bulging pockets making her hoodie sag midthigh. "Got 'em."

"Good haul." Addie gave her a thumbs-up, still feeling uneasy about ditching work, wondering what Derek was up to.

"Have a seat. I'll divide them up."

Addie wiggled around until she found a place that fit, and accepted a lapful of assorted size rocks, smoothed and rounded by constant tumbling.

"Now." Ellen sat, picked up a stone from her supply and hurled it. A second later, the most delightfully liquid *thwunk* and splash made them both laugh for no particular reason.

Addie took her turn. Another *thwunk,* more splash, strangely and wonderfully satisfying.

"Okay." Ellen consigned her next one to the deep and smoothed her hair, which the breeze promptly messed up again. "I have a confession."

"What's that?" Addie threw another rock, farther this time, enjoying the release.

"I used to be really jealous of you." Ellen tossed one high in the air.

"What?" Addie was so astonished she didn't watch for it to come down. "Of *me?* What on earth for? You've got everything."

"Paul was in love with you for years."

Addie's jaw dropped. She laughed uncertainly. "With *me?* Paul? No, no, he wasn't. Not with me. You're confusing me with someone else. We hung out together all the time as friends. With Sarah and Kevin and a lot of others. It wasn't me."

"Yup, it was." Ellen threw her next stone, then wiped her hands together, that's that. "He was absolutely crazy about you. You were his perfect woman."

"But…but that's impossible." She laughed again, incredulous rather than amused, mind racing back over their grade school years, remembering parties, movies, board game tournaments, softball and soccer and tons of plain old hanging out, trying to see now what she must have been blind to then. "He never said anything. Showed anything."

"Lucky for me."

"No, no, Ellen. I would never have—" She broke off, not sure if it was polite to tell someone you found the love of her life sexually unattractive. "I mean Paul is like a brother to me. Always has been."

"He knew that. That's why he never told you."

Addie anxiously studied Ellen's profile. Her voice and expression were unconcerned, but sometimes people could hide bitterness. Addie didn't sense any, thank God. "Wow. That is just so…weird. I never picked up on a thing."

"No. You didn't." She said the words with unusual weight, which made Addie feel a bit anxious again, and unsure how to respond.

A heron flapped over, its wingspan impressive after so many gulls and cormorants. A crow gave a guttural croak from the trees behind them, as if annoyed at the intrusion into its air space.

Addie found herself tensing again, undoing the relaxation their rock-throwing session had started. She was beginning to think Ellen had some motive bringing her here besides Bride's Prerogative to avoid work.

"Did Paul ever tell you how we got together?"

"You met on a blind date, took one look at each other and that was that."

Ellen threw another stone, watched it splash. "That's the version for public consumption. It was more complicated, and more difficult."

Addie felt a jab of disappointment. She'd loved the idea that the two of them had found true love simply, honestly and easily. Did it ever happen that way? "Complicated how?"

"Paul fought how he felt for a long time."

"No." Addie was too flabbergasted to throw her next stone. "But it's so obvious you're perfect for each other."

"Mmm-hmm." Ellen arched an eyebrow at Addie, who was clearly being sent some signal, but had no idea what it meant. "However, it wasn't obvious to him, not at first.

He'd wedged himself into this narrow mindset about who he was and about his feelings for you. He wasn't really open to me, even though he thought he was ready for a relationship, and had been dating around looking for one."

Addie pelted the water with two rocks at once, hard, as if she was punishing them. "How did you convince him?"

Ellen nudged her, blond bob fluttering around a mischievous expression. "Take a wild guess."

"Ha!" Addie's grin stretched her mouth to its maximum. "I'm shocked. *Shocked,* I tell you!"

"I knew you would be." Ellen waggled her brows lasciviously before settling back into being serious. "But that wasn't the whole story of course. One day he told me that before he could commit to me, he had to tell you how he felt about you. He thought that was the only way to finally put those feelings to rest."

"Urgh." Addie cringed, waving away Paul's imaginary speech like a bad smell. "That would have been so painful all around. For him, for me, for you…"

"I didn't know how it would go." Ellen shrugged, gazing distantly out to sea. "I was only sure of how I felt about Paul, and how I was pretty sure he felt about me underneath, and that I'd have to fight to keep him for both our sakes. So I told him if he didn't stop hedging and making excuses, in short, if he wasn't *man* enough to give us a serious shot, I was outta there."

"Really? You would have left him?" Addie gasped, horrified to think that this perfect couple might not have made it as far as this weekend's joyous celebration. Then she caught a look in Ellen's eyes. "You were bluffing."

"Of course I was bluffing!"

Addie burst out laughing. She liked Ellen more and more. "But Paul didn't know that."

"Exactly." She heaved a larger rock over the ledge and

nodded in grim satisfaction at the splash. "I gave him the ultimatum Friday, left him alone all weekend and caught up with him Sunday night. He was a wreck. Absolute mess. But he jumped, and I caught him like I said I would."

"Thank God he did."

"The point of all this is, Addie." She turned and fixed Addie with a look that made Addie brace herself. "We both took a risk for something we not only believed in but deeply wanted to happen."

Addie narrowed her eyes. Okay. She was getting it now. Someone had been talking to someone about certain decisions involving big risks. "Gee, Ellen, is there any particular reason you happen to be telling me this now?"

"Who, me?" Ellen plonked a hand to her chest, eyes innocently wide. "No, of course not. Just a bride musing on her wedding day."

"Uh-huh." Addie picked up a good-size rock, heart beating like mad, not sure what she was feeling. "Has someone mentioned something about me and a certain, oh, I don't know, other person lately? Anything?"

"No, no, not at all." Ellen spoke reassuringly. Addie didn't buy it for a second. "I have really good intuition about this stuff. You and Derek have been setting off sparks since you met. I thought maybe y'all needed a push in the right direction."

"Ha." Addie hurled the rock as hard as she could. "I wouldn't begin to know what the right direction is."

"Addie, all I know is that the only two people who walk on water in Paul's world are you and Derek."

"And you."

"Well, *obviously.*" She winked.

"Me, I was in the water yesterday." Addie mimed a sudden drop. "I sank right to the bottom."

"Don't sell yourself short. You were really important

to Paul, his first ideal of love. And Derek was kind of his savior. My life with Paul wouldn't have been possible without Derek. The close relationship Paul has with his family would not have been possible without Derek. Any kids we have would not have been possible without Derek. He is a good, good person who has had a lonely and hard life, and he needs someone really wonderful who can…" She frowned and gestured aimlessly. "I don't know—"

"*Rescue* him?"

Ellen laughed. "That's about the last word I'd think of when it comes to Derek, but I suppose there is an element of that. Anyway, I'm just saying, Addie, that sometimes we need shaking out of our usual ideas about ourselves and what we want and deserve in life."

Addie pressed her lips together, suddenly annoyed by all the talking around the issues. "Can we just be blunt here?"

"*Yes.*" Ellen spoke with exaggerated relief. "Thank you. I would love to be blunt."

"I permit you to be blunt. What exactly are you saying?"

Ellen sat up on her haunches and put her hand on Addie's shoulder, her lovely blue gaze earnest and warm. "I think you should give Derek a chance next year. Give him a sense of home. I don't think he's ever had a real one."

A jolt of adrenaline, a burst of joy, then, predictably… fear. Damn it. She was sick to death of being afraid.

"Wait a second." Addie pointed accusingly when Ellen's words sank in. "Give him a chance next year? That is *way* past what you can know by intuition. Even really good intuition."

"Okay, okay." Ellen captured Addie's finger. "Put away the weapon, I'll squeal. Derek and Paul talked last night and again this morning. I'm playing meddling match-maker. That's it."

Addie blew on her finger and holstered it. "You should never work for the CIA."

"Cracked like an egg, I know." She gestured to Addie to throw her last stone and stood. "Now, sugar, having delivered my supersecret spy message, I am going back to help. You coming?"

"Absolutely." Her stone made it farther than anything she'd ever thrown in her life, fueled by giddy adrenaline and a growing certainty.

The story of Paul and how he'd nearly blown the chance of forever happiness with Ellen affected Addie deeply. Fear had ruled her for far too long. Fear of the unknown. Fear of what could happen. Both were imagined negatives, neither were real threats.

Her feelings were real. Derek's feelings were real. His offer to see where those feelings could lead was real.

And she might just have to accept it.

THE WEDDING WAS the most beautiful thing Sarah had ever seen. It didn't hurt that she was already imagining hers to Joe. Because of course that was their next step. The Brisbanes' house was a majestic white Victorian with sage trim, built by a ship's captain in the mid-nineteenth century at the height of the region's prosperity. It sat on a lovely sloping lawn with a spectacular flower garden, where the ceremony was held, designed to make the most of Maine's short summer season—gladiolas were in full bloom in a riot of colors, black-eyed Susans and daylilies grew in profusion. Tables had been set up for the reception around the lawn, which had an expansive view of Machias Bay. The band was playing on the front patio next to a floor set up for dancing. The weather had been perfect.

Mr. Brisbane, Esq., had officiated at the ceremony, since lawyers were permitted to marry couples in the state of Maine. He'd spoken warmly of the couple, of their devotion to each other and to their families, had cautioned Paul and Ellen to be good to one other above all else, and generally reduced Sarah and many other guests to mushy sniffles, which got louder and more obvious when the couple recited vows they'd written themselves, gazing rapturously into each other's eyes. Sarah couldn't be happier for her brother and her new sister-in-law. The reception had been joyous, food and champagne plentiful, the dancing and socializing enthusiastic.

But now it was time for her.

From where she'd been standing next to the bride during the ceremony, Sarah hadn't been able to see Joe, but she could sense him behind her in one of the chairs set up for the guests, imagined that maybe he was watching her, too, that maybe he was thinking about them being up at an altar in front of an officiant reciting their own vows.

Maybe. She hoped.

The day had gone by in a blur. Sarah had done everything she could to treat Joe the same as usual, so her at-last declaration would be a surprise. And in case her certainty about how she felt about him waned, which it decidedly hadn't. Once she'd finally admitted her feelings to herself, Joe had changed permanently into the more masculine, more handsome man she'd only caught glimpses of before. Frankly she'd had trouble keeping her hands off him. Just the idea of what she'd say and do to him tonight—soon!— had her shivering and hot at the same time.

Now, at last, the moment she'd been so impatient for and so nervous about was here. Paul and Ellen had left a few minutes earlier, the guests were starting to clear out and she was happy to say that Derek and Addie had left together soon after the happy couple. Sarah so hoped they'd work out. Why she ever thought Kevin would be right for Addie, she had no idea. Why she'd thought half the stuff she'd used to, she had no idea, either. Too much of her life had been spent in a weird distorting fog. Finally she was starting to see things—and herself—clearly.

If only she could see clearly how the rest of this evening would go. She knew Joe had feelings for her, had for a long time, but maybe he'd gotten to the end of his rope as she'd just gotten to the beginning of hers. Maybe he'd trust that she'd had a true change of heart. Maybe he wouldn't. Sarah couldn't blame him either way. All she could do now was put her plan into motion and hope for the best.

She scanned the thinning crowd until she found Joe, chatting with one of Paul's friends next to the dance floor. Even her hundredth or so glimpse of him this evening thrilled her. They'd spent most of the afternoon apart— Sarah had maid of honor duties and she was terrified she'd give something away if she spent too much time with him. Joe could read her like a Nook.

Okay, Sarah. Ready, set, go.

She moved onto the dance floor and caught the eye of the bandleader, who nodded.

Now.

Squaring her shoulders, Sarah made a beeline for Joe. By the time she was next to him, the band had started her request, the last song of the evening, "It's Your Love" by Tim McGraw, which he performed with his wife, Faith Hill.

"Dance with me?" She caught Joe's hand and tugged him onto the floor, where a few brave couples had stuck it out nearly to the bitter end.

"I hate dancing."

"So?" She turned to face him, standing close, and put

her arms around his neck, aware of his tall, solid body in a way she'd never been before. "It's the last song, you can manage one."

"I don't know, Sarah."

She rolled her eyes, heart pounding, same old teasing Sarah, and yet she felt so different, so much more of a woman around him, so much calmer and more sure about who she was and what she wanted. "You can handle a slow dance. Even my two-left-feet brother can handle a slow dance. And frankly, if there's anyone who needs to be afraid right now, it's me."

His deep brown eyes had been avoiding hers. At this, he looked down at her. "You? You're a great dancer."

"It's not the dancing I'm afraid of." She started swaying, aware of the song's romantic lyrics flowing around them, the warmth of his body close to hers, the way it drew her. How could she have been so stupid for so long? Joe...

"So?" His hands remained stubbornly at his side, though he made some attempt to move with her. Not wildly graceful, but not embarrassing, either. He was a fine dancer. "What are you afraid of?"

"The dance being over. The weekend being over. You leaving me."

His mouth pressed in a line. A muscle twitched in his jaw. How had she never noticed its strength? "I'm taking a new job, not leaving you."

"Joe?"

"What?"

"Put your arms around me."

"Sarah..."

She moved closer, pressed against him. "Please, Joe."

She felt rather than heard him sigh. Then his arms came around her, reluctant at first, then firm and protective, and for the first time in her life held by a man she wanted, Sarah felt absolutely safe and absolutely content. "Thank you."

"You're welcome." He was grumpy as a bear. She ignored him and pressed her cheek to his—as far up as she could reach. His scent was so clean and masculine, his skin so just-shaven smooth, the song so romantic and beautiful. She couldn't let his mood undermine her resolve.

"Joe?"

"Yes." His tone was slightly less exasperated. Maybe she was getting to him? She hoped so. Because it was time.

She tightened her arms around his neck, pressed her forehead under his chin, unable to meet his eyes. "How about I move with you to Phoenix?"

His body stiffened. "Right."

"I'm serious, Joe."

"Why the hell would you move to Phoenix?"

"Because you'll be there." She summoned all her courage and looked up, letting her feelings show in her face. *I love you, Joe.*

His brows drew down. "What are you playing at, Sarah?"

Ouch. She kept her features from sliding into dismay, told herself to be patient. He was going to have to accept a radical change after a decade of everything being the same. It would take more than a few minutes for him to trust her. "I'm not playing. I want to be with you."

Silence for a few minutes while he searched her face. "I don't understand what you're saying."

"I'm saying…" She stopped dancing, stayed still in his arms and looked him full in the eyes while hers filled with tears. "I'm saying I love you, Joe. I want to be with you, wherever you are."

The band swelled into the final chorus. Joe didn't move.

Sarah started to feel a bit panicky. She told herself to calm down, but it wasn't working very well. "I love you."

"So you said."

"I thought...that's what you wanted from me." Panic for real this time. What if he'd only loved her for all this time because she was unreachable? What if he'd been doing the same thing Sarah had been doing for so long with guys like Kevin and Ethan and Derek?

What if he didn't really want her?

"Where is this coming from, Sarah?"

"My heart." More tears. She couldn't help it. Joy and fear together.

Still no movement, still the stoniest of stone faces.

"Joe, for God's sake." Okay, she was never going to be patient. She could only change so much.

He glanced around. The band had stopped. The guests that hadn't already left were doing so now. "We need to talk about this somewhere else."

"Yes. Okay." She took a deep breath. This could still work. "My room at the hotel."

It took Joe a few seconds to agree. The instant he did, she practically dragged him off the dance floor, over to thank the Brisbanes, and down their yard to her car, which she drove like a demon to the hotel where they were spending the night, wishing they could be back on Storness, on the beach under the stars, wishing she'd had the brains and timing to seduce him there.

But her room at the Machias Motor Inn would have to do.

She let them into her second-floor room with the view of the Machias River, and tossed her bag on the bed, kicked off her shoes and faced Joe, who was standing uneasily next to the bed. She put her hands to his chest. "Let's try this again?"

He shook his head, bemused, adorable, dark hair tumbling over his forehead. "Sarah, you are confusing the hell out of me."

"It's very simple. I'm telling you I'm in love with you."

He dropped his forehead into his palm and groaned. "Since when?"

"Since I figured it out."

"Just now?" His looked up suspiciously. "Right after watching your brother get married? After several glasses of champagne?"

"No." Tears rose. She pushed away from him. "No. Yesterday, when we were talking, when you told me you were leaving. I realized I can't live without you."

"That is nothing like—"

"No." She held up her hand to stop him. "That's not what I meant. I *can* live without you. But I don't *want* to live without you. You've been such a vital part of my life for so long, my very best friend. I'm so sorry I put you through so much, and I'm so sorry it took me this long to realize what you mean to me."

"A best friend?" His voice cracked hopefully and she realized what this was costing him. The rest of her life wouldn't be long enough to make it up to him, but she was damned if she wasn't going to try.

"So far your best friend. But from now on…" She stood very still, understanding what must happen to make what she was saying clear. Words wouldn't be enough to convince him.

She reached behind her neck, found the zipper on her dress and pulled it down.

Joe's eyes widened, then his face turned stony again, hands fisted at his side.

Her dress slid to the floor. Underneath she wore a lacy white bra with matching panties and thigh-high stockings.

"Sarah…"

"Yes, Joe?" she whispered.

"I don't…" He took a step forward, then stopped, his expression finally showing emotion. Want, fear, love, fear, desire…fear. Sarah's heart melted. *Oh, Joe.*

"I've been so slow. So selfish." She unhooked her bra, let it slide off her arms, conscious of her breasts in the cool room air. "So blind."

He blinked. Swallowed, staring into her eyes, glancing down at her body as if he couldn't help himself. Then the ghost of a smile. "Thank God I'm not."

Sarah grinned, hope shooting up inside her like a geyser. That was her Joe. He had come back to life, snapped out of whatever zombie state she'd put him in. Maybe this would be okay. Maybe not too little too late.

Down came her panties. She kept the stockings on, sauntered toward him, helped him take off his jacket. "I have a favor to ask you."

He made a sound she'd take as an appropriate response.

She put her lips near his ear, loosening his tie. "I want you to kiss me, Joe. Then I want you to make love to me until I beg for mercy."

He shook his head as if to clear his brain of fog. "I still can't take this in. I don't—"

"Shh. Don't worry. We'll take it slowly." She threw the tie across the room, put her arms around his neck and pulled his face down, kissed his mouth.

Deep desire spread through her. She understood desire. She was used to desire. What she wasn't used to was the sweet depth of emotion she felt along with it.

Joe.

She kissed him again, more deeply this time. His eyes stayed closed, his hands at his side, but his mouth moved, responded.

Then a low groan began in his chest and he enveloped her in a crushing embrace, kissing her as if he'd never wanted to do anything else. The sweetness grew and spread, and with it, hot desire she felt him return from a certain place that for men was a dead giveaway.

"Sarah." He repeated her name over and over between kisses, sliding his hands up and down her arms, over her back.

She backed up, smiling into his eyes with everything she felt for him, with all her hopes for their future together. In Phoenix or wherever else Joe was. That was where she belonged.

"Where are we going?" He was smiling now, and she knew it was sinking in, that he was starting to trust what she felt, and that the next hour spent in this motel room would be the final proof he needed.

She climbed onto the bed, lay back, inviting him to join her. "We're going to make my wish on the shooting star come true."

Joe climbed reverently onto the bed with her, wearing way too many clothes, but they would soon take care of that. He moved over her, pressed his forehead to her forehead, his heart to her heart.

"Trust me, Sarah. Both our wishes will come true tonight."

15

ADDIE GAVE A LONG, joyous whoop and ran down the riverbank behind the Machias Motor Inn, not caring that her panty hose probably wouldn't survive the trip. Her heels, she'd left in Derek's car and who cared about them, either? If she fell, her sleeveless blue silk sheath would be toast, as well. Too bad! She was happy! Incredibly happy! The wedding had been amazing, Paul and Ellen were going to be blissful the rest of their lives and she'd all but decided to chuck her entire existence and spend the next year on the yacht of a particularly hot guy named Derek Bates.

Arms came around her waist and lifted her, shrieking with laughter, spun her around, then deposited her back on terra firma. Terra mostly firma—she hadn't been shy with the champagne and the world seemed to be tilting ju-u-ust the tiniest bit.

"Mmm." She kissed Derek's most *ama*-zingly awesome lips and threw her arms around his neck, breathing hard from her run. "That was the best wedding I'd ever been to."

"It was pretty special." He was looking at her funny. Was she being funny? She didn't think so.

"They're going to be together forever, I really feel it. Really. I'm serious."

He nodded, looking totally hot in his gray summer suit. She couldn't wait to see him in his yacht captain outfit. She'd bet he looked incredibly hot in that. And naked? She already knew what he looked like naked: amazingly hot. Face it, the guy was hot.

"Sometimes, like this one time I went to a wedding and I just knew the marriage wasn't going to last." Her voice was coming out too high. That was weird. She tried to pitch it lower. "And it didn't. Well, it did for a year, and then *pthhhhhpt*."

"Yeah?" He was definitely amused now, but just as she was about to ask him what was so funny, he lunged forward and picked her up, swung her around and around again, and kissed her the way she'd always dreamed about being kissed, which come to think about it, was pretty much the way he always kissed her.

Really, he was perfect.

"I could happily suck face with you forever, Captain Bates."

"That's a pretty long time." His eyes were warm, his smile wide.

"It is, isn't it." She kissed him again, then pressed her body against him and turned the kisses slow and suggestive. "You know what?"

"Mmm, what?" He slid his big warm hands over her bottom and pulled her roughly closer, grinning down at her.

"We've never had sex in a bed."

"You're right." He quirked an eyebrow. "Though I would have been happy to the first night when you shamelessly crawled into mine."

"Mistakenly. Only it didn't turn out to be a mistake."

Addie smiled up at him. She hoped that night would never seem like one. Or any of the time she'd spent with him.

"I think deep down you knew it was me."

"Very possible." She batted her eyelashes and slid her hands under his jacket, savoring the firm curves of his pectorals. "So I'm thinking we really need to make love in a bed."

"That sounds—"

"Now!" She broke away and ran back toward the hotel, giggling madly. She felt so free tonight! So wild! She couldn't remember when she'd had this much energy, this much savage adrenaline. This much joy. Her life was about to change in a huge way, a significant way, and so was she! Gone was the drudge, gone the creature of habit, gone the slave to routines and predictable safety. She was... Neo-Addie!

It felt so damn wonderful.

Thudding steps sounded behind her. She picked up her pace, knowing he could catch her easily if he wanted to, but why not make him work harder?

He let her reach the door of their room half a second before he did, though she didn't have a key, so what good had the sprint done her except give her a chance to enjoy the joyful rush of air into her lungs, the pull of her muscles working hard, the fabulous feeling of being an alive and mobile and feeling woman who was madly in love with a wonderful man and about to declare she'd spend the next year carefree and pampered aboard a luxury yacht. A yacht! Captained by the sexiest man alive, ever.

While Derek opened the door, she assisted by wrapping her leg around his and helping herself to the enticing muscular feel of his back under his jacket, hungry to get him alone and naked. Did she mention naked?

Inside, she threw herself into his arms and kissed him,

backed him up toward the bed, conveniently located as the centerpiece of the room. She couldn't wait. The wedding had been so lovely, so very lovely, and while she'd loved every second of watching Paul and Ellen seal their happiness, the evil selfish part of Addie had just been craving *this*.

He tumbled her back on the bed, held her wrists over her head and covered her body with his. Oh, yes. He wanted the same thing she did. Bodies joined and writhing in—

"Addie."

"Mmm?" She moved her hips in a circle under him, smiling, glorying in the feeling of being pinned down by a strong man. "Can I help you, sir?"

"We need a time-out here."

"A what? Why? What are you talking about?" Her voice crept back up too high, and became strangely brittle.

"Shh. Just lie there for a minute. Take deep breaths."

"What? *What!*" She laughed at him. "I don't need to calm down. I'm in a great mood, that's all."

"Shh." He brushed his lips across hers. "Breathe."

Addie rolled her eyes, and obediently tried to slow her breathing.

It didn't work. Her lungs stuttered and fought. She started to feel a bit light-headed, a bit panicky. What was the matter with her? How did he know?

"Turn over." He released her hands, turned her over and unzipped her dress, pulled it off her shoulders and unhooked her bra.

Oh, yes. Forget breathing, now they were getting somewhere.

She waited impatiently for him to finish undressing her, for his hands to slide under her breasts, for his body weight on top of her, for the nudge of his erection searching for her opening from behind.

Instead his hands landed on her back and began stroking, top to bottom, bottom to top, following her muscles, his touch light at first, then increasing in pressure. Slowly, sensually, he massaged her. She lay waiting, unsure of what was happening, wanting to know when he'd turn this sexual.

"Relax, Addie." He started on the long muscles next to her spine, smoothing them, spending time on the knots, one inch at a time, kneading and loosening. Then her deltoids, her upper back, around her shoulder blades—light strokes, then deeper, singling out muscles and insisting they let go. On and on he worked until her breathing became even and deep without her trying. Her eyes closed, her world dwindled to his touch and the wonderful sensations in her body. She hadn't realized how much tension she'd been carrying until he decided it had to go.

"Better?" His stroking became light again; he drew the tips of his fingers over the skin on her back, covering every inch, then laid his hand in the center and pressed gently.

Addie was nowhere near where she'd been only half an hour before. She felt as if she'd gained ten pounds. Her body would leave an Addie-shaped crater in the mattress that would never rebound. But…very strangely, her heart and spirits had sunk down from their high, first to normal, and then into an odd free fall she didn't want to examine just then.

"Thank you," she mumbled. "That was wonderful."

"You're welcome." He pressed a kiss to her shoulder.

"Except I don't think I'll ever be able to move again."

"Darn." He kissed the small of her back, the top of

each buttock, then nudged her legs open, burrowed his face down and kissed between them.

Addie's eyes shot open, her dismay dissolving. "Um…"

"Yes?" His tongue joined in what his lips had started.

"Well…" She inched her legs farther apart. "Maybe I can move a little."

"Mmm." He took advantage of the new space she'd given him. His tongue was very warm and very wet and she was getting very, very hot in spite of the near stupor he'd put her in. She responded to him so strongly. It wasn't just his tongue, it was the reverent way he tasted her, the brush of his hand on her thigh, the small murmurs here and there that let her know he was making love to her as a whole woman even while touching only one special part.

A minute later he stopped and Addie felt him leave the bed. The sound of clothes being removed got one of her eyes open again. She rolled over to watch him, heart still strangely heavy.

Tie first. Derek tugged it off with practiced ease and tossed it onto the room's chair. Shoes and socks next—he took care of those standing on one foot without over-balancing. Trousers. Addie nodded appreciatively as his strong, muscular thighs came into view. Shirt unbuttoned, off. T-shirt. Off. His chest was broad and defined without being over-pumped. His abs ditto, a muscular washboard she wanted to drag herself over repeatedly.

Boxers off, and her man was naked, putting on a condom, climbing back onto the bed. She reached for him. "Welcome back."

"Nice to be back." He positioned himself over her, stroking her hair, gazing into her eyes. Addie's heart rose to meet him. It had no choice.

Then Derek kissed her, over and over again, softly, sweetly, firm lips exploring and tasting. Addie felt the last of her giddy wildness leaving, replaced by deep emotions that both filled and frightened her.

He reached down to prepare her then slid inside, taking his time, pushing in slowly. When he'd buried his last inch, he paused. Looking into his eyes she felt the most powerful connection she'd ever known, and out of that bliss, out of that loving, wonderful certainty, came understanding of a deeper, painful truth that she'd soon have to face.

He began to move, slow thrusts, slow retreats, pausing in between. Her arousal grew sharply, but he held his pace and she lay still, letting him take the lead, running her hands over the smooth firmness of his back, tracing the rounded muscle of his buttocks, cupping the hard swells of his shoulders, biceps and triceps, indulging every sensation, keeping her mind carefully blank.

Tomorrow would happen tomorrow. They still had all of tonight.

Derek didn't seem to be in a hurry, either. He took time to kiss her mouth, her temple, to bend and suckle her breasts, adoring her nipples, the tugs of his tongue and lips, the rasp of his stubble against her skin increasing the sensation and her arousal.

Out and back in, pushing to the hilt, moving his hips in a circle pressed tightly against her clitoris, then back out, and back in, a lovely, leisurely rhythm that kept her desire burning hot, but not yet desperate.

She explored the soft, thick texture of his hair, drew her fingers down the planes of his face, tasted and tested every angle and aspect of his mouth.

"I could get used to this," he whispered. "I'd like to get used to this, Addie."

No, no. Not now.

She could tell the truth, that she'd like to get used to

this, too, but he might think that meant she'd decided to go with him, and she couldn't tell him that.

So she pulled his mouth down passionately, kissed him as if it were the last time. He responded with equal passion, and that passion translated into the language of their bodies and made them move urgently against one another as if, again, it might be the very last time.

Addie went over first, holding Derek tight, arching back into the pillow, mouth open, holding stone-still through the rush of ecstasy, so he'd feel her contracting around him, so he'd know what he'd done for her.

He drew in a sharp breath, exhaled, *oh, Addie,* and plunged deep into her, hands dug in under her buttocks to merge them more closely. In and out only a few more times, then he stiffened, moaned low, and she felt him pulsing inside her, reveling in his climax with a rush of tenderness that nearly undid her.

They came down slowly. Instead of a flush of triumph, she felt a deep sadness, wrapped her arms around him and pressed her cheek against his, feeling his breath warm her shoulder.

One minutes, two minutes, she wasn't sure how long they lay there until he lifted and met her eyes, his dark with sadness. "You're not coming with me."

Addie shook her head.

"Tell me why."

"I can't handle that much change, that much risk. I was going to. I'd gotten myself all excited, all ready. I was going to tell you tonight. You saw what it did to me." She paused, determined not to cry. "I was a totally manic wreck. If it was the right thing to do, I'd be able to tell you my decision calmly. Instead I nearly fell apart."

"I sensed that." His eyes were full of pain, but also understanding, which made it even harder not to cry.

"I would love to find out what could be between us, Derek." Her voice broke. "Maybe there's another way. I mean…we can keep in touch. You could visit maybe, or I could."

"Sure." He kissed her gently, but she knew what he was thinking, because she was thinking the same thing. They might stay in touch, might retain some of the passion for a while, but without contact, without access to each other, there was nothing solid they could build. To get to know someone enough to maintain a relationship, to make any kind of commitment, there had to be something other than occasional passionate reunions. They could go on that way for years, in a limbo of impermanence.

Addie didn't want that. She wanted a man she could get to know intimately over many, many months, his moods and his routines, to face trials and joys together, discover each other's secrets and strengths, wonders and weaknesses. She couldn't do that with a man half a world away.

Derek pulled carefully out of her, disposed of the condom in the room's little bathroom and brought back glasses of water for each of them.

She watched him move, that glorious body, well-balanced and graceful, muscles flexing and contracting. He climbed back into bed and pulled her close. Addie sighed heavily. "I'm in total ridiculous denial how much this is going to hurt."

He chuckled, that deep glorious sound that was going to tear her in half every time she remembered it for the next several weeks. Maybe months. "I think we both are."

"But it's time to put on my big-girl pants and deal with reality." A tear slipped past her defenses.

"I guess it is." He wiped it carefully off her cheek and kissed her, kissed her again, sweetly, reverently. Her heart was breaking. She was surprised not to hear it cracking in her chest.

"When do you head out to sea again?"

"Thursday. I'm taking a group out of Lahaina Harbor on a three-island tour."

Addie nodded. She'd be going to the office. Sitting at her usual desk, interacting with her usual colleagues, going home to her usual apartment.

It was what she wanted. What she needed. It was her chosen life.

"After that?"

He frowned, thinking. "After that a fishing trip. Then a birthday cruise."

She'd still be going to the office.

But maybe by then she'd have enrolled in a class, met new people, broadened her horizons, interests and skills. Not the same in-a-rut-Addie, but not trying to be her polar opposite, either. Something in between. Something she could handle without losing her mind.

She lay in Derek's arms, head on his chest, legs tangled with his, thinking she'd never felt so blissfully relaxed with anyone. But if she'd discovered this now with him, it must mean she could do so again, right? Derek wasn't the only man she could find happiness with. And because he was so wonderful, he'd raised the bar for her. She wouldn't settle for ho-hum relationships again. That was another check in the plus column. Silver linings. After the worst of the pain subsided, she'd find more of them. She was certain.

Eventually she dozed, woke to find Derek stroking her awake, drowsy at first, then, wow, um…very, very awake.

"Addie," he whispered. "Wake up."

"I'm up. It's not morning."

"No. But I'm thinking since we might not be able to make love again, at least for a while…"

"Ah. Good thinking, Captain Bates." She rolled him onto his back and straddled him, holding his arms to the mattress, the way he'd imprisoned her earlier. "I agree with you. We'll make this a good time."

"A night to remember."

"Uh." Addie frowned. "Isn't that the name of the book about the Titanic disaster?"

"Could be."

"I'm not sure that's appropriate for what we're planning."

"Sure it is." He struggled up and flipped her over, making a mockery of her physical dominance. "How about this. 'As captain of the ship, it is my duty to go down.'"

Addie burst into laughter, loving that he could make her smile, even through this dense cloud of misery. Her laughter cut off in a gasp as his mouth found her between her legs.

Fear entered her heart at the same time pleasure spread through her body. Yes, Derek had raised that bar.

But what if he'd raised it to a height only he could ever attain?

16

THE SOUND OF the ocean woke Addie. She was back in Derek's arms, listening to waves tumble over rocks on the shore outside their window. A seagull laughed nearby.

Addie's eyes shot open. Registered the familiar white ceiling.

"Alarm off."

The ocean was not outside her window. Derek was on the other side of the world. There *were* birds calling, but they were pigeons on the roof of the Russian Orthodox Church opposite her apartment building, making that deep gurgle noise in their throats, as if they were forever using mouthwash. She missed the wild free call of gulls, eagles and osprey, the thrush and other songbirds. She missed the ocean and its wonderful smells. She missed Derek something fierce.

Leaving him three days earlier had been one of the hardest things she'd ever had to do. Addie preferred relationships neatly wrapped up when they ended, with literal or figurative notes of apology, regret, thanks or sympathy dutifully composed if not sent. This was a mess of loose ends, full of doubts and what-ifs. And yet, she'd stayed true to herself by deciding to come home to New York.

She'd done the right thing for herself and, ultimately, for Derek.

Eventually this ten-ton spiked weight she was carrying around in her heart would dissolve into the satisfaction of exactly that understanding.

She bloody well hoped.

"Time."

"Six fifty-five," Tick replied.

Six fifty-five. The latest she'd figured she could get up without having to rush any of her morning.

Addie dragged herself out of bed, remembering suddenly how the week before she left for Maine she'd been having trouble getting up, too. Funny. She'd been thinking about getting her Vitamin D checked or her iron. And yet, she'd felt fine—more than fine—in Maine. Plenty of energy, zest for life, you name it.

Just her rut, which she was going to get out of as soon as possible. She'd clean up those boxes of Great-Aunt Grace's and maybe look for a condo for real this weekend. September was right around the corner, there would be classes of all kinds starting soon.

In the meantime, she could get back to the kind of life she needed to keep herself sane.

In the bathroom she counted to seventeen until the shower was warm, scrubbed her hair and body, humming a melody she abruptly stopped when she realized it was Avril Lavigne's missing-you song "When You're Gone."

In her bedroom, she dressed quickly and efficiently in the clothes she'd ironed and laid out the night before.

In her kitchen she fixed and ate the same breakfast she had every morning: a banana, granola with yogurt, a half piece of toast with butter and jam—sometimes honey— orange juice, milk and coffee.

In the subway she read that day's *New York Times,* saving the crossword to do at lunch.

In her office she dealt with the day's tasks from eight-thirty until eleven forty-five when she broke for lunch to beat the rush at the cafeteria and secure her favorite table.

In the cafeteria, with the crossword section under her arm, she selected carrot sticks, a sandwich, an apple and skim milk to be sure she was getting enough calcium.

On her way to her usual table, sitting empty waiting for her, Addie came to an abrupt stop, nearly causing the woman behind her to dump her tray contents down Addie's back.

Her routines were not comforting today, as they had been the first day back, and then a little less yesterday. Today they were stifling her.

"Addie?"

She turned to find Linda Persson back at *her* usual table, with *her* usual lunch. Linda must have been sick Monday and Tuesday. Or maybe she'd decided to take a trip after all.

"Hi, Linda, welcome back. Were you out on vacation this week?" She could hear the hope in her voice, not sure why she'd care either way.

"No, no, I was out sick. Nothing serious. I'm much better now. How was Maine?"

"Wonderful. The wedding was lovely. It's good to be home, though." Sort of. For the most part. In spite of being bored and having a huge jagged hole in her heart. She took a step toward her regular table then hesitated, struck by inspiration. If anyone could make her feel good about her decision to forgo a life of constant uncertainty for a life of total stability, it was Linda. "Hey, can I join you?"

Pleasure lit Linda's face, making Addie feel guilty for wanting to have lunch with her for such a selfish reason.

"Absolutely, come on over. I'm dying to know what you thought of Maine. My friend Marcy and I are thinking of going there."

Addie set down her tray and took a seat. "Really going there?"

"Well, yes." Linda seemed surprised Addie would ask. "One of our friends from college opened a B&B outside of Portland and invited us. So I want to hear all about your trip."

"I thought you didn't like to travel."

Linda looked trapped, and then gave an embarrassed shrug. "That was partly sour grapes. I had no reason to go anywhere and it felt terrible. I'm excited about this, though, so tell me everything."

"The state is beautiful, so wild and pristine and free. At least where we were, in Downeast Maine. The seafood is delicious and so cheap compared to the city. It's the kind of place that changes you." Her voice thickened. She bit into a carrot and chewed viciously. "But I'll tell you, after a week of constant socializing I was pretty fried."

"Oh, I bet." Linda nodded. "Weddings are exhausting. But so romantic."

"Yes." Addie picked up her sandwich, trying to look nonchalant, and pretty sure she was failing big-time. "I actually met someone."

"You're *kidding!*" Linda spoke so loudly a couple of people turned to look.

"No, I'm serious." Addie was a little annoyed. Was it *that* incredible to think she might have met a guy? "A friend of the groom, who's an old friend of mine."

"Weddings are great places to meet people. All that love in the air." Linda leaned across the table, eyes hungry. "Tell me about him. Does he live close by? Is he from Maine? Will you see him again?"

"Well, actually…" Addie leaned in, too. She wanted this to have maximum impact, to enjoy Linda's shock and dismay. "He asked me to leave New York and live with him."

"Oh, my *gosh!*" she yelped. More people turned to look. "After a week? Where is he from? What does he do?"

"He's a charter yacht captain. Based in Hawaii."

Linda gasped so hard she started choking on her sandwich, and had to hold her hand up to tell Addie to wait, and then drink water a few times. "Oh. My. *God.* You have to tell me *everything.*"

Addie told her the short version, leaving out the part about Kevin and climbing into Derek's bed by mistake, though her whole body was remembering that part so vividly she kept leaving bits out of the story and having to backtrack. Linda, either very polite or totally enraptured, hung on to every word. Addie told her how Derek had taken her to watch the sunset, how he'd shown up to surprise her when she was sunbathing privately—Addie left out naked—how he'd taken her on a moonlit rowboat ride and danced with her by a river under the stars.

And then how after only three full days, he'd asked her to give up her job, her apartment, her well-ordered life, and follow him out onto the ocean to go who-knew-where for who-knew-how-long, who-knew-when.

Crazy, right?

Silence as Linda stared at her in horror and sympathy. Slowly, slowly, the pain in Addie's stomach started to lift. Here was someone who'd understand. Someone who'd be able to tell Addie to her face that she'd done the right thing. Sarah thought Addie was nuts. Ellen thought Addie was nuts. Paul thought Addie was nuts.

Linda would understand.

"Are you *nuts?*"

Addie was so shocked she sat there with a carrot stick halfway up to her mouth.

"You came back *here?*" Linda gestured around the cafeteria. "Instead of living on a *yacht*? With a guy you were completely *crazy about*? You came back *here*? *To this*? *This company* and this *cafeteria*? And that *carrot*?"

Her voice became louder with each phrase. Her face turned bright red. Around them people were falling silent. By the time she said "carrot" she was practically shouting.

Addie managed to put the carrot down.

"Yes," she whispered.

Linda looked around, noticed people staring and lowered her voice. "Will he still take you?"

Addie's eyes shot wide. "No. I mean I don't know, but no, I can't go. I'm not the type of person who can just up and leave everything I've built for myself. I can't handle huge changes like that. And boats…I don't think it's for me."

"Oh, so you mean last time you tried living with an amazing hunk on a yacht you didn't like it?"

"I never said he was an amazing hunk."

"Is he?"

"Well…" Addie wrinkled her nose. "Yes. But that's not the point."

"Agreed. The point is that you are nuts. Boats have schedules, too, they have to, to function smoothly. And after you've been on it for a while the life will become second nature like anything else. How long has this guy been at it, you think he's enthralled with every new day, with every aspect of his job?"

"I guess not."

"But he wants to be enthralled every new day. With you, Addie." She shook her head slowly, eyes narrowed. "And you said no."

Addie could only sit and blink at her.

"Go." Linda was whispering. "Go now. Just walk right out of here. Tell you what... I'll take care of your paperwork. We can give you whatever, vacation time, sick time, short-term disability, you leave that to me. If you go and change your mind in the first month or so, you'll still have a job to come back to. I'm sure you can manage your rent for a few months. But for God's sake, don't let this pass you by."

"Why are you doing this for me?"

"Because I had an offer like this. From a military man. We'd known each other a short time, but we were crazy about each other. Before he went abroad, he asked me to marry him. I was a timid homebody and panicked at the idea of living overseas, of moving whenever the military said we had to. I couldn't handle it. I've regretted that every day because no one I met after him came close. That was my chance. That was my life calling me, Addie, and I ignored it because I didn't give myself credit for being able to evolve into more than I already was. I know now I could have handled it. And if I couldn't, I could have left him, older and wiser. But this way I'll never know. And there is no greater hell to live through than that." Her eyes filled with tears. She slammed her fist onto the table. "Go to him. Right now."

"Linda, I—"

She stopped Addie with an upraised hand.

"Go now. Before you change your mind. Trust me. Go." She leaned forward and took Addie's hand, looked earnestly into her eyes. "Do not even finish your carrot."

DEREK STOOD AT the helm of *Joie de Vivre,* having steered carefully out of the tiny Lahaina Harbor on Maui. He was heading northwest with his six passengers to explore the island of Molokai. This was one of his favorite trips, a full eleven days, with the passengers designing the itinerary. After Molokai, this group wanted to visit Lanai, then Hawaii. Usually he was in great spirits at the start of a trip, and today the weather was glorious: eighty-two degrees with full sun and calm water.

It might as well have been forty degrees with dense fog and towering seas.

Up until the minute he started *Joie de Vivre's* engines, he'd been hoping Addie would change her mind. Eleven days from then he was sure he'd still be hoping. Hell, next *year* he'd still be hoping. His bookkeeper, Mary, was due to go on maternity leave after they got back and he'd made arrangements to hire a temp rather than give up hope Addie would want the job.

He and Addie had agreed to keep in touch, but his last email on Wednesday morning had gone unanswered for four days. Four miserable minute-by-minute days. Derek had considered calling, but pride kept him from the phone. Addie knew he still wanted her, knew he still wanted to hear from her, still wanted her here with him. He wasn't going to beg.

Most likely.

Derek closed his eyes briefly against the pain, shaking his head. Listen to him. He missed her so deeply it was as if mini construction workers were hard at work 24/7 jackhammering his heart. Addie had turned him from the cool untouchable captain of his own soul into an obsessed pining wimp.

"Captain." The voice of Renard, his first mate, came from over his left shoulder. Derek hadn't heard him approach.

"Yes, Renard." Derek pulled himself up tall. Apparently he'd even started slumping. By tomorrow he'd probably have developed a permanent whine and half his teeth and hair would fall out.

She was killing him.

"Trouble down in your cabin, sir."

"In my cabin?"

"Trouble with a passenger. Jenny found her when she was cleaning, asleep in your bed."

Derek's mood blackened further. He knew exactly which passenger. The stacked blonde who'd gotten drunk at the welcome onboard dinner the night before and tried to fondle him under the table while her older husband sat right next to her, too wasted to notice.

Lovely people.

"Gene can handle her." His excursion leader was expert at dealing with difficult personalities.

"I've never seen him stopped by anyone before, sir. He claims this is something only you can manage."

Derek's lips tightened. This was ridiculous. "Unless her life is in some kind of danger, there is no reason he can't—"

"I'm...afraid it is, sir."

Derek stared at Renard incredulously. "Her life is in danger?"

"Uh. No, not really." The smaller man's dark eyes flicked to one side, then returned to his. Derek had the distinct impression Renard was amused, and it pissed him off further. "Thing is, sir, she insists on seeing you."

"Right." Derek nodded curtly, wanting to growl. Stupid diva theatrics. "Take the wheel."

"Yes, sir."

Derek banged through the bridge door, thudded down the narrow wood stairs, attempting a smile at one of the passengers making her way to the top deck. Once on the main deck, he strode to the captain's quarters, located in the bow of the ship.

At his door he hesitated, listening. No voices. Gene was nowhere to be found. Damn it. He shouldn't be leaving his captain to deal with this woman alone. Unless there were witnesses, whatever happened would be her word against his.

He knocked. "Hello?"

"Yes?" The voice was strangely high, oddly false sounding. The woman last night had a low smoker's voice. Was she trying to disguise it? "Is that Captain Derek?"

Captain Derek? "This is Captain Bates, what are you doing in my cabin?"

"Waiting for you." The caricature of a voice took on a breathy quality, probably meant to be seductive.

"Ma'am, there are plenty of other places on the ship where we can talk privately if you need to."

"*Talking* wasn't what I had in mind."

Derek rubbed his jaw. There was something very weird about this. Was one of his crew playing a trick on him? They knew better than to risk their jobs or the boat on a prank while their captain should be at the helm. He'd been through all the passengers in his mind, and besides the crazed smoker lady and her husband, there was a honeymooning couple and an older pair celebrating their retirement.

So who the *hell* was—

A thought occurred to him.

A beautiful, wonderful, fabulous thought.

He tested the brass door handle. Unlocked. He pushed it open. Went inside.

Addie.

Naked.

In his bed.

Derek was there in two steps, grabbing her to him, holding her, feeling her warmth, hearing her laugh at first, then dissolve into a couple of sobs he could tell she was struggling to control.

He kissed her. Her hair, her temple, the dimple in her cheek, then he found her mouth in a kiss that lit fires all the way through his body, and cemented her already strong hold on his heart.

He meant to talk to her, meant to discuss the situation, ask how long she was there for, whether she was really going to give their relationship a serious chance or if this was just a short visit.

But she was naked. In his bed. Kissing him as if she really, really meant it, and he was only human and definitely a man.

So in a very short time, his clothes were off and he'd joined her between the soft sheets, reveling in her skin against his, her mouth on his chest, on his neck, his hands stroking every part of her he could reach.

And when he moved over her beautiful body and entered her, they stared into each other's eyes in awe of what was between them, then reached hungrily toward each other and kissed as if they'd never stop, while their bodies heated and mated and made sounds of satisfaction and of deep forever-after love.

He rolled to one side to touch her clitoris, loving the noises she made, the sharp breaths, the gasps, the way her head writhed on his pillow. And when he knew she was close, when a flush covered her body and cheeks, he plunged back into her, sending her over an edge he fell over himself only a few seconds later.

Eventually…very eventually, the movement of the boat reminded him who and where he was. Captain Bates. On duty.

But Addie was with him.

"I can't believe you're here." He nuzzled her neck, inhaling her sweet scent.

"I can hardly believe it, either." She stroked his hair,

gazing up at him, starry-eyed, the most enchanting sight he'd ever seen. "I wasn't going to."

"That part I knew." He took her hand and covered his heart. "Leaving you nearly killed me."

"I know. I kept telling myself the pain would get better, that I'd done the right thing. And then life in New York, which I thought I needed, started to feel like a prison without you."

He couldn't believe he was hearing his over-and-over again fantasy, directly from her lips this time. "You quit your job? Left your apartment?"

"I didn't quit exactly. Not yet. I took vacation, sick time and a short leave. I have a few months to see how this goes." She wrinkled her nose self-consciously. "You know I'm not a risk taker."

"You were smart. We don't really know how we're going to do." He kissed her again, tasting the exquisite corner of her lips, the sweet roundness of her chin, as sure that they were right together as he'd been of anything in his life. That he belonged on the sea. That he was meant to own *Joie de Vivre*. "Though I'm giving us good odds."

"That's my job." She stretched against him, nearly making him hard again. He had a feeling he'd have to change his schedule for the first week or so, in order to include as much lovemaking as possible. "Speaking of which, is Mary's job still open or will I be your kept woman?"

"Her leave starts after this trip. So she'll have time to show you the ropes."

"Well, Mr. Captain. I've been reading about boat stuff. We sailors call them 'lines,' not 'ropes.'"

"Is that right?" He drew his finger down her full soft lips. "I can see you have a lot to teach me."

"I should think so."

He grinned, so overwhelmed by emotion he could hardly speak. "I'm so glad you're here, Addie."

"So you can get laid regularly?" Her eyes told him she was teasing, but he wondered if she knew.

"So I can tell you in person that I love you."

Surprise widened those eyes then emotion filled them with tears. "Oh, Derek."

"Too soon?"

"Would I be here if I thought you were a passing fling?"

He grinned. He would have liked to hear *I love you, too,* but her eyes were telling him loud and clear. His cautious woman could take all the time she needed. "Listen, I better call my crew and let them know I'm being unavoidably detained."

"They couldn't have been nicer to me. Paul called Renard and vouched for me, so they let me sneak on."

"Totally against ship's protocol."

"I should have asked you?"

He kissed her, getting hard again, thinking he'd give them about three months of sea-time bliss before he started shopping for an engagement ring. "Only the captain can give you permission to come aboard, Miss Sewell."

She turned to lie facing him, draped her leg over his hip and pressed herself intimately against his growing erection. "I'd like very much to come on board, Captain Bates. Then I'd like to come again. And again after that."

"Permission granted." He cupped her face in his hands, realizing that this boat he'd loved for so long had changed with Addie a part of her.

Now she very much felt like home.

* * * * *

Is there anything sexier than a hot cowboy?

How about four of them!

New York Times bestselling author
Vicki Lewis Thompson is back in the Blaze® lineup
for 2013, and this year she's offering her
readers *even more…*

Sons of Chance

Chance isn't just the last name of these rugged
Wyoming cowboys—it's their motto, too!

Saddle up with

I CROSS MY HEART
(June)

WILD AT HEART
(July)

THE HEART WON'T LIE
(August)

And the first full-length Sons of Chance
Christmas story

COWBOYS & ANGELS
(December)

Take a chance…on a Chance!

THE HEART WON'T LIE

BY
VICKI LEWIS THOMPSON

First published in Great Britain 2013
by Mills & Boon, an imprint of Harlequin (UK) Limited,
Eton House, 18-24 Paradise Road, Richmond, Surrey TW9 1SR

© Vicki Lewis Thompson 2013

ISBN: 978 0 263 90319 5
ebook ISBN: 978 1 408 99693 5

14-0813

Harlequin (UK) policy is to use papers that are natural, renewable and recyclable products and made from wood grown in sustainable forests. The logging and manufacturing processes conform to the legal environmental regulations of the country of origin.

Printed and bound in Spain
by Blackprint CPI, Barcelona

New York Times bestselling author **Vicki Lewis Thompson**'s love affair with cowboys started with the Lone Ranger, continued through Maverick and took a turn south of the border with Zorro. She views cowboys as the Western version of knights in shining armor—rugged men who value honor, honesty and hard work. Fortunately for her, she lives in the Arizona desert, where broad-shouldered, lean-hipped cowboys abound. Blessed with such an abundance of inspiration, she only hopes that she can do them justice. Visit her website, www.vickilewisthompson.com.

To Louis L'Amour, an author who claimed that, if necessary, he could write a story sitting in the median of a busy intersection. He's my kind of guy!

Prologue

August 13, 1988, from the diary of Eleanor Chance

MY GRANDSON JACK, who turns ten this fall, can be a trial at times. I cut him some slack because he still carries the scars from being abandoned by his mother when he was a toddler. I'm not sure if that wound is ever going to heal, no matter how much love we all give him.

Truth be told, Jack and I have a special bond because I took over raising him for a couple of years until my son Jonathon married his second wife, Sarah. I've stepped back now, because Sarah is terrific with Jack and the two sons who came along after that, Nick and Gabe. The Last Chance Ranch is a happier place with Sarah living here.

But Jack is still a handful. Even so, he'll always have a special place in my heart, and that's partly because we both love to read, especially Westerns. Whenever the real world gets too complicated for Jack, he escapes into a book. I just introduced him to one of my favorites, Louis L'Amour, and he's gobbling up those stories.

I remember doing the same when I first discovered

Louis L'Amour back in the fifties. That man could spin a yarn like nobody's business. I was so sad to hear that he'd died this past June, but he left us a whole lot of good reading, and I'm grateful for that.

Winters are dark and cold in Jackson Hole, and I don't know what I'd do without my Westerns. You can bet this winter both Jack and I will be curled up in front of the fire with a book. I envy Jack having all those Louis L'Amour stories ahead of him.

I may read them all again, myself. I should probably try one of the new authors, like that Larry McMurtry everyone's so keen on. But it just seems as if nobody quite comes up to Louis L'Amour.

1

Present day

"WHAT NAME DO you want to go by while you're at the ranch?"

Michael James Hartford, aka Western writer Jim Ford, thought about how to answer Jack Chance, who was currently driving him to the Last Chance Ranch. Michael had flown to Wyoming from New York City so he could learn some cowboy basics before a publicity team put him in front of a video camera in three weeks. Nobody besides Jack was supposed to know Michael was also Jim Ford, who wrote as if he could ride and rope but…couldn't.

He wondered if he should be known as Mike while he was here. A shortened name seemed better for a cowboy, but he already had his Jim Ford persona. If he adopted too many alternate names he wouldn't remember which one he should answer to. "Michael's fine," he said. "Michael Hartford. That shouldn't tip anybody off."

"Michael Hartford it is, then. I don't think you have

anything to worry about, though. Some of the hands have read your books, but they'd never believe a greenhorn like you could possibly be the guy who writes those stories."

"Yeah, I know." Michael took the blow to his ego with good humor. His lack of cowboying skills really was an embarrassing joke.

"Besides, the picture in the back of your books shows you with a mustache. That really changes how a guy looks."

"I grow that mustache before I have to make any appearances or get my picture taken. Then I shave it off. I'll have to start growing it again next week. Between that and the Stetson, I've fooled just about everybody except my family, and they're not about to broadcast the fact that I'm Jim Ford."

"I don't get that. You'd think they'd be proud of you."

Michael laughed. "They would be if I wrote deep, philosophical literature. The Hartfords are old money, loaded to the gills with culture. They don't want to claim a pulp fiction author. That's actually worked to my advantage. If nobody knows who Jim Ford really is, then nobody knows that he's never been on a horse in his life."

"That still boggles my mind. You write as if you're a real cowboy. I would have sworn you'd done all those things. What's your secret?"

"Research." Michael felt good knowing he'd managed to get it right, despite his lack of experience. "Plus I grew up reading Louis L'Amour."

"Me, too. I didn't think I'd find his equal, but you've

hooked me real good. I wish my grandmother was still alive. She would have loved your books, too."

"Thank you. That's high praise."

"I mean it sincerely." Jack shook his head. "But I can't figure you out. The way you write, I can tell you love the idea of being a cowboy. How come you never got the itch to spend time on a ranch?"

"You hit the nail on the head. I love the *idea* of being a cowboy, but I've avoided the reality, in case it doesn't live up to my image of it." *Or I don't.* "I'm selling a fantasy, and if I discover that fantasy doesn't exist…"

"Damnation. You mean this visit could burst your bubble? I don't want that on my conscience."

"Hey, Jack, you're not the one forcing me into this. The publicity department is to blame." He blew out a breath. "No, that's not right, either. I created this stupid situation all on my own. I chose to write about a world I don't know firsthand, and then I accidentally became a big success at it."

Jack nodded. "I noticed. Your name keeps getting bigger on the cover."

"If my books weren't selling so well the publisher would never pay for a video of me playing cowboy. My secret would be safe. But they made it clear I need to do this video if I expect continued support from the marketing team."

Smiling, Jack glanced over at him. "Cheer up, little buckaroo. It won't be so bad."

"Easy for you to say. I'm going to make a damned fool of myself, and you know it."

"Maybe so, but I'll be the only one who'll know it. Your lessons will be as private as I can make them."

"Thank you for that." Michael relaxed a little. "Bethany told me I could trust you." He'd met motivational author Bethany Grace on the Opal Knightly TV talk show and they'd kept in touch. When he'd needed riding lessons on the QT he'd thought of her, because she'd grown up in Jackson Hole.

"Bethany's good people," Jack said. "Did you catch her wedding to Nash Bledsoe on Opal's show?"

"Sure did. Nash is a friend of yours, right?"

"Yep." Jack checked his mirrors before pulling around a slow-moving semi. "Nash owns a little spread next door to the Last Chance."

"Bethany mentioned that. She inherited it, sold it to Nash and the rest reads like a romance novel."

Jack chuckled. "It does, at that. Poor Nash, though, having to get hitched on national TV. There was some talk of me being the best man at that shindig, but it was way better for Nash's dad to have that honor."

Michael was beginning to get a bead on Jack's personality so he made a calculated guess. "You didn't want to do it, did you?"

"*Hell,* no. Not after I found out I had to wear *makeup.*" Jack grimaced.

"It's not so bad, little buckaroo."

"Maybe not for a city slicker like yourself, but real cowboys don't wear makeup."

"What about your friend Nash? I guarantee he had on makeup during that wedding."

"Only because otherwise he wouldn't get to marry Bethany. Bethany was beholden to Opal for letting her out of her TV contract, and Opal was determined to stage that wedding on TV."

"What a guy won't do for love." As he said it, Michael realized he had no personal experience to go by, and that was a damned shame.

"Ain't it the truth. My wife, Josie, has got me wrapped around her little finger. Between her and my kid, Archie, I'm like a bull with a ring in its nose. They can lead me anywhere."

Michael grinned. "I seriously doubt that."

"No, really. They've got me hog-tied. How about you? Is there some citified lady calling the shots in your life?"

"Nope."

"Too busy?"

"Kind of, but that's not really the problem. The high-society women I meet don't interest me, but I can't date the ones I meet as Jim Ford because they think I'm a cowboy, which I'm not." He didn't like being caught between worlds, not belonging in either one, but he hadn't figured out what to do about it. He envied a guy like Jack, who knew who he was and where he fit in.

Jack tapped his fingers against the steering wheel. "But you will be a cowboy."

Michael felt a jolt of pleasure at the possibility. But he had to be realistic. "In a week? Not likely."

"Are you doubting my ability?"

"No, I'm doubting mine."

"Well, cut that out right now. First and foremost, a cowboy faces every challenge with an air of quiet confidence."

"Of course he does, especially if he's a hero in one of my books." Michael looked over at Jack and expected they'd share a laugh over that. Instead, Jack seemed totally serious. "Wait, you're not kidding, are you?"

"No, I'm not. Being a cowboy is a state of mind. You can start working on your attitude before you ever put your booted foot in a stirrup."

"I see." Michael was fascinated. For years he'd assumed that the larger-than-life cowboys in his books didn't exist in reality. But Jack Chance was proving that assumption had been dead wrong.

AFTER A YEAR working as the housekeeper at the Last Chance's main house, Keri Fitzpatrick, former Baltimore socialite, could wield a mean mop. She'd learned the basics from her boss, Sarah Chance, and the cook, Mary Lou Simms. Following their instructions, Keri could clean windows like nobody's business and polish bathroom fixtures until they sparkled like fine silver.

But she'd challenge anybody, even a professional armed with power equipment, to eliminate some mysterious smell left by eight adolescent boys. They'd been part of the Last Chance's summer program for disadvantaged youths, and they'd moved out early that morning. She'd been cleaning nonstop ever since except for a short lunch break with Mary Lou.

The second floor, where the boys had slept in two rooms fitted with bunk beds, was warm, and she dripped with sweat. Putting her hair in a ponytail to get it off her neck hadn't helped cool her off much. She'd opted for jeans instead of shorts because she'd anticipated getting on her hands and knees for this job.

Sure enough, she'd had to clean some gunk off the baseboards. God knew what it was. She'd dealt with this last August right after being hired, but she was sure the previous year's batch of kids hadn't left a stink this bad. She'd noticed a slight odor yesterday, but had thought it would leave with the kids. Instead, it was worse.

Glancing at her watch, she gasped. The wealthy tenderfoot from New York City was due any minute. She'd been told very little about him, but Jack had said the guy was used to the best.

Keri had been raised in luxury, too. Although she didn't live that way now, she knew exactly how to prepare guest quarters for a wealthy man. She'd spit-shined his room, which was at the other end of the hall, right across from her room. The crockery vase of wildflowers she'd placed on his dresser gave off a delicate aroma.

The poor things couldn't begin to compete with the stench coming from the boys' rooms. She'd already tested the situation, and the entire top floor, including the tenderfoot's room, smelled like a garbage dump. Opening all the windows hadn't made a dent in the foul odor.

Desperate to find the source, she went through everything again—closets, drawers, even under the bunk beds. Finally she found a kitchen matchbox crammed so far under one of the bunks that she'd missed it when she'd swept and mopped. Using a broom, she nudged it free and nearly gagged. She'd found her culprit.

She shouldn't have looked, but after all this effort, she wanted to know what was in that box. As she slid open the matchbox, the smell got worse. She stared at a very fragrant, and very dead, mouse. It rested on a carefully folded tissue, and a second tissue covered the lower part of its body, so only the head was exposed.

Guessing what had happened wasn't hard. She'd been around the boys enough to understand how their minds worked. They'd found the dead mouse, decided it deserved a decent burial and put it in the matchbox. Then they'd forgotten all about it.

Now what? She could throw it in the trash, but that seemed wrong. They'd folded the tissues so carefully, and she was touched by their concern for the little creature's final resting place. Silly as it seemed, she wanted to bury it the way they'd intended.

Okay, so she would. Holding the box, she walked into the hall. She didn't dare take the smelly thing down the back stairs and through Mary Lou's pristine kitchen, so she made for the curved stairway leading to the front door. If she was very lucky she could get rid of the dead mouse before the tenderfoot arrived.

Luck was not on her side. The front door opened and Jack Chance ushered a broad-shouldered man through it. From this angle he didn't look like a tenderfoot. His jeans were slightly worn and his blue chambray shirt was faded. His leather suitcase was scuffed up some, and even his hat seemed broken in. If she didn't know better, she'd think this was a seasoned cowboy, and a nicely built one, at that.

Jack closed the door behind them. "I'll take you straight upstairs so you can get settled in before dinner."

As Keri froze in position, unsure whether to go up or down, Jack spotted her. "Ah, Keri! Perfect! You can show Michael to his room. Michael Hartford, this is Keri Fitzpatrick, our housekeeper. I'm sure she has your room all ready."

Michael Hartford glanced up. "Nice to meet you, Keri."

"Nice to meet you, too." Whoa. Cute guy. Square jaw, strong nose and dreamy eyes that were an unusual blue-gray color. He looked vaguely familiar, too, although she was sure she didn't know anybody named Michael Hartford.

She'd love to show him to his room, but not while she was holding an extremely dead mouse. "Um, Jack, before I show Mr. Hartford to his room, I need to—"

"What's that godawful smell?" Jack wrinkled his nose.

"I found a dead mouse under one of the bunks."

"It's in that box?"

"Yes, and I—"

"Let me have it." Jack started up the stairs. "I'll throw it in the trash."

Although it might not be wise to disagree with the man who signed her paycheck, Keri couldn't let him take the mouse. "That's okay. I'm going to bury it out back. I won't be a minute. The guest room is all ready." She started down the stairs.

"You're going to do *what?*" Blocking her passage, Jack shoved his hat back with his thumb as he stared up at her.

She paused on the step above him. "Bury it." Jack could be intimidating, but she'd also seen him melt whenever he was with Archie, his little son. Jack had marshmallow insides. "The boys fixed it up with tissues and everything, like it was in a little coffin."

Jack's mouth twitched and amusement flickered in his dark eyes. "Keri, those boys are gone. They'll never know what happened to the mouse. Besides, they obviously forgot all about this burial they'd planned."

"I realize that, but it was a sweet impulse, a sign they cared for this little creature. I think it proves that they made progress while they were here, and I'd like to carry out their wishes."

"Or else it was meant as a joke."

"I prefer to believe it was sincere."

"All righty, then." Jack moved aside to let her pass. "Bury it deep. Put a few stones on top. That thing stinks to high heaven and I don't want the dogs digging it up."

"I'll dig a deep hole." She gave their visitor a quick smile as she walked past him. "Welcome to the Last Chance Ranch, Mr. Hartford. Sorry about the dead mouse."

He smiled back. "May it rest in peace."

"That's the idea." She held his gaze for a little longer than was polite, but he had such beautiful eyes, especially when they were lit up with that warm smile of his. She hoped he wouldn't always associate meeting her with the smell of dead animals.

2

AFTER HIS INTRODUCTION to Keri Fitzpatrick, Michael decided he was going to like it here. Most women he knew would refuse to deal with a dead rodent, and if forced to do so, would grab the first opportunity to get rid of it. Instead, Keri had held on to the stinky mouse because she respected the impulse that had caused someone to tuck it into a matchbox.

He would have admired her spunky behavior whether she'd been pretty or not, but she *was* pretty, which made the encounter even better. He'd thoroughly enjoyed those few seconds of gazing into her vivid green eyes. The fact that she was flushed and sweaty made her eyes even brighter and her dark hair more tempting as it escaped from her ponytail and curled damply at her neck.

Her disheveled state probably wasn't her favorite way to greet visitors, but she hadn't bothered to apologize for how she looked. She'd only been concerned about the foul smell of a decaying animal. Good thing he didn't have a weak stomach.

"Sorry about that," Jack said. "Ready to go up?"

"You bet." Michael wanted to ask about Keri. The

scene with the dead mouse had charmed him, and when she'd spoken he'd heard a familiar accent. She was from back east somewhere. Not New York, but close.

He'd felt an instant attraction, and her steady gaze had told him she'd been drawn to him, too. But he didn't ask Jack about her, because that would imply he was intrigued. Maybe he was, but he was here to learn riding and roping skills, not romance the housekeeper.

Pursuing her would be a rotten way to repay the Last Chance's generous hospitality. Besides, it would be totally out of character for him. He wasn't a sexual opportunist, ready to make a move on any good-looking woman he ran across.

"The smell should fade in a bit," Jack said. "At least you'll be at the other end of the hall. The boys stayed down there." He gestured to his right as he topped the stairs. "It'll be a lot more peaceful up here now that they're gone."

"Will you miss them?"

Jack glanced at him. "Interesting that you should ask. I will miss those varmints. When they're here, I'm ready to tear my hair out, but when they leave, the place seems too quiet."

"I can imagine. All that energy must grow on you." Michael was impressed by what he'd heard of the program, which Jack had casually described during the ride from the airport.

Judging from the offhand way Jack had talked about it, he'd only intended to give Michael some background in case the subject came up while he was at the ranch. But Michael had made a mental note to donate to the cause. Jack had refused to charge anything for this week because he claimed it was an honor to tutor his favorite living author. So Michael would reimburse Jack in a different way, one the cowboy couldn't refuse.

"We had to shovel them out of here, though," Jack said, "to make room for wedding guests arriving at the end of the week."

"Right. The wedding." Bethany had told Michael that Sarah, the ranch's matriarch, was marrying Peter Beckett. Sarah had been widowed several years ago, and everyone seemed thrilled that she'd fallen in love again. "I'm still worried that I'm here at a bad time."

"No, you're here at a good time." Jack grinned as they headed down the hall. "Much as I love my mother and respect Pete, I hate all the fuss and bother that goes into the planning stages of a wedding. You're the perfect excuse to get me out of that. Come Saturday I'll dress up and play my role, but until then I'm busy with an important pupil."

Michael had an uneasy moment. "Why am I so important? I thought nobody knows who I am."

"Don't worry. They don't. But you're Bethany's friend. Nash is like family, and Bethany married Nash, so now Bethany's like family, too. So any friend of Bethany's is a friend of ours."

"I see." Apparently the right connections mattered in the West just as they mattered back east.

"Here's your room. Used to be mine before I got married, but the furniture's all different." Jack walked through a door on the left side of the hallway.

Michael followed him into a large room decorated in shades of green. He noticed a king-size bed and a spectacular view of the Grand Tetons. The jagged peaks still had a smattering of snow, even in August. "Very nice."

"I like it. Looks like Keri picked you some wild-flowers."

Michael had been captured by the view of the mountains, but now he noticed that a bouquet of Indian paint-brush and purple lupine sat on the dresser. "That was thoughtful." Research for his books had taught him what they were, because he wouldn't have had a clue otherwise.

"Yeah, Keri's a gem. She thinks of those things. Don't look for an attached bath, though. The bathroom's right next door, but connecting it would be tricky. The bathtub would get in the way of cutting a door between the rooms. I doubt you're used to walking out into the hall, but it can't be helped."

"Jack, the view from the window is spectacular. I couldn't care less about an attached bath."

"Good." Jack seemed pleased by that. "I'll leave you to unpack, then. Dinner's at six, but you can explore the place before then if you want. I have some issues to handle, but Keri should be back from the mouse funeral soon. If you need a guide, I'm sure she'd be glad to show you around."

"Great." Michael was careful not to sound too eager about having Keri do him that favor. "And thanks, Jack."

"Don't thank me yet. Tomorrow, when your butt's sore from spending hours on a horse and you ache all over, you may not be so thankful."

"I thought you said it wouldn't be too bad?"

Jack smiled. "I didn't want you to panic." Then he turned on his booted heel and left the room.

Some exit line. And thanks to that line, anxiety had him firmly in its grip. What the hell did he think he was doing? Nobody could learn to be a cowboy in a week.

Despite the help from Jack, he could end up falling off his horse during the shooting of the video. That would be embarrassing as hell, both to him and to the publicist. He should have confessed his shortcomings to the gung-ho woman who'd called him with feverish excitement to propose the video they would shoot in three weeks.

Michael could have told her the truth and suggested they drop the idea. Some still shots might work if they found a docile horse for him. But no, he hadn't said those things because he'd wanted to preserve the mystique. Ego, pure and simple.

With a sigh, he walked over to the window and looked out at the majestic Tetons. He should have come to this part of the country years ago. A summer on a dude ranch would have given him what he needed and he wouldn't be in this fix now.

But he hadn't admitted all his fears to Jack. He was deathly afraid that he wouldn't have any talent for being a cowboy, no matter how long he worked at it. By cramming his lessons into a week, he could excuse himself if he failed. If he'd taken an entire summer and failed, he'd have been forced to conclude that he wasn't cut out for the life he wrote about so convincingly.

That would be a tough pill to swallow. He wasn't sure how that would affect his writing, but he had a hunch it would make a dramatic difference. If he'd never tried to be a real cowboy, then he could hang on to the illusion that such a thing might be possible.

"Mr. Hartford?"

He turned from the window and discovered Keri standing in the doorway. "Call me Michael, okay?"

"All right, if that's what you'd prefer. Is there anything you need? I ducked out on my job, but I'm available now."

"Has the mouse received a decent burial?"

"It was quick, but I think the boys would have been satisfied." She studied him. "It's the strangest thing, but I feel as if I know you from somewhere. I don't, do I?"

He didn't dare ask if she read Westerns, but this was the very thing he'd worried about. "I doubt it. I have one of those faces. People often think they know me."

"Maybe, but I've seen you somewhere. I'll figure it out."

That settled one thing for sure. He wouldn't start growing his mustache while he was here.

"So, is everything to your liking? Have you checked out the towel supply in the bathroom?"

"I'm sure it's fine." He still couldn't quite place her accent.

"What's your pillow preference? You currently have down, but I can substitute polyester fill if you're allergic."

"Not allergic. I'm pretty low maintenance." He had a feeling she was, too. She'd hurried right back without stopping to primp.

"Then I'll quit pestering you and let you settle in. If there's anything you need, my room's right across the hall."

"It is?"

"I know. It's not the usual thing to have the employees stay on the same floor as the guests, but Sarah never planned on having more help than Mary Lou, the cook. Then the boys came, which made extra work. When they hired me last summer, they put me up here."

"Do we…uh…share a bathroom?" That could get quite cozy.

"No, we don't. That one is all yours. Last fall Jack renovated my space and installed a small bathroom. He also put one in between the boys' rooms, but it's tiny, too. The nicest one is yours." She backed toward the door. "Let me know if you need anything, though. Seriously."

"Jack said you might give me a tour of the house."

"He did?" She glanced down at her clothes. Without saying a word, she'd managed to communicate her desperate hope for a shower and change of outfit.

"But it can wait until you get cleaned up."

Relief showed in her green eyes. "Thank you. I feel gross. Give me fifteen minutes."

"I'll give you thirty. Listen, I've been trying to place your accent. Where are you from?"

"Baltimore. See you in twenty minutes." Flashing her bright smile, she turned and walked across the hall.

He gazed after her. He had a hunch she hadn't been a housekeeper back in Baltimore. Everybody had a story, and he wanted to know hers.

KERI RETREATED TO her room so she could give herself a good talking to while she showered off the grime. She was attracted to Michael, and she needed to put a lid on that inconvenient attraction ASAP. She was a member of the staff, which meant no fraternizing with the guests.

Nobody had told her that in so many words, but she'd been on the other end of the social spectrum. Her parents would have fired any maid who'd shown interest in a houseguest. It just wasn't done.

The Chances hadn't turned this upstairs bedroom into housekeeper's quarters so that she could mingle with the guests. They'd put her here because it was the only space available that also could be plumbed for a small bathroom. If she happened to be across the hall from the extremely good-looking Michael Hartford, she didn't have to emphasize the fact. God knew what he'd thought when she'd mentioned how close she was to his room.

When she took him on a tour, she'd establish more distance between them. The whole mouse incident had thrown her off and made her forget her position here. She'd even pushed the issue of burying the little rodent when Jack had clearly thought that was nonsense, and she'd made her stand in front of Michael. She'd apologize to Jack about that.

After years of being at the top of the social pecking order, she sometimes forgot that she wasn't there now, at least not in Jackson Hole. Then again, the Chance family didn't stand on ceremony with their employees. Back home, the household help wouldn't dream of calling their employers by their first names. At the Last Chance, first names were all anybody used.

That made it easy for her to forget that she wasn't in charge around here. She figured the Chances understood why she slipped up sometimes, though. They all knew that anytime she chose, she could tap into her trust fund. She was proud to say she hadn't needed to.

Eighteen months ago, on New Year's Eve, she'd scandalized Baltimore society by engaging in an epic girl fight at a ritzy party. Selena had started it, and Keri had finished it. Pictures of the fight had shown up on Facebook, and somehow Keri had become the villain of the piece.

When she could no longer be effective in her job at a Baltimore PR firm because of the gossip, she'd decided that a change of scenery might be a good idea. Wyoming had seemed far enough away to accomplish that, and she'd loved the area when the family had come for ski vacations. She'd flown to Jackson, rented a car and searched for a job.

Lucky for her, the Last Chance had taken her on, and instinct had told her to grab the opportunity. Sure, she could have lived off her trust fund while she was in Jackson Hole, but she'd wanted to see if she could make it on her own. She'd been a trust-fund baby for too long, and she hadn't realized how that steady income had undermined her confidence.

Earning a living without depending on anything but her own grit and determination had boosted her morale quite a bit. She didn't miss her old life much. She'd only intended to be here a few months, until the gossip had died down, but the place had grown on her.

Theoretically she could go back to Baltimore anytime, because according to her parents, nobody mentioned the incident anymore. But Keri found herself looking for excuses to stay at the ranch. They'd needed her when the boys had arrived in June, and now they needed her to help with the wedding guests.

Come winter, her services wouldn't be so critical. She could give her notice then, which would allow them plenty of time to find a new housekeeper. She loved living on the ranch, but she didn't intend to be a cleaning lady for the rest of her working life. What she did want was still up for debate.

She showered in record time, and true to her word, she made it out of her room and back over to Michael's in twenty minutes. She'd even managed to blow-dry her hair. Getting dressed was easy these days. Jeans, a T-shirt, running shoes. She no longer spent much time on makeup, either.

Some fancier outfits hung in her closet, but she had no reason to wear them. Once in a while she longed for a reason to put on party clothes, but people didn't do that much at the ranch, or in the little town of Shoshone ten miles down the road. She'd accepted dates with some of the ranch hands, but jeans were fine for the Spirits and Spurs in Shoshone. Those dates hadn't resulted in any wild love affairs, either.

Maybe that explained her attraction to Michael. He hailed from her neck of the woods, and she felt that gave them something in common that she didn't have with everyone here. As she rapped on his door frame to announce her presence, she cautioned herself to be very careful. She might not want to keep this job forever, but she didn't want to be booted out for inappropriate behavior, either.

Michael closed a drawer and turned. He'd taken off his hat and it lay on the bed, brim side down. She'd have to tell him to flip it the other way, which preserved the shape better.

He glanced at the clock sitting on top of the dresser. "Twenty minutes, and you're showered and changed. I don't think I know any woman who could accomplish that."

"It's the simplicity of the existence here. Ranch life can be complicated sometimes, but getting dressed for it isn't."

"Maybe not if you've been here long enough." He gestured toward his shirt, jeans and boots. "This outfit took an enormous amount of effort."

"It did? Why?"

"I didn't want to look like I just stepped out of a Western wear store, so I had someone rough these things up a bit. Everything's been artificially distressed so it looks as if I've been out riding the trails and roping those doggies."

She pressed her lips together, not sure if she was supposed to find that funny or not.

"It's okay. You can laugh. It makes me laugh, too."

"Whoever worked on it did a good job. When you walked through the front door, I thought you were the real deal."

"I'm not, but maybe Jack will whip me into shape."

"I'm sure he will, but why are you…" She caught herself just in time. Her question was inappropriate coming from a staff member.

"Why am I doing this?"

She shook her head. "Forget I asked. It's none of my business."

"Well, it's complicated."

"Really, you don't have to explain."

"I know, but it's a legitimate question. All my life I've wanted to be a cowboy. I can't really be one because my life is in New York City. But this week, I'll at least find out if I have what it takes."

"I completely understand that." Yep, that feeling of connection was snapping into place. She'd come out here to get away from gossip, but she'd stayed because she wanted to see if she had what it took to live in a completely different environment.

She was testing herself, and apparently, so was he. She admired that impulse to seek a different path from the one you were born to. Talking about that with him would make for interesting conversation. Maybe someday, when they were both back in their normal environments…but that was getting way ahead of the game.

"I believe that you do understand. I'll take a wild guess that you might have some similar reasons for being in Wyoming."

"Good guess." But she wouldn't elaborate, because the more they exchanged confidences now, the stronger the link between them. And now was not the time for making a connection. "Let's go see the rest of the house."

3

KERI WAS AN excellent tour guide, and Michael was interested in the history of the massive two-story ranch house with its sturdy log construction. But he was even more interested in Keri and why she'd left Baltimore to come out here. Whatever the reason, she'd adapted with a can-do attitude that both attracted and inspired him.

She kept the focus on the ranch, though, and he couldn't figure out how to question her without being intrusive. He learned about the grandparents, Archie and Nelsie Chance, who'd homesteaded the place in the thirties. As a storyteller, he appreciated the tale of how they'd taken a run-down place and created a gem that was now worth millions to their heirs. Jack was the oldest grandson, followed by Nick, a veterinarian, and Gabe, who specialized in showing the registered Paints bred and trained at the Last Chance. Raising cattle had been abandoned for the horse business.

Keri proudly showed off the awards Gabe had won, all displayed in a case in the large living room, which was anchored by a great stone fireplace. The leather furniture and wagon-wheel chandelier were the sort of rustic touches Michael often included in his books. He was gratified to find out that in this, too, he'd gotten it right.

But whenever he tried to turn the conversation in the direction of Keri's background, she dodged away. Close to six o'clock, she took him into a large dining room at the end of the house's left wing. His bedroom would be directly above it.

She gestured to four round tables, each of which could seat eight people. "This is where everyone gathers for lunch," she said. "That includes the ranch hands and as many members of the Chance family as are available. It's a tradition to get together for the noon meal and exchange information about ranch business."

"Do you eat lunch here, then?"

"That depends on whether Mary Lou needs my help. When the boys were here, they also ate in the dining room, so Mary Lou needed me to serve and clear."

"But now?"

"I grabbed a quick lunch in the kitchen today because I had so much cleaning to do, but tomorrow I'll probably eat here. Mary Lou may join everyone, too, at least for a few days until the wedding guests arrive. Then it'll get busy again."

Michael felt ridiculously pleased that he'd see her at lunch tomorrow. Between now and then he planned to do some research on the internet. Social media could be a pain in the ass, but through it he might be able to get a bead on Keri Fitzpatrick.

A regal woman with silver hair walked out of the kitchen. She wore jeans and a Western blouse, nothing fancy, but she had an air of command about her.

"I thought I heard voices." She walked forward, hand extended. "You must be Michael Hartford, Bethany's friend."

"And you must be Sarah Chance." He clasped her hand and felt the firm grip of a woman who was as sure of her place in the world as Jack was of his. Bethany had told him that Sarah was the reigning queen of the neighborhood, and Michael began to see why.

"That's right." She smiled at him. "Looks like Keri's been showing you around. Thanks for doing that, Keri. I've been a little distracted today. Pete wants to fly in floral arrangements from Hawaii, and I want wildflowers. I do believe it's our first fight."

Michael spoke without thinking. "Wildflowers." Then he realized he didn't have a vote. "Forget that. It's not my place to—"

"Hey, I'll take all the support I can get." Sarah glanced at Keri. "What do you think?"

"I agree with Michael. This is Wyoming. You need wildflowers, not some exotic tropical arrangement. But I'll bet Pete wants to do something extravagant because he's so happy. It's sweet, really."

"It is sweet." Sarah's blue eyes grew soft. "So maybe I'll let him order a tropical bouquet for me to carry, and the altar can be decked with wildflowers. How's that?"

"Perfect," Keri said. "Great compromise. And now, if you'll excuse me, I'll go in and see if Mary Lou needs any help in the kitchen." Just like that, she was gone.

Sarah turned to him. "How about a drink before dinner?"

"Sounds good." Not as good as following Keri into the kitchen, but he had no excuse to do that. Guests probably weren't allowed to help out, and he'd be worthless at it, anyway.

"Let's go back into the living room." She led him down the hall past a rogue's gallery of family pictures. "Pete should be here soon. He had some errands in town. Jack and Josie are coming, too. They've left little Archie over at Gabe and Morgan's house." She paused. "Here I am rattling off names, and I have no idea if you know who I'm talking about. Did Bethany fill you in at all?"

"I know the names of your sons, and Jack mentioned Josie and little Archie on the drive in."

"Morgan is Gabe's wife, and they have two kids, a girl and a boy. Nick is married to Dominique, and they have one adopted boy. All three of my sons have built their own homes on ranch land, and I love having them so close."

"You have quite a legacy here, Sarah."

"Thanks to Archie and Nelsie." She gestured around the living room as they walked in. "I married into this, so I can't take any credit for it."

"That's not what Keri said. She told me that you're the lynchpin holding everything together."

"Did she? What a nice thing for her to say." Sarah moved over to the liquor cabinet. "I do like that woman. I wish she'd stay on, but I can't expect someone with her background to be a housekeeper much longer."

"She's leaving?" Michael felt a moment of panic. If she took off tomorrow or the next day, he'd never have a chance to learn more about her.

"Oh, not right away, but she will. I think she's waiting until after the wedding, which is considerate." She opened the hand-carved liquor cabinet. "What would you like?"

"Two fingers of Scotch, if you have it."

"We do." In moments she'd poured herself a glass of red wine and given Michael a squat tumbler containing ice and his requested Scotch. "Here's to friendship."

"To friendship, and to your generosity in letting me stay here the week before your wedding."

She touched her glass to his and took a sip. "I'm thrilled you're here. Jack needed something to do this week, so your arrival is perfect. If he didn't have you to distract him, he'd be underfoot. He pretends not to like the preparation stage, but he can't keep his nose out of things, either."

Good thing Michael hadn't been drinking when she'd said that or he might have choked on his Scotch. No wonder Sarah was considered the lynchpin of the family. She understood people better than some CEOs he'd met.

She gestured toward the leather chairs positioned in front of the fireplace. "Let's sit. It's too warm for a fire, but we tend to gather here and stare at the cold grate, anyway. Habit, I guess." She settled into one of the leather armchairs.

Michael took the one next to her. "Great chair."

"Thanks."

"And even without a fire, the stonework is worth looking at."

"My father-in-law was a talented man." She turned to Michael. "I'm curious. What prompted you to ask for riding and roping lessons?"

Michael decided to give her the same answer he'd

given Keri. It was the truth, so far as it went. "Like a lot of guys, I've always wanted to be a cowboy."

She studied him for a moment. "It's not as glamorous as it looks from the outside."

"I'm sure it's not, which is why I don't plan to actually be one. But learning some of the skills will be... interesting."

She smiled. "I notice you didn't say it would be fun."

"Yeah, well, I don't know if it will be or not, but I have to try."

"I think it will be fun for you. I hope so, because you're obviously interested in giving it a shot. But Jack's a taskmaster."

"I'm not surprised to hear that." Michael took another taste of his Scotch, which was excellent.

"I think we have some liniment upstairs, and probably Epsom salts, too. Have Keri find those for you."

"Okay." He decided that was as good an opening as any. "If I'm being too nosy, just say so, but why are you so sure Keri will leave? What is her background?"

"She didn't tell you?"

"No, just that she's from Baltimore."

Sarah hesitated. "I shouldn't have mentioned that I think she'll leave. I'll blame being distracted by the wedding for letting that comment slip out. But since I did mention it, I can understand why you'd be curious. So I'll just say that she comes from a very privileged background." She glanced at him. "Probably much like yours, in fact."

"Yet she's working as a housekeeper."

"Yes, and her reasons are hers to tell."

"I don't think she will tell me."

Sarah met his gaze. "That's up to her, then."

Michael had no choice but to drop the subject. He asked about her grandchildren, a topic she clearly loved, and Keri wasn't mentioned again. Later on, Sarah's fiancé arrived, followed by Jack and his wife, Josie.

During their meal in the smaller dining room adjacent to the larger one used for lunch, Michael thought he did a pretty decent job of focusing on his four dinner partners. Pete Beckett, Sarah's fiancé, was tall, lean and had a great sense of humor. Josie, an attractive blonde, dressed like a cowgirl and wore her long hair in a braid down her back. Jack obviously needed a strong woman to balance his tendency to take charge, and Josie seemed to fit the bill. Michael liked them all, but his thoughts stayed with Keri.

The ranch cook, a middle-aged woman named Mary Lou, served the meal. But Michael knew that Keri had helped prepare it, and he kept hoping she'd show up at some point. She didn't, but he could hear the faint sounds of feminine laughter coming from the kitchen, along with a man's voice.

Michael wondered who was in that kitchen with Mary Lou and Keri. For all he knew, Keri was involved with one of the ranch hands. It shouldn't matter to him. Unfortunately for his peace of mind, it did.

THE DINERS HAD LEFT, the dining table had been cleared and Keri sat with Mary Lou in the kitchen. They'd been joined by Watkins, a ranch hand who was also Mary Lou's husband as of the previous summer. All three of them were enjoying a leisurely moment over dessert and coffee.

"Mary Lou, nobody can make a chocolate cake like you can." Keri pushed back her chair. "I'm having a second piece."

"Believe I'll have a second piece of that cake, myself." Watkins rose from his chair.

"Hold on there, cowboy." Mary Lou caught his arm and pulled him back down. "Your jeans are getting a might snug."

Watkins sighed and resumed his seat. "That's a fact, but it ain't fair." He used a napkin to wipe cake crumbs off his handlebar mustache. "Keri eats and eats, and she doesn't gain a pound. I just look at a second piece of cake and I have to let out my belt another hole."

"That's because Keri is twenty-seven and you're fifty-four," Mary Lou said. "Your metabolism is slower."

"That may be, Lou-Lou, but the rest of me hasn't lost a step." He winked at Mary Lou. Although they'd only been married a year, he'd been after her for a long time before that, and his delight at finally getting her was obvious.

Mary Lou rolled her eyes. "There you go again, bragging on yourself." But she said it with a smile. Then she glanced at Keri. "I thought you were getting more cake?"

"I don't really need it."

"Don't give it up just because Watkins will stare at you mournfully while you eat it. Be strong. Claim your cake."

"I will stare at her mournfully, too," Watkins said. "That is the best damn cake in the world."

"Oh, for crying out loud!" Mary Lou picked up his plate and hers. "I'll cut you a tiny slice, you whiny baby.

You can eat it slow. And I'll have some more, while I'm at it. Give me your plate, Keri. Might as well cut them all at once."

Keri grinned and handed over her plate. "Thanks, Mary Lou. Make it this big." She held her thumb and forefinger about two inches apart.

Watkins shook his head. "I don't know where you put it all, girl."

"It's the grave digging," Mary Lou said as she uncovered the cake and started slicing. "Keeps a person slim and trim."

"I guess I'll never live that down, will I?" Keri didn't mind the teasing, though. Mary Lou only teased the people she liked.

"You not only buried him, you erected a monument." Mary Lou set a good-size piece of cake in front of Keri, a medium-size one for herself and a sliver in front of Watkins, who made a face.

Keri picked up her fork. "Jack asked me to make sure the dogs couldn't dig it up."

Watkins laughed. "They sure as hell won't after you piled about twenty-five rocks on it. You'd need a backhoe to get that varmint out of the ground, now."

"But at least we know where she buried the little bugger," Mary Lou said. "I won't get a nasty surprise next summer when I plant my petunias." She glanced over at the door that opened onto the large dining room and lowered her voice. "Don't look now, but the greenhorn's on his way."

Keri's pulse jumped. She'd been thinking about Michael as he'd sat eating his meal with the Chance family in the formal dining room. She wondered how he'd liked the mashed potatoes, which she'd beaten until there were absolutely zero lumps. She usually didn't take such care with the potatoes.

Despite Mary Lou's warning not to look, Keri turned in her chair and her gaze met Michael's. She knew before he spoke that he'd come searching for her. Her pulse ratcheted up another notch. He was one good-looking man.

Mary Lou stood. "If you're after another slice of cake, you've come to the right place. We're all having seconds."

Michael took in the scene and hesitated for a moment. He didn't seem to have come there for cake. Then he smiled. "I'd love another piece. Thanks for asking."

"Have a seat next to Keri. I'll get it for you." Mary Lou opened a cupboard and took down another dessert plate.

Michael's presence next to Keri created a dramatic change in temperature. He also took up space, and she moved her knee so she wouldn't brush against his. She became aware of his slow, measured breathing and the scent of his aftershave. Until this moment, she'd avoided being close enough to smell it.

"Coffee?" Mary Lou asked.

"Sure. That would be great."

"Cream and sugar?"

"Just black."

His voice stroked her nerve endings, putting them on alert. She felt tension coming from him, too. If she had to guess, she'd say he was as hyperaware of her as she was of him. This would be an interesting week.

"I'm Watkins, by the way." The barrel-chested cowboy reached across the table to shake Michael's hand. "Mary Lou's husband."

"I'm so sorry!" Keri was mortified. "I should have introduced you two. I forgot Michael doesn't know everyone."

"Don't worry about it." Michael glanced at her with a smile. "I barged in here uninvited. I hope I'm not intruding."

"'Course not." Mary Lou set a piece of cake in front of him, along with a fork and napkin. "My kitchen's open to anyone on the ranch. Sooner or later, everybody comes through here."

"After tonight's meal, I can see why," Michael said. "Dinner was great. The mashed potatoes were perfect."

"Keri made those." Mary Lou poured coffee into a ceramic mug and brought it to the table.

Michael turned toward Keri again. "Well, you did a terrific job on them."

"Thanks." Keri's cheeks warmed. Men had given her compliments before, but never about her cooking. Until she'd moved here, she'd only known how to operate a coffeepot and a microwave. "Mary Lou's a good teacher."

"Apparently I am," Mary Lou said with a laugh. "You knew squat about cooking when you came, and now you're not half bad at it." She reclaimed her seat at the table.

"Yep." Watkins beamed at Keri. "You caught on real quick. Today you graduated to the mouse-burying business. Next thing I know, you'll be shoveling out stalls."

"Bring it on." Keri felt Michael's attention on her, and she tried to squash the squiggles of excitement that attention produced. "I've cleaned up after eight adolescent boys. Nothing scares me."

"Wish I could say the same." Michael picked up his fork and started eating his cake. "But Jack Chance scares the bejeezus out of me."

Watkins chuckled. "He likes doing that with greenhorns. You'll be okay."

Michael swallowed a bite of cake and reached for his coffee. "That's what I told myself, until Sarah mentioned the liniment and Epsom salts. Now I'm worried." He turned toward Keri. "She said you'd find them for me. That's why I came looking for you. I'm glad I did."

Her breath caught at the unmistakable flicker of desire in his eyes. "Yeah, you got an extra piece of cake out of the deal." She hoped Mary Lou and Watkins hadn't noticed her tone was slightly strained.

"Exactly." His gaze held hers for one more heart-stopping moment. Then he broke eye contact and went back to eating his cake and asking questions about the ranch as if nothing of significance had passed between them.

But, oh, it had. She started to pick up her coffee mug and had to wait a moment until she stopped trembling. Good Lord. She wanted this man, and he wanted her right back. They'd be sleeping across the hall from each other for a week. Keeping a lid on this mutual attraction was going to be a real challenge.

4

AFTER A COZY half-hour spent eating cake and drinking coffee in Mary Lou's kitchen with Keri sitting right next to him, Michael's defenses were down. Circumstances had presented him with rich chocolate, a tempting woman and the prospect of going upstairs with her after they'd finished their dessert. A guy could only take so much before he cracked.

On top of that, he discovered that Mary Lou and Watkins had only been married a year, which explained the friskiness going on between them. Knowing that Mary Lou and Watkins would soon be getting it on didn't help Michael's state of mind. They shooed both Keri and Michael out of the kitchen once the dishes were cleared from the table.

That left them little choice but to walk through the silent house and climb the stairs together. The intimacy of it grew with each step they took. Michael made small talk along the way, and Keri responded as if she thought his conversation was brilliant.

She wasn't fooling him, and he doubted that he was fooling her, either. They were on thin ice, but maybe if they didn't acknowledge that, they'd get to their respective bedrooms without incident. What a damned inconvenient time to lust after a woman.

They kept up the inane chatter, but the winding staircase seemed endless. She was a step ahead of him, and her scent, a combination of sweet perfume and warm woman, drifted back to him, tugging at his resolve. He considered laying a hand on her shoulder. That might be all it would take.

She'd turn back to him, and then…then he would kiss her. But it wouldn't stop with a kiss, and he knew that. He'd never made love to a woman on a staircase, and he wasn't about to do it now. Still, that didn't keep the images from bombarding him until he was hard and aching.

"Do you want me to dig out the liniment and Epsom salts tonight, so you'll have them available when you come back from riding tomorrow?"

"Sure." He shouldn't have said that. Every extra minute they spent together increased the possibility that one of them might do something that would make them both lose control. He was willing to take that risk if he could be with her a little bit longer.

"I think they're in your bathroom." She walked down the hallway, lit only by a small wall sconce.

He followed, all the while lecturing himself to get a grip on his libido. This wasn't like him. Then again, she wasn't like any woman he'd met before. She had secrets, and he had to believe they were interesting secrets. Apparently curiosity was a powerful aphrodisiac for him. He hadn't known that.

Well, then, that was the solution, wasn't it? If he

solved the mystery of Keri Fitzpatrick, he wouldn't be so attracted to her. He'd planned on searching the internet to see what he could turn up, but asking her outright was really a more honest way to approach it. His questions might be considered intrusive, but if that would keep him from seducing his host's housekeeper, he felt justified.

She stepped into the bathroom and flipped on the wall switch. "Let's see what I can find." Walking over to the sink set into a carved wooden vanity, she began pulling open drawers.

He leaned in the doorway. "It's none of my business, but wondering why you left Baltimore to come out here and be a housekeeper is driving me crazy."

"It is?" She glanced up and understanding passed between them without either of them saying a word. His curiosity wasn't the only thing driving him crazy, and they both knew it. "The answer's pretty simple," she said. "I ran away from a scandal."

"That's not a simple answer." And all it did was ratchet his curiosity up a notch.

She gave him a wry smile. "No, I guess not." Folding her arms, she propped one hip against the vanity. "I was at a New Year's Eve party at a friend's penthouse and the champagne was flowing. This cute guy and I were making out in a darkened corner when his fiancée showed up. I didn't know he was engaged."

"That was the scandal?" He had a hard time imagining that would create enough gossip to make her leave town.

"No. She threw a drink in my face, so I threw one in hers. She came at me, claws out, wailing like a banshee.

My temper got the best of me, and…well, there was smashed crystal, imported caviar ground into the antique rug, a crack in a priceless statue…in other words, an unholy mess."

Michael tried not to grin, but she'd conjured up quite a picture. He'd only known her a short while, but he sensed the fire in her. She wouldn't take kindly to being falsely accused. "And here I was impressed that you didn't faint over a mouse."

She shrugged. "What can I say? I'm Irish."

He'd thought learning her secrets would make her less intriguing. Instead, he was more fascinated than ever. "Did you win?"

Triumph shone briefly in her green eyes. Then she sighed. "I did. But in the end, I lost, because I became notorious as the New Year's Eve Brawler. I couldn't do my job without the subject coming up. That fight began to define who I was."

"What's your profession?"

"PR."

It figured that she'd be trained in the area that was currently the scourge of his existence.

She pushed away from the vanity. "There you have it, the reason I came out here." Moving to the other side of the vanity, she opened the top drawer.

"But why be a housekeeper? Why not get another PR job?"

"I just wanted to hide out for a while, do something completely different. The cliché for it is *finding yourself.* I hadn't been all that happy with my life in Baltimore, anyway, so this was a chance to explore other options."

"You came out here without knowing a soul?"

"Yep. That was exciting, in a way. I interviewed for the job here on a whim. I had no experience, but luckily Sarah and Jack took pity on me." She rummaged in the drawer. "There's a box wedged in the back of this drawer. It could be the liniment."

"For the record, Sarah's thrilled with the job you're doing."

"She said that?" Keri reached deep into the drawer and tugged at the box. It was more square than rectangular, which didn't make sense for a tube of ointment, but she might as well haul it out, anyway.

"She did. She's very happy with your work, but she also expects you to leave."

"Which I will, but I'll give them plenty of time to hire someone else before the boys descend on them next summer." She yanked at the box. "Got it!" Holding it aloft, she looked at the label.

Michael looked, too, and began to laugh. "That's not liniment."

Without meeting his eyes, she tossed the box back in the drawer. "Nope, not liniment." Her cheeks had turned a becoming shade of rose.

Michael longed to walk over there and kiss her blushing cheeks, her full mouth and her delicate throat. Hell, he'd like to work his way through every tempting spot on her sweet body. Each piece of the puzzle that was Keri Fitzpatrick only made him want to find more so he could complete the picture.

"I'll keep looking." She opened the door under the sink and crouched down to peer inside.

"That's okay." God, he was a noble SOB. "I may not

even need any. We should probably just forget about it and go to bed."

She gave him a startled glance. "What?"

Oh, Keri. Lust slammed into him. He pushed it back. "Separately."

"Oh." She blushed again. "Right."

"See you in the morning." He walked out of the bathroom before he changed his mind and closed the short gap between them. Yes, he was nobler than he ever thought he could be.

But once he was inside his room with the door closed, he reflected on what had been in that drawer. Fate had not only thrown the luscious Keri into his path, it had provided him with condoms.

KERI TURNED OFF the bathroom light and retreated to her room. Once there, she flopped back on the bed and stared up at the ceiling until her head stopped buzzing and her heartbeat returned to normal. She'd given herself away. How embarrassing was that?

A woman who wasn't thinking about sex would never have reacted the way she had when Michael had suggested they go to bed. People said that kind of thing all the time—*we should go to bed*—and they only meant it was time to turn in. That's all Michael had been saying, for God's sake. She was the one who'd made it into something else.

Sure, there was a sexual attraction between them. For the benefit of all concerned, they would ignore that attraction. No good would come of indulging themselves.

Not true, a devilish voice taunted her. *Lots of good would come. And you would, too, most likely.*

Her groan was spiced with laughter. She'd behaved like a nun ever since taking the job at the Last Chance. A woman living in her employer's house couldn't exactly invite guys up to her room. To be honest, she hadn't met anyone she'd wanted to invite in. Until now.

The whole setup was ridiculous. If she'd met Michael while on some business trip to New York and they'd hit it off this well, she would have considered a sexual relationship. Maybe not tonight, because that was a bit fast. Tomorrow night wouldn't have been out of the question.

But they weren't in New York. They were across the hall from each other in the Chance family's ranch house, where she was an employee and Michael was a guest. No matter which way she sliced it, that put him off-limits.

So she should be patient. He would leave at the end of the week, and she would leave in a couple of months. She'd get his contact information and give him hers. If the chemistry between them was more than a passing fancy they could get together later, once the barriers had been removed.

Since they were from similar backgrounds, and apparently had both yearned for a more unfettered lifestyle out West, they'd probably have many traits in common. She admired him for throwing himself into this setting with no experience. That took guts, and she appreciated a man with courage. Yes, he'd be worth tracking down later on.

Figuring out that a possible hookup was being postponed, not abandoned, should have made her feel less frustrated, but it didn't. Blowing out a breath, she levered herself off the bed and changed into her pajamas. Then she washed her face and brushed her teeth.

Unfortunately, she spent all that time straining to hear Michael moving around in his room. At one point she caught the sound of footsteps in the hall. Like a teenager with a crush, she pressed her ear to the door.

He went into the bathroom and closed the door. Calling herself crazy, she listened until he came out and started back down the hall. He paused, and she held her breath. What would she do if he knocked on her door?

She had two choices—to answer it, which might lead to the forbidden pleasures she dreamed of, or to ignore it, which was the wisest course of action and sounded dismal and sad. But he took the choice away from her by continuing into his room and closing the door. Damn.

With nothing exciting on the horizon, she climbed into bed and picked up the paperback by Jim Ford lying on her nightstand. One of the ranch hands she'd dated last fall had loaned her a Jim Ford Western to help teach her about ranch life.

She'd never read that kind of book before, and it had helped her feel more at home here. She'd liked the story, too. She'd ordered all of the Jim Ford books online, which had given her a stack of more than twenty.

Her nightly reading habit was her little secret, her stealth method of taking a crash course in all things Western. After going through them once, she'd started over, which probably qualified her as a fan.

She'd nearly finished this one, *Showdown at the Wildcat Saloon,* for the second time. Within twenty minutes she'd arrived at the last page. The good guys won, the bad guys lost and the cowboy hero ended up with the girl. The plot was more complicated than that, but the structure was similar in all the books.

That worked for Keri. She liked knowing the stories would turn out well, and the details about cowboys and ranch life had taught her many things she might not have learned otherwise. The hands at the Last Chance were too busy being cowboys to stop and explain the process to a transplant from Baltimore, but Jim Ford did a fine job.

Her only complaint was that the love scenes weren't hot enough to suit her. Maybe Western writers weren't expected to have spicy romance in their books, but she would have liked more sizzle. She'd considered writing to tell him so, but hadn't taken the time.

After finishing the current book, she glanced at the author photo on the inside back cover of the paperback. In it, Jim Ford leaned against the weathered side of a barn. She knew the photo well after seeing it in twenty-some books.

But tonight it reminded her of someone else. When she'd stared at the picture for a few minutes and couldn't place where she'd seen the guy, she turned out the light and slid down under the covers.

Lying there quietly, she could hear noises from Michael's room—the sound of his booted feet on the wooden floor, followed by the clump of the boots as he pulled them off and dropped them. She imagined him undressing, and then stopped imagining it. A sexual buzz right now wasn't going to help matters any.

Surely he was exhausted by now. He'd flown east-to-west, so his body clock was probably out of whack.

It was much later for him than for everyone else on the ranch.

But he wasn't going to bed. Instead, he turned on his laptop. That chime was unmistakable. If Jack had given him the ranch's Wi-Fi password, he could be checking his email. Or his portfolio.

Though she'd told him a lot about her life tonight, she was woefully ignorant of his, other than Jack mentioning that he was loaded. He could have inherited his money or earned it himself. She had no idea which.

Usually a person gave some indication if they had a job. They'd reference it somehow, but Michael had been curiously mum on the subject. So maybe he lived off his investments, or his parents' investments. She'd known plenty of people who did that.

She could choose that route herself, but she wouldn't. Now that she knew what hard work was, she'd discovered that she liked it. She enjoyed ending the day feeling pleasantly tired and satisfied with what she'd accomplished.

When she left this job, she'd continue to cook and clean for herself, at least most of the time. She didn't want to lose her newly acquired skills. The life she used to have, with minions handling every routine maintenance task, had lost its appeal.

Sleep began to pull her under, but in that hazy moment before she drifted off, she realized who Jim Ford reminded her of. Michael. The two men looked very much alike, except Michael was clean-shaven and Jim Ford had a mustache. Talk about a crazy coincidence. Michael Hartford knew nothing about being a cowboy, and Jim Ford was an expert on the subject.

Maybe she should loan Michael a few of her Jim Ford books. They might help him the way they'd helped her. Jack's lessons were all well and good, but Jim Ford provided the lingo. Michael also might get a kick out of knowing that if he grew a mustache, he could impersonate a well-known Western writer.

Tomorrow she'd leave a book in his room, along with a note to check out the author photo on the inside back cover. That should make him laugh.

5

By LATE MORNING on the following day, Michael was hating life, and he hadn't even made it out of the corral. If he'd had some image of galloping across a meadow on Day One, he could kiss that fantasy goodbye. He'd spent at least an hour, probably longer, learning to saddle and unsaddle his assigned horse, Destiny.

Destiny had stood patiently while Michael practiced over and over under Jack's supervision. Mastering the bridle application had taken another big chunk of time. Jack had insisted, and legitimately so, that a rider needed to know these basics before climbing aboard. Jack was also a perfectionist in this regard. No student of his would get away with sloppy habits. No, sir.

Michael couldn't very well bitch about Jack's exacting attitude, either. The guy was offering his house and his services for free, out of the goodness of his heart. If Michael had been paying him, the dynamics would have been different, but under this program Michael kept his mouth shut.

Lack of sleep hadn't helped his concentration any, either. He'd planned to work on his current manuscript for an hour or so the previous night because his deadline loomed. Usually, working helped him wind down, except the chapter he'd faced had included—of course— a love scene.

He'd thought about Keri while he wrote the blasted thing, so by the end of the writing session the scene had been hotter than he usually made them. And he'd been equally hot. At least he'd finished the chapter and could move on to some action sequences tonight.

That was assuming he could sit long enough to type. The first portion of the actual riding part hadn't been bad—getting the horse to walk and then putting on the brakes. But then had come the torturous gait called the trot.

Michael had circled the corral endlessly while Destiny jolted every bone in his body. How naively Michael had written trotting into his manuscripts over the years. His characters were constantly trotting their horses here, there and everywhere.

His characters were also experienced riders who had somehow learned how to sit in the saddle without bouncing like a teenager on a trampoline. Michael wondered how in hell they'd accomplished that feat. Jack kept telling him to sit back and just move with the horse. Yeah, right. He wondered if a construction worker just moved with his jackhammer.

At least he wouldn't have to worry about being tempted by the lovely housekeeper. After today, his privates would be out of commission. He might not be in shape to have sex for a month.

"Okay, slow him down," Jack called out from his perch on the corral fence. "Walk him around a couple of times and we'll call it quits for now and head in to lunch."

Lunchtime meant seeing Keri again. Despite feeling achy and chafed, he brightened at that prospect. As he walked Destiny through the gate Jack held open, he thought about Keri's expression last night when she'd reached into the vanity drawer and pulled out a box of condoms. She'd been flustered and cute as the dickens.

"That's what I like to see after a trotting session," Jack said. "A big ol' smile on your face. You'll be happy to know we'll work on that gait some more after lunch. You're better, but still not good enough."

Michael hadn't realized he'd been smiling, but Jack's comment sobered him up real quick. "How about trying some roping instead? You know, switch things up a little."

"Yeah, but you're so close on the trot!" Jack turned to fasten the gate. "Another hour or so and you'll have it down!"

Another hour or so and he'd be in traction. "Maybe so, but I'd rather spend some time roping. I have a scene coming up in the next chapter where the hero ropes the villain. I'll probably do a better job with it if I've thrown a rope myself."

"You're working on something now?" Jack walked beside him as they headed toward the barn.

"I am. That's why I brought my laptop, so I could write while I'm here."

"Well, that's just special. I hadn't thought about you actually writing while you stayed here. I might need to get a plaque for the door of that room after you leave."

"You're kidding, right?" Michael pulled the horse to a stop at the hitching post.

"No, not really. But I wouldn't do it because you want these lessons to be hush-hush. By the way, you can climb down from there anytime, now."

"Oh. Okay." Michael felt a little shaky and hoped to hell he didn't fall off.

"Left side, Hartford. Left side."

"Um, yeah. I was thinking about something else." He put his foot back in the left stirrup and eased his right foot free.

"Don't let yourself think about something else when you're working around horses, my friend. You're dealing with a thousand-pound animal. Anything can happen."

"Anything?" Michael thought Jack said things like that mostly to scare him. Clenching his jaw against the pain in his thigh muscles, he swung down from the saddle. He'd be damned if he'd let out a groan.

"Absolutely anything." Jack wore his dark glasses and his black Stetson, which made him look like a badass. "Death, dismemberment, you name it."

"That really makes me want to get back on old Destiny."

"Ah, I'm just having a little fun. You're safer on him than you are walking down the streets of New York City. But I'll bet you stay alert there."

"I do."

"That's really all there is to it. Be vigilant when you're around horses. Don't be scared. Be aware. Destiny's calm, but no telling what kind of horse you'll end up with for the photo shoot. Some horses spook at a blowing scrap of paper."

"It's good advice. Thanks."

"You're welcome. Don't want you getting killed." He grinned. "Aside from my concern for you as a fellow human being, I'd miss out on more Jim Ford books."

"You're all heart, Jack."

"So they tell me." He gestured toward Destiny. "Take off his saddle, and we'll have a short lesson in grooming before we turn him loose in the pasture. We'll rope this afternoon if that's what floats your boat."

Thank God. "I appreciate that."

"I suppose you'll need to rope somebody, if that's what you'll be writing about."

"A post will do fine. I don't need to actually—"

"Oh, I think you do. For authenticity's sake."

Michael glanced at him. "Are you volunteering?"

"Hell, no. I'll volunteer one of the ranch hands. Tell me how big your villain is, and I'll find somebody that size."

"He's about your height."

"Hmm. Okay. Maybe Jeb, then."

"How are you planning to explain this little exercise without telling him I'm a writer?"

Jack gazed at him. "I see your point. We don't generally rope people around here. Jeb might very well question what we were up to." He sighed. "Guess I'll have to do it, after all."

"You don't have to. A post will work."

"No, it won't. There's a world of difference between roping a post and roping a man. I want you to get it right."

"Okay." Michael worked hard to keep from smiling. "If you insist." His day was looking up.

He followed Jack's instructions and brushed Destiny's glossy coat before turning him loose in the pasture. Destiny seemed as glad to be free of Michael as Michael was to be through with Destiny, at least for today. Michael looked at the experience from Destiny's perspective and realized that having a beginner rider bouncing on your backbone might not feel so good.

Following Jack's lead, Michael washed his hands and face in the deep sink located inside the barn. As they walked up to the ranch house, Michael felt almost like a cowboy. His clothes were dusty, he smelled of horse and he walked slightly bowlegged thanks to his riding lesson.

Like Jack, he kept his hat on as they mounted the steps, crossed the covered porch and went through the massive front door. On the way down the hall he pulled the brim a bit lower. Yeah. He was getting into this. He wondered if Keri would notice the difference.

KERI HAD A basket of hot rolls in each hand when Jack and Michael strode into the dining room. And they were definitely striding, not merely walking. Jack had always had that cocky way of moving, and now Michael had picked it up.

She was mesmerized by the sight of Michael, who obviously was in the process of getting his cowboy on. She'd promised herself to stop mooning over him, but how could she help it if he ramped up his sexy quotient when she wasn't looking? He even wore his hat with more authority. He'd spent the morning with a powerful horse between his legs, and she knew from her year at the ranch that riding could turn a regular guy into a conquering hero.

His gaze found hers and he smiled. Wow, did he ever look like Jim Ford when he did that. She'd left the book in his room, but he might not see it until this afternoon when he was finished working with Jack.

After returning his smile, she snapped out of her daze and delivered the rolls to two of the tables. Then she walked back into the kitchen. The ranch hands were hungry and she couldn't dawdle. Platters of fried chicken and bowls of potato salad and coleslaw sat on the counter. Mary Lou opened the large commercial oven and took out the first of the apple pies.

She set it on the only vacant space left on the counter and glanced at Keri. "Are you okay? You seem a little distracted."

"I'm fine. Sorry for the delay." She picked up two platters of chicken and hurried out the door. Mary Lou had come to depend on her to serve lunch, and unless she moved the main course out, no counter space was available for dessert.

Sarah used to help, but she'd done less as Keri took over her duties. This week Sarah was so involved with wedding plans that she wouldn't have been much use, anyway. Both the ceremony and the reception would take place at the ranch, and the details surrounding that production were endless.

Once Keri was back in the dining room, she couldn't help noticing where Michael had ended up. He and Jack had chosen the table where the ranch foreman, Emmett Sterling, sat with his daughter, Emily—who would be foreman someday—and her husband Clay Whitaker, who ran the stud program for the Last Chance. Four ranch hands rounded out the eight-place table.

Michael fit right in. The clothes he'd paid to have distressed were a little dirty from being out in the corral, which gave them more legitimacy. He joked with the people at the table as if he'd been part of this world forever. Not every city boy could pull that off, but Michael seemed to be a natural at it. Maybe he didn't need to read the Jim Ford books, after all.

She approached his table with a platter of chicken and a bowl of potato salad. The ranch hands ate family style and passed the serving dishes around. In fact, lunch at the Last Chance had always seemed like a big family gathering to Keri, and she loved the idea that everyone was on equal footing here.

She wasn't treated as a waitress, which meant she could pause beside Michael's chair and ask him how the morning went.

"Great." He gave her another one of those smiles that made him look like Jim Ford without the mustache. "Jack's teaching me a lot."

"Good. By the way, I left a book in your room, something that you might enjoy. I put it on your nightstand."

"Thanks. What is it?"

"A Western by Jim Ford. It's the perfect thing to read while you're here."

Michael must have swallowed wrong at that moment, because he launched into a coughing fit. One of the ranch hands got up and pounded him on the back while Jack offered him a glass of water. Keri stood and waited for the fit to be over, because she couldn't simply walk away as if she didn't care that he was choking. He wasn't turning blue, so she wasn't terribly worried, but it was a spectacular fit, all the same.

At last he settled down, took off his hat and wiped his eyes. "Sorry about that." He looked up at her. "Thanks for loaning me the book."

"I'm sure you'll like it."

"I'm sure I will."

"Well, I need to get back to the kitchen." She turned to go, but not before she caught a look passing between Michael and Jack. She didn't have time to interpret it because not everyone had food, and hungry cowboys looked forward to this meal. For many of them it was the highlight of their day.

Much later, after the pie had been devoured with many words of praise for Mary Lou's cooking, the ranch hands began filing out of the dining room. Keri was clearing the dishes when Jack approached. Michael wasn't with him.

"I didn't know you were a Jim Ford fan," he said.

"I am. Jeb loaned me one of his books and I've been hooked ever since." She decided this was the perfect time to talk about the mouse incident. "About that mouse. I probably shouldn't have made a stand in front of a guest. I apologize."

Jack waved a hand dismissively. "You were right to give those boys the benefit of the doubt. I'm too cynical sometimes."

"You could be right, too. It might have been an elaborate joke."

"It doesn't matter. The mouse has been decently interred." Jack shoved his hat back with his thumb. "How long have you been reading Jim Ford?"

"Since last October. I ordered every book that was available. They helped me understand ranch culture and I thought maybe they'd help Michael, too." She paused. "You know what's amazing? Michael actually looks like the picture of Jim Ford in the back of his books, except for the mustache. Is that wild or what?"

Jack opened his mouth as if to say something, but he closed it again. "Yes," he said at last. "I noticed that, too. Weird, huh?"

"Yes, totally weird." But she'd seen something in Jack's eyes that made her start to wonder. Michael couldn't possibly be Jim Ford. Considering Jim Ford's expertise, that made no sense.

Yet something was up. She could sense it. Jack and Michael had exchanged that significant glance at the table, as if they shared some kind of secret. She began weaving all kinds of scenarios. What if the real Jim Ford was an ugly old man who didn't photograph well? What if he'd asked Michael to masquerade as Jim Ford, and now Michael had to learn some ranch skills to make the charade believable?

She decided to keep her eyes and ears open. If that meant keeping tabs on Michael Hartford, so be it. That wouldn't be a hardship at all.

6

Roping looked so easy in the movies that Michael had expected to pick it up really fast. He played a mean game of racquetball, so he considered himself as co-ordinated as the next guy. But he soon discovered that *building a loop,* as Jack phrased it, was much harder than it looked. And he had to build a loop before he could throw it at anything.

"You're making it too big," Jack said. "Start smaller."

"A small loop looks wimpy."

"A big loop that's snarled around your ankles looks a hell of a lot worse. You wouldn't want anybody to think you're compensating for something with that big loop, would you?"

"Hey!"

"Just sayin'. Make one about half that size and see how you do."

Michael found the smaller loop worked much better. He made the rope spin in a circle next to him for a couple of seconds before it went all wonky again.

"Nice job. Keep playing around with that size while

I check on Bandit. He pulled a tendon and I want to see if the swelling's down any."

Michael kept his eye on the twirling rope. "Bandit's your horse?"

"My stallion."

"Oh, ho!" Michael was proud of himself for keeping the rope turning in a perfect circle as he talked. "A *stallion,* you say? Now who's compensating, Jack?"

"Nice comeback! Now you're starting to sound like a cowboy." Chuckling to himself, he started toward the barn.

Smug bastard. He'd earned the right to be, though. Michael envied his confidence and skill. He decided to throw all he had at this practice session so he'd have something to show for it when Jack came out of the barn.

Jack had said Michael would start by roping a nearby post. Then he'd progress to roping Jack. Michael gathered the rope, built his loop a little bigger and tossed it at the post.

He missed, but he'd expected that. He missed five times in a row, but on the sixth try, he roped the post. Okay, then. After he'd roped it three out of five attempts, he increased the size of his loop. He was getting the hang of it, now.

The rope spun in a circle wide enough so that it would fall neatly over Jack, hat and all, when he reappeared. Twirling the loop, Michael moved a little closer to the barn. He heard Jack's boots on the barn's wooden floor. Any second now he'd step into the sunshine, and then Michael would nail him.

His timing had to be perfect. Jack appeared. Michael let fly with the rope. It sailed toward Jack's head, knocked off his hat and dropped toward his shoulders.

"Pull on it!" Jack yelled.

Michael yanked the rope. It tightened quickly, but by then it was around Jack's knees.

"Shi-i-i-t!" Jack went down hard.

"Damn!" Dropping the rope, Michael ran forward. "Sorry! Are you okay?"

Jack pushed himself onto his knees, shook his head once to clear it and grinned up at Michael. "Congratulations, greenhorn." He leaned over and loosened the rope around his knees. "You just roped yourself a man."

"Yeah, but I knocked you down." Michael extended his hand to help him up. "I didn't mean to do that."

"Effective, though." Jack allowed Michael to pull him up. Then he dusted off the seat of his jeans. "Can't say I've ever had that particular experience. Can't say I'd want to do it again, either. But you'd want your hero to do that on purpose."

"Guess so."

"Sure you would. The hero takes the villain by surprise, waits until the rope drops to the guy's knees and then bam!" Jack smacked his fist into his palm. "The bad guy goes down, your hero runs over, gives him a right hook to the jaw and your villain's subdued."

Michael nodded. "That works. Thanks, Jack."

"You're welcome. Now I've made my contribution to art for the day."

Michael coiled the rope. "How's Bandit?"

"Doing okay. Come on in the barn and I'll introduce you."

Following Jack, Michael realized that even though

this was his first full day, he was starting to feel at home around here. The scent of hay mingled with the earthy smell of horses was familiar to him now. Sure, his muscles were sore and would probably tighten up on him later. But he'd taken his first two lessons in cowboying and hadn't done half bad.

"This is Bandit." Jack tucked his dark glasses into his shirt pocket, opened the stall door and walked up beside a big horse with distinct black-and-white markings, including a black circle around each eye. His right front leg was wrapped in a bandage. "Bandit, this is Michael, the tenderfoot I was telling you about."

"I'm happy to meet you, Bandit."

"Come on in," Jack said. "He likes to be scratched on his neck, like this." He demonstrated and stood back.

Michael mimicked Jack and scratched Bandit's silky neck. Maybe it was his imagination, but the horse seemed to exude power and confidence, much the way Jack did. "I take it you breed him."

"Yeah, we do." Jack stroked Bandit's nose. "He commands a high stud fee, which helps keep us in the black. So he gets the royal treatment around here."

"I'll bet he would, anyway."

Jack smiled in acknowledgment. "He would. We all have our favorites around here, and Bandit's mine. We've had some great times together over the years."

A moment ago Michael had been feeling a part of this environment, but that last statement told him how much of an outsider he was. He'd lived in apartments all his life, where the only animals he'd known well had been small dogs that walked down crowded sidewalks on leashes.

Jack had spent many solitary hours riding this majestic horse over the untamed acreage of the Last Chance Ranch. Michael had written about such rides, but that wasn't remotely the same as doing it. Now that he'd had a small taste of ranch life, he wanted to vault over the beginner stage he was currently in and take those long rides in the shadow of the Grand Tetons.

"We should probably talk about Keri," Jack said.

"What about her?" Michael glanced around to see if anyone else was in the barn.

"Don't worry. I checked. We have some privacy. That was the main reason for getting you in here." Jack continued to stroke Bandit's nose. "Keri's read everything you've written. Furthermore, she thinks you're the spitting image of Jim Ford, except for the mustache."

Michael blew out a breath. "Damn. She's going to figure this out. She's too smart not to." He debated his choices. "Can she keep a secret?"

"I would say so. I haven't noticed any blabbermouth tendencies."

"And she knows what it feels like to be embarrassed by negative publicity."

Jack glanced over at him. "She told you about the girl fight?"

"Yeah."

"Man, I would've loved to see that. She keeps a lid on her temper most of the time around here, but I found out the hard way she's murder in a snowball fight."

"I'll bet." Michael could picture her, cheeks pink from the cold, pelting the enemy with deadly accuracy.

"Anyway, she must like you. She doesn't broadcast

that information much. Other than you, she's only told me and Sarah, so far as I know."

"Well, I did ask her why she'd left Baltimore."

"She could have dodged the question or made up some bogus answer." Jack combed Bandit's forelock with his fingers.

"I think she feels a kinship to me because we're both from back east," Michael said. "And she knows I have a similar background. I can put myself in her shoes and imagine what she's been through."

Jack chuckled. "That could be true, but she also plain likes you. I haven't seen her look at any of the hands the way she looks at you."

Hearing that gave him a jolt of pleasure, but he didn't want Jack getting the wrong impression. "Just so you know, she hasn't said or done anything inappropriate."

"That sounded kind of protective." Jack's grin flashed. "I think maybe you like her, too."

"Yeah, I like her, but that's as far as it will go. I give you my word on that, Jack."

"Oh, for Pete's sake. This is the Last Chance, not the Waldorf Astoria. You told me on the drive from the airport that you can't seem to hook up with any-one you like."

"Yes, but hooking up with someone is not why I'm here."

"Hell, I know that! But if the opportunity presents itself, don't be such a damned puritan, okay? Near as I can tell, poor Keri hasn't been getting any since she arrived. Seems to me you could do each other a lot of good."

"I can't believe you're saying this."

"Apparently I have to. Otherwise you and Keri will spend a miserable week sleeping right across the hall from each other and doing nothing about it."

"Probably because she respects you and doesn't want to get fired! And I don't want to abuse your hospitality! Those are legitimate reasons. And I'm not a damned puritan."

"Okay, okay. I appreciate your code of honor, but I'm giving you permission to bend it. I'm giving her permission, too, but I can't very well talk to her, seeing as how I'm her boss and it would embarrass both of us. So I'm talking to you, sunshine. You can pass the word on to her."

Michael stared at him. "Pass the word on?"

"Well, use some finesse. You're the guy with the gigantic vocabulary, so I'm sure you can manage. But you'll have to tell her I said it was fine so she won't be afraid I'll fire her."

"That'll be an interesting discussion." Michael was having a tough time imagining it. He couldn't think of any subtle way to broach the subject.

"You'll figure it out. And if she's willing, and you'll have to be the judge of that, then cut loose a little while you're here. Trust me, it'll be good for you."

Michael nearly choked. "Are you telling me I need to get laid?"

"You said it. I didn't. But from the way you were whining about your situation yesterday afternoon, I'd have to answer in the affirmative. I didn't think this trip could help you any in that department, but then I noticed Keri had that certain look in her eye, and I recalculated your chances."

Michael scrubbed a hand over his face. "God."

"I'm not, despite rumors to the contrary. Oh, and FYI, there's a box of condoms somewhere in that bathroom."

Michael decided against mentioning that he already knew about those. "Any more tips?"

He was being sarcastic, but Jack didn't seem to notice. "Not at the moment, but if she's been reading all those Jim Ford books, she probably has a cowboy fantasy going on. You might want to play to that."

"I don't see how I can. Once she finds out Jim Ford's a phony, she's liable to be disappointed in both the books and in me."

"Look, she knows you're a tenderfoot, and she likes you, anyway. I'm guessing when she finds out the truth, she'll take pity on you."

Michael groaned. "Oh, that sounds even better."

"It could be. She's spent a year around cowboys. Ask her for pointers. Take it from ol' Jack—women love giving pointers to a man. Then the more you act like a cowboy, the more she'll feel proud of you and turned on at the same time. You're in an ideal position, my friend."

"I don't know if I agree with that. I think I could get squashed like a bug."

"Why should you? You have talent. You just managed to rope me without half trying."

"Oh, I was trying, Jack."

"See what you can do when you put your mind to it? You're more of a cowboy than you think you are. Just follow your instincts. And for God's sake, have fun. You take things way too seriously."

"I do?"

"Yeah, and I know all about the dangers of taking life too seriously. You miss all the good stuff. Don't do that."

THE DINNER HOUR came and went without Keri having any excuse to interact with Michael. She'd set the Epsom salts and the liniment on his bathroom counter, so he had no reason to ask for her help. She had cleaned up all the dinner dishes with Mary Lou and Watkins, both from their meal in the kitchen and the one served in the dining room.

With nothing left to do, she walked back through the house and climbed the stairs to the second floor. Michael's bedroom door was open and she could hear him moving around in there. But she couldn't think of any conversation she might need to have with him, so she opened her door and was halfway in when he called to her.

"Keri?"

The sound of his voice jump-started a familiar response of tingling heat that flowed despite her efforts to stem it. She had a thing for this guy, and apparently her hormones would dance to his tune whenever they had a chance. She turned. "Do you need something, Michael?"

"Yes." He stood in the doorway of his room, and his eyes, the gray-blue color of a jay's wing, focused intently on her. "I...need to tell you something."

"Is there a problem with your room?" She didn't think so, but it was her job to ask.

"No, it's about Jim Ford. Would you come in for a minute?"

A minute. He didn't have a lengthy discussion in

mind. But her pulse rate jumped at the thought of crossing his threshold. "Sure." She noticed that he hadn't said *Jim Ford's book.* He hadn't had time to read it, anyway.

No, he'd said *Jim Ford.* Her suspicion grew that for some reason he'd been asked to play the part of Jim Ford in public appearances. Maybe he was a wealthy actor she'd never heard of, although living close to New York most of her life, she knew the names of most of the famous actors on Broadway.

Once she walked into his room, he motioned her to the only chair, a wingback upholstered in a sturdy green plaid. He sat across from her on the edge of the bed. When he moved, a slight wince and crinkling of the corners of his eyes betrayed him. He needed that soak in the tub and some liniment before he went to bed.

But he'd given this "minute" with her priority, and she couldn't imagine why. Being here with him was exciting, though—the most excitement she'd had all day. His clothes looked much more lived-in than they had yesterday. Jack had put him through his paces.

No matter what he wanted to talk about, she was happy to sit and look at him. He had great shoulders, the kind a woman could take comfort from. His body was lean, but solid, too. She'd been surrounded by lean, solid male bodies for a year, but Michael's drew her more strongly than any of the others'.

Part of it was the combination of his clothes, which branded him a cowboy, and his accent, which reminded her of home. He was an enticing blend, which made him more exotic than any man she knew. But that wasn't all of it. Beneath his calm exterior, she sensed an undercurrent of primitive passion.

She'd sensed that undercurrent the minute he'd walked through the ranch house door. But until now, she hadn't admitted it or examined why she was so drawn to him. For years she'd battled that same untamed yearning.

Because of her polished society upbringing, she'd resisted those feelings and had blamed her Irish heritage for saddling her with inappropriate urges. Michael wasn't Irish, at least not that she knew, but that same hidden fire flashed in his eyes. It was there, now.

"So." He rested his hands on his jeans-clad knees, and tension radiated from him. "About Jim Ford."

"If I've caused a problem by bringing you his book, I apologize. I don't know why you're here, and I may have stumbled on something I shouldn't have. You can give me back the book, and we'll never talk about it again."

His glance flicked over her, and his mouth curved into a wry smile. "I don't think that's going to work. You're too intelligent, and I'll never be able to maintain my cover."

"You've been hired to impersonate him! I knew it!"

Humor glinted in his eyes. "That's one way of looking at it, but—"

"I won't give you away, Michael. I understand what it's like to have things you want to keep under wraps. You can trust me."

"I'm counting on it, because I'd rather not have anyone know I'm out in Wyoming learning how to be a cowboy."

"Of course. And I'll help you in any way I can. Have you read all of Jim Ford's books? Because I have, and I can fill you in on anything you might not know."

"I haven't read them."

"Then you'll really need my help, because I—"

"I wrote them. I'm Jim Ford."

Her mouth dropped open. Then she said the first thing that entered her mind. "No, you're not."

7

KERI WAS SO cute in her refusal to believe him that he almost laughed, but she wouldn't have appreciated that, so he controlled himself. "Yes, I'm afraid I am. I have the manuscripts on my laptop to prove it. My full name is Michael James Hartford, and I pulled the pseudonym Jim Ford out of that."

She still appeared to struggle with the information. "But Jim Ford is a cowboy. He's an expert. I've used his books to learn about ranch life, and everything he writes rings true to what I've found here. You—pardon me for saying so, Michael—but you're clueless!"

"That's a pretty accurate assessment." He tried not to get distracted by how beautiful she looked sitting there in the wingback. She'd worn a kelly-green blouse with her jeans today, and it matched her eyes. Her hair was in a ponytail, as it had been yesterday, but that only added to her appeal because it showed that she was no hothouse flower. She was a woman who was ready to take action, whether that meant defending herself in a girl fight, striking out on her own in Wyoming or hurling snowballs for fun. She would be an uninhibited lover, and he ached to experience that.

If Jack was right and Keri wanted him, she'd be the first woman he'd taken to bed who knew the real Michael Hartford. Every affair he'd had since he'd begun publishing the Jim Ford books had been based on a lie.

But at the moment, she didn't seem particularly interested in getting it on with Michael Hartford, aka Jim Ford. She looked confused and bewildered, like a kid who'd been told there's no Santa Claus.

She cleared her throat. "So all the while you've been writing the Jim Ford books, you've been making it up."

He couldn't keep from smiling. "That's what fiction writers do."

"Oh, for heaven's sake! I know that much! But what about your bio? It says you're a cowboy."

"No, it doesn't, not if you read it carefully. It says that I love the West and all it stands for—hard work, rugged living, honesty and straightforward dealings. It doesn't say I'm a cowboy or even that I live on a ranch."

"Then you're misleading people."

"I suppose you could say that, but they wouldn't buy the fantasy if I told them the truth about my life." This conversation wasn't going well.

"But you must have at least ridden a horse before."

"Nope. Not until Jack put me up on Destiny today."

"So it goes without saying that you've never roped a steer, shot a rifle or slept in a bunkhouse."

"Nope."

"How could you write like that, as if you'd done those things millions of times?" Her tone was more accusatory than curious. A spark of that Irish temper flared in her eyes.

"Lots and lots of research."

She continued to gaze at him as if he'd recently landed in a spaceship from a faraway galaxy. She didn't look as if she trusted him much, either. "So all this time, as I've been reading your books and picturing you as this accomplished cowboy, you've been...what?"

"Living on Central Park West."

"Do your books make that much money?"

"God, no. It's picking up, but that's not what pays the bills. I have a trust fund. The Hartfords are old money, and they wish to hell I'd stop writing trashy Westerns and go back to serving on the boards of prominent investment firms. It's what the Hartfords do."

She nodded. "I know that story. But I still don't understand why you didn't take some of that mega-money, buy a ranch and live the way your characters do. You obviously love the idea of it." She sounded impatient with him.

So here was the sticky part, where he could lay himself bare and risk being rejected as a coward, or make up some other story to explain his behavior. He was a pro at making up stories.

But he also was tired of lying to cover his ass. "I was afraid I wouldn't be any good at it."

"Really? But you already knew so much about this life."

"Book learning, as they used to say in the Old West. It's not the same."

"No, but you're a smart guy. You'd catch on. I was a

horrible housekeeper for the first couple of months, but people cut you some slack if you're trying."

He took a deep breath. "It's more than that. Sure I was afraid of making a fool of myself, especially after Jim Ford developed this reputation as a seasoned cowboy. But what if it turns out that I love the fantasy and not the reality? What if I don't like ranch life?"

Her eyes widened. "Oh. I didn't think of that. If the real thing ruined your fantasy, you wouldn't be able to write about it so lovingly, would you?"

"No."

"So why risk that now?"

"Couldn't avoid it." He told her about the PR campaign and his connection to Bethany. "She said I could trust Sarah and Jack to keep my identity secret while I learned enough to make it through the video."

"You can. You can trust me, too."

"I know."

"How do you know? We just met yesterday."

"Jack vouched for you."

"He did? That makes me feel good." She smiled, but then her smile faded. "Wait, if Jack vouched for me, then you two must have discussed whether to tell me your secret. Now I get why Jack was quizzing me about my Jim Ford books after lunch today. He was afraid I'd catch on."

"That's right. We decided I should tell you rather than you stumbling on to something when you were cleaning my room and finding out that way."

"I appreciate that."

This was his golden opportunity to segue into the

other topic, the more loaded one. His heart rate picked up. "That wasn't all that Jack had to say this afternoon."

Her cheeks turned pink. "If he mentioned that I overstep sometimes, he would be right. I've learned how to cook and clean, but sometimes I forget that I'm the hired help, not the mistress of the house. Old habits die hard."

"I'll bet, but that wasn't what we talked about. He… got the impression that you were…attracted to me." God, this felt like junior high. *He said you liked me. Do you like me?*

Her blush deepened and she looked away. "Okay, now I'm totally embarrassed. I'll talk to him tomorrow and assure him that I'm not making a play for his important guest. In fact, I should go back to my room right now." She stood quickly and started toward the door.

Michael left the bed. "He doesn't care."

She turned back to him, her face suffused with pink. *"What?"*

"He mentioned it because he thinks that would be fine. More than fine. He—"

"He *wants* me to make a move on you? That sounds bad on so many levels!"

"No! He didn't say that! This is coming out all wrong."

She folded her arms, and now she made no attempt to hide her temper. "No shit, Sherlock. Maybe you'd better tell me Jack's exact words instead of paraphrasing."

He thought about some of Jack's comments and winced. "I'm not sure that's a good idea."

"You can hardly make things worse."

"You have a point, there." He blew out a breath. "He

said that near as he could tell, you haven't been getting any since you came to work here."

Her green eyes glittered with fury. "That is none of his damned business, and first thing tomorrow, I'll tell him exactly that. I don't care if he fires me. I'll—"

"Keri, he meant it kindly. He noticed the chemistry between you and me and figured we'd both resist out of respect for him."

"Well, *duh*. I may forget my position sometimes, but I would never in a million years..." She peered at him. "Maybe you'd better tell me what you said to Jack on this topic."

"I told him I couldn't imagine how I'd ever broach the subject to you, and he claimed I have such a big vocabulary that I shouldn't have any trouble. Obviously he was wrong."

She kept her arms folded protectively over her chest, but her gaze grew speculative. "So basically, after Jack gave us the green light, you were ready to go along with his suggestion, assuming I agreed."

He tried to think of a way to reply that wouldn't land him in more hot water. But in the end, he decided that his new vow of complete honesty dictated that he could only give one answer.

"Yes." He looked into her eyes and hoped she'd see the desperate longing he felt every time she was near. "I've been lusting after you ever since you marched out of the house with that dead mouse."

Her mouth twitched as if she wanted to laugh but wouldn't let herself. "Smelly rodents turn you on, huh?"

"No, but a woman who's willing to dispose of them without freaking out certainly does. And if she's doing it out of a sentimental attachment to some adolescent boys, that's even more appealing. I figure a woman like that has character, and character turns me on."

Her rigid posture relaxed a little, although she didn't uncross her arms. The real change registered in her eyes. Hot indignation had been replaced by a different kind of heat. It flared for a moment, but she quickly looked away, as if she didn't want him to see. But he had, and that hot glance gave him hope.

"You've given me a lot to think about," she said.

"I'll bet."

"I left the Epsom salts and the liniment on the bathroom counter for you."

"I noticed. Thanks." He could be wrong, but that sounded as if she was about to make her getaway.

"Have a good night." She turned and walked out the door.

"Keri, wait." He followed her.

She turned, but kept her hand on the door into her room.

"If your answer is no, that's understandable. I'll only be here a week. You might consider that a bad deal all the way around."

She had the brass to look him up and down, as if considering her options. "Thanks for giving me a graceful way out. Even a woman who hasn't been getting any for the past year likes to give herself time to think things over."

"Keri, Jack didn't mean anything by that remark. He's a guy, and that's the way we talk."

"Uh-huh."

"I thought of something else, too. I'll only be here

for a week, but after you quit this job and move back to Baltimore, then—"

"Don't you think that's getting way ahead of ourselves?"

"Yeah." He rubbed the back of his neck. "Forget I mentioned it."

She didn't look as if she'd forget anything, especially not the lame parts of this conversation, which had been most of it. "For the record, have *you* been getting any lately, Michael?"

He felt warmth climbing up from his collar. "I'm kind of in your same boat."

"Hmm." She smiled. "That could make for an interesting combination. Good night." She opened her door, walked inside and closed it with a soft click.

He'd maintained control until her *interesting combination* remark. That got to him. He turned back to his room, his cock growing harder by the second. She was going to make him sweat out her decision, which meant he was in for another frustrating night.

But she hadn't said no. And the gleam in her eyes before she'd closed her bedroom door had definitely hinted at yes.

KERI CLOSED THE door and leaned her forehead against it as thoughts swirled in her mind. An hour ago, she'd had a crush on a hot guy who'd come to the Last Chance for a crash course in cowboy skills. Sure, she'd been frustrated that she couldn't pursue him because of her job, but there'd been some comfort in that, too. She could fantasize without repercussions.

Jack was absolutely right. She hadn't been getting

any for the past year, and she'd become used to being guy-less. Being without a man had given her time to think about where her life was going, and where she wanted it to go.

Until tonight, she'd figured on returning to Baltimore sometime this fall. But when Michael referred to it as a done deal, she was reminded of what waited for her there—more of the same. She could probably get her old job back and fall into the routine she'd left. She'd be a city girl again, wearing high heels to work and attending cocktail parties in sparkly dresses.

She remembered the constant hum of downtown Baltimore, the wail of a siren, the rattle of a jackhammer, the blare of a taxi, the rumble of a delivery truck. Walking over to her window, she raised it and listened. A cool pine-scented breeze billowed the curtains.

In the distance, an owl hooted. Some little night creature rustled in the bushes. Those sounds soothed her, whereas the mechanical noises in the city put her on edge. She'd never admitted that to herself before. When she ventured down to the harbor she felt closer to nature, but at the Last Chance she was immersed in it 24/7.

She edged closer to a decision that would change everything. She thought of her parents, but even when she'd lived in Baltimore she hadn't seen them all that often. She had friends in the city, too, but amazingly, she was more in sync with the people she'd met here. The life she'd once led seemed distant and unfamiliar. This place was her reality now, not the world she'd known back east.

Michael might be leaving in a week, but as she stood at the window gazing into darkness more complete than she'd ever find in the electricity-filled city, she knew what was right for her. She'd have to return to Baltimore to settle a few things, but after that, she was coming back to Wyoming.

That left her with another decision—what to do about the man across the hall. He'd thought she might guess his identity, but he was giving her too much credit. She'd been so firmly convinced that Jim Ford knew his stuff that she might never have figured out who Michael was.

Going over to her bedside table, she picked up the paperback she'd finished the night before and opened it to the author picture in the back. If she squinted so the mustache was blurry, she could clearly see that the man was Michael. Same broad shoulders, narrow hips, square jaw and sensuous mouth.

And he wanted her. As she studied his picture, sexual tension coiled low in her belly. He didn't just *want* her. He'd admitted to *lusting* after her. She believed him. He'd had that untamed look in his eyes when he'd said it. Her body had reacted to that look—it still hummed with anticipation.

Now that she knew who he was, she understood why he might have a wild side. After all, his characters did. She knew those guys, which gave her some insight into Michael. His characters were men of action, which she found very sexy. That's why she'd wanted more detail in the love scenes. That energy carried through a more explicit scene would be incredibly arousing.

Thinking about how he could improve those scenes aroused her even more. She was making herself squirm a little, to tell the truth. Relief was right across the hall. All she had to do was walk over there, and—her imaginary sexual adventure screeched to a stop when his door creaked open.

Was he coming back to mount another offensive? Her heart hammered as she waited to see what happened next. Footsteps padded down the hall. That was logical. He'd have to pick up condoms before knocking on her door.

She held her breath and listened for the sound of his returning steps. Instead, she heard water thundering into the tub. He hadn't gone after condoms. He was going to soak in Epsom salts.

If anything was going to happen tonight, she would have to initiate it. That was fair. He'd braved the first conversation, and she hadn't made that discussion easy on him.

When she pictured Michael and Jack discussing her lack of sex, she got angry all over again. But Michael was right about one thing. Jack had meant well.

He'd taken the only route he could think of to remedy a problem. He'd clumsily but effectively removed a barrier between two people who weren't getting any. And now, thanks to Jack's meddling, they had a golden opportunity to get some.

The more she thought about that, the more touched she was. Maybe Jack should have minded his own business, but he hadn't, and it was done, now. What a shame if his efforts went to waste.

Her heart began to pound as she envisioned what she was about to do. But she'd learned a valuable lesson in the past year. If she wanted something, she had to be willing to take the risk of going after it. She wanted Michael.

Putting down the paperback, she stripped off her clothes and took her silk bathrobe out of the closet. If she planned to seduce him, she would do it right. She hadn't brought many luxury items to Jackson Hole, but this emerald-green bathrobe had made the trip.

Next she took her hair out if its ponytail and fluffed it around her shoulders. A quick check in the full-length mirror on the back of her closet door told her that she looked…untamed. Her blood heated, much as it had when she'd hurled herself into the girl fight.

Except this time she wasn't flying into a rage over an insult. She was turning loose a more basic, primitive desire, one she'd kept in check, afraid the intensity would intimidate a lover. But now…there was Michael.

Leaving her room, she walked barefoot down to the bathroom. If he'd locked the door, then she'd have to rethink her plan. But the knob turned easily, and she walked right in.

Michael sat up so fast that water sloshed over the edge of the tub. "Keri! What the hell are you doing here?"

"Do you really have to ask?" She feasted her eyes on the first naked man she'd seen in quite a while. Michael was worth the wait.

His powerful chest heaved as he stared at her. She stared right back, enjoying the way drops of water clung to his dark chest hair and glittered in the overhead light. She followed the line of his damp body hair down to his navel and beyond, where his pride and joy rose from the water in a gratifying display of the lust he'd mentioned earlier.

She was glad he made no move to cover himself with

a washcloth. She might have caught him by surprise, but he was quickly adjusting to the possibilities of the situation. His eyes grew hot, burning with the same intensity that made her heart hammer.

Without taking his gaze from hers, he reached forward and pulled the plug. As the water drained away, he stood, his body glistening with water and radiating sexual power. He stepped out of the tub and surveyed her green robe. "Is that silk?"

"Yes."

"Unless you want to get it wet, you'd better take it off." His voice was tight, as if he was holding on to his control with difficulty.

Her blood pounded hot through her veins. "We have to get the condoms."

"Right behind you."

She turned, and there was the box, sitting on the counter. "Were you so sure of me, then?"

"No. Not sure at all. I never thought you'd come in here."

"Didn't you?"

He swallowed as his glance raked over her. "Only in my fantasies."

"We can go back to your room."

"I don't think so." Hooking a finger in her robe's sash, he pulled it free. "We're staying here."

8

TALK ABOUT WHIPLASH. He'd given up on getting any response from her tonight. He'd told himself that most women would want some time to think about whether they wanted to have a temporary fling with a guy they'd just met.

Apparently he'd misjudged. She'd walked right in on him as if she had every right in the world to do so. Damned if he was going to argue the point. No, what he had in mind was kissing her. And then…yeah, and then.

He cupped her face in both hands. God, her skin was soft. He looked into her green eyes, exactly the color of her robe. "Did some guy buy you the bathrobe?"

"No."

"Good." It shouldn't matter, but it did.

"I bought it for me. I like the feel of it on my bare skin." She slid her hands up his chest to his shoulders.

He shuddered at the caress. *Thank you, Jack.* And that was the last thought he'd give his host tonight.

He stroked his thumbs over her cheekbones. "I admire a woman who knows what she wants and goes after it."

"That's why I'm here." She clutched his shoulders. "Now kiss me before I go crazy."

"Would you really?" He leaned down and nibbled her lower lip. "I'd like that."

Her breath came in quick little gasps. "I've been known to smash crystal."

"No crystal here." He outlined her mouth with his tongue. "Do your worst." Holding off was driving him crazy, too, but it was a good kind of crazy. He didn't plan to leave this room until he'd used one of those condoms, and in the meantime, they could play.

Now that he knew the outcome, he wanted to savor the lead-up. They were two powder kegs ready to blow, and once they let loose, there would be no stopping them. This would be his only chance to build the suspense. As a bestselling author, he knew something about that.

"My worst?"

"Yeah." He feathered kisses at the corners of her mouth. "Bring it. Show me what you've got."

He wasn't even slightly prepared for what happened next. Sliding down his water-slicked body, she took his cock in her mouth. He swore softly as she reduced him to a blithering idiot. It seemed her worst was also her best.

"Enough." Somehow he found the fortitude to pull her upright before the inevitable happened. Then he gave her a long, slow and very deep kiss. She tasted of sex, and he was fast losing the battle to make this first encounter last. He wanted her wild, sassy, sexy self *now*.

But she'd thrown down a gauntlet, and any man worth his salt wouldn't ignore the challenge. Sinking to his knees, he cupped her smooth bottom and bestowed a similar, long, slow and very deep kiss on the moist cleft that was the entrance to all things wonderful.

Then he breached that entrance and reveled in her moans of pleasure. He brought her close to the edge, could almost taste victory, when she clutched his head and forced him away from paradise.

"Fair is fair." She gasped out the words, but they were clear enough. "You wouldn't let me, so I'm not letting you."

He had a good argument for why she should let him give her a climax. She could have several to his one. But if she wanted to stay even, that was okay, too. He stood and sought her mouth again. His lips were wet from all that he'd enjoyed, and she couldn't seem to get enough of kissing him.

They both became a little frantic after that. He grabbed for the condom box, but she was the one who took out the packet, tore it open and dressed him up. While she did that, he concentrated on not coming and ruining the entire enterprise.

They had a brief, breathless discussion about location, and they ended up on the floor with her on top. The floor was damn hard, and his muscles hadn't recovered from his morning ride, but once she lowered herself over his aching cock, he didn't notice or care. As she leaned over him, he finally paid proper attention to her sweet breasts, which fit exactly into his hands and tasted like wine on his lips.

She set the rhythm, and he rose to meet her as if they'd created this dance long ago. They fit together so perfectly that he found himself thinking of fate and destiny. He tried to hold her gaze, but she looked away, as if the force of this passion scared her a little.

He understood. It scared him, too. Then she pumped faster, and he forgot to be scared or even to think. There was only the pleasure, the rushing, crashing, incredible power of it driving him to lift into her, over and over.

A shred of sanity remained, enough for him to wait until he felt her convulse around him. Then he surrendered to a climax that bulldozed the breath right out of him, leaving him panting and dazed. She slumped forward, and he held her close.

As he slipped his hands under the silk of her robe to caress her warm skin, he realized she'd never taken off the robe. Its cool, smooth texture had billowed around them as they'd come together again and again, seeking their bliss. He was glad. If she kept the robe, it would always remind her of this moment.

That's when he admitted that he wouldn't be satisfied with the brief time they'd have together. He'd probably known that all along, but he'd pretended not to know. She might have done the same thing. But whether she realized it or not, he certainly did. This night had changed the game for both of them.

KERI SPENT THE night in Michael's bed, and a very fine bed it was, too. Choosing his king over her double had been a no-brainer. To make up for interrupting his soak in Epsom salts, she'd rubbed liniment into his sore muscles.

That had naturally led to a more interesting massage that resulted in another round of incredible sex. They'd both had a long day, so the addition of a couple of mind-blowing climaxes guaranteed that they'd sleep soundly, wrapped in each other's arms.

But Keri had neglected to bring her alarm clock over to Michael's room, and when she opened her eyes, the sun was up. Way up. The aroma of coffee and bacon told her that breakfast was being cooked without her. For the first time since arriving at the Last Chance, she'd overslept.

Struggling out of Michael's sleepy grip, she climbed out of bed. "I have to go."

He opened his eyes, but he wasn't fully awake. "Go where?"

"Downstairs. To my job. Mary Lou is cooking breakfast without me." She glanced at a small clock sitting on the nightstand. "Good grief. I should have been down there an hour ago!"

Michael sat up, the sheet pooling around his hips. His hair was mussed and his face was shadowed with the beginnings of a beard. He looked sexy and rumpled, the kind of man any woman would want to crawl back into bed with. "They'll make allowances," he said.

"You don't know that!" She caught a glimpse of his privileged upbringing in that statement, but she'd had a year to get over that attitude. "I doubt that Jack gave us carte blanche to ignore the ranch routine." She tied her robe with a jerk on the sash. "I'll see you later."

"Keri, wait."

"I can't. Last night was great, Michael. Really great. But I have to go." She ignored the plea in his stormy blue eyes and left the room. No matter what Jack had said, he'd still expect a day's work out of her.

Michael might see things differently, but he was a

product of the world she'd left. He was used to people *making allowances*. Once upon a time, she had been used to that, too. But she wasn't a spoiled little rich girl anymore, thank God.

Her new lifestyle had taught her to shower and dress in record time, so she was down in the kitchen in a matter of minutes. Her hair was still damp, but her clothes were clean and so was she.

Breakfast in the cozy kitchen, a meal she usually helped prepare, was in full swing. No doubt Watkins had already left for the barn, but Sarah and Pete sat at the oak table with full plates in front of them. They were involved in a deep discussion, probably something to do with the wedding. Keri could have dealt with having them there when she apologized to Mary Lou for sleeping in.

But Jack stood at the counter pouring himself a cup of coffee. She wasn't as sure that she could deal with Jack.

She met his dark gaze and caught a glint of curiosity there. She wasn't sure what he'd seen in her expression, but the corner of his mouth tilted up.

Her first impulse was to mumble some excuse and leave the room. Her second impulse was more worthy of her. She remembered that she was Keri Fitzpatrick, of the Baltimore Fitzpatricks. A Fitzpatrick didn't run and hide her head when she was caught in an awkward situation. A Fitzpatrick woman braved it out.

Her chin lifted. "Good morning, Jack."

"Morning, Keri." He smiled. "Sleep well?"

Jack Chance had *such* a devilish streak. "I did, thanks." She glanced at Mary Lou, who had turned from the stove at her entrance. Mary Lou also looked curious. "Sorry I didn't make it down in time to help you this morning, Mary Lou."

Sarah interrupted her private discussion with Pete. "Don't worry about it, Keri. I helped her. It felt good to wield a spatula again. Listen, Pete and I need everyone's opinion about the music for Saturday."

And just like that, the subject shifted away from Keri's late arrival to wedding plans. It could have been unintended, but Keri had been around Sarah Chance long enough to know that Sarah was a master at guiding social interactions into safe waters.

She wondered if Sarah had talked with Jack. Mother and son were very close, and it was always possible that Sarah had an idea of what was going on. Then again, she was extremely observant, so she might have figured things out on her own.

Pete, however, seemed oblivious. He simply followed Sarah's lead and opened up the discussion of wedding music to the group. "We planned to have Watkins play his guitar for the ceremony, but he's suggested adding the new guy, Trey Wheeler, and making it a duo. What do you think? Too much?"

Mary Lou laid down the spoon she'd been using to stir a big kettle of soup intended for lunch. "I don't think you can ever have too much guitar music. Trey and Watkins were jammin' in the kitchen the other night, and it was wonderful. Remember, Keri?"

"I do remember. I loved it. What songs are they going to play?"

"Just don't let them play 'Achy Breaky Heart.'" Jack

picked up his coffee mug and took a sip. "They purely love that tune, but it's not wedding material."

"It would be good for a laugh, though," Sarah said.

Pete leaned back in his chair. "Yeah, but are we going for laughs? How about 'I Cross My Heart'?"

"That's a good choice," Jack said. "But I don't want to get in the middle of this discussion. I'm taking my coffee and heading down to the barn." He started out of the kitchen, but then he paused. "Hey there, Michael. What's up?"

"Morning, Jack."

Keri gulped. Just when she was hoping that any potential awkwardness had been avoided, here came another dose of embarrassment through the kitchen door. She wished he'd stayed upstairs a little longer, but he hadn't, so she turned toward him with as much nonchalance as she could muster.

"Sleep well?" Jack asked oh-so-casually, repeating the question he'd put to Keri.

To Michael's credit, he didn't look at her. "Sure did. The Epsom salts and liniment did the trick."

Good Lord. Keri had to glance away and press her lips together to keep from laughing.

"Excellent news." Jack cleared his throat. "Well, I'm off to the barn. Meet me down there whenever you've finished breakfast. We'll saddle up Destiny."

"Good. Can't wait."

"That's what I like to hear. See you soon." He left the kitchen.

"Pull up a chair, Michael," Mary Lou said. "Keri, you go ahead and sit, too. There's bacon left and at least two helpings of the egg casserole Sarah and I made."

"Let me get it." Keri moved over to the stove. "You've already started lunch."

Mary Lou smiled at her. "I can wait on you this once. Go ahead and keep Michael company while he eats."

"Yes, please do," Sarah said. "Pete and I have to leave. We're driving into Jackson for some last-minute decorations, and you'll be happy to know, Keri, that we're also buying new sheets for the bunks. After two seasons of adolescent boys, we need something less worn for the wedding guests."

"New sheets would be lovely." Keri slid into the chair Michael held for her. The scent of his shaving lotion was nice, but it was the underlying aroma of liniment that stirred her the most. He must have put on more this morning. She vividly remembered helping him apply it last night, and what happened after that....

Michael nudged her knee with his, and she snapped back to the present.

Mary Lou hovered over her expectantly. "How many pieces of bacon, sweetie?"

"Two is plenty." She had a bad feeling that Mary Lou had been trying and failing to get her attention while she was daydreaming about sex with the man who currently sat right next to her. "Thank you." She directed the comment to both Michael for nudging her and Mary Lou for serving her.

Sarah tucked her napkin next to her plate and pushed back her chair. "You're looking especially pretty this morning, Keri."

"You do look great." Michael gave her a warm glance, probably warmer than he should have.

Sarah had a knowing gleam in her eye. "Maybe you should sleep in more often."

And now Keri was blushing for sure. She'd worked so hard not to get flustered, but a girl had only so much fortitude in these situations. "Thanks, but I don't like shirking my responsibilities."

"Which is laudable." Sarah rose from the table. "You've been extremely conscientious, and I appreciate that. But you and I both know this isn't a permanent career path for you."

Keri sighed. "No, it's not. I've learned so much, though. It's been good for me to have this job, in so many ways."

"A little physical work is always good for a person." Mary Lou scooped a helping of casserole onto Keri's plate. "Keeps you connected to the basics."

"That's exactly what this job has done for me," Keri said. "I wouldn't have missed the experience for the world."

"I'm glad." Sarah beamed at her before turning to Pete. "Ready?"

He drained his coffee mug and stood. "Let's do it."

"Don't forget to buy those extra chafing dishes while you're in Jackson," Mary Lou called after them. "For the wedding buffet."

"They're on the list!" Pete called back as they walked out of the kitchen.

Mary Lou glanced at Keri. "I also know you'll be leaving this job eventually, but thanks for staying through the wedding."

"Of course!"

"Normally Sarah helps when we have a big event, and I swear she'd try to do it, but we can't have that."

"No, we can't. Besides, I want to be on hand for the wedding. I'm excited for her, and for Pete. I've only known them for a year, but I feel as if it's been longer."

Mary Lou nodded. "That's the kind of people they are. They make you part of the family."

"It's a gift," Michael said. "I've only known them for a couple of days, and I already feel right at home. It'll be hard to go back to New York at the end of the week."

"Do you have to?" Mary Lou asked. "I don't think anybody needs that room in the near future, and I'm sure you'd be welcome."

"That's nice to hear, but I have to go back. There are some…some things I have to do."

"All right, then. If you must, you must. Speaking of things to be done, I have a couple of letters I was planning to write while the soup simmers, so if you'll excuse me, I'll get to it."

"By all means," Keri said. "I'll watch the soup for you."

"Thanks." Mary Lou walked back into her apartment.

After she left, the kitchen was silent except for the soft bubbling sound coming from the stove. Keri had been spared a morning-after discussion because she'd had to leave Michael's bedroom in such a rush. But she'd bet they were about to have one now.

However, they had to be careful. A normal discussion would carry into Mary Lou's apartment, but if they murmured softly, that would seem suspicious, too.

As if they'd choreographed it, they turned to each other at the same moment and started speaking.

Michael grinned, and it was the cutest expression she'd ever seen. He looked so damned happy. "You first."

"No, you." Every reservation she'd had about continuing this affair under the noses of Jack and Sarah disappeared when she saw the banked heat in his eyes, which seemed far more blue than gray this morning.

"Okay." He angled his head in the direction of Mary Lou's apartment, as if acknowledging their need for caution. "I wanted to thank you for locating the Epsom salts and the liniment for me."

"You're welcome." She winked at him. "It was my pleasure."

"You're very good at what you do."

"Thanks for the compliment." Heat sluiced through her at the look in his eyes. "It's wonderful to be appreciated."

"I plan to make a habit of the Epsom salts and liniment while I'm here."

She pressed her napkin to her mouth to keep from giggling. When she had control of herself, she leaned toward him. "I absolutely think you should. It's so good for you."

"I know." His tone became more urgent. "Sure wish I could take a treatment right now."

"But Jack's expecting you any minute."

"Yeah, he is." He scooted back his chair and picked up his plate.

"Hey, you didn't finish your breakfast."

"No." He stood and gestured to the prominent jut of his fly. "But as you can plainly see, I have to leave."

She gazed up at him. "Pity."

"Isn't it, though?" He winced as he walked over to the sink and dumped his food down the garbage disposal. "If I had time for a treatment, I might not have so much trouble walking right now."

"Think about Destiny. That'll take your mind off your problem."

He turned back to her. "The horse or the concept?"

"I meant the horse."

"I was hoping you meant the concept. I don't think it's an accident that we both ended up at this ranch together."

"Michael, I—"

"Gotta go. See you at lunch." He walked slowly and deliberately out of the kitchen.

She sat there staring at the empty doorway. Maybe he'd come back, pop his head in and say *just kidding*. But he didn't, and she was left with the conviction that he'd jumped way past this week and was already planning a reunion once they were both on the east coast.

If so, she needed to let him know that she wouldn't be living there from now on. She didn't want him building castles in the air. He was a storyteller, so he might be prone to that.

But damn, he'd looked so happy this morning. She hated to burst his bubble. But as she'd concluded last night, she wasn't a city girl anymore.

9

WHEN MICHAEL ARRIVED at the barn, Jack had already mounted a black-and-white Paint, one that was smaller than Bandit and didn't have the eye patches. Destiny was tied to the hitching post by his lead rope.

Jack walked his horse toward Michael. "Go get Destiny tacked up. We're heading out today."

Michael squinted as he looked up at Jack, who was wearing his shades again. Michael had pricey sunglasses in his room, but he hadn't worn them. He figured they'd fly off his face and get crunched in the dirt within the first five minutes of bouncing around on Destiny.

This morning, though, he wished he'd worn them, after all. Jack would have a harder time reading him if he had on shades. "Am I ready for that?"

Jack grinned. Despite his dark glasses, there was no mistaking the mischief in his expression. "You tell me. If you're too exhausted from your night's activities, we can always—"

"I'll saddle Destiny." Michael lengthened his stride

as he headed for the barn. Now that his erection had subsided, he moved damned well, if he said so himself.

He'd made a joke out of how much the liniment had helped, but apparently it had. Either that or great sex loosened up a guy's muscles better than anything else. He was more than willing to believe that.

Jack had left him alone to saddle and bridle Destiny, which he appreciated. After practicing so many times yesterday, he remembered what to do. Accomplishing it by himself and swinging up in the saddle made him feel like a semi-proficient rider.

Once Destiny started to move, though, he discovered a few twinges that hadn't bothered him until now. Yeah, he was saddle sore. Not incapacitated, though.

Jack rode up beside him. "Nice work."

"Thanks. Which horse is that?"

"This here's Ink Spot. Bandit's not up to a trail ride yet, so I'm giving this boy some exercise. How're you feeling?"

Michael nodded. "Good."

"You're looking good, too. More relaxed and loose. I always say there's nothing like a—"

"Jack, I don't want to talk about it."

That typical Jack grin appeared again. "You don't have to say another word, buddy. But just know that I'm happy for you."

"So we can drop the subject?"

"Absolutely. I can tell by the look on your face that you're a very satisfied man this morning. No discussion necessary."

"Glad to hear it. Now let's—"

"And Keri looked like a very satisfied woman, too."

"Jack, for God's sake."

"Just making a comment."

Michael sighed and waved a hand at Jack. "Okay, you're obviously very proud of yourself and need to have your say. Go ahead."

"Matter of fact, I am proud of myself, and I'll tell you why."

"I'm sure you will. Just don't get graphic or I'll have to punch you, and then I'd probably fall off this horse."

"Nothing graphic on my mind. Just an observation." Jack rested both hands on the saddle horn and sat back, almost as if he'd taken a spot in one of the porch rocking chairs. "When I met you at the airport, you were a man living in his head. I can imagine why that is. You're a writer, so a lot goes on in that head of yours."

Michael adopted Jack's posture, hands resting on the saddle horn, butt sitting easy on the saddle. It felt… right, as if he was supposed to be sitting in that saddle talking to Jack on this bright August morning.

"The thing is," Jack continued, "to be a cowboy, you have to live in your body, too. Riding is great for that. But good sex is even better. In fact, the two have some things in common. You have to feel the motion of the horse when you're riding the same way you sense the motion of a woman when you're making love to her." He paused and looked at Michael. "Your jaw's kind of tight. Is that too graphic for you?"

"You're skating on the edge, my friend." But Michael understood exactly what Jack was saying, and he was right. Having a vivid imagination was both a blessing and a curse. Michael could conjure up stories like nobody's business, but sometimes he forgot to come down from the clouds and experience reality.

"That's about all I had to say, anyway." Jack sat up straighter and gathered the reins in one hand. "I'll make a prediction, though. You'll find being on the back of a horse a much easier proposition today, and not only because of the practice in the corral yesterday." He clucked to Ink Spot. "Let's ride."

Michael hoped that prediction would be true, but when Destiny broke into a trot, he bounced the way he had before. He thought about what Jack had said, and then he thought about the effortless way he and Keri had moved together in the king-sized bed.

There had been nothing intellectual about that experience. They'd communicated on a purely physical level as they explored different rhythms and found the one that worked. Wow, had it worked.

The heated memory of what he'd shared with Keri cushioned the jolting discomfort of Destiny's trot. And sometime later, Michael realized he wasn't bouncing anymore. Instead, he was moving with the motion of the horse. His body knew what to do if he stopped trying to think his way through the problem.

Once he could relax and enjoy the ride, he paid attention to his surroundings. Dry grass warmed by the sun smelled faintly like the old books in his family's library. They rode past a stand of evergreens, and he picked up the crisp scent of pine and the warble of songbirds flitting among the branches. The creak of leather and the steady beat of hooves had a lulling effect.

Across the meadow, the snow-topped Grand Tetons rose against a blue sky. A hawk wheeled overhead, probably searching for breakfast. No wait, that wasn't a hawk. Michael shaded his eyes and looked up. White feathered head, big wingspan. A bald eagle.

Michael looked at Jack ahead of him on the trail. Jack was watching the eagle, too.

"Do you see many of those?" Michael called out.

"We have a pair of them nesting on the edge of the property. A woman named Naomi Perkins is camped out there while she studies them. That could be one of them. I'm sure there are others in the area, too."

"I've only seen pictures of them." Michael had expected to see wildlife while he was out here. He hadn't expected to be dazzled by it. He watched the eagle until it was only a speck in the sky.

Meanwhile Destiny, who'd picked up on the fact that Michael wasn't paying attention to him, had stopped to munch on the dry grass beside the trail.

Jack was several yards ahead of them by now. He turned in the saddle. "Pull his head up. Don't let him eat like that." Jack continued along at a good clip.

"Right." But Destiny was a deeply stubborn animal who wouldn't give up his snack easily. By the time Michael wrestled him away from the grass, Jack was more like thirty yards away.

Nudging Destiny's belly with his heels, Michael clucked at the horse the way Jack did when he wanted to get the animal moving. Destiny's ears pricked forward and he seemed to notice for the first time that he was lagging behind.

Michael nudged him again, and a quick walk turned into a trot. They weren't catching up, though, so Michael made that clucking sound to speed up the process.

Destiny surged forward in a rolling gait that covered the ground much faster. After the first shock of the faster pace, Michael discovered he *loved* it. He didn't know if they were galloping or not, but this was how he wanted to ride, rocking gently in the saddle with the wind in his face.

Jack turned in the saddle, flashed a quick grin, and took Ink Spot's speed up to match Destiny's. "How do you like cantering?" he called over his shoulder.

"This is cantering? I thought we were galloping."

"Nope. Galloping is much faster, and we won't be doing that." Jack slowed Ink Spot to a trot, and finally to a walk. "We'll head back now, and walk them in." He turned Ink Spot in a semicircle, cutting through the grass to head back the same way.

"Works for me." Michael guided Destiny along the same route and paid attention so Destiny didn't pause to chew on grass now that they were moving so slowly.

Jack regained the trail and swiveled in his saddle. "Congratulations, cowboy. You've ridden a trot and a canter. It wasn't always pretty, but you stayed on. I think by the time you leave you'll be good enough to fool them during the video."

"I guess." Michael had forgotten all about the filming. He'd been immersed in this experience for its own sake, testing himself to see if he could hack it. So far, he'd done okay. And this was only Wednesday, his second full day of lessons. He might have the makings of a cowboy, after all.

"You know what?" he said. "Let's not worry too much about what skills I need for the video. Just teach me everything you can in the time we have."

Jack pivoted in the saddle again. "You want to learn how to pen cattle?"

Two days ago, Michael would have been too intimidated to even try something like that. But that was two days ago. "Do you have time to teach me?"

"I can show you some of the basics. I can't turn you into an expert in two days, but the cutting horse does most of the work, anyway. We can start this afternoon, and we'll have all day tomorrow. You'll get the idea."

"Then yes, I'd like that."

"All righty." Jack smiled. "After you get comfortable with it, like maybe tomorrow afternoon, you should invite Keri down to watch. It impresses the hell out of women."

"That wouldn't be my motivation, Jack."

"Maybe not, but when it comes to the ladies, a cowboy uses all his tools."

DURING LUNCH, KERI noticed that Michael seemed more relaxed around the other cowhands. His riding lesson with Jack this morning seemed to have gone well, judging from the way Michael was joking around with everyone. Yesterday he'd seemed worried that he wouldn't make the grade, but he'd gained confidence in the past twenty-four hours.

She couldn't help wondering if his high spirits came partly from his new relationship with her. She hoped not. His remark about destiny bringing them together continued to worry her. They might need to have a discussion about that tonight, just to make sure they understood each other before they got in any deeper.

Thinking about what else might happen tonight made

her hot and bothered, so she shoved those thoughts away. When Michael said hello, she returned his greeting with a casual smile. Jack might know what was going on, but the rest of the crew didn't need to find out. They probably wouldn't, though, because everyone was focused on the upcoming wedding on Saturday.

Keri couldn't believe it was Wednesday already. She had the upstairs in good shape, though. Once Sarah and Pete brought home the new sheets, she'd make up the beds for the wedding guests, who were mostly Pete's friends.

Meanwhile the ranch hands were making minor repairs to the barn and the corrals so the place would look perfect by Friday afternoon. On Saturday they'd set up the tents and the dancing platform for the outdoor reception. The wedding itself would be held in the ranch house living room.

Keri wouldn't be in charge of creating that venue. Jack's sister-in-law Tyler Keller was a professional party planner, and she in turn would get plenty of help from Sarah's daughters-in-law when it came time to decorate. Keri just had to make sure the area stayed clean.

That reminded her that Sarah had asked for every last bit of soot to be cleaned out of the fireplace, because they planned to fill the cavity with greenery and flowers. As she helped Mary Lou clear the lunch dishes, she asked for some tips on how to do it.

"Don't use the regular vacuum cleaner," Mary Lou said. "Let me go get the old wet/dry vac from the laundry room." She set down a load of dishes and left the kitchen. In a few moments she was back with the canister and a hose. "Go ahead and get started. I can finish up here."

"Okay."

"And change out of that white shirt. You're going to get filthy. Do you have something old to wear?"

Keri paused to think.

"Never mind. I have an old shirt you can put on. I use it whenever we repaint." She left again and returned with a button-up shirt covered in paint splatters of various colors. "It's ugly, but it's clean."

"Thanks, Mary Lou." Keri took the shirt and the vacuum cleaner and left the kitchen. Michael and Jack and a few of the hands were still in the dining room, and as Keri walked by she heard enough of the conversation to gather they were talking about cutting horses.

That made sense. The Last Chance was famous for their well-trained cutting horses. She'd watched a demonstration this summer and had found the maneuvers fascinating but tricky. She doubted that Michael was up to that kind of riding yet, but maybe he planned to watch someone else do it.

After dropping off the vacuum in the living room, she climbed the stairs to the second floor. In her room, she pulled off her white T-shirt and put on Mary Lou's shirt. It hung on her, but that didn't matter.

As she started out of her room again, she heard boots on the stairs. Adrenaline sent her heart racing—only one person had a reason to come up here.

Michael topped the stairs and came down the hallway toward her. "Interesting outfit."

"It's Mary Lou's shirt." Her breath hitched at the heat in his eyes. "I'm going to clean out the fireplace."

"I wondered. I went looking for you and found the vacuum cleaner, but you were gone. I decided to see if you were up here."

"You were looking for me? Why?" Silly question. His expression told her exactly why.

"Because I was going crazy all through lunch." He stepped closer. "I needed this." He drew her into his arms.

She told herself that she should resist, but being held in those strong arms felt like heaven. "I'm not sure we should—"

"Just one kiss. I have to get down to the barn. Jack's going to start teaching me how to ride a cutting horse."

"He is? Listen, be careful. That's tricky."

"That's why I want to learn." His head dipped. "I like tricky."

Well, she liked *this*—his warm, clever mouth seducing her, his tongue teasing her with promises of what he'd do to her later tonight, his hand slipping under the hem of the loose shirt to cup her breast....

Before she realized what he had in mind, he'd flipped open the front catch of her bra and was stroking her nipple with his thumb. His kiss deepened, and he pulled her against the hard ridge of his penis.

Now she *really* should resist. But instead of pushing him away, she'd somehow shoved her hands in the back pockets of his jeans and urged him even closer.

His kiss turned from a full-on assault to soft nibbles. "If I don't let you go right now, I'm going to drag you into my bedroom and strip you naked."

She gulped for air. "That would be bad. You'd never hear the end of it from Jack."

"That's for sure." He squeezed her breast. "But it would almost be worth it."

She forced herself to slip her hands from his pockets. "Let me go, Michael." Her voice didn't carry much conviction. "I'll see you tonight."

He groaned and leaned his forehead against hers. "That's hours away."

"But then we'll have hours together." She rested her palms on his chest and felt the wild beat of his heart. If she pushed gently he'd probably release her, but she couldn't make herself do it. His warmth made her want to nestle closer, not pull away.

"Okay, I'm going to be strong." Drawing in a shaky breath, he stepped back and gazed at her, his eyes the blue-gray of storm clouds. "I'll be upstairs as soon as I can possibly get away tonight."

"Me, too." She trembled, still not in control of her impulses. "I think Sarah knows."

"I think so, too, but she doesn't seem to disapprove. If anything, she seems happy about it."

"Well, she won't be if I start slacking off." She said that as much to remind herself as to inform Michael.

He took another deep breath. "And I have to get down to the barn." Reaching out, he brushed a finger over her cheek. "See you tonight."

"It's a date." She waited until he'd started down the stairs before she reached under the shirt and hooked her bra in place.

Her body was moist and achy from his touch, and she was honest enough to admit that if he'd tried to maneuver her back to his bedroom, she'd probably have let him do it. He tempted the hot-blooded Irish lass she kept hidden most of the time. When that side of her cut loose, no telling what might happen.

10

MICHAEL HAD TROUBLE sitting through dinner with Sarah and Pete that night. And it wasn't only because he was eager to get upstairs and be with Keri. He ached all over, and the longer he sat, the more his muscles stiffened. In his zeal to practice riding a cutting horse, he'd stayed in the saddle way too long this afternoon.

He'd admitted to a few aches and pains, and Pete had been generous with the Scotch. The liquor had helped, but he still hurt. He hoped to hell his enthusiasm for riding hadn't ruined what promised to be another night of great sex.

When dinner was over, he winced as he rose from the table.

Sarah noticed. "I recommend a long soak in Epsom salts," she said. "And tomorrow you need to tell Jack to ease up on you."

"Jack's not to blame." Michael hobbled to the doorway. "I'm the damned fool who wanted to stay out there. I was having fun and didn't realize what I was doing to myself."

"I'm glad to hear you were having fun, at least."

Sarah gave him a sympathetic smile. "Epsom salts, plenty of liniment and a good night's sleep. You'll be better in the morning."

"I'm sure I will be. See you both for breakfast." He made his way down the hall and climbed the stairs with effort. He knew Keri wouldn't be in her room yet. If the meal had just ended, Keri would be helping Mary Lou with the cleanup.

That was okay with him. He'd soak in the tub and hope that it restored him to vibrant manliness. He wanted to be a tiger in bed tonight, but at the moment he felt like a slightly drunk pussycat.

Not long afterward, he slipped into the warm, salted water with a groan. Yes, this was going to help. He put a rolled-up towel behind his neck and slid as far into the water as he could, considering the length of the tub and his six-two frame.

Closing his eyes, he drifted in the soothing water and his tortured muscles stopped screaming at him. He didn't want to go to sleep, but the combination of the warm water and the lingering effects of the Scotch tugged at him. Maybe just a little nap....

The water had cooled by the time he slowly came awake. But that wasn't what had roused him from sleep. Although he lay still, the water rippled around him, and something wonderful was happening to his cock. So nice. He hated to open his eyes, in case he was dreaming the sweet massage and opening his eyes would make it stop.

But the pressure felt real, and finally he looked. Keri, without a stitch on, knelt by the tub, one arm braced on the edge and the other hand lazily stroking his very happy johnson. She gazed at his growing erection with interest, as if conducting a scientific experiment.

"Having fun?"

Her glance shifted to his face, and her green eyes were lit with the passion he longed to see there. "You're awake."

"Some parts more than others."

She kept toying with him. "The water's getting cold. Cold water won't help much. You need to change the water, or—"

"Do something with what you're building there?" He checked out the stiff evidence and figured he was more than ready to party.

"I don't want to put a strain on you. Sarah mentioned you were in bad shape." But her fondling continued, and the flame danced in her eyes.

"I'm in terrible shape. I need you to keep that up for a really long time."

"Michael, be serious. Are you hurting?"

"Yeah. My nuts ache like you wouldn't believe."

The corners of her mouth tipped up. "I could just keep doing this and relieve the pressure."

"To hell with that." He sat up and discovered that the pain was still there, but not nearly as bad. The potential explosion threatening in the region of his groin, however, was a more urgent matter.

Her forehead creased in a cute little frown. "Think you can make it to the bedroom?"

"Probably not. Did you happen to bring a condom in with you?"

"Well…yes." She gestured toward the counter. "I left it over there."

"That's my girl. Stand back. I'm getting out." As he navigated out of the tub with some decent dexterity but a few moans and groans thrown in, he could tell she was trying not to laugh. "It's okay," he said. "You're allowed to make fun of me. It was my own stupid fault."

She handed him a towel. "I think you're brave. I admire a man who goes all out."

"You do?" He tossed the towel aside. "Then you're going to love this." He grabbed her and lifted her to the counter so abruptly that she squealed. That gratified him. He didn't relish playing the role of the invalid.

Dropping to his knees sent shooting pains through his body, but he ignored them. The reward for doing it would be worth whatever it cost him. "Prop your hands behind you."

"Michael, I don't know if you should…" Her protest died away as he settled her knees over his shoulders, cupped her bottom and drew her gently to the edge of the vanity.

Her sigh was deep and heartfelt. "Oh, Michael. Michael, that's…good." After that, words seemed to fail her as her moans of delight blended with the liquid sound of his tongue and his mouth as he feasted on her many treasures.

She didn't yell when she came, which was a good thing because he didn't know how well sound carried in this house. But she arched against him and moaned his name low in her throat as the spasms rocked her.

Heart pounding with triumph, he licked the juices heated by her passion. Her passion for *him*. She'd said his name. She knew who knelt between her thighs and sought her essence.

When he stood, he clenched his jaw against a cry of pain. But his throbbing cock demanded satisfaction. He found the condom she'd left on the counter and put it on.

She watched him, leaning back on her hands, her eyes heavy-lidded in the aftermath of her climax, her body limp, pliable. Lust pumped through him like molten lava, urging him to take her with abandon. Grasping her ankles, he lifted them to his shoulders.

Her eyes widened.

"Yes." He gazed down at her, so open, so vulnerable. She wouldn't be able to move. But he could. "Just like this." And he shoved in deep, lifting her off the vanity.

She gasped.

He wanted to take her, but he didn't want to hurt her. "Keri, did I—"

"No!" She began to pant, softly, seductively. "No, it's good. It's good. Don't stop."

That was all he needed to know. He grasped her bottom to keep her steady and began to thrust. Dear God. This was intense. He looked into her eyes, and saw his own raw hunger reflected there.

He pumped faster, and she began to whimper. Faster yet, and she let out a high, keening cry. He no longer cared who could hear as he drove into her again and again. He felt her tighten around his cock. Then she came, breathing hard, and he rocketed forward, seeking, seeking, and finding...yes...*yes.* With a groan he sank forward, into her, as his cock pulsed in a glorious, liberating rhythm.

He stayed braced against her for several long seconds as he slowly recovered from the rocket-ship ride of making love to Keri Fitzpatrick. As a guy with an imagination, he'd harbored quite a few sexual fantasies. He had a feeling she could make every single one of them come true.

DESPITE MICHAEL'S AMAZING performance in the bathroom, Keri was worried that he'd end up crippled by tomorrow if he didn't slow down. When they finally made it into his big bed, she insisted on massaging him with liniment. He made some mild protest about feeling like a damned baby, but he stretched out on his stomach with a sigh of relief.

By the light from the bedside lamp, she worked the cream into his muscles, which gave her the perfect excuse to admire his body. He might be a writer, but he had the physique of an athlete. His broad shoulders tapered to slim hips and a sculpted backside. His thighs and calves had the definition of a runner.

"Where did you get all these muscles?" she asked as she worked on his back with her fingertips and the heels of both hands.

"Gym membership. Didn't prepare me for this, though."

"Horseback riding is its own thing." She scooted down and began massaging his thighs.

"No kidding." He moaned softly.

"Am I hurting you?"

"Not really. It feels good, in an intense sort of way." He inhaled slowly and exhaled even more slowly, as if breathing through the pain. "Do you ride?"

"Yes, if I have time. When the boys are here, I'm usually busy with them and don't ride much. Part of my job was teaching them to clean up after themselves."

"Did they learn?"

"They got better at it."

"Maybe you need to teach me."

"Nah." She used firm strokes on his calves. "You're an honored guest."

"Everybody else works on the ranch. I feel like a spoiled rich guy."

"You're not so bad." She moved back up to his thigh muscles. She guessed those needed the most attention from the way he'd moaned earlier. "You hung up your towels and picked up your clothes."

"But I didn't make my bed."

"No." She smoothed her hand up over the swell of his butt. Nice buns. "But I liked doing that. It reminded me of all the fun we had."

"Maybe we should make the bed together, so we can both enjoy those memories."

"You know perfectly well that we'd never get it done." Somehow her massage had turned into a caress. He really did have spectacular butt cheeks.

"So were you turned on by making my bed?"

"Maybe." She was getting turned on now, that was for sure.

"Did you stretch out on it and wish I could be there, buried deep inside you?"

"It's possible I did, just for a moment."

His voice roughened. "Did thinking about that make you wet and achy?"

"Yes." Giving in to temptation, she leaned down and kissed his firm butt. Not satisfied with that, she licked the spot, and kissed him again.

"You do realize you're driving me insane when you do that."

"I hope so." She kissed the other side. "Because I really want to make another memory in this bed right now."

"How convenient." He rolled away from her and gestured toward his penis, which stood at rigid attention. "Apparently, so do I."

Things moved quickly after that. She soon found herself on her back looking into Michael's beautiful eyes as he aligned his body with hers.

"I'll suit up in a minute," he murmured. "Once I put that condom on I'm like one of Pavlov's dogs. I have to go for it. But first I want to take some time to just look at you." He rubbed his chest lightly over her breasts and lifted up so he could see his handiwork. "I like it when your nipples perk up and take notice."

"Me, too." She took a quick breath. "I like it when you suck on them."

His gaze grew hot. "Is that a request?"

"Well, as long as you're looking, you might as well sample what I have to offer."

"What an excellent idea." As he slid farther down, he made plenty of skin-to-skin contact. Braced above her, he focused on her breasts. "So perfect. I can't decide which to taste first. Choose for me, Mistress Keri."

Heat surged through her as she cupped her right breast and lifted it toward him. "This one, if you please, kind sir."

"I would be most pleased." Dipping his head, he kissed the very tip of her nipple. Then he swirled his tongue around it. And again, a fleeting caress.

"More." Her throaty plea came unbidden.

"Ah, Keri." Leaning down, he opened his mouth and closed it over her nipple. His cheeks hollowed as he drew her in.

She felt the tug all the way to her womb. Using his tongue to increase the pressure, he began a rhythmic sucking motion, and her body clenched in response. She arched against him, wanting....

As if in answer to her unspoken need, he shifted his weight to one arm and reached between her thighs. His touch was smooth, gliding in on a rush of moisture.

Yes. She moaned as his fingers worked their magic. So good. So very...with a gasp of surprise, she came, the tremors rolling through her in quick succession as she gulped for air.

He lifted his head from her breast and gazed into her eyes. His hand slowed to a gentle, easy rhythm, and he smiled. "Again, Keri. I want to watch this time."

Her body was his to command. She spontaneously tightened around his fingers and lifted her hips.

"That's it," he murmured, deepening his caress. "You're so beautiful like this, with your breasts all rosy and your eyes getting darker the closer you get." His breathing roughened. "I could almost come, just looking at you."

His intensity turned his eyes to a deep gray. She was mesmerized by the heat in those eyes as he probed the very core of her sexual being.

"But I won't come." He stroked her with deliberate intent. "I'd rather watch you. Now you're closer yet. I can feel it right there." He thrust his fingers deep again.

She began to whimper.

"Soon, Keri, soon. I can see the climax in your eyes. I can feel it in your body. Almost there. Now, Keri. Now!" He pumped faster.

She erupted, lifting off the bed with a cry of surrender. Murmuring words of encouragement, he continued to pleasure her until she sank back, dragging in air and drained of every ounce of tension.

She closed her eyes and savored the gift he'd given her. Then she opened them and gazed up at him. "That was…amazing."

"For me, too."

She took a shaky breath and reached to stroke his cheek. "But I'll bet you're about ready to die of frustration."

"Pretty much." His voice sounded strained.

"Then let's do something about that. Lie back and let me take care of you for a change."

"I hope you're not talking about liniment."

That made her smile. "No." She brushed her fingertips over his chin, darkened with the beginnings of a beard. It made him look a little dangerous and a lot sexy. She ran her tongue over her lips. "I have a different therapy in mind."

11

MICHAEL DIDN'T THINK there was a man alive who could resist a woman who offered to give him a tongue bath. She licked him from stem to stern, with her dark hair curtaining her face and tickling his skin. He hadn't realized that his nipples were so sensitive, or the inside of his elbow, or the spaces between his toes.

The experience was erotic as hell, probably even more so because she didn't lay her tongue or a finger on his extremely erect cock. He just prayed he could hold himself together long enough for her to reach that pivotal point. She had to go there eventually.

In the meantime, she made him moan, and gasp and sweat. If she kept avoiding the main event, she was going to make him beg. Maybe that was the idea.

He struggled to catch his breath. "Keri?"

"Mmm?" From her position down at his feet, she looked up the length of his body. She had to peer around his stiff rod to make eye contact.

"Are you going to…"

She smiled. "Yes, Michael, I am."

"When?"

"I wanted to build the suspense so it would be super good."

He nearly choked. "If you build it any higher, I'll be able to break bricks with my cock."

"Well, then." She did a little maneuver that allowed her to settle her plump breasts on his shins. "I'll move to the next phase." She slid up his body with a maddening lack of haste, but at last she lay with her breasts cradled against his thighs and her warm breath against his shaft.

His pulse rate skyrocketed. She adjusted her position, and one of her nipples grazed his balls. He almost came from that alone. Gritting his teeth, he fought back the orgasm that prowled like a tiger in a cage.

She kissed the base of his cock. He wanted to see, but he was afraid the visual would do him in. Ah, hell. He was nearly a goner, anyway. Stuffing a pillow behind his head, he looked down to where she lay. From that position, she'd never be able to carry out the job he had in mind for that full mouth of hers.

He started to make a suggestion, but before he could, she braced her forearms on the bed and began to glide upward. As she rose, she flattened her tongue against the ridged underside of his penis. He groaned and fisted his hands in the sheet. He wouldn't come, he wouldn't come, he wouldn't come.

He didn't, but it was a close call. A drop of moisture trembled on the tip. When she reached that point, she licked it off, and he groaned again, a little louder this time.

Meeting his gaze, she winked at him.

"You're a devil." He sounded as if he'd swallowed barbed wire.

"This is for your own good." Then she finally, *finally* closed her mouth over his johnson. But she wasn't finished with him yet. Circling the base with her thumb and forefinger, she created the equivalent of a cock ring.

He'd had a vague idea of the concept, but she showed him exactly how it worked. She drove him into a frenzy with her tongue, her lips, even her teeth. When she knew he was about to come, she squeezed the base of his penis until his breathing slowed a little. And then she took him back up again—and again.

He went a little nuts—laughing, moaning, writhing against the mattress—until the moment she let go and took him in all the way to the back of her throat with the strongest suction she'd used so far. His climax roared through him with the force of a tsunami. He came, and came and came.

She took it all. As he gasped for air and stared at the ceiling, he heard her swallow. That, he thought, had to be the most intimate bedroom sound in the world. He was one lucky sonofabitch to be here with Keri listening to her swallow like that. At this moment, he wouldn't trade places with any guy, anywhere, not even someone dominating the bestseller charts.

CUDDLING AFTER SPECTACULAR sex rated high on Keri's list, and fortunately, Michael also seemed to be a fan.

"I don't want to fall asleep, though." He gathered her against him, spoon fashion.

"You should sleep." Snuggling into the warm curve of his body, she felt relaxed and cozy. She'd planned for falling asleep in his bed this time. Before her little ambush in the tub, she'd left her cell phone on his bedside table and had set the alarm. "You'll have another big day tomorrow."

"Yeah, but I'm having a big night tonight." He wrapped his arm around her and cupped her breast. "That's more important to me than my big day tomorrow."

"Uh-oh." Guilt washed over her. "Am I distracting you from what you came out here to do?"

"Nope." He lazily fondled her breast. "You're helping."

"Maybe a little bit, by rubbing liniment on you, but you could do that for yourself, and you'd get more sleep without me around."

"No, I wouldn't. I'd know you were right across the hall and I'd lie awake with a stiff cock all night."

"Yes, but we've taken care of that. Twice, in fact. Much as I love being here in your bed, I should probably go back to my own room." She started to pull away.

His grip tightened. "Don't you dare leave, especially out of guilt. You're the reason I rode so well this morning, so stop thinking you're a hindrance. Jack predicted I'd do better after having good sex, and—"

"Wait a minute. Jack recommended going to bed with me because it would make you a better rider? Now I'm insulted!" She tried harder to squirm away, but he held her fast.

"No, he didn't do that. Stop struggling and check your Irish temper for a second, okay?"

"This better be good." She relaxed against him again, because it was what she really wanted to do, anyway.

"Oh, it is good." He loosened his hold and kissed her shoulder. "Win-win. Jack said I had to get out of my head and into my body if I wanted to learn to ride well. Yesterday I couldn't do that, but after being with you last night, I got much better at it." He cupped her breast again. "Sex with you keeps me grounded."

"That's nice to hear, but let's get back to the part where Jack predicted your riding would improve after having sex with me. When did he say that?"

"Ah, I see what the problem is. You think he said that yesterday and that's why he wanted us to get together."

"Well, isn't it?"

"No. Okay, maybe a little bit, but that was an afterthought, I'm sure. He didn't make that remark about sex helping horsemanship until this morning, after he figured out we'd had a fun time last night."

"I'm not sure I believe it helps all that much. He might be trying to justify this arrangement."

"Oh, it helps. You know how we just instinctively move in rhythm with each other during sex?"

"Yeah." And talking about it was getting her hot. She didn't think that was possible after all they'd done tonight, but she couldn't deny the tension coiling within her.

"I had to let my body feel the rhythm of the horse and go with it. I was thinking about you, and how great we felt together, and suddenly I was sitting a trot without bouncing."

"Huh. That's cool." Keri sighed and nestled closer to his warmth. "Okay, I feel better now."

"Actually, you feel outstanding." He stroked her breast. "Silky soft. I love touching you."

"FYI, touching me is producing certain results. I'm not saying we should do anything about it, but—"

"But we could." He nudged her with his growing erection. "Incredibly enough."

"I know." She pressed against him, reveling in her power to arouse him again. "I hope we don't kill each other with too much sex."

"If we do, I'll die a happy man." He slid his hand between her thighs. "Mmm. I think you're ready for another round."

"Told you." She started to turn toward him.

"Stay there. Stay right…there." And he withdrew his hand.

She missed his caress, but she was eager to find out exactly what he had in mind. Cool air wafted over her as he moved away.

Foil crinkled, latex snapped and he was back. "I want to try it like this, on our sides." He grasped her hips, angled his body and eased into her from behind. "I couldn't do this, except you are so…wet." He moved slowly until he was deep inside. His breathing came faster, now. "How's that?"

"Different." She hadn't thought she was a fan of this position, but now that he was there, filling her, she thought she might like it, after all. And he seemed to love it.

He cradled her breast, as before, but now they were intimately connected as he lightly pinched her nipple. His fingers began a rhythmic kneading motion as he began to move within her. He was slow at first, almost careful.

But then he stroked faster, and the world shifted. Having sex like this was a step away from civilization and a step toward primitive lust. She felt it, and judging from the energy he put into each thrust, he felt it, too.

From this angle, her passage was narrower, which meant she felt the slide of his penis more intensely. Surely he did, too, which would explain his ragged breathing and his eagerness to pound into her over and over. She trembled on the edge of a climax that drew nearer each time he drove forward. Then he released his hold on her hip to reach around and slip his finger into her cleft. He pressed down, and she came in a rush amid wild cries of completion.

He kept his hand there, steadying her as he plunged into her with abandon until he shuddered against her, moaning softly, holding her tight to receive all that he had to give. Their breathing slowed, and they lay still, coupled together in an ancient posture.

She'd never before felt taken, but she felt it now. She and Michael were knocking down the barriers between them one by one. With each barrier that fell, they became more vulnerable to being hurt when they eventually had to part.

And they would part. His life was in New York, in the heart of the publishing world, while hers, once she handled some details in Baltimore, would be in Jackson Hole. If she had any sense, she'd pull back. She'd protect herself and protect him, too, from risking too much.

But being with Michael was so good. And he'd said that she was helping him become a better cowboy. That was all the rationalization she needed for indulging in sexual pleasure the likes of which she'd never known.

LATER, MICHAEL LAY on his back beside Keri. They held hands but they didn't speak, almost as if they both needed time to process what was going on. He couldn't be certain of her state of mind, but his was certainly on tilt.

He'd never experienced intimacy like this. The reason was obvious. He'd known this might happen before they'd begun the affair. He'd finally gotten naked with a woman emotionally as well as physically. Until now, no lover had truly known him, known the wildness deep in his soul. He wasn't sure if it was Keri or the ranch, or maybe the combination of the two that brought it out.

Because of that, he wasn't sure he could trust his feelings for her. He thought they might have a future, but what if the dynamic changed once they were both living back east? Would he be the same uninhibited person if they met up in New York? Would she?

She gave his hand a squeeze. "I have a question for you."

"Shoot." Considering the direction of his thoughts, questions made his heart thump a little faster. He wondered if she had some of the same thoughts.

"Why don't the characters in your books ever have oral sex?"

He laughed. Of all the burning questions he imagined she might have, that wasn't one of them. He wasn't even sure how to answer.

But she was obviously interested in this topic because she layered on another question. "Didn't the people back in the Old West do that stuff?"

"I haven't given it much thought, but I'll bet they did. Couples have been enjoying oral sex throughout history, so the Old West wouldn't have been that different."

"How about sex with the woman astride?"

This was the strangest conversation. "I'm sure they

did that, too. Ladies of the night were popular back in those days, and the more innovative ones probably made the most money."

"But nice girls stuck with the missionary position, I suppose."

He rolled to his side and gazed at her. "I don't know that, either. People are endlessly inventive in the bedroom. Who knows what they did when the candles were snuffed?"

She turned to face him and her green eyes sparkled. "Do you suppose their men took them from behind once in a while?"

"I wouldn't doubt it. For one thing, if a woman's pregnant, especially if she's pretty far along, I've heard that's the most comfortable way to have sex."

"I hadn't thought of that. It would be. And just because a woman has a big belly doesn't mean she doesn't want an orgasm now and then. Or that he doesn't want to enjoy the pleasures of his lovely wife."

He was transfixed by the image of making love to her when she was pregnant with his child. How dumb was that? Their relationship might not survive past this week, let alone blossom into a permanent commitment that resulted in her being pregnant with his kid.

Even so, the image of taking her to bed when she was in that special condition wouldn't leave him. He felt a tenderness that had absolutely no basis in fact. For one thing, she might not even *want* children, let alone children who carried his genetic code.

Finally he asked the obvious question. "Why are you so interested in the sex lives of people in the nineteenth century?"

"Because I read your books."

"I know you do." That's what had landed them in this briar patch, or more accurately, in this bed of roses. He now owed a huge, impossible-to-calculate debt to his publisher for causing him to meet Keri. Fortunately his publishing house would never know the role it played, so he wouldn't have to make any kind of grand gesture.

"I'm only one reader, and I know you must have thousands."

"I do, now. I didn't in the beginning, but business is picking up."

She smiled. "It should. You're a terrific writer."

"Thanks." He was a little embarrassed to be having this discussion while he was naked with a woman he'd recently... Oh, yes, he certainly had. And he'd loved every single thrust into her warm body, every taste of her juices on his tongue, every whimper she'd uttered when he'd touched her in those secret, fragrant places. He'd loved the way her pupils dilated when she was ready to come. He loved the way she arched into his caress, and how she quivered when he—

"I wish you'd put more hot sex in your books," she said.

He blinked, disoriented. "What?"

"You have a really sexy style—strong, masculine, commanding. I wanted to see that masterful behavior in the bedroom. I wanted the scenes to crackle, with the cowboy hero taking charge and stripping her naked, or maybe the heroine pushing him back on that coverlet and straddling him. I wanted you to make me squirm in my bed while I was reading those pages, but...you pulled your punches."

He stared at her. "The stories aren't about sex."

"Everything's about sex."

He started to contradict her, but then he realized she was right. Sampson and Delilah. Anthony and Cleopatra. Napoleon and Josephine. From the famous lovers of the past to current scandals in the headlines, sex changed lives and altered the course of history.

"I wondered if maybe Jim Ford wasn't very creative in bed," she continued, "so those scenes would necessarily be boring. But you're not boring in bed, Michael."

"That's something, at least." He faced another decision—whether to make excuses or tell her the truth. He opted for the truth. "I didn't know if I could write good sex scenes, so I skimmed over them."

She held his gaze. "You can write good sex scenes. I know that you can after spending two glorious nights in your bed. You only have to give yourself permission to let that side of you come out in the writing. And after all, it's only Jim Ford doing it. Nobody knows Jim Ford, really."

"You do."

"And I'll never tell."

He wasn't worried in the least that she would tell. No, the real worry was whether or not he was capable of writing a sex scene that conveyed the intensity he'd experienced with her. If he failed, he'd know it from her expression.

He'd suffered through bad reviews before, but always once removed, something he saw in print or online. Because he didn't interact much with readers for fear they'd discover his identity, he'd seldom had someone criticize him to his face.

Not that Keri would attack. She would be kind, regardless of whether she liked what he'd written. But if he hadn't met her expectations, he'd know it. That could be rough.

Still, she'd issued a challenge no writer worth his salt could ignore. They talked a little more about the subject, but he didn't agree or disagree that he should beef up those scenes. Privately, he knew he was going to give it a shot and then decide if he'd show her what he'd done.

He waited until she finally drifted off to sleep. Then he slipped out of bed and pulled his laptop from its case. If he planned to do this thing, he'd best do it now, when his nostrils were filled with the scent of her and his body throbbed with remembered pleasure. Lying naked in his bed, she'd provide all the inspiration any man should need. God help him, he wanted to please her in this, too.

12

KERI WOKE TO the peppy phone melody she used as an alarm. It didn't take her long to remember where she was. Michael's big body spooned hers, and his arm was tucked around her waist. When she tried to reach her phone the weight of his arm held her back.

She tried to ease away, in case he was still sleeping. He pulled her close. Obviously *not* sleeping. "Let me go, Michael."

"I don't want to."

"I'll bet you don't." She rubbed her fanny against his hard penis. "But we don't have time for that."

"Sure we do. You proved that you can get dressed in twenty minutes." His hand moved down her belly headed for an obvious destination.

Laughing, she grabbed his hand and stopped its downward movement. "And that's all the time I gave myself when I set the alarm. Sorry, Romeo."

"Damn."

She brought his hand up to her mouth and kissed it. "I can change that tomorrow morning and give us a little more time."

"I guess you'd better. I expect to be waking up this way tomorrow, too." He sighed and flopped onto his back.

"How much extra time will you need?" Moving to the edge of the bed, she grabbed the phone and shut off the alarm.

"An hour."

She rolled to face him. "An *hour?* You want to wake up an hour early so we can have sex?"

He grinned at her, his smile very white against his beard-darkened face. "You're right. That's not enough. Make it two hours."

"You're insane." Smiling, she climbed out of bed and tossed the sheet over the lower half of his body.

He surveyed the result. "Oh, look, a circus tent. It's the Greatest Show on—"

"Sorry, but this part of the circus is leaving town." She started toward the door.

"If you could see yourself, you'd understand why I'm in this condition."

"I don't know what you mean." She pivoted and glanced down. "It's just plain old me."

"There's nothing plain about you." He propped his hands behind his head. "You're all pink, tousled and sleepy-eyed. Take a look in the mirror when you get a chance. You're the most ready-for-sex woman I've ever seen in my life."

She rolled her eyes. "Nice try, but I'm still leaving. Have a good day." She headed for the door again.

"Thanks. You, too. Oh, and Keri?"

"What?" She turned back to him with a show of impatience. She thought he was adorable with his stalling routine, but she couldn't let him know that or he'd drag her back to bed.

"I wonder if…well, if you have time, if you'd take a look at the sex scene I wrote last night. I labeled the file *Sex Scene* so it would be easy for you to find on my laptop."

She stared at him as two things registered. He'd been writing while she slept, and he valued her opinion. He valued it so much, in fact, that he'd immediately attempted to correct the flaw she'd pointed out in his books.

Praising her sex appeal was one thing. Men complimented women on that all the time. But Michael had listened to her suggestion about his work and had put his ego aside to act on that suggestion. That took a special kind of guy.

"You might not have time, though," he said. "It's okay if you don't."

"I'll make time." She walked over to the bed and picked up a condom from the nightstand. "I'd be honored to read your scene." She handed him the condom.

"What's this for? I thought you were leaving?"

"I'll dress a little faster today. I hear the circus is in town." And she climbed back into bed.

"STAY WITH HIM! Stay with him!" Jack shouted encouragement as Michael focused on the constantly shifting motion of Finicky, one of Gabe Chance's prime cutting horses. Michael had tried to talk Jack out of using this valuable horse for a beginner, but Jack had insisted that either the horse or the rider had to know what he was doing or they'd have chaos.

Finicky, a chocolate-and-white Paint, was obviously the knowledgeable one in this pairing. Jack had released four steers into the corral, and Finicky was charged with singling out one of them and herding it into a pen. Michael was simply along for the ride, but if he didn't concentrate he'd land on his butt in the dirt. That had happened once already, and he didn't want it happening again.

"That's it," Jack said. "Now you're feeling it. See if you can let go of the horn and stay on. Holding on to the horn will not impress the ladies."

Finicky swerved with the precision of a Formula One racer, and Michael almost didn't make the turn with him. "I'm not ready for that, Jack."

"Sure you are. Stop thinking and let yourself feel the motion of the horse. He'll telegraph his moves if you're paying attention. Remember the analogy we talked about yesterday."

Michael knew exactly what analogy Jack was referring to, and fortunately he hadn't shouted it out where anyone passing by could hear. But Keri was a dangerous topic for Michael right now. If he thought of her, he pictured her reading what he'd written last night, and he broke out in a cold sweat.

He wanted to master this cutting horse business, though, so he let go of the horn and tried to anticipate Finicky's next move. He failed to do that. Next thing he knew, he'd slid neatly out of the saddle and landed with a thud in the middle of the dusty corral.

Jack hopped the fence and came over to collect the horse and hold out a hand to Michael. "What's the problem, buddy? You were doing great yesterday. Did something go wrong upstairs?"

"Nope." Michael picked up his hat and slapped it against his jeans to knock off some of the dust. "All's well."

"You're not thinking about that, though, are you?"

"I might've made a mistake."

Jack frowned. "I hope you're not talking about doing it bareback, because that's not acceptable."

"For God's sake, Jack. I wouldn't take that kind of risk. Give me some credit."

"Well, when you used the word *mistake,* my mind naturally went to that kind of mistake. What did you do, then?"

Michael took a deep breath. "I asked her to read a scene out of my current manuscript."

"You did?" Jack beamed at him as if Michael were a star pupil. "That's *great.* She will totally love that you asked her to do that. What a way to make points. Well done."

"Yeah, but…" Michael settled his hat on his head. "What if she doesn't like it?"

"Why wouldn't she? Is it too bloody? Did you have some bad guys hack up a sweet old grandma or something heinous like that?"

Michael laughed. "I don't write about sweet old grandmas getting hacked to bits. You should know that."

"You haven't so far, but there's always a first time. If you were dumb enough to let her read something like that, no wonder you're falling off Finicky, here." He reached over and stroked the horse's nose.

"It was a sex scene."

"Oh, well, then. You're in high cotton, my friend. She'll think she inspired you."

"She did."

"Then you can't lose. She'll feel a part of your creative process and get turned on in the bargain. I don't know what you're worried about. That was a brilliant move. If I'd have thought of it, I would have told you to do exactly that."

Michael scratched Finicky's neck. "She said my sex scenes weren't hot enough."

"Really?" Jack cocked his head as if mentally reviewing sex scenes by Jim Ford. "I thought they were fine, but I don't read your books for that. I like the gunfights."

"She likes the sex."

"That's natural, and there's nothing wrong with making them hotter, especially for your female readers. You might increase your audience that way. You should listen to Keri."

"I did, but now I'm worried that she won't like what I wrote."

Jack clapped him on the shoulder. "I'm sure you wrote that scene just fine. I guarantee she's already read it, so you can't change the situation now. What's done is done."

Michael nodded. "You have a point."

"And this afternoon you want to impress her with your riding abilities, so you need to get back on that horse and think about what you actually did in bed last night, not how you wrote about it later on."

Michael tugged his hat brim down. "That's good advice, Jack. Let's try this again." He swung into the saddle.

"Now you're talking like a cowboy." He gave Finicky a whack on his flank, and the horse went back to work cutting cattle.

Focusing on the sensation of moving effortlessly toward a climax with Keri, Michael began to sense the rhythm of the horse. He couldn't carry that analogy too far. Keri was not a horse and he was certainly not her rider. But the cooperative effort had some similarities.

Writing was a mental exercise, and he'd been thinking again. Once he settled back into his physical body, he could let go of the horn and shift his weight with Finicky's abrupt changes in direction. After a while, it felt like dancing, except he was in the position of follower. That was new, but he'd get used to it.

And sometime this afternoon, he'd put on a show for Keri. Jack had recommended it, and the more Michael hung out with Jack the more he saw the wisdom of following Jack's recommendations. The guy knew about horses and women. Michael was more than willing to learn more about both subjects.

As THE LUNCH hour approached, Keri struggled with logistics. She wanted time alone with Michael, both to tell him how great his scene had been and to satisfy her craving for at least one kiss. Reading that scene had made her want him with a desperation that was alarming.

After much thought, she could see no solution other than taking Mary Lou into her confidence. They'd made a cowboy favorite—ribs, baked beans and coleslaw. The hands would file in any minute, and Keri needed an ally.

She checked the simmering beans. They smelled

wonderful, as always. Lately Keri's senses had been more alert than ever in her life. Food smelled amazing and tasted even better. She paid more attention to the birds singing outside the kitchen window. Her skin was more sensitive to touch, and wherever she looked she saw beauty.

Mary Lou pulled the first pan of ribs out of the commercial oven. "Bring me the platters, Keri. It's time to get these ready to serve."

"You bet." Keri took the platters out of a bottom cupboard and helped Mary Lou load them. "I have a big favor to ask."

"Sure, honey. Name it."

Steam from the ribs surrounded them. The kitchen was hot, and tendrils of hair had escaped Keri's ponytail to curl damply at her neck. Ordinarily she'd be wishing for a cool breeze, but today the fiery need for Michael that burned within her made the external temperature unimportant.

"I need a moment alone with Michael."

Mary Lou chuckled. "I had a feeling he'd be what the favor was about." She used tongs to load another platter. "How can I help?"

"When the hands start coming in, I'll head out into the backyard. If you could tell Michael to come out and find me there, I'd be very grateful. We won't be long. I won't leave you in the lurch."

"You won't." Mary Lou took the last pan of ribs out of the oven. "I'll get Watkins to help me put out the food. That man will do anything I ask him."

Keri moved the filled platter and replaced it with an empty one. "Really? How did you manage that?"

"It's very simple." Mary Lou leaned close to murmur her secret. "Blow jobs."

Keri grinned. "You go, Mary Lou."

"Don't tell him I said so."

"I wouldn't dream of it." Keri couldn't imagine having that conversation with the stocky cowhand under any circumstances, but it was extremely cute that Mary Lou thought she might. "Thanks so much for letting me duck out for a minute."

"I'm glad to help. I like seeing two young people in love."

"Oh, it's not love." The minute she said that, the statement felt false. But she didn't have time to mentally debate the issue.

"In lust, then. One can look a lot like the other."

"Yes, it can." Keri didn't want to get confused about that.

"I hear them coming in. Go on out back, and I'll send Michael to find you when I see him."

"Thanks, Mary Lou." Keri squeezed her arm. "You're the best."

Mary Lou winked at her. "That's what Watkins says, too."

Keri walked through a side door and out onto a little deck where Mary Lou often took her morning coffee break. A set of steps led down to the yard, where Mary Lou's small garden was protected from critters by a chicken-wire fence and bird netting. Keri knew she would miss a great deal about the Last Chance when she ended her employment here, but leaving Mary Lou might be the hardest part of all.

Her thoughts about her future were a jumbled mess.

She wanted to move permanently to Jackson Hole, but she hadn't decided where to look for a job. The city of Jackson was the logical place to start if she wanted a PR job, but she'd rather stay in a more rural area like this one.

Oh, well. Her decision to stay was brand-new, and it wasn't like she was leaving tomorrow. She'd figure it out. But her feelings for Michael complicated things. By remaining here, she'd put a lot of miles between them. If she returned to her old life, they could see each other on weekends.

Much as she now wanted that, she couldn't face living the way she had before, not even for the prospect of being closer to Michael. So while she'd worked today, she'd given more thought to what kind of job she could get here that would suit her training. One possibility would be perfect. But she didn't know if Bethany Grace needed a personal assistant.

The self-help author, who was currently honeymooning with her new husband, Nash Bledsoe, would eventually return and set up housekeeping with Nash on the Triple G, a small ranch next door to the Last Chance. In addition to her writing career, Bethany planned to host retreats for burned-out CEOs.

Nash would give riding lessons and lead trail rides for those who wanted that experience, and Bethany would conduct mini-seminars on living a balanced life. Keri could manage Bethany's schedule and provide some PR for the retreat venture. But until Bethany and Nash came home, she couldn't find out if her idea was viable or not. Bethany might already have someone in mind for that job. Keri decided to ask Jack and see what he knew.

The back door opened and she turned as Michael walked out. He looked more like a broad-shouldered, lean-hipped cowboy every day. Even the tilt of his Stetson seemed more authentic.

He smiled, crossed the deck in two strides and bounded down the steps.

She hurried over to meet him. Wasting no time, she threw her arms around his neck and kissed him so enthusiastically he lost his hat. He didn't seem to care. With a moan, he pulled her close and thrust his tongue into her mouth.

She couldn't seem to get close enough. Burrowing against him, she felt the rapid beat of his heart and the ridge of his cock. His breathing roughened and he cupped her bottom to press her tighter against his fly.

Erotic visions flashed through her mind. Maybe, in the shadow of the trees, they could…no. She'd promised Mary Lou she wouldn't be out here long.

I like to see young people in love.

Mary Lou's words came back to her. But this was lust. This deep craving was about sex. Maybe, given enough time together, they'd—

Michael lifted his mouth a fraction but held her firmly in place. His breath was warm on her kiss-moistened lips. "Let's skip lunch."

"I can't."

He groaned. "Damn. Guess I should be grateful for what I have, huh? One more kiss. Then we'll go in and—"

"Wait." She pressed her finger against his mouth. "I need to say something, first. Your scene is wonderful."

He drew back to look into her eyes. "It is?"

She nodded. "Women readers are going to love it. *I* loved it. Reading it made me hot."

The corners of his mouth tilted up. "I seduced you with a few paragraphs of my deathless prose?"

"Yeah, you sure did."

"If this is your response, I'll cancel my riding lessons and head back to the computer. Jack claims you'll be turned on by watching me penning steers on Finicky this afternoon, but obviously he doesn't know what he's talking about."

"You want me to watch you ride?"

"Not anymore. Writing a sex scene is a hell of a lot easier for me than trying to stay in the saddle of a cutting horse." He nudged her gently with his hips. "And apparently the writing works just fine."

"But I want to watch you ride."

"No, you don't. If I look like a fool, then I'll lose all the ground I gained with that sex scene. Instead of watching me ride, go read that file again."

He sure could make her smile. She noticed that his eyes always seemed more blue than gray when he was teasing her. The longer she held his gaze the more she wanted to stay right here, tucked against his warm body. She plain liked being with him.

He took a deep breath. "You need to get back inside."

"We both do. You have to eat lunch so you'll be fueled up for your cutting horse demonstration."

"Let's forget about that. It was all Jack's idea, not mine."

"I want to watch. Tell me what time."

"He mentioned four o'clock, but—"

"I'll be there."

"I'd rather have you in my room, reading that scene. I look much better on paper."

"You look good no matter what you're doing."

His eyebrows lifted. "Thanks. You, too. We seem to have a mutual admiration society going."

"Seems like it."

He looked into her eyes for a long moment, and when he spoke, his voice had lost every trace of teasing. "Maybe we should talk about that."

She'd meant to lead up to this subject, not drop it like a bombshell, but instead she blurted it out with no finesse whatsoever. "I've been meaning to tell you. I'm moving here. Permanently."

Shock registered in his expression. He clearly hadn't been expecting that. "Oh."

"I thought you should know."

"Yeah. Yeah, that is good to know." The warm light had left his eyes. "Well, let's get back, so we don't cause any problems." He released her and picked up his hat from the grass.

"Michael, what we've shared has been...*is* important to me."

"I know." His wry smile tore at her heart. "For me, too. But life goes on, doesn't it?"

13

MICHAEL THOUGHT HE'D done a pretty good job of acting normal at lunch, but Jack had spent enough time with him to figure out something wasn't right. He started asking questions as they walked down to the barn after the meal was over.

"You had a chance to talk to Keri before lunch, right?"

"Yeah."

"Did you ask her to come down around four and watch the team penning?"

"I told her about it." Michael kept walking. He felt like a first-class fool for thinking he and Keri were building a relationship that had potential. When she'd announced she was leaving her job here, he'd assumed she'd go home to Baltimore where she'd be a short train ride away. Apparently she'd changed her plans.

"Is she coming or not?"

"I don't know. Probably."

"You're mighty sparse with the info, buddy. What's up?"

Michael glanced at him. Keri had said she was moving here permanently, but she hadn't said whether she planned to keep working as a housekeeper at the Last Chance. Even if she had said that, he wasn't the person to tell Jack about it. "Just a little misunderstanding, that's all."

"She didn't like your sex scene?"

"Oh, no. She loved it. You were right about that. She appreciated being asked to read it and as a result of reading it, she was turned on."

"Excellent! So what's the problem? When Mary Lou sent you out to find Keri you were riding high. Happy didn't even begin to describe the expression on your face. Now you look as if you just finished watching *Old Yeller*."

"Sorry."

"Me, too. Finicky likes you a lot better when you're cheerful."

That made him chuckle, in spite of himself. "I wouldn't want to get on the bad side of Finicky, that's for damned sure."

"I didn't think so. No matter what sort of misunderstanding took place out behind the house, you want Finicky to be in a good mood, so put on your happy face, little buckaroo."

Michael sighed. "Jack, did anybody ever tell you that you're a royal pain in the ass?"

"Once or twice."

"Well, I'm telling you again."

"Duly noted." Jack clapped him on the shoulder. "I have an idea. Before we go back out to the corral, let's muck us out a few stalls. You will be amazed at how that improves a fellow's disposition. I've been remiss in not introducing you to that particular type of therapy."

"Is that what you call it? Therapy?"

"I do, and I'm not the only one. You ask any cowboy how he works through his problems, and he'll give you one of four answers. He rides like hell, gets drunk, picks a fight or shovels shit. Since we're not going to run any of our horses in the middle of a hot day, and I'm not prepared to get you plastered or fight with you, that leaves us with mucking out stalls."

Michael considered that option. It sounded pretty good, actually. Something sweaty and mindless. "How do you know there are stalls to be mucked out? Maybe the other guys have taken care of it already."

"My friend, when you own as many horses as we do, there will *always* be mucking to be done. Horses eat an uncommon amount of food and horses poop an uncommon amount of shit. The opportunity for that type of therapy never ends."

"Then lead me to it."

AROUND THREE-FORTY-FIVE, Keri walked down to the barn and the corrals. She felt terrible about the abrupt way she'd informed Michael about her recent decision to stay in Wyoming. When he implied that they needed to discuss their future, she could have agreed with him and then waited until they had more time together before hitting him with her revised plans.

Of course, if she'd told him sooner, instead of reveling in great sex and pushing that other issue aside, he'd never have made that comment in the first place. She wondered how much would have changed between them if she'd laid out her future plans earlier, as she'd intended to.

Michael probably would have wanted to continue having sex. Guys seldom turned down that option if they were attracted to the woman in question. But he might not have been so open with her, and he might not have asked her to read the sex scene. Maybe he wouldn't have written it in the first place.

In her heart of hearts, she believed he'd created that scene for her, as a present. She'd asked for something, and he'd decided to grant her request. If that hadn't been his motivation, why show it to her? It definitely had been offered in the spirit of a gift.

Her heart ached when she remembered how his eyes had dulled when he'd heard her news. She didn't think he'd reached the stage of wanting a commitment, but no doubt he'd hoped they could continue what was obviously working out well for both of them. He might have had a hazy idea that it could develop into something serious eventually.

Her timing had been terrible, just terrible. First she'd kissed him as if she couldn't imagine life without him, and then, when he'd naturally followed up on that enthusiasm with a rational statement about what might come next, she'd shot him down. Talk about mixed messages.

She would apologize once she had a chance, but that wouldn't fix anything. The damage had been done, and she'd been the one responsible. If he wanted to end their relationship now and save himself potential heartache, she wouldn't blame him.

All things considered, she expected Michael to be in a somber mood when he put on this demonstration, assuming he put it on at all. Instead, he was grinning as he stood in the middle of the corral with Jack and Jack's younger brother, Gabe. Gabe had inherited his mother Sarah's fair coloring and was currently sporting a mustache.

Each of the men held the reins of his horse, and they seemed to be having a jolly time hanging out together. From the way they were laughing, Keri thought they were trading insults or bawdy jokes as they waited for the steers to be brought in.

Several other cowboys lined the corral railing, along with Emmett Sterling and his daughter, Emily. Putting a foot on the bottom rail, Keri pulled herself up to lean on the top rail beside Emily. She and Emily had liked each other from the first day Keri had arrived at the ranch.

Emily's blond hair was tucked up under her hat and she was chewing on a piece of straw. Keri got a kick out of that. Emmett had the same habit, and his daughter was mirroring him, either consciously or unconsciously.

Emily took the piece of straw from her mouth and glanced over at Keri. "Hey there, girlfriend. Gonna watch the greenhorn do his stuff?"

"I thought I would." She looked around for Emily's husband, who ran the stud program for the ranch. "Where's Clay?"

"He had to straighten out a shipping problem and he's stuck inside on the phone. Somehow a canister of sperm arrived unfrozen and spoiled. Clay expects the shipping company to pay for it, but they're giving him a song and dance."

Keri smiled. "They've picked the wrong guy to mess with."

"Yes, indeed. I know from personal experience that he's very persistent." Emily's blue eyes shone with pride. She was obviously crazy about Clay Whitaker.

"The Last Chance is lucky to have him."

"Yep. And so am I." Emily gestured toward the corral. "I hear Michael's really coming along with this riding gig."

"I hope so. He wants to learn."

Emily hesitated. "This is clearly none of my business, but word around the ranch is that you like him a lot."

"I do."

"Good." Emily looked happy with the answer. "I can see you two together."

"Uh...we're not exactly *together*." And wouldn't ever be.

"Okay, didn't mean to imply anything. Whatever the deal is, you'd make a cute couple. Your accents are almost the same."

Keri latched on to that remark with gratitude. She blinked innocently. "What accent?"

"Yeah, right. Don't get me started. You have the accent. We don't. End of story."

"Easterners set the standard." She smiled at Emily. "Everything else is a variation." It was a running joke between them, and Keri welcomed the chance to kid around, even about something as silly as accents.

"Not a variation. An improvement." Emily winked and returned her attention to the corral. "Here come the critters."

Six white-faced Herefords, the small herd the ranch kept for training purposes, trotted into the corral. The men mounted up. Michael swung into the saddle like a pro.

Keri didn't recognize all the Last Chance horses, but she knew the one Michael was riding. The chocolate-and-white gelding was featured in many framed pictures sitting in the ranch's trophy cabinet, a cabinet Keri was in charge of dusting.

She turned to Emily. "Gabe's letting Michael ride Finicky?"

Emily nodded. "He and Jack wanted Michael to learn on a well-trained horse, and Finicky's the best. Michael looks good on him."

"Yes, he does." Keri realized she'd said that with a little too much enthusiasm when Emily grinned at her. "They all look good," she added quickly. "Are Jack and Bandit going to participate?" Everyone on the ranch knew Bandit, the most valuable stud on the ranch, had been laid up recently.

"No, Bandit's not up to it yet, although I'm sure he's bored silly. Jack probably wants to give him a little outing without doing anything strenuous first. Jack can keep an eye on things while Gabe and Michael work the cattle. I love watching Jack on Bandit, though. He and that horse are a unit. As for Gabe, he can ride any horse and make it look like a champion."

"Who's he up on?"

"That's Rorschach. It's tough to tell them apart if you're not down here every day like I am. It's especially hard when they're both black-and-white, like Rorschach and Bandit. Rorschach doesn't have the eye patches. Or the attitude."

"I see what you mean about Bandit's attitude." Keri's

gaze followed the horse as he pranced around the corral, neck arched and tail flying like a flag. He didn't seem to be favoring his leg at all. "I think Jack encourages him."

Emily laughed. "You think?"

But impressive as Jack and Bandit looked circling the corral, and as obviously accomplished as Gabe was on his horse, Keri couldn't take her eyes off Michael. Seeing him now, she couldn't believe he was a novice. As he sat easily in the saddle, his back straight and his hands loose on the reins, he looked every inch a cowboy.

She turned to Emily. "I'm excited to see this demonstration. I've never watched team penning, before."

"You're in for a treat. Gabe's a super rider, and he'll get the most out of Rorschach. Finicky's a great horse, and he'll get the most out of Michael. The pairing is brilliant, really. Michael should have a lot of fun if he can stay on."

"He might not?" Keri's stomach churned.

"He probably will. But I'll bet that's why Jack's there, in case things get crazy and Michael needs a quick pickup."

Keri hadn't even considered that Michael might get dumped in the dirt, caught in a whirlpool of churning animals and sharp hooves. Her heart beat faster as her anxiety level rose.

"Don't look so scared. He'll be fine."

"He'd better be," she muttered. If Jack had put Michael in danger just so they could all show off, she would never forgive him.

As the penning operation began, she clenched her jaw and tightened her grip on the rail. At one point she felt a little dizzy and realized she was also holding her breath. And praying. This wasn't fun at all.

Michael, however, seemed to be having a blast. He was concentrating hard, but that didn't stop the grin from popping out whenever he and Finicky executed a tricky maneuver. As dust flew and cowboys whooped, the two men and their horses cut a steer from the milling herd and worked it neatly into the pen.

They repeated the feat again with no mishaps, and Keri began to relax. But the third steer wasn't so cooperative. Finicky was determined and turned a corner with such blinding speed that Michael lost a stirrup and started to slide.

Keri gasped and clutched Emily's arm.

Jack shouted something to Michael, who grabbed the saddle horn and righted himself. Finicky seemed to take no notice of Michael's behavior. He focused on the steer and pivoted like a dancer as he blocked the animal's attempt to escape. Gabe worked the steer's other side, and Michael eventually regained his stirrup and became part of the action again. They penned the steer.

"There, see?" Emily glanced at Keri. "He stayed on."

"Just barely." She blew out a breath and let go of Emily's arm. "Sorry if I left a bruise."

"Nah, I'm tough."

Jack called for a break and rode over to talk with Michael and Gabe. Keri was reminded of a coach coming out on the baseball field to consult with his players. Both Gabe and Michael nodded. Then they all laughed.

That laughter did more to sooth Keri's jangled nerves than anything else. "I guess everything's okay if they can laugh about it."

Emily glanced at her. "I'll bet you've never been in love with a cowboy before, have you?"

"I'm not..." She didn't finish the sentence because Emily gave her a look that said she wasn't buying any denial on Keri's part. For emphasis, Emily held up her arm, with little pink spots where Keri had grabbed her.

Keri sighed. "No, I've never been in love with a cowboy before." She was beginning to wonder if she'd ever been in love before, period. No man in recent memory had affected her with this bone-deep yearning. Or this paralyzing fear for his safety.

"The thing is, they're modern-day knights. That means they take physical risks to challenge themselves, and you have to be okay with that. Sometimes they get banged up, and you have to be okay with that, too, because they don't take well to being fussed over."

"I already know that about Michael." She remembered Michael's stubborn insistence that he was fine, when she knew he had to be in pain. "But he's not really a cowboy yet."

"Oh, I think he is." Emily turned back to the corral where Gabe and Michael prepared to pen another steer.

"How can you tell?"

"He didn't quit after the humiliation of having to reach for the horn."

"What was humiliating about that?"

Emily looked at her. "Grabbing the saddle horn is not macho. I suspect he was willing to go down rather than hold on until Jack yelled at him not to be stupid. So now he wants to prove he can finish the event without doing that again." She smiled. "That's typical cowboy thinking."

Keri groaned. "I don't know if I can watch the rest of this. If he falls, then he could get trampled."

"Jack and Gabe are there to keep that from happening."

"But you just said cowboys sometimes get banged up." The image of Michael lying on the ground, bloody and unconscious, made her sick to her stomach.

"They do get banged up. And I won't kid you. He's not perfectly safe in there. I hope you stay, though. If he's like most cowboys, he's doing this for you."

14

MICHAEL WOULD BE damned if he'd grab the saddle horn again, despite what Jack had said at the break. In fact, Jack had mentioned several things. He'd alluded to Michael's inability to write any more bestsellers if a horse or a cow stepped on his fingers. He'd added that choosing image over safety was ridiculous and that impressing a woman wasn't worth getting stomped on by critters.

Jack was probably right about all of that. Maybe if Keri hadn't said she was staying in Wyoming, which essentially meant she wouldn't be seeing much of him in the future, he might not have felt so hell-bent on showing off. But if he was going to become only a memory, he wanted to be a good one.

Of course, he wouldn't be such a good memory if he got himself trampled right in front of her. So he couldn't let that happen. That meant he had to stop thinking and simply feel the motion of the horse beneath him. As Jack had said, it was a lot like having sex with a woman.

All afternoon he'd considered how Keri's announcement would affect their sexual relationship for the rest of this week. By choosing not to live in Baltimore she'd changed everything. He couldn't blame her for that choice. He certainly didn't want her to be miserable in Baltimore just so they could see if they were meant to be together.

But now, instead of anticipating a continuation of their affair, he would leave knowing it was over. Tomorrow the wedding guests would arrive, and he and Keri wouldn't be alone upstairs. That didn't completely cut out the possibility of sex, but…it wouldn't be the same.

It wasn't the same, anyway. He might be able to act as if nothing had changed when they were in bed together, but everything had. He'd foolishly started to fall for her, but he was finished with that nonsense.

As he waited for Gabe's signal to start working the cattle again, he glanced across the corral at Keri. Pain sliced through his heart, and he cursed softly. He hadn't *started* to fall for her. He'd fallen, and hard. He couldn't let her see that.

If he called a halt to their affair, that protective move would telegraph his feelings. He might as well write it out in glowing neon. As he thought of that, he knew how tonight would go.

Tonight would be all about physical gratification, and he would be fine with that. She'd be fine with it, too. He'd make sure she was so blissed out by multiple orgasms that she never noticed his emotions weren't in play. Yep, if he was going to be a memory, she'd need a fan and a bucket of ice whenever she thought of him. Guaranteed.

That decision brought a focus he'd lacked before. When Gabe nodded, Michael was ready to go. No more overthinking his actions. He'd let his body do its thing and simply roll with it.

When it came to the team penning, Michael was stunned by the spectacular results. He didn't miss a single cue Finicky gave him. Neither did he kid himself that he was a pro who could ride any cutting horse in the world. Finicky's expertise was a big part of the smooth operation. But at least he wasn't a hindrance this time.

When it was all over, he got plenty of compliments from the cowhands lining the rail. Jack and Gabe both rode over to shake his hand. When he happened to look at Keri, she gave him a thumbs up and a big smile. He might be the only one who noticed that her smile trembled a little bit.

The thought crossed his mind that she might be battling some feelings for him, too. Maybe ending their affair wouldn't be a walk in the park for her, either. In that case, maybe he should ask her what she wanted, rather than assuming they'd head upstairs tonight for their last hurrah.

Hell, he was back to overthinking his decisions. If she didn't want to have sex with him tonight, she would say so. She'd never been particularly shy with him.

He rode Finicky through the corral gate on his way to the hitching post in front of the barn. Clay Whitaker had arrived, and Keri stood talking with him and Emily. As Michael rode past them, Keri glanced up and he touched the brim of his hat the way he'd seen Jack and the other cowboys do when they met a woman.

She smiled again, and this time there was no doubt. It was the saddest smile he'd ever seen in his life. She *was* miserable, and he couldn't ignore that and pretend he didn't see her distress. He wasn't built that way.

But now wasn't the time to deal with it. He'd ridden Finicky hard, and the horse deserved a good rubdown and a handful of oats. Gabe and Jack had already tied their horses to the hitching post.

"Great job," Jack said as Michael rode up.

Michael laughed. "Are you talking to me or the horse?"

"The horse, but you weren't so bad, yourself." He pulled his saddle and blanket off and started into the barn.

"Thanks!" Michael called after him.

Gabe lifted his saddle and blanket off Rorschach. "You hit your stride after we took that break."

"Yeah." Michael dismounted and tied Finicky to the rail. "I finally got in sync with this amazing horse. I'm sure he could do the job without me, though."

"He could, but he wouldn't. He's trained to do this with a rider on board. He's not a sheepdog."

Michael unbuckled the cinch. "Well, I'm honored that I got to be that rider, Gabe. Thanks for letting me pretend to be the real deal for an afternoon."

"Hey, you're well on your way to becoming the real deal. You've got the right stuff. Are you sure you don't want to stick around a little longer?"

"Unfortunately, I can't." He glanced at Gabe. "Wish I could, but I have to get back." He had a meeting with his agent and his editor on Tuesday to discuss the details of his next contract, which should include a sizable bump in his advance money. On Wednesday he'd be on a plane to California, where the video would be made.

"Could you schedule another week or two out here before the snow flies? I hate to see you go months without riding when you're so close to really getting it."

"I'll think about that." He wished he could, but with his book sales increasing, his publisher had pushed up the publication date for his next release. That meant some long hours at the keyboard. "Thanks for the invite. And the confidence in me."

"You bet." Gabe left for the barn.

Michael followed soon after, and he met Jack coming out with a bucket full of grooming supplies. He lowered his voice. "Don't look now, but Keri's headed this way."

"Oh?" Michael hoped he looked unaffected by that news.

"If you want to take your time putting your saddle away, I could send her in there so you two can have a more private discussion."

"I can talk to her out here."

"I dunno. She looks like a woman who would like to have a word, and that usually requires privacy."

"Okay." Belatedly, Michael realized they should talk and establish how things were going to be between them tonight. Maybe she would be the one to call it off. God, he hoped not. He wasn't ready to let her go quite yet.

He continued into the cool shadows of the barn and put his saddle and blanket away. Some shape he was in for a close encounter with a woman. He and Jack had worked up a sweat shoveling manure earlier that afternoon.

The therapy had worked like a charm, too. Michael had relaxed into the rhythm of a working ranch, and his stress had melted away, until the moment he'd looked over at the corral fence and spotted Keri. Then he'd tightened up again.

Needing to move, he walked down the wooden aisle between the stalls. He'd let this woman get to him, and that was entirely his fault. He'd wanted her from day one, and once the barriers were gone he'd been only too eager to enjoy the charms of Keri Fitzpatrick.

That wouldn't have been a mistake if he'd thought of it as a brief affair. But he hadn't done that. When he'd seen the possibility for more, he'd let his imagination have at it.

Shaking his head, he admitted that he'd pictured a romantic reunion at Penn Station. Somehow he'd always imagined her coming to New York, instead of him traveling to Baltimore. In his mind, they'd walked through Central Park, wandered the halls of the Metropolitan Museum, held hands during a Broadway play and eaten pasta at his favorite little place on Restaurant Row.

They'd also made love in his apartment—in the bedroom, in the living room and even in the kitchen. Oh, yeah, he'd mentally placed Keri firmly in his life and in his bed. Only problem was, she had no intention of going there.

"Michael?" She stood in the doorway of the barn, a shadow outlined in golden light. She didn't seem quite real, and he felt her loss as if she'd already disappeared from his life.

"I'm here." He walked toward her, the sound of his boots on the floorboards echoing in the stillness.

"Jack said I should come and find you." She stepped into the barn, and the soft glow from the lights set at floor level along the aisle made her look more ethereal than ever.

He had an overwhelming urge to hold her and convince himself she wasn't some figment of his overactive imagination. Closing the distance between them, he gathered her close. "I've missed you."

She didn't ask what he meant by that strange comment. They'd only been apart a few hours. But they'd been separated by a gulf wider than hours. She seemed to understand that as she wrapped her arms around his waist and held on tight. "I've missed you, too."

His plan to stay emotionally distant crumbled. Instead, he told her the naked truth. "I wish there was a way we could be together."

"So do I." She gazed up at him, anguish in her green eyes. "But I can't live back there anymore. I didn't know that for sure myself until after we'd…after…"

"After we'd made love." He dared to put that name on it, even if doing so would only make things worse.

"Yes." She hugged him closer. "I wanted to talk about my decision, but it never seemed like the right time. And then…I picked a *horrible* time. I'm so sorry, Michael."

He smiled, remembering the way she'd practically knocked him down with her passionate greeting in the backyard. "I liked the first part of that discussion."

"That's what was so wrong about it! First I attacked you like a crazed rock star groupie, and then I lowered the boom. That's twisted."

"You were only being honest. Just because you love my writing and kind of like me, too, that doesn't mean you should arrange your life around those things."

"A part of me wants to."

He slid his hands down to cup her bottom and squeezed. "I'll bet I know which part."

"No, you don't, smarty pants. Not that part. It's my—"

"Don't tell me." He looked into those green eyes and silently commanded her to hold her tongue. If she admitted that she felt the same way about him that he felt about her, they'd both be lost. "You know I have to go back."

"I know," she said quietly. "There's no better place to be if you're a bestselling author."

"And it's my home. My family's there. This has been a lot of fun, but I'm not a cowboy."

"Emily thinks you are."

"Was she the one you were talking to at the corral?"

Keri nodded. "She says you're a cowboy because you kept going even after humiliating yourself by grabbing the saddle horn."

"Good God. Is *that* the benchmark? Being humiliated and forging on, anyway?"

"According to Emily."

"I say she's full of it. A real cowboy wouldn't have been humiliated in the first place."

"That's where you're wrong, Michael. In the year I've worked at the Last Chance, I've seen cowboys humiliated all the time. They make stupid mistakes like the rest of us. But any cowhand worth his salt will laugh it off and keep going. Which you did today."

He gazed down at her. "Thank you for that. And while I'm at it, let me thank you for every wonderful thing you've done since I arrived—and there are dozens. You're a treasure, Keri Fitzpatrick, and I'm going to miss you like hell."

"You say that like you're leaving tonight. Have you changed your plans?"

"No, but under the circumstances, I wasn't sure how you wanted to handle everything going forward."

Her eyes took on an impish glow. "I'd like to handle them the same as always. Lovingly and often."

He groaned. "I am seriously going to miss you."

"How did *you* want to handle things going forward?"

He was tempted to echo her smart-aleck remark, but instead, he found himself confessing his original plan. "I'd intended to make tonight all about sex."

She wiggled against him. "That sounds promising."

"What I mean is, *only* about sex. No emotional involvement. Just raw sex, lots of orgasms, especially for you, and maybe even some kinky stuff thrown in, since I'll never see you again after this week."

"Kinky stuff? What kind of kinky stuff?"

"I hadn't decided." He peered down at her. "Don't tell me that whole scenario appeals to you?"

"Not the *whole* scenario, but you couldn't deliver that, anyway."

"Who says?" He wondered if she doubted the kinky part. He could come up with kinky if he wanted to, especially when inspired by a lusty woman like Keri.

"You couldn't have sex without emotional involvement, so don't even try it."

Oh. He sighed. "You're probably right. It sounded good when I was planning my strategy."

"But I'm intrigued with the idea of kinky sex."

He'd kept his cock under control until she said that. Now it rose to the occasion. "Let me see what I can do about creating something."

"It's our last night alone upstairs." She rubbed against him.

"I'm well aware of it. Are you aware that you're alone in the barn with a very aroused cowboy?"

"Yes." She eased out of his arms and backed away. "And I'm also aware that Jack and Gabe are waiting for us to finish our conversation so they can put the tack away and go home to their wives."

"Good point."

"But I really like the fact that you referred to yourself as a cowboy." She continued backing toward the open doorway. "That's progress."

"It was a slip of the tongue. I still have a long way to go."

"Maybe I can help you get a little closer tonight."

He fought down the urge to go after her and drag her into an empty stall. Gabe and Jack's dinner plans didn't seem like a priority right now. "How could you do that?"

"I'm not sure yet, but I have some time. I'll work on a few ideas. I'll see you upstairs around nine."

"I'll be a basket case by then."

"That's the idea." She blew him a kiss and left the barn.

He stood there, breathing fast and willing his erection to subside.

"Hey, Michael!" Jack's voice drifted from the open door. "We saw her leave. You decent?"

"If you're asking if I'm dressed, the answer is yes. If you're asking if I'm a kind and generous soul, the jury's still out."

"I figure you're as kind and generous as the rest of us around here." Jack walked down the barn aisle, the bucket of grooming supplies dangling from one hand. "How'd it go?"

"She wants kinky. Wait! Forget I said that. I don't know why I told you that!" Michael rubbed a hand over his face. "Jeez. I can't believe I blurted that out. I'm obviously losing it."

Jack seemed to find the subject hysterical. "You mentioned it because you know old Jack can give you some suggestions."

"No! Don't give me suggestions. I don't want to talk about it."

Jack shrugged. "Okay." He turned and started back down the aisle carrying the bucket.

"Like what?"

Jack turned back, his grin wide. "It's basic, but you can't go wrong with some thin strips of rawhide and a can of whipped cream."

"Where can I get the rawhide?"

Jack motioned toward the tack room. "There's a roll of it in there. Take what you need. As for the whipped cream, raid Mary Lou's refrigerator. Just don't let her catch you."

15

KERI HAD SOME concept of what a dance-hall girl should look like from watching movies. She had enough of an idea that she might be able to recreate it for Michael's benefit. She had one dress that sort of fit the bill. It was long, black and tight, with a slit in the skirt that reached midthigh. The neckline plunged a satisfying amount, too.

If the evening was as wild and lusty as she hoped, the dress would be ruined. She'd paid a small fortune for it, and heaven knew why she'd brought it with her to Jackson Hole. But in the new life she envisioned for herself she wouldn't need a dress like this ever again, so she might as well sacrifice it to a good cause.

She'd been afraid their last night alone up here would be filled with angst and regret, but as she dabbed perfume everywhere she could reach, she no longer feared that. Tonight they were going to celebrate who they were. They were going to play. And then they would have fabulous sex. They would end this affair on a high note.

She'd piled her hair into an elaborate updo and had

added a couple of fabric flower hair ornaments she'd
also brought from Baltimore for some unknown reason.
She wore an emerald necklace that she should have left
in the safe back home and several rings that belonged in
a bank vault. Anyone who didn't know would assume
it was all costume jewelry.

Michael would know, of course, but they could pretend it was fake. To emphasize that idea, she'd put on
more makeup than she'd worn since arriving in Wyoming. Eyeliner, mascara and green eye shadow, all applied with a heavy hand, made her look like a lady of
the night. Hot red lipstick added to the image.

Under the dress she'd put on a black lace garter belt,
sheer black stockings and nothing else. No bra, no panties. She would have killed for a pair of fishnet hose,
but she didn't have any. As a final touch, she slipped
into glittery silver heels that added a good two inches
to her height.

Finally, knowing she was already ten minutes late,
she opened her door and walked across the hall. He'd
left his door slightly ajar. Heart pounding, she pushed
it open.

He lounged in the room's single upholstered chair.
He'd pulled it over to the bed, which he'd stripped of
its comforter. Then he'd propped his booted feet on the
dark green sheets, as if he didn't give a damn if he got
them dirty or not. She'd bet he'd cleaned his boots before doing that, but still…the pose was effective.

He wore his hat pulled low and didn't look up when
she entered. His shirt was open, baring his lightly furred
chest. He'd discarded his belt and opened the top but-

ton of his jeans. He looked like an image from a fantasy cowboy calendar.

Moisture sluiced through her, and because she wore no panties it dampened her inner thighs. She pitched her voice low. "Hi, there, cowboy."

He lifted his head to gaze at her, his expression giving nothing away. "Howdy, ma'am."

She slid her hands over the smooth fabric covering her hips. "Want some company?"

"I might."

She ran her tongue over her ruby-red lips as she strolled over to his chair. When she propped her foot on the edge of the seat, the side slit fell open. It almost, but not quite, revealed all. "I'll make it worth your while."

"I do believe you will." Slowly he lowered his booted feet and uncoiled himself from the chair. His glance traveled from her silver heel, braced on the chair, up the length of her stocking-covered leg. His muted swallow was the only sign that she'd affected him at all.

She had to give him credit. He seemed cool as a cucumber, while her pulse was thrumming wildly out of control. She was breathing hard, too, which made the black silk over her breasts tremble.

He focused on her cleavage. "Nice dress."

"Just an old rag I found."

Reaching out, he trailed the back of his hand over the emerald necklace and down to the edge of the daring neckline. "An old rag?"

"Worthless."

"Then you won't care what happens to it, will you?"

She lifted her chin. "Not a bit."

In one swift move, he grasped the front of her neckline and yanked down. The dress came apart as if made of tissue paper. She'd had no idea it was so fragile.

Now it really *was* an old rag that hung in tatters, allowing him to see her quivering breasts, the black garter belt, and a dark triangle of curls already damp and ready for him. If he looked closely, and he seemed to be doing that, he might notice her thighs were slick, too.

Stepping back, he surveyed his handiwork. "Lie down on the bed."

"Should I take off—"

"No. Like that. Exactly like that."

She stretched out on the quilt, glittering heels and all. As he walked toward the headboard, he pulled something from his back pocket and looped it around her wrist. It was a thin strip of leather that reminded her of the trendy bracelets for sale in Jackson.

But this wasn't a trendy bracelet. She gulped for air. He was tying her wrist to the bedpost. And she was going to let him.

MICHAEL HAD NEVER done anything like this in his life, and his cock was so hard from the excitement of it he wondered if it might crack from the strain. Keri made no protest as he tied her wrists to the bedposts.

Then he tied her ankles, which left her open to his greedy gaze. He could come just looking at her. She breathed in quick little pants that made her whole body quake. That was delicious by itself, but he was enthralled as he drank in the sight of her stocking-covered legs spread to reveal exactly how much she wanted him. He stood at the foot of the bed, concentrating on that view, while he stripped off his clothes.

When he finally freed his cock he groaned with relief. He was tempted to forget about the whipped cream and dive into the banquet she presented. But he'd braved Mary Lou's kitchen to steal a can of it, and not using it now would mean he'd wasted all that effort.

He'd wanted the whipped cream to be a surprise, so he'd tucked it under the bed. He reached for it now and Keri's eyes widened.

Then she began to laugh. "Oh, my God. You're going to be in big trouble with the housekeeper if you get that all over the sheets."

"It's okay. I'm planning to bribe the housekeeper."

"Oh?" Her green eyes sparkled as bright as the emeralds she wore. "With what?"

"She'll find out really soon." He smiled.

"You know, it takes guts to steal Mary Lou's whipped cream."

"Are you going to turn me in?"

"No, cowboy," she murmured. "I won't squeal on you."

"Thanks." He climbed onto the bed. "But you can squeal now, if you want." And he sprayed mounds of whipped cream on each breast.

She did squeal, and she pulled against her bindings. "That's so cold!"

"Then let me warm you up." By the time he'd cleaned all the whipped cream from her breasts, she was pulling at the leather for a different reason. And begging.

But he had more plans for the whipped cream. Leaving her writhing on the bed, he walked to the foot, climbed in between her spread legs, and aimed the can's nozzle.

"Michael! Don't you dare put that cold stuff on my—" She squealed again as he sprayed her liberally with sweet clouds of white. "Michael! Do something!"

"Oh, I plan to." He went to work, and she quickly seemed to forget about being cold. He'd figured on licking away all the whipped cream, but all he really wanted was her moist, juicy center, so when he reached that, he left the rest to decorate her thighs.

She was nearly ready to come, though, and he wanted to set her free before she did. She complained mightily as he interrupted his feast to untie her, but she'd thank him later when she didn't have rope burns. As he settled into position again, she clutched his head and held him exactly where she wanted him.

He thought that was only fair after the way he'd imprisoned her. Besides, he was more than happy to stay right there, doing exactly what they both wanted. She tasted like heaven. He didn't even care that she pulled on his ears when she came. Nothing mattered but loving her, and loving her some more, until she lay panting and spent on a very sticky sheet.

He kissed his way up her body. She was pretty sticky, herself. Finally he reached her red, red mouth and hesitated. "Will that lipstick come off on me?"

She dragged in air. "Probably."

"Ah, hell. I don't care. We're both going to be a hot mess when this is over." And he kissed her with all the passion in his heart. It was a memorable kiss to start with, blending as it did the distinct flavors of sex, lipstick, and whipped cream.

He sank into the kiss and eased down onto her sticky body. She was a whipped cream disaster, and something about that turned him on even more. Sex, he suddenly realized, shouldn't always take place between scrubbed and polished bodies on freshly laundered sheets.

Sex should also be wild and messy and sticky, and if it was connected with other sensual delights, like food, so much the better. He wished he'd brought other items from Mary Lou's refrigerator so he could smear those on Keri, too.

He continued to kiss her as he slapped a palm on the nightstand and located the condom he'd put there. His hands weren't as sticky as the rest of him, at least not yet. Much as he hated to interrupt this all-encompassing, very flavorful kiss, he had to do that if he wanted his own climactic reward.

And he did want it, desperately. He longed to merge with her in every way, with his lips, his tongue, his hands, his arms, his legs and, most of all, his cock. When he pushed forward and locked himself in tight, she sighed happily.

"Perfect," she said.

"I know." Covering her mouth with his once again, he pumped slowly, almost reverently. He'd never thought about it before, but opening herself to him was so very generous. She was letting him inside her body. No, not just *letting* him inside. She welcomed him there.

With each thrust, she lifted her hips to greet him. She wanted this connection as much as he did, and that was some sort of miracle, wasn't it? She was willing to be vulnerable with him. She'd allowed him to tie her up, for God's sake. And squirt her with whipped cream.

As he rocked easily back and forth, knowing that he would come, but not ready to rush the process because he liked it too much, he faced the truth. He was in love with her. Besides that, unless he was a lousy judge of people, she was in love with him.

Right now, as they enjoyed their mutual passion in this sticky bed, being in love was a wonderful thing. Next week, when they weren't together anymore, it might not be quite so wonderful.

The answer to that problem was blindingly simple. He couldn't believe he hadn't thought of it before, but sometimes the most obvious solutions were the easiest to overlook. It would be all right. They would be okay.

With that issue solved, he gave himself up to the power and glory of making love to Keri Fitzpatrick. Of course they wouldn't end their relationship on Sunday. That would be stupid. Michael was many things, but stupid wasn't one of them.

"ACTING ON IMPULSE is not a good idea." Keri sat in the middle of the mess they'd made of the sheets as early morning sunlight slowly brightened the room. She couldn't believe what she'd just heard come out of Michael's mouth. "I know you're not stupid, so—"

"Thank you for that. I'm not stupid. Some have even called me brilliant. And moving here is the smartest idea I've ever had in my life."

She gazed at him as he paced the room wearing only his jeans. He'd been awake since four and he'd spent the time while she slept writing. The moment she'd roused herself enough to realize he wasn't in bed with her anymore, she'd sat up and discovered him typing away at the small desk.

Although he'd seemed lost in his imaginary world,

he must have sensed that she was awake, because he'd shut down the computer. Then he'd told her that the ranch inspired him, and that *she* inspired him. He no longer wanted to live in New York City.

"You've been here less than a week," she said. "And you've lived in New York your entire life. What about your family? Your friends?"

He shrugged the broad shoulders that looked so damned good naked. "I'll visit them, or even better, they'll visit me. They all have plenty of money. Money shrinks distance between people."

She yearned to follow him into this fantasy, but one of them had to keep a clear head. "I think you have it backward. Stay in New York. Visit here. Give yourself some time to—"

"I don't need time. I need this place." His expression grew more intense. "I need you."

Oh, boy. She understood. She really did. They'd had some amazing sex, and she was falling for him, too. But that didn't mean he should abandon everything and everyone in his former life and move far from the center of the publishing world just to be with her.

She took a long, shaky breath. "I love hearing that you need me. But changing your entire life on the spur of the moment doesn't make sense."

"You did."

"Yes, but I…I wasn't coming here to be with someone. That puts more weight on the situation."

"And that scares you?"

"A little. You like Jackson Hole in August, but will you like it in February, when it's twenty below, not even counting the wind chill factor?"

He smiled. "We'll keep each other warm."

How she longed to sink into that smile, to believe in his vision of the future, to welcome this decision with the joy he obviously expected from her. But she couldn't do it. He could be setting them both up for a fall.

"Winter on a ranch in Wyoming is nothing like winter in New York City. You're sometimes cut off from the basics like food and gas. Keeping the animals warm is a constant concern."

He met her gaze. "I'm sure it's not New York, and I'm ready to experience the difference."

"Are you, really? It took me a year before I knew for sure this was where and how I wanted to live. You can't possibly—"

"You're wrong, Keri. I can feel the chains coming off with every breath I take. My family is so damned proud of their heritage, which dates back to the effing Mayflower. Leaving New York would be unthinkable for them. All my life I've bought the premise that Hartfords always live east of the Hudson. But I belong here. On some level I've always known that."

"You're so good with words." Her heart ached. "I would love to be convinced by that argument, but Michael, you don't really know what you're talking about. You arrived on Monday afternoon. This is only Friday morning. You've experienced a tiny sliver of life on this ranch during August. You need more time, more exposure to the seasons, and more exposure to living a rural existence."

He exhaled, obviously impatient with her stance. "I'm beginning to think you don't want me here, Keri."

"No, that's not it! Of course I want you here. I'm…

fond of you." If she mentioned the *L* word, that would only make things worse.

"Fond of me?" He studied her as if considering the meaning of that.

"Very fond." It was all she'd allow herself to say right now.

"If you're so *fond* of me, why are you throwing up these roadblocks?"

"I'm worried that you're making a rash decision that will turn out to be a huge mistake. If you move out here and discover it's not for you, then what?"

"That's not going to happen."

She was so afraid he was doing this mostly because of her, and changing an entire life for one person, especially one he'd known a few days, sounded like a recipe for disaster. "Okay, let me ask you this. If I changed my mind and decided to go back to Baltimore, would you still move here?"

His hesitation said it all.

"Please give this some more thought before you plunge ahead." She climbed out of bed. "You need to move here because it's the right place for you, not because you want to be with me. I shouldn't be your reason."

He looked as if he wanted to say something, but then he shook his head and turned away. "You're right." He walked over to the window and stared out at the mountains. "I sometimes let these flights of fancy get the best of me." His words sounded reasonable, but his tone and his body language were defiant.

If he'd looked at her while he'd admitted his impulsive nature, she might have believed that he intended to rein it in. Instead, he had his back to her, and what a rigid back it was, too.

Judging from his posture as he stood at the window, she didn't think he was calmly considering his options. She feared he was bitterly disappointed because she hadn't thrown herself into his arms and celebrated this wonderful decision with him.

It would have been so easy to do. And so unwise. "I need to get down to the kitchen."

"Yes, I know." He didn't turn around.

"Michael, I hope you understand why I didn't jump on your idea with cries of glee."

"I do."

"Well, good." She waited a moment longer to see if he'd turn around. Nope. "I'll see you downstairs," she murmured.

"See you then."

16

THE FIRST WEDDING guests, the O'Connelli family, arrived around ten on Friday morning. Michael had just finished grooming Destiny after a short trail ride on his own, a gratifying sign that at least Jack had confidence in him. Keri was another matter.

Besides giving the okay for a solo ride, Jack had also prepped Michael on the eccentric O'Connellis. He wasn't startled when a Volkswagen bus covered with peace signs and other New Age symbols pulled into the circular drive in front of the ranch house.

Free spirits Seamus O'Conner and Bianca Spinelli had combined their last names when they'd married in the seventies, creating the surname O'Connelli. Morgan, Gabe's wife, was one of seven O'Connelli siblings. Seamus and Bianca had arrived for Gabe and Morgan's wedding three years ago in this same bus.

The following year, another of the O'Connelli daughters, Tyler, had become Jack's sister-in-law when she'd married Alex Keller, Josie's brother. With two daughters living here, the vagabond O'Connellis had become regular visitors to the Last Chance.

Tyler's twin brother, Regan, had come for the wedding, and so had his seventeen-year-old sister, Cassidy. The four O'Connellis, who had spent a good part of their lives crammed into a Volkswagen bus, were apparently delighted to be given a room upstairs that included four bunks.

The other four-bunk room was reserved for Pete Beckett's two brothers and their wives, who often traveled together and were used to sharing quarters. The remaining room upstairs, a small one with a twin bed and a tiny attached bath, would go to Pete's aunt Georgia, who reportedly was quite spry for eighty-nine.

As people came rushing out of the house to greet the arrivals, Michael took Destiny out to the pasture and lingered there after he turned the horse loose. He wasn't in the mood to be social. Not just yet.

In the wee hours of the morning, when he'd thought that his life was finally beginning to make sense, he'd looked forward to the hustle and bustle of the wedding weekend because he and Keri would experience it together. Now he wished to hell he'd planned to leave today. Participating in the cheerful festivities wouldn't be easy after discovering that the woman he loved was merely *fond* of him.

Okay, maybe she was more than fond, but she wasn't willing to commit to what she was feeling, and she sure as hell hadn't leaped onboard with his new plan. Instead, she'd tried to talk him out of it with some ridiculous argument about extreme weather and the problems of rural living. As if any of that would matter to him if he could be with her.

He was a writer who spent hours alone in imaginary

settings. When he left those imaginary places and re-joined reality, having her there would be far more important to his happiness than whatever lay outside the door. But she'd told him to make his decision without factoring her into it.

He couldn't do that. He'd fallen in love with the place and the woman at the same time. Knowing that she wanted to stay here made for a perfect situation, if only she'd admit that she loved him as much as he loved her. He'd thought so last night, but now…well, if she wouldn't say it, why wouldn't she?

Maybe because she didn't want to be the reason he moved to the Jackson Hole area. But she was a huge part of it. If she'd been heading back to Baltimore, he wouldn't have considered moving here. Where she lived would factor into his decision, but he couldn't say the same about her. She'd been willing to end their relationship so that she could stay in Wyoming.

No matter which way he looked at her reaction to his plan, the conclusion remained the same. He was head over heels, and she was less so. That sucked.

But the Chances had been terrific to him ever since he'd arrived, and he would shake off this rotten mood and do his best to be upbeat for the next couple of days. Tonight everyone was headed to the Spirits and Spurs, the bar in Shoshone owned by Jack's wife, Josie. Michael had been invited a couple of days ago, but he'd begged off, saying that this was for family, not some stranger from back east.

His real reason, of course, had been that he'd hoped to spend time alone upstairs with Keri while the place was empty of guests. That wasn't such a good idea anymore. Another night in bed with her, and he was liable to make an even bigger fool of himself than he already had. Might as well ask if he was still welcome at the Spirits and Spurs tonight and see if he could forget his troubles for a few hours.

BEING RIGHT WAS no fun at all. Keri believed with all her heart that she'd done the right thing by trying to convince Michael to take his time. He was talking about making such a drastic change. But she hated the distance she'd created between them.

And there certainly was distance. He'd avoided her gaze when he'd come down for breakfast, and he'd left with only a brief goodbye. Later, as she'd bundled up the sticky sheets and remade his bed, she'd wondered if they'd ever make love again. Something told her they might not.

She'd put the sheets in with a load of towels and her ruined dress was shoved into the depths of a garbage bag. Their night of mildly kinky sex would remain a secret, but she longed for a smile or a wink from Michael to let her know he remembered that part of the evening and not just the awkward discussion that followed in the morning.

She'd tried to blame all the wedding activity for keeping them from exchanging any private words, but she knew that wasn't the reason. Lunch had been a chaotic affair with all the extra guests, but that should have made it easier for him to find a moment to say something to her. No one would have noticed.

He'd made no effort to connect ever since she'd left his room this morning, and she missed him more than she could have imagined. Someday soon, after he'd left here and had given himself a chance to gain perspective, he'd realize that her advice had been good. But picturing that moment of clarity didn't keep her from feeling sad that they were estranged now.

She was fairly certain he hadn't planned to go to the Spirits and Spurs with the wedding party, but she wasn't surprised when he went, after all. She and Michael could have had some time alone upstairs while the others were partying, but apparently he hadn't wanted that.

After everyone was gone, she closed herself in her room and took a long hot shower. It didn't relax her as much as she'd hoped, but she put on some light flannel pajamas and climbed into bed. Her usual evening entertainment, reading a Jim Ford book, would only make her feel more unhappy, so she switched off the light.

Closing her eyes, she tried a few relaxation techniques with no success. Her brain insisted on replaying the events of the day. Judging from Michael's behavior since this morning, she could expect the same tomorrow, and then on Sunday he'd leave.

She couldn't let him do that without making one more attempt to reach an understanding. She decided to write him a note and put it on his pillow. Maybe he'd rip it to shreds, but she didn't know how else to let him know that she'd acted out of love.

No, she couldn't say that. If she mentioned love, he'd take that as a sure sign that he should move here. He wouldn't give himself time to think about the decision.

She'd have to find a way to indicate she cared about him without using the *L* word. She'd been in PR, for

God's sake. Although she wasn't a professional writer like Michael, she was no slouch with the English language.

But as she sat down with a pen and one of the monogrammed notecards her mother had sent her for Christmas, she struggled. She ruined three notecards before she finally came up with something that sort of worked. She read it over one more time to be sure.

> Dear Michael,
> My reaction to your plan seems to have greatly disappointed you and destroyed the friendship we had. But I still believe what I said—that a major decision like this needs to be considered from all angles. I didn't say that to be a wet blanket or because I don't care about you. I do care, and I want you to be happy.
> Yours,
> Keri

She'd debated a long time over how to sign off. She certainly wasn't going to say *with love* or anything mushy. *Yours* was a common closing, and didn't have to mean anything more than *at your service*. If it meant something more personal to her, he wouldn't have to know that.

Slipping the notecard into its cream-colored envelope, she tucked the flap inside and wrote his name on the front. Then she walked quickly across the hall to his door.

Her heart pounded with anxiety, even though she'd seen him leave with the others and was certain he wasn't there. As she opened the door and confirmed that, bittersweet memories made her sigh with longing. Last night when she'd walked in, he'd been waiting with rawhide strings and whipped cream. Tonight, he'd been eager to get away from her for a few hours.

He hadn't left any lights on, but the moon shining through the window allowed her to find the switch on the bedside lamp. Once she turned it on, she could see that the room was as neat as she'd left it this morning, as if he didn't want to cause her any extra trouble. Last night he'd been willing to spray whipped cream on the sheets.

In another two days, it would be even neater, because no one would be staying here. She probably shouldn't think about that. Michael might be keeping his distance, but at least he was still in the vicinity. She could catch glimpses of him here and there. Yes, she was pathetic, but he would never know that.

She leaned down to lay the envelope against the pillow sham. Then she changed her mind. Tonight Michael would get turn-down service.

Removing the decorative pillows, she folded back the sheets. Then she turned on the other bedside lamp. She left the envelope propped against the pillow on what had become his side of the bed when they shared it. As an afterthought, she pulled one of the lupine blossoms out of the vase she'd refreshed that morning, shook the water off the stem and laid that on top of his pillow. A peace offering.

If all that didn't convince him that she meant well, he wasn't going to be convinced. She went over their conversation this morning and tried to think of how it could have turned out better. Maybe if he'd offered his plan as a possibility instead of a certainty, she wouldn't have been so alarmed.

But he'd proclaimed his intention boldly, leaving no room for discussion. When she'd tried to initiate discussion, he'd been closed to other options. His comment of *you're right* had sounded almost belligerent. Sometime during the night he'd made up his mind and that was supposed to be the end of it.

She might have let him stumble on if she hadn't been so closely tied to his decision. But he wasn't just moving to Wyoming. He also was moving to be with her. If it turned out to be the wrong thing for him, he could break both their hearts. Smoothing the folded sheet one last time, she returned to her room.

Several hours later, after she'd finally dozed off, she heard everyone come back. Footsteps on the stairs, murmured conversation and muffled laughter were followed by calls of *good night*. Then, instead of one pair of feet coming down the hallway toward Michael's room, there were two. And one of them stumbled a bit.

"Almost there," said a male voice that was not Michael's.

"Thanks, buddy. 'Preciate it."

Keri squeezed her eyes shut. The crazy idiot had decided to drown his sorrows, which meant he'd feel like crap tomorrow.

"Glad to help out, dude." The voice sounded too young to be one of Pete's brothers or Seamus O'Connelli, so that left Regan, Tyler's twin. "You were a riot, tonight."

Michael chuckled. "Was I?"

"I've never seen anyone stand on a table and recite Shakespeare's sonnets while balancing a mug of beer on his head. You got into it."

"Know why I did that?" Michael asked.

"Can't imagine, but it sure was funny." A door creaked open.

"I'm in looove."

Keri gasped. Dear God, was he, really? No, probably not. He was drunk and didn't know what he was saying.

"Congratulations," Regan said. "Okay, a little more... there we go."

The rest of the conversation was lost to Keri as Regan helped Michael through the doorway and into the room. She lay in the darkness, pulse racing, while she lectured herself not to dwell on an offhand remark by someone who was plastered. No doubt he'd meant it as a joke, something to amuse his new friend Regan.

But what if he'd meant it? Liquor acted like a truth serum sometimes. But he still shouldn't move to Wyoming on the strength of that, should he? Even if he loved her, he might still hate living in Wyoming year-round. Then what? They'd have a mess.

Oh, but the very thought that he might actually love her...that hovered in her mind, a glittering possibility that she dared not believe in. If she reached for it, would it disappear?

A door creaked again, and footsteps retreated as Michael's rescuer headed for the far side of the second floor. Another door opened and closed far down the hall, and all was quiet except for the erratic thumping of her heart. She needed to go to sleep, but that wasn't going to happen anytime soon.

Eventually she turned on the light and picked up one of her Jim Ford books. Opening it to the back, she gazed at Michael's author photo for a long time. She'd always been drawn to his eyes, even in a small black-and-white picture. Those eyes seemed utterly sincere. They weren't the eyes of a man who would say something he didn't mean, even in a drunken stupor.

Yet as she started rereading the book, she remembered that this man had allowed his fans to believe he was a seasoned cowhand. She understood his reasons, but maybe he wasn't as sincere as he looked. Maybe he was capable of blurting out words of love he didn't mean.

She continued to read, captured as always by his effortless prose. The clean crisp sentences had been part of the charm of his books. His style had convinced her that he was, in fact, a cowboy because he sounded like one.

After she'd read a few pages, she was startled to hear Michael's door open again. His steps whispered along the floor, and she guessed he was navigating the hallway in his bare feet. He walked into the bathroom and closed the door. Seconds later, the shower came on.

The man she'd thought was passed out in a heap on his bed was awake and in the shower. Putting down the book, she listened while the shower ran. He'd been known to fall asleep in the bathtub. Would he fall asleep in the shower?

She was about to check on him when he turned off the water. Moments later, the bathroom door opened and he returned to his room. She relaxed a little. He couldn't be in very bad shape if he'd managed a shower.

Switching off her light again, she eased down under the covers. A cool breeze through her open window soothed her and she closed her eyes, determined to get some sleep. The next day would be busy and she couldn't afford to be tired.

The knock at her door was so soft that she wasn't sure if she'd heard it or imagined it. Then it came again.

Adrenaline pumped through her. Only one person would knock on her door at this time of the night. Sliding out of bed, she left the light off as she went to the door. She opened it slowly, and his slurred declaration of love rang in her head as she gazed at him.

He wore only his jeans, and his dark hair was still damp from the shower. He wasn't smiling. "I saw your light under the door when I came out of the bathroom," he said quietly. "I figured we woke you up, and I apologize for that." He sounded a little hoarse, but not particularly drunk anymore.

She took a quick breath. "Apology accepted."

"Hang on." He lowered his voice even more. "There are more apologies where that came from."

"Oh?" She looked into his eyes, but could read nothing there.

"I apologize for putting you on the spot about me moving here, and for being such an ass when you offered me some helpful advice. I realize now you had my best interests at heart."

She swallowed. "Are you saying that you'll give the idea more thought before doing anything?"

An emotion flickered in his eyes. They looked very gray tonight. "Depends on what you mean by *anything*."

"I mean—"

"Never mind." A hint of a smile touched his mouth. "I know what you mean. I promise to give the idea more thought, but right now there is something I'd like to do, with your permission." The flicker in his eyes became a gleam.

She'd seen that gleam before, and the implication made her tremble with excitement. "What's that?"

"I'd like to thank you for your note."

That threw her a little. "You're…you're welcome."

"No, I want to *really* thank you. May I come in?"

17

MICHAEL HELD HIS breath while he waited for her answer. He wasn't convinced that she was as invested in this relationship as he was. She might have decided by now that he was too moody and not worth the trouble of further involvement.

But she'd written him that note, turned back his sheets and placed a flower on his pillow. She might not love him as much as he loved her, but apparently she still cared about him a little. If she'd let him, he'd build on that.

Obviously she hadn't expected him to show up at her door. The flannel pj's covered in little bouquets weren't what women usually wore to entice a lover. They did entice him, all the same.

She glanced down the hall, as if considering the reality of all the people sleeping upstairs tonight.

"We'll be quiet," he murmured.

Her green-eyed gaze lifted to his, and mischief danced there. "Do you think that's possible?"

"In my world, anything is possible." He grimaced. What a cheesy line. "Okay, maybe not anything. This won't be a sexual marathon. I'm not up to it. I've had quite a bit to drink."

"I know."

"You do?" He had a horrible thought. He'd assumed their stumbling around had been what had woken her up, but they'd been talking, too, mostly about his sonnet reciting stunt, and then he'd said…oh, hell. "When Regan and I came in, could you hear what we—"

"Couldn't make out the words. Just heard you both laughing and mumbling some kind of nonsense."

Something in her expression told him that might not be strictly true, but he'd let it go. In his boozy fog, he'd assumed she was asleep until he'd glimpsed her light on after his shower.

But in spite of all his boorish behavior recently, she seemed to be in a forgiving mood. Smiling, she moved back from her door and opened it a little wider. "You can come in."

"Thank God." He stepped inside and closed the door behind him.

She'd left the light off, which might be better. Lights only alerted others to activity that was none of their business. In the cool silky darkness, he turned his attention to getting her naked.

"Nice pj's," he murmured as he worked at the buttons of her top. His coordination wasn't quite up to par.

"Let me." She gently pushed his hands aside and made short work of the buttons. "I wasn't expecting company tonight." Slipping her arms free, she let the top slide to the floor.

"I know." He cradled her breasts in both hands, once

again struck by her generosity. "After the snotty way I behaved today, you could have refused to accept any."

"But you see, I invited you." She arched into his caress and wound her bare arms around his neck. "On monogrammed stationery, no less."

"I noticed that." He nibbled on her bottom lip and fondled the breasts she thrust so eagerly into his hands. "What's the S stand for?"

"Sexy."

"Knowing you, I'd buy that." He brushed his thumbs over her tight nipples. "Knowing who your family is, I don't."

"Suzanne. My mother's name."

"Keri Suzanne Fitzpatrick." Leaning back, he looked into her eyes. They shone even in darkness, somehow gathering in the soft light flowing in from the window. "You said in your note that you wanted me to be happy."

"I do."

"Making love to you would make me very happy."

"Me, too." Unwrapping her arms from around his neck, she reached down and untied the ribbon holding her pj bottoms. They fell to the floor. "So let's."

His cock twitched. Considering all the beer he'd consumed tonight, he'd wondered if he'd be able to get it up at all. He'd planned to focus on her and not worry about whether he could fully participate.

He followed that plan. After shucking his jeans, he guided her down to the bed and revisited his favorite places. He spent more time visiting some than others, and she was obliged to cover her face with a pillow to muffle her cries of release.

In the process, he discovered that there was life in his

cock, after all. Fortunately he was an optimistic kind of guy, and he'd shoved a condom in the pocket of his jeans. She had to find it, though. His coordination continued to be a little questionable.

He also required her help in putting on the little raincoat. Consequently, he decided against trying any fancy positions. Besides, the missionary had lots of pluses going for it, in his opinion. He'd never understood why it had a reputation for being boring.

Braced above her, he slid inside the warm sheath of her body with gratitude and joy. He wasn't even slightly bored. Then he kissed her, and she kissed him back. Yes, she definitely liked him. A woman who kissed with that much enthusiasm wasn't indifferent.

But he'd scared her this morning with his news, and he'd take that as a lesson learned. If he wanted her, and he did, then he had to behave like a rational human being. Then maybe she'd believe that he loved… ah…so sweet…loved everything about her…mmm… especially…most especially…this.

KERI HADN'T SLEPT much, but the next day she drew energy from knowing that she and Michael had mended the rift between them. Whatever the future might bring, at least on this special day of Sarah and Pete's wedding, they would enjoy that unspoken connection that had united them from the moment they'd met.

The morning and early afternoon passed in a blur. Then, before anyone was quite ready for it, they had less than an hour before the ceremony. Keri and Mary Lou shooed everyone away so they could shower and change.

Then the two of them tucked any remaining wild-flowers in vases and straightened the rows of white folding chairs arranged in the living room. All the furniture had been stacked in the backyard and covered with a tarp, although the sky remained clear.

Mary Lou adjusted the white satin runner that defined the center aisle. Then she walked to the back of the room and stood, arms folded. "Beautiful."

"It is." Keri shifted one bouquet of flowers on the hearth, which was a mass of red, yellow and purple wildflowers. "There. Perfect."

"Sarah married Jonathan in this room," Mary Lou said.

"She did? Does Pete know that?"

Mary Lou nodded. "He's the one who suggested they have the ceremony here. I've never met a man who's less jealous of the guy who preceded him. I never thought Sarah would find someone who could measure up to Jonathan, but Pete...well, he's just special."

"I agree." Keri walked around the chairs to stand next to Mary Lou. "You know why this looks so wonderful?"

"The wildflowers," Mary Lou said.

"That's a big part of it, but I think it's beautiful because it was created with love by Sarah's daughters-in-law. I watched Dominique, Morgan and Josie work together. Then Tyler showed up to help, and Bianca O'Connelli, and Emily."

"Don't forget Cassidy," Mary Lou said with a chuckle. "She's a seventeen-year-old ball of fire. I loved how eager she was to help do whatever we needed.

She'd race to get string, vases, duct tape, with her red hair flying."

"Yep, she's a cutie. I think she's after my job."

"She's young, but she's a hard worker, and according to her mother she isn't set on going to college, at least not yet." Mary Lou glanced over at Keri. "How soon are you planning to leave?"

Keri decided she could confide in Mary Lou, so she described the job she hoped to create working with Bethany Grace. "And Jack said it's a great idea, and he'll put in a good word with Bethany when she gets home. He's almost positive she doesn't have anybody hired for that position."

"That's terrific!" Mary Lou's face lit up. "So you'd be right next door, so to speak."

"I would."

"Okay, now I don't feel so sad about you leaving. I think you'll get that job with Bethany and then you'll be over at the Triple G, and we'll see you all the time."

Keri's heart squeezed. She hadn't realized that she'd be so missed. "Now I'm even more determined to convince Bethany to hire me."

"Well, if you need a reference, send her straight to me."

Keri smiled. "Thank you. I will."

"Now let's make sure all's well in the kitchen. We don't have much time left."

Keri followed Mary Lou back to the kitchen and they worked until it was nearly time for the ceremony. After tidying themselves as best they could, they walked back to the living room. Many of the chairs were already filled. They stood to one side and waited until the other guests had been seated before slipping into a spot in the back row, which had been provided for the ranch hands. The boss lady was getting married, and no one could be left out. By a stroke of luck, Michael was also in the back, and he took advantage of the vacant chair to Keri's right.

Watkins and the new hire, Trey Wheeler, played old country favorites as the guests settled themselves. Trey had turned out to be a top-notch horse trainer and a fine musician. Having two guitars instead of one provided a more resonant sound and had been a good decision, in Keri's estimation. During the ceremony, Tyler would add her talented voice to the guitar music.

Watkins and Trey made an interesting combination. Watkins was stocky, mustached and middle-aged, while Trey was young, lean, and muscled. Keri noticed with amusement that most of the women in the room watched Trey instead of Watkins, even though Watkins was a better guitar player.

Pete, who stood by the hearth with his two brothers and the minister, looked as if he'd won the lottery. Any minute Keri expected him to levitate.

As excitement grew, Watkins and Trey launched into "Here Comes the Bride." First down the aisle was the tiny flower girl, Morgan's daughter, Sarah Bianca, or SB for short. She flung rose petals everywhere, even pausing to launch them into the faces of the guests leaning toward her with cameras raised.

Mary Lou put her mouth next to Keri's ear. "Did you bring tissues? I'm going to bawl. I just know it."

Keri dug in her pocket and came up with one she handed to Mary Lou while keeping a second one for herself. She'd expected to cry. Sure enough, when Sarah appeared, flanked by her three handsome sons, Keri's tears began to flow. Regal as always, Sarah wore a long, ice-blue dress and carried a bouquet of the orchids Pete had ordered flown in from Hawaii. She was radiant.

Jack, Nick and Gabe wore ice-blue vests under their Western-style jackets. Sarah linked arms with Nick on one side and Gabe on the other, while Jack walked protectively behind. Each man's jaw was clenched against the emotion glittering in his eyes. All three had lived through the loss of a father and now manfully celebrated their mother's happiness in finding someone to love.

But Keri had come to know the Chance boys, and she didn't think they were giving Sarah away. They would never do such a thing. It was more of a provisional loan that depended on Pete's ability to keep her deliriously happy.

Judging from Pete's expression when he caught his first glimpse of Sarah, he was more than ready to do that. He looked as if he wanted to rush forward and escort her to the altar himself. But he wisely refrained. Those three broad-shouldered cowboys would have stopped at nothing to keep him from interfering in this special moment with their beloved mother.

By the time each of them had embraced Sarah and stepped back, there wasn't a dry eye in the house. Keri dabbed at her tears with her left hand, because her right hand was now clutched in Michael's left. She had no idea when he'd taken hold of her hand, but he didn't seem about to let it go.

She didn't mind. Holding on to him during this emotional ceremony felt good and right, so long as neither of them attached too much significance to it. And yet, that wasn't so easy as Sarah and Pete pledged to love and cherish each other.

Their promises were heartfelt, but Keri reminded herself that Sarah and Pete were rooted in this place and had been for years. They knew exactly what they were doing by creating this union. They were grounded in reality, not banking on some half-baked dream to carry them through.

Keri tried to keep that in mind, but the ceremony was magic, and some of the fairy dust fell on all of them. Looking at Pete and Sarah, it was hard to refute the power of love, or the belief that, as Michael had said, anything was possible.

When the vows had been said and the minister invited Pete to kiss the bride, the room erupted in cheers and applause. Keri joined in. She was so glad she'd stayed for this. As the jubilant couple turned and hurried down the aisle, Michael caught Keri's chin and turned her in his direction.

"Thank you for sharing this with me," he murmured right before he kissed her. The kiss was brief, but potent nonetheless.

She hadn't expected it, and she looked up at him, a little dazed. "I have to go. Mary Lou needs help in the kitchen."

"I know." He smiled and traced her mouth with the tip of his finger. "But you can come to the reception later, right?"

"Sarah told us to. She doesn't want anyone missing the party."

"Then save me a dance." He squeezed her hand and

before she could say anything about that, he was gone, swallowed by the crowd following Sarah and Pete out the door to the tents set up for the reception.

The next two hours flew by, with Mary Lou, Keri and a couple of extra servers hired for the occasion making sure the buffet tables were stocked and the bar well supplied. Keri was dressed for practicality in jeans, a T-shirt and a serviceable apron. Party clothes hadn't been part of the plan. She hadn't stayed on at the Last Chance so she could party tonight. She'd stayed so that Sarah could have a fabulous wedding free of worries about her staff.

But then Watkins appeared with strict instructions from the boss lady. Tyler's husband, Alex, a former DJ, had taken over the music duties, so Watkins had been commissioned to get Mary Lou out on the dance floor. Rumor had it that Michael was searching for Keri for the same reason.

She was carrying a kettle of ranch beans when Michael found her. He took it gently from her hands, set it on the nearest sturdy surface, and reached behind her to untie her apron.

"This is ridiculous," she protested. "I'm a part of the staff, not a part of the guest list."

Michael pulled her apron off and tossed it next to the kettle of beans. "I have my orders from Sarah. If I don't get you out there for at least one dance, she'll send all three of her boys to carry you to the dance floor. I doubt you want that."

Keri laughed. "No, I don't. I'm familiar with public embarrassment, and it's not all it's cracked up to be."

"Then you'll come along like a good girl?"

"I'll come along, but I can't promise that I'll be a good girl."

Michael glanced at her over his shoulder as he tugged her toward the wooden platform. "Even better."

As it turned out, when they stepped onto the dance floor, Alex had cued up "The Heart Won't Lie," sung by Reba McEntire and Vince Gill. With a sense of inevitability, Keri moved into Michael's arms.

They danced, snuggled close together as the words about love and loss flowed around them. How easy it would be for her to murmur in his ear and say that she wanted him to move to Wyoming, that she wanted to be with him and that she loved him.

She resisted. She refused to do or say anything that would influence him in this so-very-important decision. One word from her, and he'd abandon his promise to think it through.

He rested his cheek against hers, and a few times he turned his head to press his lips to the soft spot beneath her ear. "I could stay like this forever," he murmured.

At times like this she felt the same way, but no matter how sweet it sounded, neither of them could stay like this forever. She'd come to realize that he was a romantic. Romantics sometimes talked that way, which wasn't a problem until they started believing it, too.

_18_

MICHAEL CARRIED THE sweetness of their dance at the reception with him for the rest of the evening. Neither of them made it upstairs until well past midnight, and he knew she had to be exhausted. But it was their final night together, and he had to hold her one last time.

So he coaxed her into his room, gave her a massage, because this time she was the one who needed it, and made slow, gentle love to her until she came apart in his arms. Then he swallowed her cries so the others staying upstairs wouldn't hear.

Perhaps he'd hoped that the combination of the emotional wedding and good sex would change her opinion that he needed to proceed with caution. If so, he didn't get his wish. Her actions were loving, but she didn't beg him to move to Wyoming ASAP so they could be together.

But at least they shared a bed on their last night together. Without knowing for sure how deep her feelings ran, he couldn't say if that would ever happen again. He might come back in two months and discover that she'd fallen for a real cowboy.

That kind of thinking could easily drive him crazy, but he couldn't force her into a commitment she considered premature. Difficult though it would be, he had to leave her here, take care of business in New York and then see if he had anything to come back to.

She left his room early on Sunday morning. Although he knew that cleanup duties would be massive today, letting her walk out the door was torture. He stopped himself from asking for one more kiss and watched her cross the hall, her robe tied tight in case anyone else was up.

He'd bet no one was. Last night had been a blow-out of a party. God, but he hated to leave. If not for the damned video, he wouldn't. But filming was scheduled for next week, and he'd come to the Last Chance specifically to prepare for that.

So he packed, went down for a light breakfast and then headed to the barn so he could say goodbye to Destiny, his main guy, and Finicky, the superstar who'd let him pretend to know what he was doing. Keri must have spotted him going there, because he hadn't been in the barn talking to Destiny more than five minutes before she showed up.

"I thought we should say our goodbyes now, when nobody's around." She came toward him dressed in her usual outfit of jeans and a scoop-necked T-shirt. This one was the color of her emerald-green eyes.

"That's probably a good idea."

"Or silly. Most everyone has guessed about us."

"Must be the constant grin on my face." He met her halfway. As he slipped his arms around her waist, he couldn't banish the thought that he had no guarantees with this woman. He might never hold her this way again.

She gazed up at him. "Are you growing a mustache?"

"I am. For the video. You might not want to kiss me and risk razor burn."

"Why not admit who you are and forget about the mustache?"

"Because…" He stared at her in stunned silence. "I have no idea why not," he said at last. "That's an excellent question."

"You didn't want anyone to know before because you weren't a real cowboy, but you're a good part of the way there. You can pull it off."

"I suppose I could. Of course, my family will have a fit if I out myself as a Hartford of the Hudson Valley Hartfords." As he said that, he realized he no longer cared. He'd been willing to break with family tradition and leave New York, so why not go all the way?

Yet he hadn't been prepared to do that until now, and maybe that was a reason, a very good reason, she'd accused him of not thinking things through. If he intended to make Wyoming his home, then he should get rid of all the hang-ups from his past.

Her green eyes filled with understanding. "It's not easy to disappoint your family. Trust me, I know this."

"I know you do." And he had more work ahead of him in building an authentic life if he expected to deserve her. He already had some ideas about how he could do that. "Listen, can I send you a copy of the video after it's finished?"

"I'd love that. Is Jack driving you to the airport?"

"Yeah, he insisted."

"Then I'll give Jack my Baltimore address before you leave, so you'll have it."

"Baltimore?" He hoped to hell she hadn't been playing him like a fish. "Lady, you have me totally confused. Why am I sending the video to Baltimore?"

"Sorry, didn't mean to be confusing. I'm planning to talk with Jack in the next day or two and give my notice."

"Wow, that's quick."

"I'm impatient to get on with my plans. Bethany and Nash will be home from their honeymoon next week, and I don't want to risk having her hire somebody else to do the job I'm angling for."

He nodded. "Smart thinking."

"If all goes as I hope, I'll be in Baltimore tying up loose ends when your video's finished. I don't want you to send it here, because I want to see it right away."

"Glad to hear that. I have a feeling all of this will work out exactly the way you want it to." If only she'd factor him into her plans, he could talk about his goal of moving here. But that might make her freak out again, and they'd reached a kind of détente on that subject.

"I think it will, too. Mary Lou's excited that I might only be moving as far as the ranch next door. I was touched that she cared so much."

"I'm sure everyone will be rooting for you to get the job with Bethany. I know I am."

"Thanks, Michael." She gazed up at him. "I know you are, too."

He sighed and pulled her closer. "I don't want to say goodbye."

"Then don't." She reached up and cupped his face

in both hands. "Just kiss me, and then I'll walk out of here. No drama."

"Right. No drama." Leaning down, he closed his eyes and pressed his mouth to hers. His heart jerked in his chest. This could not be the last time he kissed her. It just couldn't.

She answered his kiss with tenderness. Then she eased out of his arms and turned. Without another word, she walked out of the barn. Everything that mattered to him went with her.

MICHAEL'S VIDEO ARRIVED shortly after Keri returned to her Baltimore condo, so she was doubly glad she'd asked him to send it there. It came via FedEx, and she nearly destroyed the packaging in her haste to get it out of the box. Then she fumbled with the disc as she attempted to load it into her player. Apparently this separation had made her desperate for the sight of Michael James Hartford, aka Jim Ford.

By the time she put the disc in the machine and hit Play on her remote, she was hyperventilating and couldn't even sit down to watch it. She stood right in front of the screen, the remote clutched so tightly in her hand that her fingers grew numb. If she'd thought his presence in her life wasn't important, she'd been kidding herself.

The segment started with a book cover that faded to an almost identical scene of rolling hills punctuated by a single tree with a hangman's noose dangling from it. Michael had recorded the voiceover describing the dramatic scene as it played out in the book.

Hearing that deep familiar baritone gave her goose

bumps. She had the fierce urge to see him in person. She needed to touch him and verify that he still existed in her world.

The video continued, and Michael came riding over the hill. Her reaction was immediate and visceral. The tug deep within her soul proclaimed that *this* man was the one she was meant to love.

To hell with logic. To hell with everything except a primitive need to eliminate whatever distance, emotional or geographical, separated them.

Then he began to speak, and she became a little shaky. She slowly lowered herself to the floor while she kept her attention focused intently on the screen. He looked into the camera, but he seemed to be gazing directly at her.

She realized that was the intent, and each viewer would feel as if he spoke directly to them. Well, they could all harbor that delusion, but she knew the truth. He was talking to *her,* damn it!

At first she didn't notice that he'd forsaken the mustache because he looked the way he always had, clean shaven. But the mustache was supposed to be part of his Jim Ford persona, or it had been until now.

"I have a confession to make," he said. *"Last week I learned to ride a horse and throw a rope. Until then, I'd been a city boy who wrote about things I'd dreamed of but never experienced."*

Her jaw dropped. In their last conversation, she'd casually asked him why he didn't reveal who he really was, but she hadn't expected him to tell everyone he hadn't been a cowboy before and was just becoming one now. Admitting that took nerve.

He continued, *"Last week opened my eyes to new possibilities and new challenges. I'm relocating to Wyoming so I can live the way I've always hoped to. I'll write under my real name, but I'll also keep Jim Ford somewhere on the cover of the books until everyone's adjusted to the change, including me. Oh, and I'm ditching the mustache. It interferes with kissing pretty women. And there's one in particular I look forward to kissing."*

He followed that with a smile so full of optimism and joy that it broke her heart. He'd told her of his long-term goals, and she'd had no faith in his ability to make a decision that fast. She'd been privileged to be the first to know, and she'd tried to talk him out of being extremely smart and very brave.

Fortunately, he'd ignored her advice and was barreling ahead with the courage of his convictions. Perhaps it was time for her to admit that not everyone needed time to think through a major life change. Some people, like Michael, were blessed with imagination and the insight that allowed them to see clearly when the right path opened up before them.

And she loved him for being so exceptional in that regard. She loved him for many other reasons, too. She just plain loved him, and it was time she told him so.

MICHAEL CURSED WHEN the apartment security guard called on the house phone to say a visitor was in the lobby. He'd been struggling with a scene in his new book and he'd nearly figured it out. Whoever it was could come back later when he wasn't writing.

"Tell them I'm not available, Jake," Michael cut in

before Jake could say who the visitor was. It didn't matter. It could be the Queen of England for all he cared. He had a scene to wrestle with and he was so close to making it work. "Have them come back tomorrow around ten."

That's what a security person in the lobby was there for, to screen anyone wishing to visit the building's occupants. Michael cherished that about the place and made regular use of the service.

"All right."

A minute later, Jake called again.

Michael considered not answering. He'd have to discuss this with Jake later and let him know that no meant no. Luther, the previous security person, had been very good at getting rid of unwanted visitors. But Jake had only been on the job a couple of months. Michael would have to answer and get rid of this persistent person himself.

"The young lady is prepared to wait in the lobby until you see her, Mr. Hartford."

"Look, she needs to come back tomorrow, Jake. Please convince her that—"

"Her name is Keri Fitzpatrick."

Michael's brain stalled. Disbelief was quickly followed by hope, followed by caution. She'd told him she'd be in Baltimore for a month, which was why he'd sent the video there.

But she'd never said anything about getting together while she was in Baltimore. She could have, but she hadn't, so he'd resigned himself to not seeing her, even though they would be just a train ride apart for the duration.

Maybe this was a spur-of-the-moment thing. Maybe she had business in New York and had stopped by for old time's sake. He shouldn't expect that this visit would have any special significance.

"Mr. Hartford? Shall I send her up?"

"Yes, send her up."

Even though he told himself not to get excited about seeing her, his heart pounded wildly as he waited for her to arrive at his door. He took several long slow breaths in an attempt to appear calm. Then the doorbell chimed, and his heart clicked into double time again.

Still, he did his best to look casual when he opened the door and found her standing there in her little black suit and four-inch heels. "Keri! It's good to—"

"I love you."

He opened his mouth to respond, but nothing would come out. His brain had turned to mush and the rest of him wasn't holding up well under the shock, either. He was afraid he was shaking.

"I love you, Michael," she said again. "I didn't want to say it while we were in Wyoming, because I had this stupid idea that I could ruin your life."

He wasn't aware that he'd moved, but suddenly he was holding her and kissing her with wild abandon as emotions he'd kept dammed up for weeks burst free. At last, gasping for breath, he lifted his head to gaze into her sparkling green eyes. "The only way you can ruin my life is by staying out of it. As it happens, I love you, too." And with that, the shaking stopped, as if when he proclaimed his love, his world had settled into place.

She smiled and wound her arms around his neck.

"So that wasn't just the booze talking when you were stumbling down the hallway?"

"So you heard that." He wasn't sure whether to be upset or grateful that she had.

"I did hear it." She looked into his eyes and let him see the love in hers. "Which reminds me. I'd like to do something, with your permission."

"What's that?"

"I'd like to thank you for making that video."

He started to grin. "You're welcome."

"No, I mean I *really* want to thank you. May I come in?"

Joy radiated through him. "You may. In fact, I insist." Sweeping her up in his arms, he carried her over the threshold and kicked the door shut behind them.

"That felt sort of symbolic."

"Oh, it was extremely symbolic." He smiled down at her. "You realize we'll have to plan quickly if we want to get married in the Last Chance living room before the snow flies."

"We can do it." Not a single doubt lingered in those green eyes. "As a very smart man once said, anything is possible."

Epilogue

TREY WHEELER HAD learned that winter could arrive in the Jackson Hole area anytime after the first of September. So he wasn't surprised when Emmett Sterling, foreman at the Last Chance, asked Trey and Watkins to clean and oil the tack in preparation for putting most of it away for the season.

Trey welcomed the job. He enjoyed working in the old barn, which had stood on the property for more than a hundred years. He craved that kind of tradition because he had so few of his own. He also liked Watkins. Not only was Watkins a top hand, he'd greatly improved Trey's guitar skills.

He and Watkins got along, and they hadn't been able to sit and talk since Pete and Sarah's wedding. Cleaning and oiling tack would give them that opportunity. The afternoon was cool, but they were cozy inside the barn, surrounded by the wholesome smell of horses and leather.

"So how did you like playing at a wedding?" Watkins picked up a bridle and began inspecting it for any places in need of repair.

"I liked it." Trey used saddle soap to clean one of

the working saddles that had seen plenty of use and abuse this summer from those crazy adolescent boys. Trey had been hired on in the middle of that session. He'd been working at a newer ranch closer to Jackson, but he'd always hoped something would open up at the Last Chance, and here he was, in a historic barn, cleaning tack.

"That's good, because they want us to provide the music for another one."

"Sign me up. I'm ready. Whose is it?"

Watkins chuckled. "Emmett's. But don't discuss this with him, because he's expecting something small. Or let's say, he's praying for something small."

"I take it Pam's not going along with that?" Trey had come on board soon after Emmett had proposed to Pam Mulholland, who owned a bed-and-breakfast down the road.

According to the gossip Trey had picked up since then, Emmett had been dragging his heels because Pam's wealth intimidated the hell out of him. Then a rival had come to town, and Emmett had been forced to put up or shut up.

"Pam was married to a real bastard. Now she finally has the love of her life, and she doesn't want some quiet ceremony with a couple of witnesses. She's rented out the entire Serenity Ski Lodge for the second weekend in December."

"Holy shit." Trey stopped in mid-motion. "That must have cost a small fortune."

"I'm sure it did, but Pam has a large fortune, and she wants a large party. I don't think Emmett's been given very many details, though, because she doesn't want him to freak out. So just keep this under your hat."

"But we're supposed to play at this ritzy lodge?"

"Yes, we are. Pam liked what she heard from us at Sarah and Pete's shindig, and she wants more of the same. She's already booked our rooms, and she's paying us, besides."

"Aw, hell, Watkins. She doesn't have to do that. We'll play for free, especially if we're getting a vacation out of it."

"She insisted, and threatened to turn into bridezilla if we didn't take the money. She—uh, never mind. Here comes Emmett. Mum's the word."

Emmett sauntered over, a piece of straw stuck in the corner of his mouth. He leaned casually against the wall and gazed at Watkins and Trey. "Did I hear you talking about my wedding?"

Watkins glanced up, his expression filled with innocence. "We were just discussing how happy we are for you."

Emmett chewed on the straw for a while before taking it out of his mouth. "Pam's up to something. I'm not sure what, yet, but I'll bet Mary Lou knows." He stared pointedly at Watkins.

"She might." Watkins picked up a rag and began oiling the bridle. "You could ask her."

"I was thinking you could ask her, considering you're married to her."

Watkins glanced up from his work. "She might tell me, but then she'd have to kill me."

Emmett sighed. "Okay. I'll go right to the source."

"Mary Lou?"

"No, Pam."

Watkins kept polishing the bridle. "Good luck with that."

"Thanks. I'll need it." Emmett glanced at Trey. "Take my advice, son. Don't fall in love. It gets you into all kinds of trouble."

Trey smiled at him. "I'll remember that." But Emmett's advice had come too late. Trey was already in love, and he didn't even know her name.

* * * * *

Look out for
Mills & Boon® TEMPTED™ 2-in-1s,
from September

*Fresh, contemporary romances
to tempt all lovers of
great stories*

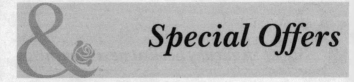

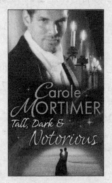

Join the Mills & Boon Book Club

Want to read more **Blaze®** books?
We're offering you **2 more** absolutely **FREE!**

We'll also treat you to these fabulous extras:

- 🌹 **Exclusive offers and much more!**
- 🌹 **FREE home delivery**
- 🌹 **FREE books and gifts with our special rewards scheme**

Get your free books now!

**visit www.millsandboon.co.uk/bookclub
or call Customer Relations on 020 8288 2888**

BS/ONLINE/K1